The Single Sister
Experiment

The Single Sister Experiment

Mimi Jefferson

URBAN CHRISTIAN

www.urbanchristianonline.net

URBAN CHRISTIAN is published by

Urban Books
1199 Straightpath
West Babylon, NY 11704

ISBN-13: 978-1-60162-987-6
ISBN-10: 1-60162-987-7

First Trade Printing May 2007
First Mass Market Printing April 2009
Printed in the United States of America

10 9 8 7 6 5 4 3 2 1

*This is a work of fiction. Any references or similarities to ac-
tual events, real people, living, or dead, or to real locales are
intended to give the novel a sense of reality. Any similarity
in other names, characters, places, and incidents is entirely
coincidental.*

Distributed by Kensington Publishing Corp.
Submit Wholesale Orders to:
Kensington Publishing Corp.
C/O Penguin Group (USA) Inc.
Attention: Order Processing
405 Murray Hill Parkway
East Rutherford, NJ 07073-2316
Phone: 1-800-526-0275
Fax: 1-800-227-9604

This book is dedicated to my mother, May,
for reasons too numerous to list.

Acknowledgements

God sends the right people at the right time. I want to express my appreciation for the people who have come along to walk this road with me:

To my husband, for believing in the project before it started making sense.

To my friend, Melissa, for her unconditional love and prayers.

To my pastor, Thomas L. Jones, for sowing the seed.

To Clifford, Ollie, Morris, and Emily, for your enthusiastic support.

To all the people I know and those I don't know who prayed for me.

To Joylynn Jossel and Urban Christian for the hard work done behind the scenes.

From the Author

Dear Readers,

About five years ago, I had a conversation that literally changed the course of my life. I was at a restaurant with a friend. Throughout our lunch his cell phone kept ringing; different women were calling him. After answering the phone one time he looked at me and said something like, "I haven't spoken to her in weeks, but I bet I could convince her to have sex with me again. She will probably resist at first, asking me where I've been and why haven't I called. But eventually she'll give in."

Later on he answered the phone again. After hanging up with yet a different woman he said something to the effect of, "You know you women don't know your power. You are selling yourselves too short."

I was alarmed. I heard how he was talking to the women on the phone. They had no idea he really believed they had power they had failed to tap into. Had I failed to tap into my power? Did all women have it? I know it makes absolutely no sense, but that night I started writing what is now the first chapter to *The Single Sister Experiment*.

I told myself that if someone gathered all the

single women in the world and told them just how powerful they were, lives would change. We women needed to meet, talk, and eventually unleash our undiscovered power. I knew there was no way that all single women could get together in one place, so I created a fictional meeting place.

Within a few days of beginning *The Single Sister Experiment,* I shared the first few pages with friends as well as strangers. The reaction I received confirmed what I was already thinking: *The Single Sister Experiment* is not just a novel, it is a ministry.

My prayer is that somewhere during the course of reading this novel you see yourself as God sees you. We are created for Him for His purposes. When we follow God we are powerful. When we follow another we are powerless.

I look forward to discussing the experiment with you. If you would like me to come to your book club, church, or women's group to discuss the novel or even lead you through one of the ceremonies you will find taking place within these pages you are about to experience, please visit me at www.MimiJefferson.com for more information.

Sincerely,
Mimi Jefferson

Prologue

Joan Dallas imagined the calm turquoise water splashing up against her bare feet as she slipped out of her too tight, but too cute to leave at the store, peep toe pumps. By this time Sunday, instead of being stuck in her office, she would be spending her time staring at the Pacific Ocean while draped over a lounge chair so soft that it could be mistaken for a bed. A red bikini would be covering her well-proportioned frame, a mai tai would be in her right hand, and if she had it her way, Chris Kahu would be in the left hand.

Joan clicked the print key on her computer, completing the lengthy accounting report two weeks before the deadline. She pushed away from her desk and swiveled around in her chair in order to view the street through the oversized windows that covered the back wall of her office. She wasn't going to miss this scene. For an entire week she would not have to deal with extra long red lights, ignorant traffic cops, or out of control drivers.

The famous Kulani Hotel would normally be out of her price range. However, Chris Kahu, a native Hawaiian and photographer she dated while he was visiting relatives in Houston, promised the beachfront view from her hotel suite would be so breathtakingly beautiful, that it would bring her to tears. Therefore, Joan decided to ignore her budget this one time. She planned on vacationing like a celebrity; exchanging the daily grind for breath-taking views, two-hour long massages, and elegant dinners.

Chris had insisted that he and Joan go Latin dancing on each one of their six dates. Now Joan loved to dance to hip-hop and R&B music, but she was completely unfamiliar with Latin dancing. The first time she walked onto the dance floor she could feel sweat pouring down her back from nervousness. Joan estimated the club had around three hundred people in it and she felt like each one of them was staring at her. This became true when she tripped over Chris's feet and landed on the floor, taking two other people down with her.

She was so embarrassed that she started crying. Chris picked her up, put his well-defined arms around her waist, placed her head on his chest and rocked her to the music until she was ready to try again. Under his careful instruction, by their third date she was comfortable enough to twirl around, wearing a short dress and extra high heels like the other women.

Joan stared at Chris's business card. She hated herself for waiting until the day before her flight to call him. It had been seven months since their last date. After she dropped him off at the airport he told her to give him a call if she were ever in Honolulu. *But did he mean it? People say stuff like that all the time.*

"Wait a minute," Joan said to herself, remembering the book she had just read by bestselling author and talk show host, Dr. Kashia Snow. She said all women had the ability to be a PATCH, which stood for Perfectly Able to Create Happiness. But before you became a PATCH, you had to start acting like one. PATCHES do not whine and wait for stuff to happen. PATCHES were to act as if they were fearless, sexy, successful, and gorgeous, whether it was true or not. Because if she kept pretending, one day she would wake up and realize that she was no longer pretending to be a PATCH, but that she had the official seal.

With that, Joan picked up the phone and dialed Chris's phone number.

"Hello, Ms. Dallas," Chris answered.

Joan wanted to scream with joy; Chris had answered the phone using her name, which meant he had taken the time to program her number into his cell phone.

"Hello, Mr. Kahu," Joan copied his professional tone. "I'll be in Honolulu all next week. I would like to get together to—"

Chris interrupted. "Salsa, samba, mumbo, and the rumba are my specialties. It would be my pleasure to assist you."

"Yes, Mr.Kahu. Can you fit that into your schedule?" Joan cooed.

"Gladly. Where will you be staying?" he asked eagerly.

Joan held her breath. "Kulani."

"Did you get the oceanfront suite?"

"Didn't you tell me to?"

"Here I thought I was going to be spending the next week alone. Now I get to be captivated by my beautiful black butterfly. When do you arrive?"

"I'm taking the overnight flight at ten P.M. tomorrow. I should arrive in Honolulu at nine-thirty A.M. Sunday morning."

"I'll be there to pick you up," Chris said.

Just then Joan's assistant, Miriam, walked into her office. "Excuse me, Ms. Dallas," her assistant said.

"Uh, look, Mr. Kahu, I have to go, so I'll talk to you later." Joan hung up the phone and looked directly into her assistant's eyes. All PATCHES know the best way to convey confidence is with eye contact.

"Sorry, Ms. Dallas. I didn't mean to interrupt your call."

Joan liked the way "Ms. Dallas" rolled off her assistant's tongue. Miriam, originally from Brazil, had a thick accent.

"Can I leave a little early?" Miriam asked. "My husband just called and told me he can't pick up the twins, so I need to make it to the babysitter's house by five."

"Sure, Miriam I'm about to leave myself. I still need to stop by the dry cleaners and pick up my son."

"You are very lucky. I would love to go to Hawaii by myself. Shoot, I would settle for being able to go to the restroom by myself."

Joan placed Chris Kahu's business card back into her purse. "You know I was a little hesitant to go alone after Tisha and Lila cancelled out on me, but now I'm looking forward to it. I can do whatever I want and go wherever I want, without anybody else's input. "

Miriam shook her hips as if she were slow dancing. "With whoever you want." She winked.

"Exactly," said Joan.

"Well I have three bits of advice," Miriam said before closing the office door. "One, use a condom; two, don't bring him back with you; and three, take lots of pictures for the horny and hopeless." Miriam laughed and then turned to exit the office. "Oh yeah, before I forget, Dr. Wright left this for you." Miriam extended her hand that held a piece of paper in it.

Dr. Wright was Joan's first and only boss since graduating from college. Joan had gone on dozens of interviews before answering an ad that stated, "Passionate Doctor needs Passionate Manager." Dr. Wright and Joan hit it off immediately.

In the eight years they worked together, Dr. Wright and Joan expanded the one office into three, housing seven other allergists along with their staffs. When asked to describe Joan's job description, Dr. Wright responded, "I take care of the patients and my Joan takes care of everything else."

Dr. Wright believed if given the opportunity she could find the right combination of medication and environmental changes to control almost any allergy. Her big break came when local Houston newswoman, Samantha Redden, mentioned on air that Dr. Wright was the only doctor in town who could help her with a severe pollen reaction.

Within a few months, Dr. Wright had throngs of doctors that wanted to be associated with her, a six-month waiting list for appointments, and patients from all over the country.

Joan took the piece of paper from Miriam's hand before Miriam walked out of the office and began to read it.

You have been with me since the beginning. I could not have done any of this without you. You are the best! That's why I've decided to give you a raise. We will discuss the details when you get back. Have fun!

Joan had worked through her lunch that day so she decided to go to the break room and pop a bag of popcorn to munch on during the ride home. She put her shoes back on, stepped out of her office door and walked dead-smack into the delivery guy's muscular chest. She stepped back slowly as he walked forward into her office, closing the door behind him.

"I'm sorry; your secretary is not at her desk. I was getting ready to knock when you walked out. I was told you had something that needed to leave today," the medium-height, medium-build man said.

Joan had not minded stumbling into him at all. She had wanted to meet him since he started handling their deliveries when Dr. Wright and the other doctors decided it was more cost effective to switch from a large national delivery service to a small local one three weeks ago. He not only worked for the service, but he was also part owner.

Joan turned around to retrieve the accounting report she had just finished from her printer. She placed it in an envelope and then bent over her desk to address it. She could feel his eyes covering every inch of her body. Joan was glad she wore her crème suit. The long pleated skirt fit her every curve.

Then Joan remembered she had forgotten to tell Miriam to call the delivery service. She turned toward him and held the envelope in her hands with a smile on her face. "Who told you I had something outgoing today?" she inquired.

He moved in closer and looked around the office. "Are we alone?" he said quietly.

"Yes, why? Do we need to be?"

"No, not really, but when I ask you what I ask you, I would prefer that there not be an audience, especially if you shoot me down. I've actually wanted to talk to you for a while now. I was here on other business and saw that your secretary was out so I decided to go for it."

Joan looked him up and down. "You don't seem like a man that has to worry about women shooting him down."

"Well, I guess I'm out of practice. I only move when I see something worth moving to."

"And you see that?" Joan flirted.

"Do I ever? You seem like a woman that is about business." He looked at the name plate on her desk and added, "Ms. Dallas."

Joan batted her eyes and handed him the envelope. "You know my name but I don't know yours."

"I'm sorry. I'm tripping. I'm Curtis, Curtis Rodgers and I'm in desperate need of having your phone number."

Joan acted as if she wasn't so happy that she could do cartwheels. "I'm out of town next week, but you can call me the following week." Joan gave him her business card from the stack off her desk. He then placed it in his wallet.

Since he did not make a point to leave, she asked him what she had wanted to ask him since the first day she saw him. "My friends and I are giving a pool party." Joan looked directly into Curtis's eyes. "It's not until the end of the summer, but I can't help but ask you now that it appears to me you would look good next to a pool."

He stepped back and smiled. Joan could tell he was turned on by her assertiveness. "See, I knew there was something different about you." He licked his lips. "I would love to join you next to a pool or anywhere else you happen to be."

"I look forward to speaking with you soon," Joan replied seductively.

"Likewise." Curtis winked and then walked out the door.

As if things couldn't get better than a week in paradise and a raise, Curtis was as attracted to Joan as she was to him. She couldn't help but laugh out loud as she thought about how fine he was, and more importantly, how jealous her girlfriends would be when they saw the Morris Chestnut look-alike on her arm at their annual book club pool party.

Last year she had made the mistake of inviting a sweet, but skinny, guy named Walter. When Walter arrived shirtless next to the hunks they had picked out just for the occasion, Joan was so embarrassed. *But that won't happen this year,* Joan thought as she prepared to leave her office.

Joan closed the blinds then retrieved her purse from the closet. Her hunger pains would have to wait. Now, it was four-thirty, too late to pop a bag of popcorn. If she could get to the parking garage in the next five minutes, she could still beat the rush hour traffic. Realizing she had forgotten to log off her computer, she reached across her desk and grabbed the mouse.

Suddenly, she was no longer in her office, but instead surrounded in darkness.

"What in the world is going on? Where am I?" Joan screamed. She could hear voices; some appeared to be right next to her while others appeared to be miles away.

One minute, each of the women who were now surrounded by darkness, were living their lives as if it were a normal day, and the next, they were in a pitch-black auditorium that appeared to go on endlessly. Some of the women were screaming and others were shaking vigorously, but most were scared into silence.

Joan could hear the rapid beating of her heart as she forced herself to wake up from what she hoped was only a nightmare. All of a sudden, a faint speck of light highlighted a small portion of a stage. The screaming women became silent and the shaking women became still.

This is too real to be a dream, Joan decided. *I must have died and went to Hell.*

Joan watched anxiously as a petite, elderly black woman dressed in a long, flowing white robe walked slowly into the only light, now radiating in the building.

"Good evening, ladies," the woman spoke. "I know you are wondering who I am and why you are here."

The intensity in her voice made Joan grow even more fearful. She tried again to look around

the room, but all she could perceive was black-
ness.

"My name and position are of no importance to
you," the woman continued. "Be calm. I mean no
harm." She paused, as if giving the women a chance
to internalize her last statement. "My beautiful
sisters, you have lost your way. The world you
have created for yourselves is simply out of control. You are lost. We have proposed an experiment
so that you may be found."

Who in the world is "we"? Joan wondered. Sweat
was pouring down her face and sliding down her
stomach. She could hear someone close to her
gagging as if they were vomiting. No longer able
to keep her composure, Joan leaped out of her
seat and yelled, her voice echoing loudly throughout the building.

"Lady, I don't know who you are and I don't
care," Joan said. "However, I do know one thing,
and that is, whatever help you are trying to provide, I don't need. So, can I please just be zapped
back to where I was?"

Just then, another voice sounded out. "Joan, is
that you? It's me, Tisha."

Joan not only heard her best friend, Tisha's,
voice, but Tisha's cousin, Lila, also a friend of
Joan's, called out to her.

Abruptly, the darkness lifted and the women
could now see each other. Hundreds of thousands
of women were neatly seated stadium style underneath bright signs that listed their places of residence. Each of them were clothed in a white linen
robe, same as the woman onstage.

At first, the woman appeared to be relaxed, but
now, the women could hear the displeasure in her

voice and see it on her face. "No one is leaving until I am finished saying what I have been sent here to say," the woman informed them. "Therefore, I suggest you *all* sit down and listen."

Joan immediately took her seat.

"As you know, there is a problem with you and the men in your lives. On numerous occasions, we have heard your cries," the woman continued.

Shockingly, each woman heard a quiet voice in her ear sounding as if it were her own.

"All men are dirty dogs. All they want to do is make babies their broke butts can't take care of. I'm tired of giving up my goodies to these no-good trifling players who act as if they would rather be tortured by a hive of honey bees than make a commitment to one woman."

Finally, Joan heard herself from one night when she was pleading out to God as her tears fell. *"Father, can you help me? I'm tired of being lonely. What am I doing wrong?"*

As the voices died out, the woman on the stage continued speaking. "All of you want to marry kings, but are you conducting yourselves as queens?"

An enormous movie screen slowly lowered behind the woman. Joan tightly grabbed the arms of her seat, embarrassed by what she had heard, and afraid of what she might see.

Joan's eyes gravitated toward the first picture to appear. It was Jamal, Joan's first sexual experience when she was only fourteen. She sat numb, unable to move or react. The men were pictured in the order in which she had slept with them. The final picture was of Scott, an accountant she had met three months prior.

She had no idea her rule of "no more than two

to three new experiences a year" had resulted in a total she was too humiliated to finish counting. She shook her head back and forth in disgust when she realized she could not recall all of their names. Without warning, the pictures of the men disappeared and images emerged.

Soon Joan witnessed herself engaged in a fist-fight with a woman named Raquel, who she had a lengthy feud with over James, the man who had fathered each of their sons. The following imageries covered Joan's two-week trip to Jamaica, which landed her in hotel suite after hotel suite with men she had met days, or sometimes hours, before. Her eyes started to water as she observed herself aggressively seducing a man she knew was married.

Simultaneously, each woman viewed her own personal video, their eyes serving as the projectors for the flashbacks they witnessed. Many of them were smiling as they watched fond memories, while others, like Joan, had shame covering their faces as they viewed a dose of reality that was anything but pleasant.

"Sisters, you don't begin to know your power!" the woman said with authority. "There was once a man walking in the desert, weak and near death because of thirst. One day, the man saw a rock with one glass of water on top of it. The man jumped for joy. The gift to him was priceless. He savored each drop as if it were his last. While he was very thirsty, he managed to have the discipline to save half the glass of water. The second day, when the man woke up and walked to the rock, there were two glasses of water. He could not believe his luck. On the third day, there were six. By the seventh day, the man grew to expect the water."

The women nervously shifted from side to side in their seats, knowing exactly where the woman was going with her story.

"The man started to bathe with the water," the woman stated. "He even washed his camel with the water. He would have given it away if there would have been anyone to give it to. Sometimes he would just pour it out if it had gotten a little old. After all, he knew more was coming tomorrow, and better still, he didn't have to do anything to get it." She paused and then abruptly stated, "Refuse to bed a man who has not made a commitment to you and God."

Joan sucked her teeth. "You expect us to just give it up cold turkey?" Joan immediately regretted that remark once she saw the expression on the woman's face.

"Give up what?" the woman responded, coarsely. "I guess you all are satisfied passing from one man to the next. I suppose you would rather share your men than to have one for yourself. Do you not want a husband and father for your children, or are you content with just having a baby's daddy? These men will never know your value unless you start acting like you are valuable. This is why we have brought you here today. This is operation SSE, the Single Sister Experiment.

"We want to know how your men would react if each of you would stop giving yourselves away and demand to be treated like the priceless gifts you really are. Many of you believe when you lie down with a man you're offering your body, but I believe you're giving up much more. Don't you want to know what would happen in your lives if you stopped giving up your precious water?

"Of course, all of you could go on doing what you have been doing and continue to hurt like you have been hurting. Is this drastic? Yes, it needs to be. Is it going to be difficult? Yes, more difficult than you can imagine. You will figure out who lied to you. Beloved, some of you will endure a painful self-analysis as you discover the lies, the liars, and your true self."

The woman folded her hands, paced a couple of times and then said, "I went shopping one day and purchased a bookcase from one of those warehouse supply stores. I opened the box and immediately disregarded the manufacture's instructions. They were just too long and too extensive. I thought, 'hey, I'm smart enough to do this by myself.' I pulled all the parts out and put the pieces together that seemed right. One of my friends stopped by so I implemented his ideas as well. I could see we had done something wrong halfway through the process, so I called one of my relatives who had a bookcase similar to mine. I took his advice and moved on. Then I looked on the Internet to see what other people had to say. At the end of the day, I called it quits. The bookcase was leaning on one side. The panels were weak and could not support the weight of even my smaller books. The one who created the bookcase gave me the instructions, but I chose not to follow them.

"Surly a great philosopher knows exactly what you should be pursuing in your life. Perhaps a famous television personality knows how to lead you from earth to heaven. Maybe you should start following a novelist, celebrity, or a scientist from one of the elite universities who is known for his extensive scholarly works. When will you grow tired of listening to that nonsense?"

Joan remembered how she and her friends had followed Dr. Kashia Snow.

"Ladies," the woman pointed out, "God is not some egomaniac who is trying to stop you from having fun. He is a lovingly Father who deeply desires to protect His children. Tell me, is this God's best for you?"

Joan thought back to what she had heard and seen and replied, "No."

"You are not alone, my sister," the woman said to Joan. "We want all of you to have everything God has waiting for you. We want you to find husbands. We want the family unit together and strong. However, you can't attract a godly man until you become a godly woman. I think it's that time, don't you?" The women nodded their heads in agreement. "I think it's time these brothers got real thirsty. Are we in the midst of a drought, ladies?"

"Yes! Yes!" the women enthusiastically shouted.

"In order for this experiment to work, we need the complete cooperation from every last one of you," the woman told them.

The women looked around at each other, and then they started to stand up one at a time. Within seconds, the entire auditorium was standing hand in hand and quietly weeping.

Joan's eyes were closed tightly, fighting to hold back the tears that were pooling in her lids. When she opened them, she found the woman had stepped off the stage and was now standing in the center aisle.

"You have been created by God for His purposes," the woman said, pointing to Joan and the rest of the women. "He is the manufacturer. Ladies, from this day forward you will follow the manufacturer's instructions. You will study and meditate on the instructions. You will journal concerning the instructions. You will be changed by the instructions. I'm speaking of the Bible, the Word of God, or as I like to call it . . ." She paused and held up her Bible, "Basic Instructions Before Leaving Earth."

After asking the women to get on their knees, she told them to repeat after her. "God, I know that you love me as no one will ever love me," she stated as the women repeated her words in unison. "Today I surrender my life to your complete control. I pray for guidance as I seek to grow into the woman you created me to be."

Joan walked over to Tisha and Lila and they all linked hands firmly. She knew she was going to need the support of her sister network like never before.

"This is the first phase of the experiment," the woman said. "I or one of my colleagues will visit each of you as we believe it is warranted. I know you may have more questions, but I am not at liberty to answer them at this time. In a few moments, you will be returned to your lives as you left them. Until next time, my sisters, be blessed," the woman concluded.

In less than a second, Joan was back at her desk. Clearly shaken up, she walked outside her office in search of a sign indicating something out of the

ordinary had taken place and that the whole auditorium scene was not just a figment of her imagination. To her disappointment, everything and
everyone looked the same. But little did she know,
her life as she once knew it wasn't.

Chapter 1

Tisha looked around her car in disbelief. Just a moment ago she was in a dark auditorium, now she was back in her Lexus driving down Beltway 8.

Within seconds of returning to her car, Tisha heard what appeared to be car horns blowing one after the other. She immediately glanced in her rearview mirror to see what all the commotion was about. Just then three separate drivers in succession zoomed past her, each one making her aware how displeased they were with her driving by continuing to sound their horns even after they had passed her.

Tisha looked at her speedometer. She was only going thirty-five miles per hour on a highway where it wasn't uncommon for drivers to take their chances and drive upwards of eighty miles per hour.

Tisha took a series of deep breaths in an attempt to calm herself down. She could feel her grip on the steering wheel weakening due to the perspiration coming from her hands. If she didn't get off the freeway soon, she feared her nerves were going to cause her to lose control of the car.

She looked in her rearview mirror again scared of what she might find. She breathed a sigh of relief realizing her path was clear to change lanes and she was close to a place where she could exit the freeway. Without thinking, she pressed hard on the gas.

As soon as she exited the highway she noticed a gas station on her right side. Tisha pulled into the gas station. Before she could maneuver into a parking spot she felt an unmistakable feeling in her throat. She quickly put the car in park, opened the door, and held her head out seconds before the vomiting started.

A man working for the gas station was emptying a trash can near where Tisha was parked. He heard her gagging and turned around and asked, "Are you okay? Do you need some help?"

She finished vomiting, closed her door and drove away, leaving him standing there with a worried look on his face.

Tisha noticed that no one was parked in a parking spot adjacent to the gas station so she slowly pulled in. Then she swished some water from her water bottle in her mouth and tried to wipe the sweat off her body with couple of napkins from her glove box. She made sure all of the windows were rolled up and each door was locked. Then she turned up her CD player as loud as it would go.

Satisfied no one would hear her, she started

screaming louder than she ever had in her life. She couldn't stop thinking about how she felt when she first arrived in that auditorium. She was too scared to speak, move, or even breathe. Tisha was sure she had died and God was finally punishing her for living her life for the last six years as if He didn't exist.

Six years ago Tisha's mother died of breast cancer. Tisha stood by her mother's hospital bed day after day. She refused to give up hope even when the doctors said there was no hope. She had gone to church as a child. She remembered how people would give testimonies about how God had healed them or somebody they prayed for, so she believed that if she earnestly prayed, God would heal her mother too.

But Tisha's plan was not God's plan. Tisha could not understand why God had allowed her sweet, generous mother to die a long, painful, cancerous death while pedophiles and murderers get to live perpetrating their crimes on helpless people.

Tisha started to beat the stirring wheel with her hands as tears slid down her face. The day of her mother's funeral, Tisha vowed she was finished with a God she could not understand.

She stopped going to church, reading her Bible, and praying. Every time she came near someone talking about God, she would change the subject or leave. It wasn't as if she stopped believing in God, she stopped trusting that He knew what was best for her.

Tisha met her boyfriend, Marcus, three days after her mother died. She was in the drive-through line at Chick-fil-A. Tisha was yelling and cursing at the lady working the window because each time she repeated the order back to Tisha she left something out. Tisha was hot when she pulled around the corner to get her food, and before she knew it, she had bumped into the car in front of her; the car belonging to Marcus.

She thought he would get out of the car and cause a scene; instead he pulled off to the side of the parking lot. Tisha followed him. She saw his free-flowing locks and lean body before she saw his handsome face. He walked slowly to her and said, "It looks like you need a hug."

Tisha couldn't believe it, but she actually let him hold her. She had not allowed herself to cry about her mother until that day in Marcus's arms. He seemed to understand that anybody who was getting that angry at a fast food clerk must really be going through something major. His caring instincts were what drew Tisha to Marcus. When she was near him, all was right with the world.

She didn't have to worry about the fact that her father was losing weight and that he sometimes sat on the porch believing his wife was going to drive back home at any moment. She didn't have to hear people tell her that she should be happy her mother was in a better place and free from pain. The fact that she was almost thirty years old and had never kept the same job for more than a year didn't matter either.

Marcus's calm nature and quiet disposition allowed her to escape. He never preached to her. He only took her for long rides on his motorcycle, bought her expensive presents, and made love to her so perfectly that every tense muscle in her body would relax. He was not just the love of her life, but the calm breeze she needed to preserve her sanity.

Tisha pushed the driver's seat to a laying down position. All the time she had been angry with God she knew she was wrong; she could feel it in her body. She would get anxious and couldn't keep still. In order to rid herself of the feeling she would call Marcus. If he was not available, she would shop, which was why she owed money to practically everyone she knew. When she couldn't find a way to shop she would surf the Internet, watch TV, clean, talk on the phone, anything to try to find some peace.

Tisha cupped her face in her hands and cried until her eyes were sore. She wasn't ready to admit what she felt in her heart. *God was her peace.* God had given her another chance to live her life according to His plan through the experiment. But if she did that, she would be opening herself up to be hurt again. She didn't know if she had the strength to risk that.

Tired of thinking, Tisha decided to call her friend, Joan, and her cousin, Lila. Maybe this whole experiment thing didn't really happen. Maybe God wasn't really trying to get her attention. Maybe it was all an illusion brought on by the vitamins she had recently started taking.

She looked around and saw a pay phone several feet from her car. Unfortunately, her cell phone company was someone else she owed. She parked as close as possible to the pay phone. She felt weird as she stepped out of the car. Normally, she thought she was too cute to use a public telephone, but the money Marcus had given her to pay the cell phone bill went to a man selling a burgundy Gucci knock-off handbag that looked so authentic she decided the already overdue cell phone bill had to wait until her next payday.

Tisha's petite frame was sporting a seven-hundred dollar weave, a teal Marc Jacobs's V-neck sundress, a bronze Coach handbag, and bronze Jimmy Choo stiletto sandals. If anybody would have been close to her, they would have had a nose full of her Vera Wang perfume.

Tisha thought about asking her father for the money to pay the cell phone bill, but each time she asked him for money he would get really sad and start talking about how Tisha's mother spent her whole life saving so that her one and only child could go to college. Before the conversation was over, they would both end up in tears as their thoughts consumed with memories about the woman they both loved dearly.

Tisha spent one semester in college and then dropped out. Tisha had been a flight attendant, a fashion stylist, a massage therapist, customer service representative and now she was a used car saleswoman. The Lexus she was currently driving came from off the lot where she worked. She couldn't afford it, but everybody thought it was hers and she didn't bother to tell them the truth.

Tisha used a shaking hand to dial Joan's work phone number, using a napkin to press the number keys on the phone more people than she could have imagined had touched. Joan's work phone rang three times then went to voice mail. Tisha placed more coins in the pay phone and then dialed Joan's cell and home numbers. Joan did not answer either one.

She dialed her cousin's Lila's number.

"Hello," Lila answered the phone.

"Hey, Lila, it's me."

Recognizing her cousin's voice, Lila said, "Finally! I've been trying to call you and Joan for the last forty-five minutes." Lila was practically yelling. "Ever since I got back from—shoot I don't know that place—that really strange, very weird place!"

Tisha could feel the tears form in her eyes. The experiment was not an illusion; it was real. The God she hated had interrupted her life in such a major way that she could no longer ignore Him.

Lila's voice went up higher. "Tisha, you do know what I'm talking about, right?"

"Of course I do. I saw you, remember?" Tisha said quietly as tears fell from her face.

"Yeah, Tisha, but for a minute I thought it was all in my head, you know, like I had this really real dream."

"I wish it was a dream," Tisha said.

"I've been scrolling the news channels and radio stations, but nobody has any news about this *experiment*." Lila continued. "I was sitting right here on my living room sofa. I dropped off Jasmine at my mom's house at a quarter after three. Then I drove to Stanley's steaks on Highway Six. I got my to-go order and drove home. I took my food into the living room and sat down on the sofa. It was exactly four-thirty; I remember looking at my watch and thinking it's Friday, Dr. Kashia Snow's talk show comes on in thirty minutes.

"When I got back from the meeting it was still

four-thirty. And my steak and fries were still pip-
ing hot. Now that we are back, time is moving as
usual."

Tisha could feel herself getting light-headed.
"Lila, what am I going to do? Marcus is probably
wondering where I am right now. He's all set for
us to spend the night celebrating his birthday.
And you know what that means?"

Lila sighed, "Sex."

"He told me he went by Victoria's Secret yesterday and bought me a few pieces of lingerie.
How am I supposed to explain this to him when I
can't even explain it to myself?"

"Call Marcus and make up an excuse. Tell him
you suddenly got sick or something. Then let's all
meet at your place. You talk to Joan yet?"

"No, she's not answering the phone. And I
called all three of her numbers. I don't know what
she could be up to," Tisha exhaled. "I guess I can
call Marcus, but I don't think I can drive to my
apartment. I don't even know where my apartment is right now, you feel me? I'm at a freaking
Exxon station off Beltway Eight and Richmond."

"I know what we can do; I'll call a taxi to drive
me to you. Then I'll drive your car to your apartment. By that time Joan should have called one of
us and she can meet us at your place."

Tisha knew this was not the time to wonder
why Lila was constantly finding a way to get out
of her house and into her apartment, especially
since Tisha actually needed her to come over this
time. She did not want to face the experiment alone.
But a part of her really wanted to know what was
going on in that big beautiful house Lila shared
with her live-in boyfriend, Steve, and her daughter,

Jasmine, that had Lila leaving every chance she got.

"Thanks, Lila, I would really appreciate it," Tisha said.

"Are you okay, Tisha? You seem spooked. I thought you would be cursing up a storm and beating up stuff, but you sound like somebody gave you a tranquilizer."

"How could my life have changed so completely so quickly? One minute I'm driving to my boyfriend's house so we can celebrate his birthday and then the next . . ."

Lila interrupted, "Everything changes."

"Yes, Lila . . . everything." Tisha paused for a moment. "I'm just so angry."

"At that woman who was talking to us?" Lila asked.

"No, it's nothing, Lila," Tisha lied. It was unacceptable to be angry at God and the last thing she needed was a lecture about it. So she kept her feelings about Him to herself.

"Do you have any food at your apartment? Or do I need to gather up some snacks and bring them with me?" Lila asked.

Tisha could not believe Lila was talking about eating at a time like this. Any other time Tisha would have made a rude comment about Lila's excess weight only to have Lila make a comment about Tisha's excess shopping, but she was in no mood to play the dozens. "Go ahead and bring your snacks," Tisha said. "I'm going to call Marcus; I'll see you when you get here."

Tisha put more coins in the phone and dialed Marcus's cell number.

"Marcus, it's me," she said after he answered.

"Baby, you sound sick. Are you okay?" Marcus responded.

"No, I'm not okay. I don't feel good at all. It's a real bad headache."

"I can tell; you sound bad. So that means we are going to have to postpone our celebration," Marcus responded. "That's okay; I probably need to work on updating my business plan this weekend. I just found out I have a breakfast meeting with a potential investor first thing Monday morning. It won't be long, Tisha; your man is about to leave his old firm and start his own!"

"Congratulations and happy birthday, Marcus." Tisha tried to sound upbeat.

"Thank you, my love. You want me to bring you some of that soup you like?"

"No, I think I'm just going to lie down."

"All right, I'll call you in the morning. I love you, Tisha."

"I love you too Marcus." Tisha hung up the phone and stepped back into her car.

Could she risk losing Marcus? In the six years they had been together, he never talked about marrying her. Marcus had been married and divorced twice before he started dating Tisha. Once she over heard him say to one of his friends, "Marriage is what ruins relationships."

Marcus didn't think much of Christians either. He believed they were nice people, yet delusional if they really believed everything in the Bible was true.

Tisha closed her eyes as she sat in her car. She tried to imagine her life without Marcus. She couldn't. Tisha opened her eyes. A life without Marcus wouldn't be worth living. She would try the experiment, but if the experiment meant she would lose her man, then she may have to lose the experiment.

Chapter 2

The plain white ceiling alarmed Joan as she opened her eyes. Anxiety circulated throughout her body as segments from the day before became vivid, but she still wondered if it could have all been a dream. Joan looked around her bedroom wondering if one day soon she would be exchanging her condo for a hospital room and straitjacket.

As she sat up in bed, the morning light brought some relief. Her custom-made oak dresser was firmly in its place, the wood as shiny as it always had been. The track lighting over her canopy bed was just that, lights, and not the menacing eyes they had appeared to be the night before. Last night had seemed endless. Her heightened senses caused her to stay awake for hours listening to noises she never knew her home made.

Joan looked at her cell phone on the nightstand. She had turned it off as soon as she returned from being with the woman in the auditorium. When she got home she unplugged her home phone. She was not in any condition to have a conversation with anybody.

Suddenly there was a knock on Joan's bedroom door.

"Momma, wake up, my waffles are stuck in the toaster!" the little voice beamed from the other side of the door.

"Come in baby." Joan smiled at the sight of her son in his pajamas and the guilty expression on his face.

"Momma why are you sweating?" James Jr. asked.

Joan looked down at her chest. Her T-shirt was stuck to her body. She could feel the moisture on her forehead and underneath her arms. She placed her hand where she had slept; it was drenched.

Joan looked back at her son, noticing the puzzled look on his face. "Baby, Momma just had a bad dream, that's all." She waited to see if he was accepting her explanation.

"What happened to your hair?"

Joan turned to an adjacent wall to look into the mirror, then instantly tried to pat her hair into place. "Baby, Momma just forgot to wrap her hair last night, that's all." Joan avoided her son's eyes. "Now what are you doing making waffles?" Joan asked. "You know you're supposed to wait for me."

"Momma, I didn't want to—" The doorbell interrupted him.

"I got it, Momma." James Jr., hoping to divert attention from his latest toaster episode, hurried to the door to get the garbage ready for pickup;

door-to-door garbage pickup was just one of the luxuries management provided.

Joan looked at fourteen different complexes before deciding on the three-bedroom condo. The contemporary yellow building in the midst of downtown blandness made a statement of, "I'm young and hip, therefore I need to be near the new basketball stadium, baseball stadium, and a host of trendy restaurants and clubs." The all-glass foyer with waiting doorman stated, "I'm a successful professional who can afford to spoil myself."

Getting out of her bed, Joan's eyes gravitated toward the closet where three pieces of luggage were neatly placed outside the door. She had left them there days before in anticipation of the vacation she now knew she had to cancel. She walked to the kitchen quickly, not wanting to think of what she had planned to do on her first solo trip to Hawaii.

As Joan pried her son's waffle out of the toaster, she formulated her plan. Instead of going to Hawaii she would spend the week in a hotel, starting today. She needed time to think without the risk of getting interrupted. She would take James Jr. to her mother's, just as she had planned to do while she went to Hawaii. Next Sunday she would pick him up, and Monday morning she would return to work. That is, if she had not officially gone crazy.

Joan put the waffle on a plate, added some butter and syrup and gave it to her son, who was in the den watching television. She called her travel agent to cancel her trip. Thankfully, she had purchased vacation insurance. Joan looked online and found a nice hotel that was miles outside of the city. No one would find her there. She called and made reservations at the hotel, then she e-mailed Chris Kahu to inform him she would not be coming to Hawaii tonight after all.

James Jr. fell asleep the first two minutes of the five-minute drive to his grandmother's house, leaving Joan alone with her thoughts. She did not want to deal with the aftermath of telling anyone, especially her mother, that she was no longer going to Hawaii. Joan had moved into the dorms at Texas Southern University as soon as she graduated from high school and had not lived with her mother in over ten years, but she still expected to have a detailed account of Joan's every move.

Tisha would have to wait on finding out the truth too, Joan decided. While they had been best friends since middle school and shared almost everything, Joan believed what she needed to do now she had to do alone.

It was 10:00 A.M. when Joan glided into her mother's driveway. Her childhood home looked like a museum towering with history. Most of the homes on this corner of Third Ward were nothing fancy in a cosmetic sense, but were so large and well-structured that they made new homes look like dollhouses.

It was the beginning of the summer, sunny, and warm. When Joan was a child, by this time on Saturday morning a group of boys would be outside playing kickball on one side of the street while a group of girls were on the other side practicing cheers. Now, the street was quiet. All of Joan's old friends were grown and had moved out.

James Jr. woke up when Joan opened the door on the passenger's side. Leaning over, Joan gave him a kiss. As she looked into her six-year-old's eyes, she wanted so badly to tell him she was sorry for being such a messed-up mother and she wanted to promise him she would do much better from that day forward. Instead, she reached for his hand while he jumped down from her SUV, gave him his bag, and then watched as he jogged up the walkway.

His identical features forced her thoughts to settle on memories of his father, even though she tried to stop them. James Sr. obviously was not worried about her, and she did not need to waste any time being worried about him.

As was customary, a smile flashed across her son's face as he met his grandmother at the door. The two of them waved good-bye to Joan. She got back into her vehicle, waved, and then drove off.

Joan started scrolling the radio stations. The dj's were still pulling childish pranks, gossiping about celebrities, and playing way too many commercials. The traffic lights were still turning red, yellow, and green. The people in their cars were still eating, talking on their cell phones, and driving recklessly. It was as if it was an ordinary Saturday morning for everyone except Joan.

She scrolled the stations again, stopping at a place she never would have before, the local Christian radio station. Joan turned it up so she could hear each lyric. The song playing was about a young man driving to meet his parents after a difficult period. He was driving too fast and lost control of his car. At that moment he knows he can't help himself and calls out to Jesus. He realized he had lived his life outside of the will of God. After reaching a point where he couldn't help himself, he relinquished control. The man with the beautiful voice kept saying, "Jesus Take Over."

Joan turned the radio off before the song was over. She refused to allow the tears that were building up in her eyes to fall down her face. She exited Highway 59 behind a truck carrying several horses in a large trailer. The animals appeared to not have a care in the world. The person who owned them made sure they had plenty to eat and bought a covering to protect them from nature's elements. They didn't have to worry about whether they were going crazy or not, or if they had, in fact, been kidnapped and were now part of some strange experiment in which they had to stop having sex and relive their past all while developing what appeared to be an impossible relationship with God.

Joan could not believe she was accessing the benefits of being a horse as she navigated into her favorite parking spot at the mall. She needed to pick up a few things before heading to the hotel.

Opening the glass door, the complexity of what she was facing was thick in the air as she passed woman after woman walking, talking, and shopping, just the same as they did any other time she was at the mall. Even though she desperately wanted to know if any of them had been in the same dark-filled auditorium with the strange woman as she had been, she would not dare ask.

Taking long strides, she stayed focused on reaching her destination, which was a small Christian bookstore she often passed on her way to her favorite department stores. She had made mental notes to go in it several times before, but never seemed to find the time to do so.

"Hey Ms. Dallas," Joan looked up at the familiar face now blocking her path.

"Hi, oh, how's it going—?" Joan stammered.

"Miriam, your assistant," she filled in Joan's obvious blank.

"Oh forgive me, Miriam, my body is here but mind is already in Hawaii."

"I can see that. Where are you going? Saks, Gucci, or what do you call it, yes, Victoria's Secret?"

"A bookstore." Joan tried not to sound annoyed.

"Oh, I see, may I join you? My husband has the kids today. All day!"

Miriam seemed delighted. Joan didn't know what to say so she started walking again. The bookstore was only a few steps away.

"What books are you looking for?" Miriam inquired.

"The Bible," Joan said reluctantly. She wasn't ready to admit to herself why she needed to go to the bookstore and she certainly hadn't wanted to admit it to anyone else.

Miriam stopped in front of the bookstore. Joan turned to face her.

"Joan, you never struck me like that. Are you religious? Me, I'm not religious, just spiritual," said Miriam.

"What exactly does that mean?" A man who

was walking into the bookstore butted into their conversation.

Joan and Miriam looked up at the man who was dressed in a blue suit with a red tie. He was holding the biggest Bible Joan had ever seen. He had a wooden oversized cross around his neck.

"Excuse me sir, I believe in God," said Miriam with conviction.

"Yeah, a God you made up in your head. I got news for you, sweetie. That God does not exist. The Bible talks about people like you," the man stated.

"The Bible has lots of errors and contradictions," said Miriam.

"Really? Here's a Bible, find me one," said the man, holding out his Bible.

Miriam stepped back. Joan waited for Miriam to speak.

"Sir, I believe there are many paths to heaven. No one religion is right. I sometimes read the Bible and the other holy books," said Miriam.

The man raised his voice, "So you believe Jesus Christ was a lunatic?"

"No, I believe Jesus was a great teacher. I follow him as well as others," said Miriam.

"No, either Jesus is the Son of God who came to save the world, like he said, or he is a nut case with a messiah complex. Pick one!"

Two women walking by stopped and joined the conversation. One of them said, "That's the problem with you Christians; you guys are so narrow-minded."

Joan remained silent, realizing she was the only who seemed not to have much to say.

"I bet you won't say that when you're burning

in hell. 'Enter through the narrow gate. For wide is the gate and broad is the road that leads to destruction, and many enter through it.' Matthew Seven, look it up," said the man.

A short, elderly man wearing gray slacks, a white shirt, and a maroon tie with RICHARD on his name tag walked up to them. "Can I help anyone find something today?"

The man and the two women declined his offer and continued on their way, leaving Joan and Miriam standing there.

"Joan, I think I'm going home now. That mean guy talked so much he gave me a headache," Miriam said as she walked away.

"I'm just looking," Joan responded with a smile after realizing the man was waiting patiently on her response.

Nodding, the gentleman walked back into the store. Joan followed him. She took a quick glance back at him, hoping he did not realize she did not belong in a place like this. She imagined he was a deacon who went to church every Sunday, knew every gospel song ever written, and regularly gave to the poor.

Joan was embarrassed as she looked at the rows and rows of Bibles. She had no idea the selection would be so big. The only Bible she ever owned was given to her by her maternal grandfather, Grandpa Tyler. She kept it on top of a table in her living room except for when she had male company, and then she would tuck it inside a drawer underneath several layers of clothing. Sometimes when she saw the old Bible, she felt fuzziness in her stomach, like her grandfather was in the room disapproving of her actions.

As Joan stood in the bookstore the woman in the white robe's words entered into her head. *"Ladies, from this day forward you will follow the manufacturer's instructions. You will study and meditate on the instructions. You will journal concerning the instructions. You will be changed by the instructions."*

Joan could not see herself doing that with the old Bible her grandfather had given her. That's why she needed a new one that didn't carry memories of her grandfather along with it.

Grandpa Tyler always insisted that when Joan and her brother, Travis, spent any time with him, they went to church. Joan was baptized at the age of ten. Being the proud grandparent, her grandfather sent her to get her hair done, even though her stubborn grandmother told him repeatedly it was a waste of money. He argued she needed to be pretty the day Jesus came into her life. Joan did not know whether to laugh or cry as she thought about the look on her grandfather's face when she came out the water. Until that moment, he seemed to not really understand the water would ruin her carefully done Shirley Temple curls. Not wanting to admit defeat, he quickly changed his perplexed look to a smile and proceeded to take snapshots while her grandmother, Betty, made her way around several people to get a good look at his face.

"Are you sure I can't help you?" the man asked Joan after noticing her confused state.

Joan wanted to cry. Her grandfather had died soon after she was baptized. What would he have thought to know she had barely opened the Bible since then?

"Miss, can I help you?" the man repeated.

Joan snapped out of her daydream to find Richard staring at her.

"I'm sorry, sir, maybe this was a bad idea." Joan turned to leave.

"Please, miss, let me suggest something."

Joan turned around. She looked down not wanting to look into his eyes. He could probably tell she had not attended any church long enough to say she was a member, and when she did go, she was more concerned with the single men who were present and how cute she looked in her new suit than getting much out of the service.

Joan waited, hoping he would start talking.

"I suggest everybody starts out with the New International Version or NIV Study Bible and the Commentary that goes along with it. I also suggest purchasing Strong's Exhaustive Concordance and Vine's Expository Dictionary of New Testament Words," Richard explained. "The Bible was originally written in Greek, Aramaic, and Hebrew and to get the correct meaning, you often need to know something about the original languages." Richard took a deep breath and pointed to the back of the store, "On that table in the back of the store, you see it?"

Joan nodded.

"There's a list of churches and Bible studies you might want to attend," Richard added. "They are organized by location. There's also a flyer for a class called Bible Study Methods at the College of Biblical Studies. It's on the Southwest side. You ever heard of it?"

Joan shook her head.

"Well, the class is free. I highly recommend it to anybody who does not want to be told what's in the Bible, but they want to find out for themselves."

"Thank you," Joan replied as she walked to the back table, and randomly picked up a few flyers. The man had been so nice that she didn't want to appear rude. Then, she grabbed the books the salesmen recommended and stood in the checkout line.

Joan stood behind two teenage boys who had obviously witnessed the incident at the front of the store between the man and Miriam. One of the boys had everything in his hands that Joan had it hers.

"Hey Michael, if I decide to be a Christian, does it mean I'm going to be angry like that man was?" one of the boys asked his friend.

"You know, when I first believed, I was a lot like him."

"You are joking."

"I wish. Over the last two years I have learned there are better ways to share my faith. I'm still passionate about God's Word, just a whole lot more patient."

"Good, because if you would have came at me like that, I might have punched you."

They two friends laughed heartily. Joan wondered if she would ever laugh again.

She was glad when another register opened, because if she had to stay in that store any longer, tears were surely going to fall from her face.

Chapter 3

Pleased to finally have something to feel good about, Joan closed the door to her hotel room and sat her luggage down. At the last minute, she decided to splurge on a suite, and looking at the king-sized bed, feathery burgundy sofa, and oversized bathtub, it had been worth it.

She instantly wanted to call Tisha to brag, but changed her mind when she realized she would have to explain everything else as well. The temperature was approaching 100 degrees outside. Joan turned the air conditioning to its coldest setting.

Lowering herself into a sitting position onto the bed, Joan placed her Bible, pen, and an Italian leather journal with her initials she had received from her staff as a gift but never used, down on the bed.

Not knowing where to start, she left everything on the bed and walked to the bathroom, hoping she would know what to do next when she re-

turned. Joan looked in the bathroom mirror. Her
dark brown skin, spotless complexion, soft features, and shoulder-length bob looked back at her
innocently. Joan recalled what the woman in the
auditorium had said, *"The world you have created
for yourselves is simply out of control. You are lost."*
Joan agreed with the woman that she was lost,
but she didn't know why God would care. She
had forgotten Him. Hadn't He forgotten her?

"What happened to me?" Joan asked herself
out loud as she grabbed an oversized towel from
the rack on the wall and placed it on the sink's
countertop.

She splashed water on her face. As she was ap-
plying her makeup removal cream, she looked
back into the mirror. Getting a glimpse of her new
reflection, she jumped back and screamed.

She opened her eyes wider, as if that would
make the eight-year-old girl with two thick braids
dressed in a blue-and-white polka-dot short set
and wooden clogs disappear. With happy energy
and a toothless smile, the girl spoke in her child-
like voice.

*"My daddy's coming to get me at three-thirty this
afternoon. He said I needed to be packed and ready to
go or we might miss our flight. We are going to have so
much fun this week going to amusement parks and
stuff. I was packed as soon as school got out, for summer break, and that was almost two weeks ago."*

Joan forgot the shock of seeing the girl and remembered how on that day she had waited and
waited for her father to arrive. When he was two
hours late, her mother had told her that he was
not coming, but she refused to give up hope. She
stayed on the couch in the living room close by

the front door, loudly singing the Mickey Mouse song in an attempt to stay awake as the hour grew later. She remembered waking up tucked tightly in a bed that felt too much like her own. She lay there for hours refusing to open her eyes and face the fact that she might not be in the hotel room right next to Disney World like her dad had promised.

"My daddy is an airline pilot. He goes on trips all over the world. That's why he doesn't live with us. Once, he took me up in his own plane to see the peaks of the Colorado Mountains. He's coming to get me next summer just as soon as he gets settled in his new place."

Dropping to the cold tile floor in a fetal position, Joan rocked back and forth as she remembered that day and all the days like it. Her father lied to her and she lied about him. With tears falling from her face and too emotional to stand, she crawled to the bed. Buried under the sheets, she felt trapped by the bad memories and feared what other dangers the experiment held.

"Joan, write about your father," a female voice whispered in her ear. Joan would never forget that voice. It belonged to the woman from the auditorium.

Joan jumped off of the bed to look around, but she saw no one. She started to run to the door but realized even then she would have nowhere to go. She wanted to scream but decided not to. If someone heard her and responded, she would not know what to say. Once they came to her rescue, they might think she was losing it and haul her off to a mental ward.

Not knowing what else to do, and hoping the

whole time the woman would not speak again, she cautiously picked up her pen and turned to the first page in her journal. Initially, she had no idea what she was going to write. To her surprise, the words poured out effortlessly.

Every single time he told me something, I believed it, Joan wrote in her journal. *I loved my dad so much and wanted more than anything for him to love me too. Every year around my birthday I would run home from school, hoping to find a card in the mail. Sometimes he sent one, and sometimes he didn't. Once, he sent me the same card two years in a row.*

Against what Joan had hoped for, suddenly, the woman spoke once again. "I want to help you through this, Joan. I am delighted you have allowed yourself to feel what you refused to so long ago."

Not frightened this time due to the fact that Joan was full of emotion and could use someone to talk to, she replied. "Who are you? Where did you come from?"

"Joan, I'm here to help you, my dear."

"But I don't want to do this. It hurts. I was better off just leaving it where it was," Joan said as her eyes filled with tears.

"No, Joan, leaving it where it was . . . burying it . . . is why you are here today. You have not decided to lock yourself in this room for the next week to give up and fail to face the truth."

"This is just too crazy. I can't believe all this is happening. I feel like I'm on a bad episode of the *Twilight Zone.*"

"I know you don't want to do this right now." Joan was about to speak, but the woman cut her off and continued to speak. "Write about the father-daughter dance."

Joan felt a burst of embarrassment, realizing, once more, this woman knew her business in its entirety.

After quickly scanning her brain for a way out of the situation and finding none, Joan picked up her pen and started to write. The moment her pen hit the paper, she felt her body tense up twice as much as before. Suddenly, the memories flooded into her mind when only moments ago they had been so distant

I was so excited, Joan wrote in her journal. *I was in the eighth grade and my grandmother made me a beautiful silver dress and bought me my first pair of high-heeled shoes. My cousin did my hair in soft pin curls. My mom even told me I could wear a little lipstick.*

I looked at this handsome man in my doorway and fell in love instantly. Joan stopped a moment to wipe away the tears from her face and then she continued to write. *He was more beautiful than I could have imagined. I walked around that dance like I had the cure for the common cold in my possession, introducing all my friends, and my enemies, to my father.*

At the end of the night, he told me he loved me and gave his word that although he lived in another state, he would make sure we spent time together. He apologized for all the other times he had misled me. I didn't need any of them, though. I forgave him for every disappointment the moment I laid eyes on him at my doorstep. He was mine and I was his. That night, I flew in my dreams. Joan paused to take a deep breath.

He didn't call until three weeks later to tell me he had a new job, a new wife, and a baby on the way. He thought I would be happy for him. "I'm going to send you a ticket just as soon as we get settled in," he said on the phone that day. The ticket has yet to come.

Consumed with anger, Joan forgot the weirdness of the situation, put the pen down, and began speaking to the woman as if she was in the room with her and not just the sound of her voice in her ears.

"I didn't hear from him again until my eighteenth birthday," Joan ranted. "Yeah, he had sent Christmas and birthday cards when he felt like it, but it was not until then that I heard his voice again. I hung up the phone in his face." Joan threw her hands in the air. "You know he had the nerve to call himself a deacon. How can a person lead other people when they cannot lead their own family? Isn't there something in the Bible about that? I mean, how can a person go to sleep every night not knowing if their child is sick, hungry, dead or alive? All the times I needed him to be there for me and all I got was one short dance.

"You know how little kids say stuff like, 'I'm going to tell my daddy?' Well, I had no daddy to tell. I hated having to turn in my permission slips and enrollment cards year after year with my father's name, address, and phone number left blank. I would try to make sure mine was at the bottom of the stack so only the teacher would see it."

Joan started pacing the floor, tears falling from her face. She then continued.

"Once, Tisha and I stole her daddy's car to visit some boys who lived three hours away. The car broke down on our way back home. She had to call her father in the middle of the night to come get us. As soon as he saw her, his face lit up. Not concerned with the fact she had stolen his car, he was just happy to see his daughter; glad she was safe. The first thing he did when he showed up was run and hug her, and then he hugged me too."

Collapsing on the bed, Joan sighed. "You know what, lady?" she said to the invisible voice. "That was the first and last time a man has ever hugged me just to hug me, and not because he felt obligated since he had just had sex with me or because he had hopes of having sex with me in the future.

"Every night, Tisha's father gave her a hug when he came home from work." Streams of tears rolled from Joan's swollen and tender eyes as she lay on the bed exhausted. "I could hear his voice whenever I was on the phone with Tisha at six-thirty P.M., which is when he came home from work. 'Where's my baby girl?' he'd ask. Tisha would act irritated. 'Daddy, please!' she would say.

"Sometimes at six-thirty, I still catch myself looking at the clock, thinking how wonderful it would have been if my daddy couldn't rest for the evening until he had given me a hug." She covered her mouth with her hands, contemplating how she had allowed those words to slip from her lips.

"One time, Joan, you really, really needed your father," the woman said. "It was somewhere around the time of your fourteenth birthday."

Joan abruptly stopped pacing the floor. She could not believe how relentless the woman had become. This was an even uglier recollection; one Joan had banned from her memory a long time ago.

"Go ahead, my dear . . . write," the woman ordered Joan.

Feeling like a caged animal, Joan looked around the room. If only she could see the woman, maybe she could make her understand. Only a few times in the last fifteen years had she allowed herself to think back to the incident. Now, this woman wanted her to relive it in detail.

"What good is this going to do?" Joan pleaded. "I mean, we both know what happened, right?" Joan felt herself getting nauseous and beams of sweat started to appear on her forehead. Joan waited for the woman to speak, but she said nothing.

"Let me just get a glass of water," said Joan. She had never drank a glass of water slower. She contemplated getting another glass, but decided against it. She could not win; she exhaled longer than necessary and then reached for her pen and wrote the following:

The summer had been long, hot, and boring, especially since Tisha was visiting her grandmother and since my brother spent summers with his father. I had been sitting in the house watching music videos for weeks, so when a moving truck pulled up across the street with two girls who looked to be around my age, I quickly ran out the house to introduce myself. The girls' names were Sabrina and Shauna. Sabrina was fourteen years old and her sister, Shauna, was fifteen.

I showed them around the neighborhood and bought us candy and gum from the corner store with some of my birthday money. I wanted to ask them if they wanted to go swing at the park or gather up some snacks and have a picnic, which was exactly what me and Tisha did whenever we got bored, but they didn't look like the swinging or picnicking type. They had long, black, wavy hair and pimple-free honey brown skin. And if that wasn't enough, they both had the body I was still waiting for.

Joan felt like she was experiencing it while she wrote it. The feeling of rejection, humiliation, and shame were the same now as they had been that day.

We had just turned onto Orion Street, four houses down from where Jamal, David, and Chris were playing basketball, but that didn't stop the boys from holding up the game to watch us, or should I say watch "them," walk down the street. Tisha and I never got a response even close to the one Sabrina and Shauna received when we walked down this street, which was often since all of the boys we liked lived on Orion Street and were always outside playing basketball, talking, or listening to music.

Jamal was the first to speak. "Man, they look good enough to eat," he shouted. As we got closer, I could see they had a hungry look in their eyes, like they hadn't eaten in weeks and Sabrina and Shauna were Quarter Pounder hamburgers with cheese and a carton of hot salty fries.

Sabrina and Shauna kept walking and talking, acting as if they didn't notice the boys were jocking them hard. When we reached where the boys were standing, Shauna walked up to David, smiled, and grabbed the ball he was holding. In an attempt to get closer to her, he pretended to try to get it back. Not to be outdone by his older brother, Chris walked up to the sidewalk where Sabrina and I were standing and started playing in Sabrina's hair like it was something he did on a regular basis.

Jamal grabbed a ball off the curb and started shooting hoops, concentrating hard like he was in a three-

point contest at the NBA all-star game. I knew Jamal, who had been in my homeroom for the last three years, wasn't the least bit concerned with me.

While I was trying to think of a way to get out of there before getting my feelings hurt, David said, "I think it's time to go old school. Let's play hide and seek?"

Instantly, the boys shouted in unison, "Hide and go get!"

Shauna and Sabrina started laughing. Sabrina then said, "We are too old to play such a childish game. Besides, we just moved here and wouldn't know where to hide." As if she didn't know that was the point.

As I eased away, my fast walk turned into a slow jog. While turning the corner, I heard Jamal say, "I'll play, but I'm not getting her. Where did she go? Oh well, she ain't nothing to get no way." The group erupted in laughter. Luckily, I made it to my front door before the first tear fell.

To my surprise, Sabrina and Shauna came knocking on my door early the next morning, as soon as my momma had driven off for work. I was going to tell them I didn't want to hang out with them, but before I could open my mouth, Sabrina was on the sofa and Shauna was in the kitchen pouring herself a bowl of cereal. Next thing you know, we had spent the morning cracking up on cartoons and watching game shows.

I don't know who, but somebody decided they were going to give me a makeover. Sabrina went in my closet, found some of my old shorts, and cut them until they were so short my butt cheeks were hanging out. Shauna took one of my T-shirts and tied it high in the back so my stomach would show. Sabrina then made up my face, gave me her big silver hoop earrings to wear, and pressed out my hair.

Eventually, we got tired of looking at me and sat down to watch some more TV. We soon dozed off, and at close to one o'clock I heard what sounded like a knock at my back door. Scared, I couldn't move. The knock came again, harder the second time, waking Sabrina and Shauna. Without any hesitation, they hopped up off the sofa and opened the back door as if our guests, David, Jamal, and Chris, were expected.

Jamal, seeing me and my new look spread all over the sofa, took notice.

"Damn, Joan, you all that," he said, licking his lips. "You're what I call DL to the fullest." Noticing the clueless look upon my face, he said, "Dark and lovely." I tried to stop the smile, but it started at my feet, traveled through my body, and was on my face in a matter of seconds. Jamal plopped down next to me. My heart hadn't had a chance to slow. It was beating fast and hard. No longer because of the knock at the back door, but because a real live boy had given me a compliment.

While staring at Jamal, with him returning my gaze, I heard what sounded like glass shattering. I rushed into the kitchen to find Shauna, Sabrina, Chris, and David taking turns pouring a liquid, I assumed was alcohol, into my momma's favorite glasses.

I knew I was playing with fire by having them in my house. But it would be several hours before my momma would return home, so I didn't sweat it. I quickly looked out the window in the kitchen to make sure Mr. Robby, my nosy next-door neighbor, wasn't around.

Coming up behind me, Jamal grabbed my waist and said, "Don't stress, baby. We made sure Mad Rob didn't see us." I could smell the Colgate on his breath and the Dial soap on his body. He grabbed my hand and led me back to the sofa where he sat me on his lap. "Joan, I'm sorry about the way I acted yesterday. I was just mad because I had been losing the basketball game, and I hate losing." Jamal and I were both motionless except for the vibrations from his pounding heart that radiated from the middle of his body and transferred to mine.

After exiting the kitchen, Sabrina told me to tell Shauna, who was upstairs in my bedroom with David, that she was going over to Chris's house. Right after that, Sabrina and Chris left my house.

"Alone at last," Jamal said, smiling as he got up to lock the door.

After returning to the couch, Jamal put his hand underneath my shirt, which caused my body to react in a way that was foreign to me. Next, he laid me on the sofa and started kissing me where he had been touching me. He whispered to me that I was pretty and had a nice body. It felt so sweet that I wanted to lay there forever.

After petting for about thirty minutes, Jamal turned away, saying he was tired of just kissing and was ready to go home. Frustrated with the fact he wanted to leave, I asked him what he would like to do.

"You'll only get mad if I tell you," was his response. After assuring him I wouldn't, he said he wanted me to kiss him down below, and then he pointed to the front of his jeans. He promised if I did, we could kiss more afterwards.

"I don't know how," I said, hesitantly.

"Don't worry. I will teach you."

After making him promise not to tell anyone, I dropped to my knees.

When the front door opened, I was in a kneeling position before Jamal with him in my mouth. My momma let out a high-pitched scream that sounded like nails scratching a chalkboard. With the swiftness of a cheetah,

Jamal jumped up and ran out the back door. I still can't figure out how he made such a quick escape.

My mom had this look in her eyes I couldn't quite read, but I knew I had better run too. She would have caught up with me if it had not been for Shauna and David running through the hallway from my room and out the door. That moment of confusion gave me just the time I needed to safely lock myself in my bedroom. From the other side of my door, my mother kept getting louder and louder and knocking harder and harder.

"Joan, get your butt out here!" she yelled.

I thought she was going to break the door down. I was shaking and trembling as sweat poured profusely down my face. I didn't know what to do. Frantically, I searched until I found an old letter my father had written me a while back.

Joan stopped writing to catch her breath. Just writing about the situation brought back the feeling of fear and anxiety she had experienced when it happened.

Joan then said aloud, "I actually thought he was going to answer the phone. I can't believe it as I'm writing it, but I actually thought he was going to come get me." Joan shook her head and then began writing again.

As my mother was still yelling for me to open the door, I yelled back to her that I was calling my daddy. I'll never forget her response.

"Haven't you figured out you don't have a daddy?" she said. "I clothe you! I keep a roof over your head! I feed you! Your daddy doesn't give a damn about you! You go ahead and call and see what happens!"

During Momma's ranting, I dialed the number that was on the letter. The man who answered the phone was real nice. Boldly, I told him, "I want to speak to my daddy." I'm sure he could tell I had been crying, which is probably the reason why he tried to help me.

I had never used the number before. All that time I thought the number was to my daddy's house, but actually it was a place of employment. The man that answered the phone said he had just started working there and did not know my dad. He called several of his coworkers over to the phone to see if they knew him. Only one did. She said he had quit months ago and she did not know where he went. I hung up without saying thank you or good-bye.

By that time, I had heard Mr. Robby come over to see what all the commotion was about after seeing people flee from our house. He eventually took my mom to his house to calm her down.

As I lay on the floor thinking of the best way to kill myself, the realization hit me that my father was a liar and had been lying to me all my life. I guess my mother was waiting for me to figure it out on my own. I know I should have known it before then, but it wasn't until I was sitting topless with the phone in my hand and tears covering my face that I realized the truth and gave up hope. In all ways that counted, he died that day.

"What kind of effect did it have on you growing up?" the woman asked Joan.

Joan replied, "I don't know. Up until I met you, I thought I was doing okay. I didn't go around crying nonstop, talking to people who were invisible, or seeing people in the mirror."

Ignoring her sarcasm, the woman calmly said, "You always know, Joan. Take a few minutes and tell me what it was like to have a father who was alive, and yet did little to acknowledge your presence."

Joan dropped her head into her lap and placed her hands over her eyes in an attempt to suppress the tears.

"Why didn't he love me?" Joan broke down. "There is so much I never got to know about him. I never watched a television show with him. I don't even know what he likes to eat for breakfast. For the love he gave me, I could be a prostitute lying out in the street.

"My momma always told me women had to be strong, especially black women. She said we all have problems, but you must keep pressing forward. So, that's what I did. I never stopped. I just kept going. I went to school everyday. I worked my way through college. I did the best I could do. I didn't cry. Tears were not going to make my daddy love me. Therefore, I stopped crying and never complained. I just kept living. I thought if I lived fast enough and hard enough, somehow and one day it would all be okay."

Joan took a deep breath, now realizing that no matter how fast and how hard she had run, it was, now, all catching up with her.

Chapter 4

The third day of the experiment, and after another restless night, Joan awoke, but did not move. If getting out of bed meant another day in the experiment, she would just as soon stay tightly woven underneath the hotel's soft sheets. She did not want to think this morning; last night she had pondered question after question to no avail.

Did the absence of her father have a direct correlation to the many men in her life? What was he doing now? Could he be alive and well? Wouldn't it be nice if that creepy woman left her alone today? Did he have a good reason for doing what he did? Could her mother answer more questions for her? Why had she not thought of any of this before?

Joan was certain of only one thing as she stiffly sat up in bed—what lay ahead would be the most challenging test she ever had to face. All of that would have to wait, though. Right now, she was about to escape, if only for a moment.

She grabbed the hotel's room service menu.

The wine list was the first to catch her attention. A few glasses too many of merlot and maybe the woman would disappear. Then she looked over at the clock on the night table and realized it was only nine in the morning. At the bottom of the menu was a picture of the restaurant's strawberry cheesecake. Joan had made this dessert for a coworker's baby shower several years prior, now her staff demanded that she make it for all their celebrations. She had learned the show-stopping recipe from her great-aunt, Alice, her grand-mother's sister.

Joan started spending her summers working with Aunt Alice in her bakery in Marshall, Texas. After the incident with Jamal, her mother no longer trusted her to be at home during the summer while she worked. She had enjoyed her time with Aunt Alice so much that that she still found herself dreaming about going to culinary school and eventually owning a successful bakery like her aunt.

Joan counted the years since her grandfather's funeral, which was the last time she had seen her aunt, and realized she had not spoken to her in five years.

Just then, her cell phone rang, disrupting her thoughts. Looking down at the caller ID and see-ing it was her mother, she couldn't answer it fast enough, fearing something might have happened to her son, and she'd never know if she didn't an-swer the phone.

"Hello," Joan answered.

"Hello, Joan." The calmness of her mother's voice produced a sigh of relief from Joan. She was worried something may have happened to her son.

"What's up, Momma?"

"I was just calling to tell you Jr.'s daddy came and picked him up last night."

"What!" Joan exclaimed.

"Joan, please, it's not right to keep that boy from his daddy. Besides, Jr. called him on his own. I didn't know anything about it until James Sr. was standing at my door."

Joan knew she had no right to doubt her mother. In her mother's younger years, though, when she was raising Joan and Travis, she was known for getting rid of anybody, including her children, if one of her male companions happened to stop by and needed some of her assistance. Time after time she and Travis were whisked off so quickly they barely had time to pack a change of clothes. She must have decided she was going to be a better grandmother than mother, because from the day James Jr. was born, she had made herself completely available. She rarely missed a school performance, track meet, or basketball game. When Joan called her to keep James Jr. she always did, even if she already had plans in place and it meant canceling them.

"Well, did he leave the number?" Joan asked, trying to remain calm.

As her mother called off the numbers, Joan quickly wrote them down. "Thanks, Momma. I'll talk to you later."

"Wait a minute. How's the vacation going? I know you're showboating in that teeny-weenie bikini you were telling me about. If I had your figure—"

"Oh, Momma, I need to go. I'm already late for

my hula class." With that said, Joan hung up before her mother could say another word.

Joan eyeballed the phone number she had scribbled on the hotel's notepad, hoping it did not mean everything she knew it must. James Sr. had finally settled down and bought that huge house he always wanted. The number had the same area code and exchange as Lila's. Lila and her live-in doctor boyfriend lived in a very upscale subdivision in Pearland, a city minute outside the city. It was a gated community along a series of man-made lakes. All the homes on the block were spacious with perfectly landscaped yards. Each home had access to a golf course, athletic club, full-size basketball court, football field, and walking trail.

Did the similarity in phone numbers mean he had settled down in the same area as Lila? Did he marry Raquel? Should she call? What if Raquel answered the phone? The last thing she needed was a verbal exchange with that woman.

Joan was twenty-two when she met James Sr. and he had been her weakness since the day she laid eyes on him, which was on the day she had been speeding through a school zone. All of a sudden she heard the siren from his patrol car. When he stepped out the car, her heart fluttered in anticipation and her urgent need to go to the restroom passed.

James was not handsome, but his manly demeanor, deep Barry White voice, and well-kept 6'5" body more than made up for what he was lacking in facial features. After Joan explained her reason for speeding, he burst out laughing, revealing perfect white teeth and an engaging smile.

When he asked why she just did not stop
somewhere, she felt even sillier trying to explain
why she would rather drive recklessly to get to
her home than to use a public restroom. He
looked down sweetly at her as if he were sorry he
had laughed at her. He then went on to tell her he
was on his way to lunch at a restaurant around
the corner and that he was sure they had
sparkling clean restrooms. Gladly accepting his
invitation to join him, Joan followed closely behind his police cruiser as if he were her own personal escort.

The restaurant did not look like much on the
outside, but inside, the décor was one of spectacular vaulted ceilings, mirrors on every wall, elaborate paintings, and carpet so plush she could not
help but slide her sandals off, after she sat down,
and squish her toes around in it. The unfamiliar
South American food was delicious, and when she
had trouble deciding which dessert to order, being
that she was a dessert enthusiast and wanted to
taste them all, he insisted she order all five that
were on the menu. Now, this may have sounded
ridiculous to some, but to Joan, it was a sweet
gesture. As she bit into the *dulce de leche* soufflé,
coconut flan, Brazilian nut shortbread, plantains
with crème, and pear empanadas, she knew she
had to marry James, especially if he was anywhere near as sweet as the splendid desserts.

That first day, James told Joan all about Raquel,
his live-in girlfriend at the time, and how they
had known each other since their days at Sterling
High School. She was the head majorette and he
was on the football and basketball teams. They

shared a three-year-old son and his initial intentions were to marry her one day.

He said Raquel was a wonderful woman, but she was a hairstylist, and although she was successful and well paid, the fact that she had not finished from a four-year university was something he could not overlook. Being a highly educated man, he had always envisioned himself with a highly educated woman. He had a bachelor's degree in political science, a master's in criminology, and was in the process of getting his doctorate. His plan was to retire from the police force and then teach at the college level.

He expressed that while he had tried to introduce Raquel to the finer things in life, she would rather have fried pork chops and grape soda than filet mignon and cabernet. She couldn't cook or keep the house clean, and she still had not yet lost the weight from her pregnancy.

Over the next few months following the time they first met, Joan made it her business to become anti-Raquel. She flaunted her flat stomach and hard body in James's face with tight dresses and jeans. She went to wine tastings, visited food shows, subscribed to food magazines, and attended gourmet cooking classes. She even went as far as to start researching the best schools in order to obtain her master's degree, making sure she left the literature where he could find it.

She had a professional clean her home twice a week and she kept her refrigerator and pantry filled with James's favorite foods. She was fanatical about making sure his food was cooked to perfection, even throwing out whole meals if they did not meet her high expectations. Upon learning his favorite pies were sweet potato and pecan, she created a sweet potato pecan pie and named it after him. He liked it so much, he asked her to make one at least once a week.

Within six months, Joan was pregnant. When James broke the news to Raquel, which he had to do since Joan was adamant about having the baby, she insisted he move out. James eagerly moved in with Joan, and within two weeks he asked her to marry him. They lived together for three months before the one thing Joan feared the most happened—Raquel showed up at their apartment with a moving truck to reclaim her man.

It was literally a tug of war as the two women pulled at James. Joan begged him to stay while Raquel begged him to leave with her. When James stood clueless as to what to do next, the women began to punch one another. Joan won the fight, but in the end, Raquel won the man.

Against her better judgment, Joan continued the relationship with James during her pregnancy, claiming she could not bear to be alone during such a crucial time. After giving birth, her excuse for remaining with James was her son needed both of his parents. Time and time again she tried to leave James. She dated and had sex with a number of men in an attempt to free her mind of him, but whenever James called, she canceled any plans she already had in place to be with him. He would stay for a night, a week, a month, but he always went back to Raquel.

Several months ago, James stopped calling to speak to Joan. The only time he would call was when he wanted to pick up or drop off James Jr., never bothering to stay for dinner or spend the night like he had done in the past. When Joan paged him or called him, he would come up with a quick excuse to get off the phone if she had no news to report about James Jr. When she asked what had changed, he told her she was delusional and he was acting the same as he always had. Hurt by his words, Joan started making excuses as to why James Jr. could not see his father. Not long after their last conversation, she moved into the downtown condo and left no forwarding address or telephone number.

Eventually, he caught up with her. One day, when she and her son were pulling up into the parking lot for his Saturday basketball game, she noticed a truck resembling James Sr.'s a few rows ahead.

Leaving her son in the car with his grandmother, Joan approached the gym to peek inside and saw two proud parents, James and Raquel, softly taking turns kissing their tiny newborn baby, as Morris their other child played near by. Now she understood why James suddenly had a change of heart several months back. He finally had the baby girl he always wanted. Carefully holding his baby and with his arms around Raquel, he seemed to be a new person. Joan could not recall one time when he had held her in public.

Angry and refusing to be humiliated any further, she went back to the car and asked her son if he wanted to pick up his two best friends and go to the beach, knowing he hated basketball anyway and would never turn down a day at the beach.

Joan snapped back to reality when her cell

phone rang, displaying the now familiar number on her caller ID.

"Good morning, Joan." She hated her body for reacting the way it did from the mere sound of his voice.

"What can I do for you, James?" she responded, trying to sound busy.

James took a deep breath in preparation for the mouth lashing he had become accustomed to when Joan was not happy. She wanted to cry at the sound of the squealing baby in the background and Raquel asking James if he wanted more coffee.

"Jr. called. He wants to stay here while you're—"

Joan interrupted. "Yeah, his grandmother already called. Just drop him over there on Sunday."

"Really?" James asked.

Joan pretended not to notice how surprised he sounded. "Is he still asleep?"

"Yeah, we stayed up late last night playing video games. He beat me twice."

"Tell my baby I'll see him on Sunday," Joan said.

Quickly, Joan hung up the phone, not wanting to hear James thank her for not acting like the cursing, shouting, out of control, desperate woman she usually did.

She threw her cell phone at the wall so hard it cracked into pieces. Immediately, there was a knock at the door. Fearing someone on the hotel's staff heard the loud noise, she quickly picked up the pieces of the phone and tossed them in the trash. She tried to think of a believable lie for the noise as she smiled and gently opened the door.

"What's up, baby?"

She was not prepared for what greeted her on the other side. It was lying, handsome, "sweat out your perm but you don't give a damn, never going to talk to you again" Darren standing in her doorway.

"What are you doing here, Darren?" Joan said, poking her head out of the door to see if anyone else was with him. Once she saw Darren was alone, she leaned back inside, his stare awaited her.

She liked the way he was gazing at her, as if she looked appealing to him in her satin forest-green pajamas.

Darren's parents owned real estate throughout the country. One minute he was in New York, the next Atlanta, and then Miami. The problem was that he never told Joan when he was leaving even though they were supposed to be in a relationship.

They had planned a weekend getaway a year ago. Joan was packed and ready to go but Darren never called or showed up despite her frequent phone calls. He phoned days later saying he was golfing in Santa Barbara. He offered to buy her a plane ticket so she could come join him, but by that time, she had enough of his behavior. She told Darren it was over and he could no longer come in and out of her life whenever he pleased, and now he stood before her.

Joan placed an irritated look on her face. "I thought I told you to get lost and stay lost."

Joan had never met a man who walked with such boldness as Darren Quentin Foster. She always wondered if it was a front or if he really believed he was King of the Universe.

He spoke today as he always had . . . direct and with confidence. "My frat is having a convention here. I saw you getting on the elevator the other day. I called out to you, but apparently you had something on your mind or else you need a hearing aid." He grinned broadly at Joan.

She glared back at him, admiring his thick lips, cinnamon colored skin, and broad shoulders. She looked at his suit, first noticing the quality and then wondering if he still had that rock-hard six-pack hid away underneath it. She glanced at the sparkling stones in the face of his watch, only to notice his big hands. Happy hands she used to call them, because each stroke of his hands would induce a deeper state of bliss. She had thoughts of him picking her up and placing her on top of the cherrywood dresser so he could insert his reliable stress reliever inside her stress-prone flesh.

Without being invited, he walked into her hotel room. As the door closed behind them, he picked her up, and sat her on the bed, reminding her of what an exciting, fearless lover he used to be. Reminiscing back, she remembered trying to do everything within her power to look normal in a crowded restaurant while Darren was hidden underneath the table supplying her body with spasm after spasm of pleasure.

As Darren lowered himself on the bed, he pulled her to him, embracing her tightly and kissing her firmly on the lips. Instantly, Joan started to feel her tense muscles loosen. His hands caressed her thighs and his tongue made circles on her neck. Allowing herself to become more relaxed, she reclined on the bed and quietly moaned in delight.

"What are you doing?" Joan suddenly heard a familiar voice in her ear, only it was much louder this time.

Jumping up like Darren's touch was fire, Joan ran out the door and stood in the hallway with her back pressed up against the wall. Darren ran after her with a puzzled look on his face, jarring the hotel door with the latch. He then stood in front of Joan, but she refused to gaze into his eyes.

"Listen, um . . . Darren, you have to go," she stammered. "Please forget me and move on with your life." Darren had heard this before, only to convince her to change her mind. Therefore, it did not surprise her when she looked up and Darren appeared not to have heard one word she had said.

He closed in on her, putting one hand tightly around her waist and used the other to bring her face to his face. With his lips right next to hers he moaned seductively, "Baby, why are you tripping? Don't you know I need to be near you?" He pulled himself closer to her body and cupped her bottom with both of his hands. He whispered seductively, "Don't you need to be near me?"

Joan said nothing; she only moved her face away from his lips. The grip he held on her body so was tight she could feel his heart beat. Part of her wanted to push him away, but the part of her that wanted to be securely in Darren's arms was stronger.

Darren looked down both sides of the hallway, seeing they were alone, he slid his hands underneath her pajama bottoms and moved his head so he could kiss her neck.

Joan prayed something would happen to get her out of this situation because she was not strong enough to get out of it herself. As if an answer to her request, a housekeeper tripped coming out a door across the hall, sending her and the cart to the ground. Darren hurried to help her.

Desperate to help herself, Joan ran inside her suite, quickly locking the door behind her. Upon entering, Joan spotted Darren's shiny platinum watch on the nightstand; he must have taken it off while they were kissing. She was angry now. Darren came knocking on her door with the intent to have sex. His goal was to have his way with her and then move on to the next event he had planned for the day.

As much as she wanted to grab the watch and throw it at Darren, along with some expletive phrases that would hurt him as much as he had hurt her, she knew the only person she should be angry at was herself. Darren only treated her the way she had allowed herself to be treated. But this is where it would all end.

She walked across the hallway with tears falling down her face and delicately handed the watch to Darren, who still had an innocent look on his face. Without a word, Joan slowly returned to her room and climbed into bed.

She opened her purse and pulled out a picture of her, James Sr., and their son. She used to put the picture under her pillow and hope somehow, some way, they would be a real family one day.

Joan picked up a pillow off the bed and imagined that it was Raquel's face. She punched the pillow twice softly. She felt silly at first but before she realized it, she was on her knees crying profusely as she punched the pillow wildly.

She was supposed to be James's wife. She was

the one that was supposed to give birth to the daughter he always wanted. She was the one who was supposed to lie next to him every night. She was the one he was supposed to kiss when he left for work. She was the one he was supposed to make love to in their very own house in their very own room. It was supposed to be her, not Raquel!

Joan punched the pillow across the room and it landed on the floor. She got out of the bed and started slamming the pillow on the floor repeatedly. The pillow burst, but still she did not stop. She threw what was left of the pillow across the room again. Then, a sudden pain in her right arm caused her to lie back on the floor in agony.

Tears and mucus were running down her face. Her eyes were so sore she could barely see. She whispered while rocking back and forth, "Why do I have to be alone? Why do I have to cry myself to sleep at night? Why does he not want me? Why not me? I gave him everything I had. No woman could love him more."

Joan cried until she was exhausted. Eventually the pain in her arm subsided. She washed her face and blew her nose on the pillow she had been hitting and placed it in the laundry bag. She walked to the bed, picked up the remote, and turned on the television, hoping to get lost in someone else's pathetic life.

Chapter 5

I was flipping channels and feeling sorry for myself most of yesterday, Joan wrote into her journal. *I started out watching a reality show where they perform dangerous stunts for money, but that got boring real fast. Seeing people make fools of themselves used to cheer me up, but yesterday it made me feel worse.*

Eventually, I settled on a Christian television station. Two hours into watching music videos and a children's play, I saw a commercial promoting a women's conference. To my surprise, it was being held at a church I had never heard of despite the address being several blocks from my condo. I can't say exactly why, but I did not hesitate to call and provide the operator with my credit card number to register for the conference.

After placing the receiver back on its base, I instantly became nervous. I hadn't been to church regularly in years, and I knew it wasn't a norm for infrequent churchgoers like me to attend conferences. I was suddenly con-

cerned with not having anyone to talk to, what I should expect, and what to wear. The church was close to my house but far from the hotel and I started to wonder how long it would take me to drive; not knowing exactly where it was located. I didn't want to risk being late on top of everything else. The operator I talked to said I could pick up my ticket at the church's bookstore the day of the conference or anytime before the conference during the church's regular business hours.

Therefore, in an attempt to calm my nerves, I decided to take a test drive so I could pick up my ticket and at the same time get a good look at the church.

As I approached the exit leading to the church, faster than I expected, my heart started beating at an accelerated pace. I could not believe just thinking about going into a church made my body react the way it did. I wanted to turn around. I did, once. But eventually I pulled up into the parking lot.

With the exception of about ten scattered cars, the lot was empty. That is why I went at one in the afternoon; I didn't figure very many people would be there.

I slowly drove around the building twice like a robber casing a bank, wondering how I could have missed it—the building—seeing I had driven that route several times before. I had to have passed it dozens of times on my way to and from taking James Jr. to his Boy Scout meetings on the very next block.

I parked close to the bookstore entrance but not too close. I was so nervous about walking in that I actually sat in the car twenty minutes before convincing myself to get out of the car.

I wanted to see if the people looked friendly. I wanted to see how they were dressed. I wanted to know if I would fit in, I guess.

Eventually, I realized the only way to find all this out was to enter the church. I slowly approached the building, my heart racing the entire way. As I opened the plain metal door and stepped inside the foyer, I walked very slowly, hoping I would not embarrass myself.

The first thing I saw was four middle-aged women dressed in suits approaching the door as I entered. Each of them looked at me, and then looked away like I was simply a speck of dirt on an otherwise clean wall.

Suddenly, my favorite pale blue sleeveless sundress seemed out of place. Once they passed me, I turned around and looked at my reflection in a nearby window so I could see what they saw. To me, I looked fine. Everything was covered up and in place.

Gathering what little self-confidence I had left, I continued walking. Before I had a chance to walk two steps, one of the ladies walked back towards me, looked me up and down again, and then suspiciously asked me why I was there.

No, she did not say, "May I help you?" she said, "Why are you here?" I could not say anything. I just stood there and looked at her.

I felt like the other women were hiding around the corner to offer protection just in case the harlot in the blue dress got out of control. I felt naked and exposed. I had not uttered a single word to these women, but it was as if they knew I did not belong. Aware of the tension my presence was causing, I walked out the door before she had the chance to say another word.

I cried for the duration of the ride back to the hotel. The more I drove, the angrier I became. By the time I reached the hotel, I had a major headache.

I couldn't stop thinking that I had just as much

right to be in that church as they did, yet this so-called woman of God practically pushed me out the front doors. I bet she hasn't been a Christian all of her life.

Every single event where I had allowed other people to control how I thought of myself started to surface. That's why I had to pick up the pen and start writing.

Joan stopped writing and closed her eyes. She then took a deep breath and proceeded.

How many days am I going to waste like this? I have spent all my adult years in some imaginary competition trying to prove to the rest of the world Joan was okay or that Joan was better than okay.

Look at me. Yesterday I had a fight with a pillow. Apparently I am far from okay.

I only bought a Mercedes-Benz SUV because most people I know would give their right arm to be able to afford it. I have a closet full of designer clothes, shoes, and handbags. Only problem is figuring out which of them I purchased because I liked them, and which did I buy because I allowed some person, magazine, or commercial to influence me. I didn't even know Manolo Blahnik shoes existed until Sarah Jessica Parker told me. I'm looking at this loud orange Hermès leather handbag. What was I thinking? I should have put that money in Jr.'s college fund.

I wish I would have found the bookstore in that church like I had planned. I'm so upset at myself for allowing that woman to make me feel inferior. I've decided I'm going to the conference tomorrow, and I don't care if I don't know any of the hymns or when to stand or when to be seated. If I can't find the scriptures in the Bible as fast as everybody else, that's fine too. I don't care if they can tell I haven't been to church in a long time.

So far, looking to other people for guidance hasn't produced much for me. It's time I started looking higher . . . much higher. Today, I am releasing myself of the burdens of everybody else's expectations.

Chapter 6

It was now the fifth day into the experiment for Joan. She felt the need to prepare herself for tonight. She refused to go into the church like she did yesterday, timid and lost. She was determined to walk into the church today confident and unashamed.

Joan closed the shades, turned off the lights, sat on the floor, and called on God to give her the strength she needed to get through the day. Afterward, Joan took a seat on the edge of the bed and read a few Psalms, the ones her grandfather used to quote to her . . . Psalms 23, 91, and 103.

Her past started to creep up on her. Dark images floated in and out of her head. Finally, she prayed. It took a while for her to get started. Joan remembered how her grandfather could pray so eloquently, it sounded as if it was poetry. She started off trying to pray like her grandfather, but eventually she started talking to God like He was her Father who loved her instead of a distant relative she was trying to impress with flowery words. She felt really good afterward. Joan cried too, but these were happy tears.

Joan had always known God was there watching her, but she denied it because she was not living right and had no intentions of changing her lifestyle. But now that she was ready to change sides, she did not have to try to run from God anymore. She could sit still and soak up His presence.

She managed for only a few moments to think of nothing but God's love, protection, and forgiveness. When it was time to open her eyes, she felt lighter, less tense, and knew that it was time to stop avoiding the inevitable. She had spent her life on the surface refusing to examine the choices she'd made. But now it was time to dive deep to find out how Joan became Joan.

She retrieved her journal and turned until she found an empty page. She then began to write.

Dear Mother,

I was taught to respect my elders and that's why I find it so hard to speak ill of you. I love you dearly and I appreciate everything you have done for me, Travis, and my son. But, Mother, you made mistakes in your mothering, mistakes I have to admit to myself right here, right now, today.

While growing up, I sometimes felt as if you wished Travis and I were never born. We have never been enough for you. You always had to have a warm body in your bed, even if it meant sacrificing your dignity. I wish one time, just one time, you could have been complete with us alone, but your smile was only genuine when you had a man to share your life with. We never really seemed like gifts to you at all, just things that happened during your quest to find a good man.

I can hear you now on the phone talking with one of your many girlfriends. "Girl, one day I'm going to get me a good man. You can take that to the bank and cash it." Every single time you brought a new man home, you actually thought he was "the one," the one who would stay and validate your existence. Over and over, I watched you cleaning the house with meticulous detail, ironing his sheets, making his lunches, rubbing his back and moaning way too loud while underneath him. It was as if you were in a constant state of panic, doing everything you could to ensure he would not leave.

Because of all I witnessed, I have spent my entire life making sure I would never be like you. I promised myself I would never give a man the satisfaction of leaving me. I made sure I got an education so I would never have to depend on a man financially. I taught myself to never love them so I would never have to depend on them emotionally. I've never had only one man. I've always made sure I had a backup and sometimes a backup for my backup. My plan was to never allow a man to play me. Instead, I planned to play him first. Unlike you, I would never be left alone to put the pieces back together. My pieces were never going to fall apart in the first place.

I convinced myself I would be the one in control, yet all I ended up with was an illusion. The pieces I said would never fall apart did. I just never stopped long enough to admit it.

I've gone through many of them, Momma. I

did it for the same reasons you did—so one of them would stay and realize what a wonderful, bright, beautiful wife I would make.

During the entire time I silently hated you, I was becoming you. Deep in my heart, I know you were just doing what you knew how to do; what made sense at the time, same as me. But I'm tired of that. I'm tired of running from man to man, searching and constantly coming up short. I'm tired of being that woman who's good enough to hook up with but not good enough to marry. I'm tired of pretending everything is okay when it's not. I'm tired of knowing deep in my heart I'm worth more but accepting less. I'm finished with all of it. I know for a fact that peace cannot be found in a man, job, designer handbag, crowded club, or vacation. I know because I've been there and done that. I can't keep doing the same things expecting different results.

So now I'm doing a new thing; something I should have done a long time ago. These layers of pain that are my life, I'm giving them all to God. I believe He will take the time to scrape each and every one of them away.

Joan

Somewhere during the time Joan was writing the letter to her mother, she forgave her. She forgave her mother because one day she was hoping her son would forgive her. Of course she would never give the letter to her mother, though. While it was addressed to her mother, it was written for Joan.

The time had come to face them—all the men she had slept with. She knew God would forgive her, but now was the time to forgive herself. She tore out a piece of paper from her journal and began to write. *Jamal, Todd, Marcus, Reginald, Frank, Sean, Tyler, Brian, Charles, Nathan, Robert, Michael P., James T., Lamar, Michael S., Steven, the three guys in Jamaica whose names I can't remember, Walter, Lamar, Melvin, James H., Darren, Chris, Payton, Carlos, Scott . . .*

Joan looked at the names then she began to weep. Her eyes gravitated to the second name on the list. The first man she ever loved was Todd. What she found with Todd was what she was looking for in all the rest of the men. She knew this was significant and she needed to journal like the woman had taught her, but she was afraid to leap into another painful memory.

Joan could not get her fingers to cooperate, fumbling the pen she held while shaking considerably. She cried a deep mournful cry that made her eyes burn, her breathing strained, and her heart accelerate, but still she found the strength to write.

When I was fifteen I used to hang around this girl named Tiffany who lived a few blocks from my house. Me and the other girls on the block were in love with Tiffany's older brother, Todd. He was nineteen, handsome, athletic, and obtained a full civil engineering scholarship to a university in town. Twice his picture was in the local newspaper. I cut out the articles and stapled them to my wall. I even used to write him love letters and hide them underneath my bed.

He had this black pickup truck that the kids in the neighborhood used to pile up in the back of for him to take us on the freeway. The wind would feel so good whipping against our faces and through our hair.

It was the weekend Tiffany and the rest of her family, except for Todd, was out of town visiting relatives. Knowing exactly what time he got off from work, I rode my bike past their house a few times, wearing the shortest pair of shorts I could find, hoping he would at least wave at me before he went inside.

To my surprise, he looked over at me and smiled. He asked if I wanted to go grab something to eat. I left my bike in their garage and practically jumped in the truck. My insides were dancing as he held my hand the whole way there. I felt like the luckiest girl alive, and when he pulled up to the stoplight, reached over and tongue kissed me, I knew I was. When we returned back to his house after eating at Burger King, I hoped he would ask me inside, and he did.

He led me upstairs to his room and I followed behind him like a little puppy dog. Once in his room, he started removing my clothing. I didn't protest.

I had heard my first time would be painful. So I didn't let him know that the sharp pains my body experienced as he entered me were excruciating. He panted and moaned like he was having the time of his life. Following his lead, I did the same. I can still hear him and see the lust in his eyes.

Joan stopped writing for a moment, tried to shake off the shame, and then finished writing.

Once finished, he cleaned off all traces of himself with a warm rag, placed my clothes back on my body, brushed my hair into place, and told me to go home and not tell anyone what happened.

Joan put down the pen and journal and took a deep breath.

"Tell me what's missing, Joan?" the woman whispered in her ear for the first time that day.

Joan knew she should have told the whole

story. She should have learned by now to admit everything, but she had grown accustomed to living her life telling lies to herself and everybody else. She did not want to admit the rest, but she knew she had to do so. Joan spoke to he woman what she should have written in her journal.

"While Todd was putting on my clothes, he smiled and said, 'Jamal told me you would be good.'" Joan took a deep breath. "After the incident with Jamal, I sort of got a reputation. My days of being ignored by the boys were over."

"How did you feel about that?" the woman asked.

Joan desperately wanted to lie but she knew she could not. "I loved it, and I had a clue as to why Todd had invited me to his house that day. I knew he played ball with Jamal and the rest of the boys, and I hoped Jamal had told him what I did to him. If he would have wanted to play a board game, I would have been satisfied with that, and if he wanted to watch TV, that would have been fine as well."

The woman interrupted. "He wanted to take your clothes off and sleep with you, and then did not even have the decency to be gentle each of the six times you were together."

Joan resisted the urge to defend herself. "While some of them were hardly pleasant experiences, it was the closeness of the act I was drawn to," Joan stated. "I looked into his eyes. I felt loved and protected. I saw the beams of pleasure my body was supplying to his, and that I enjoyed. Todd was the first man who made me feel really special."

The woman said, "What you found with Todd . . .

special feeling . . . is it the search for that same feeling that led to the other men?"

"Yes," Joan spoke quietly, "it didn't matter to me if it was all made up. I never acknowledged it wasn't real. I told myself I had left them so I wouldn't have to feel the pain of the truth."

"So, Joan, what is the truth?" the woman asked.

"In the meeting you said God is a loving Father who deeply desires to protect his children." Joan took her finger past each name. "Protection from this. Who would I be if I would have obeyed God? So much of my pain is a result of this list— there is only one good thing that came from it."

"Your son," the woman said.

"Yes, but he deserves better," Joan continued. "I never lived in the same house as my father. I promised myself I would do better for my children. But thanks to me, James Jr. is no better off than I was."

"When you go to the conference I want you to pay special attention to what the minister has to say about mercy," the woman said. "Joan, you cannot change the past but you can decide to do things differently in the future."

Joan grabbed a set of hotel matches and an ash-tray out of a drawer. She then tore the list of men she had sex with into small pieces and placed the pieces into the ashtray. Finally, she lit the pieces of paper and watched the fire consume them to ashes.

Chapter 7

Joan pulled the pantsuit she had just purchased out of the garment bag and proceeded to try it on. The pale green pantsuit with matching sandals was perfect for the conference. It was conservative, yet stylish, and the linen fabric made it ideal for the Houston heat Joan decided as she turned around in the mirror looking at her body from every angle. Last night she had combed through her luggage looking for something to wear to the conference that evening. But everything was too tight or too revealing, so she had spent the morning shopping.

Satisfied with her new look, she started to undress. Before she had the chance to finish, the telephone in her room rang, startling her because she had not heard a phone since destroying her cell phone.

She cautiously picked up the phone. "Joan Dallas, you could have called your girl or something. Lila and I have been trying to find you for all week!" the voice on the other end exclaimed. "I tried calling you on your cell, but it just goes straight to voice mail. You told me you were staying at the Kulani in Hawaii, but when I called there, they told me you never checked in."

Joan imagined Tisha's head moving in circles as her hair moved from side to side as she talked. Tisha was not what most people would call pretty just seeing a picture of her face. However, since she kept her weave undetectable and bouncy, carefully pieced together every outfit, and flawlessly made up her face several times a day, she routinely convinced herself and everyone around her that she was drop-dead gorgeous.

"I called your mother, brother, and the people at your job, and they all seem to have thought you were in Hawaii too. I've been looking for you since Friday. The only reason I finally found you is because Marcus ran into Darren at that Kappa convention last night," Tisha said without taking a single breath.

It felt weird hearing her best friend's voice. Each time Joan had picked up the phone to call her, she put the phone back down. She didn't want to risk it. What if this whole experiment thing had been in her head, a figment of her imagination? She didn't want to know if she was losing her mind. Tisha was blunt and just one conversation with her would have made it clear.

At only 110 pounds, Tisha could say anything to anybody. People jokingly referred to Tisha as Lady T. Lady T was a pet bulldog that used to terrorize children and dogs on Tisha's block in her childhood home. She was as sweet as she could be most of the time, but if someone crossed her by stroking her ears too hard or if another dog came too close to her owner's house, she would bark and snarl so viciously that much larger dogs and scared witless children would quickly run away.

"I know, Tisha, I know. I'm sorry," Joan apologized. "I just needed to be by myself for a while."

"By yourself? Are you really by yourself, because I've never felt more crowded? This woman, who I can't even see sometimes, got me tripping. She keeps popping in and out, making me do stuff I don't want to. I don't care if I need it or not. It's all too much. I can't even talk about it with anybody but you and Lila because anybody else would send me to the nearest mental ward. Joan, I'm tripping. I'm tripping I tell you!"

With a sigh of relief, Joan collapsed on the sofa. It was true! It was true! Tears fell from her face as the reality of it all settled in. It was not all in her mind. Tisha's words had rescued her, much like the time when they first met.

Joan was almost twelve and had gotten a relaxer that caused her hair to fall out. Roslyn, the school bully, had never spoken to Joan until she saw her step off the bus with her new makeshift air-fro. Roslyn stopped Joan as she was walking and stood right in front of her. It was only seconds before the rest of the children were gathered around. Roslyn was making fun of Joan's hair while the rest of the children laughed, but that all stopped when Tisha made her way through the crowd and stood right in Roslyn's face.

"You know, Roslyn, if you spent as much time on your homework as your dumb butt does trying to fight people who haven't done anything to you, maybe you wouldn't be repeating the sixth grade for the third time," Tisha spat. The crowd who had initially been laughing at Joan started laughing at Roslyn. "Girl, we will have graduated and your silly self will still be here." Tisha's stinging words caused Roslyn to run away with tears covering her face. Joan's hair grew and so did her and Tisha's friendship.

"Girl, I thought I was going crazy," Joan said in a voice laced with laughter. "I didn't want to talk to you or anybody else about it. I was afraid this was all something of my own making. You just don't know how good it feels to know she has been talking to you too. I've been waking up and going to bed each day more confused than I was the day before. Tisha, the way I'm shaking and crying right now, I must have really thought I was losing my mind."

"Joan, don't you remember talking to me and Lila in the auditorium?"

"Yeah, but I thought it was a dream or something, I don't know. I thought I was losing it, really."

"Yeah, I know, Marcus is convinced that I'm losing my mind," said Tisha.

"Wait a minute, how are you explaining this to him?" No response. "Tisha, you *have* told your boyfriend things have changed in that department, right?" Joan inquired.

Tisha still said nothing. "Tisha, are you there?"

"Well, I tried to," Tisha said, "but he is stressed out about his job. He's past ready to leave his firm and start his own business but he can't seem to get enough funding. Just last Monday he had a meeting with a potential investor—he was so excited. But just as they were about to draw up the contract, the investor got scared and reneged. It just hasn't been the right time to tell him that he can no longer depend on his favorite form of stress relief. Besides, what am I supposed to tell him?" Tisha switched to a sarcastic tone, "Hey, baby, you are going to laugh when I tell you this. The other day I was zapped into never-never Land with a woman who knows all my business. I have been drafted, you see. I'm about to start living like a saved woman as a part of this experiment. Each day this woman pops in and out of my world, having me to relive things I thought I had pushed out of my mind forever. As a part of this experiment, I have to pray, meditate, and keep a journal. Oh yes, I almost forgot . . . I also have to stop having sex with you—for good."

In her normal voice, Tisha said, "I want him as much as he wants me. I've been making excuses not to have sex with Marcus all week, but how many headaches can a girl have? Last night he looked so good in his T-shirt with those rock-hard thighs and big hands, and he had on that cologne I can't get enough of."

"You didn't!" Joan exclaimed.

"No! But I sure wanted to. We had been kissing for a while and then right when we had assumed the position but before we started, that voice— that woman—started calling my name and asked me what I was doing. Joan, I couldn't have been more embarrassed. I can't believe after just that little bit of time I was already caving in. Even more so, I can't get over how she's watching everything we do. I've been trying to pray, meditate, and keep a journal, and I'm still restless. I don't know if I can go on like this. How long are we going to be in this experiment anyway? And when will we know it's over? What if we go through all this and never get married?" Tisha continued without allowing Joan to answer. "After spending the last few days with that woman, I'm not even sure I want to get married, or where I want to work, or what I want to drive for that matter.

"Joan, I was about to go to my sushi bar and have tuna encrusted with sesame seeds like I do every Wednesday, but then I had to question whether I was going because I wanted to, or because I liked the idea of being trendy enough to go eat sushi. Joan, I don't know if I like sushi or not." Tisha released a disgusted huff.

A smile came over Joan's face. Knowing Tisha was going through exactly the same things she was going through was comforting. Joan hated to admit it, but she should have called Tisha the minute she came back from the meeting with the woman. Her misery had needed a little company.

"Tisha, we are supposed to be leaning on each other to get through this. Before, I didn't believe this was actually happening, but now I see I suffered alone needlessly. We should have been depending on each other all along. But I was too afraid—I was going crazy."

"Are you sure we're *all* not just going crazy, Joan? I feel crazy. Don't you feel crazy? I mean, this crazy thing could just be contagious."

"Well, I feel quite better now since I'm going to that conference at Miller Street Church."

Tisha continued speaking as if she hadn't heard a word Joan just said. "Girl, I've been crying all day and I can't shake this restlessness; and forget trying to work. I can't sell cars in this condition. I'm going to mess around and lose my job if I call in sick again. Joan, how are you doing it? What drugs are you on that allow you to function?"

Joan had an answer for her instantly but hesitated a few seconds.

"Jesus," Joan finally whispered.

"Jesus! That Spanish guy you met at the park?" Tisha asked, confused.

"Tisha, quit tripping. Jesus Christ."

"Joan, are you turning into a holy roller as a result of all of this?"

"Well, if that's how you want to look at it, I'm a functioning holy roller while you are sitting at home paranoid. Perhaps you need to put a little holy in your roll."

"Oh no you didn't, Ms. Dallas! I tried reading my Bible, but it was so hard to understand . . . this, thou, thee. I felt like I was in Mrs. Sumner's eleventh grade English class trying to figure out how Shakespeare was the greatest ever when he couldn't even speak the language."

"Shakespeare is wonderful once you get into it, and Bibles come in different translations. I have the NIV, which stands for New International Version. You need to get a study Bible with a commentary. A commentary helps explain the passages and gives you background information. It really helps me understand what's going on. Something about reading the Bible calms my spirit. I've been reading every morning and every night. Some things I understand, but a lot of it I don't."

"So why even bother?" Tisha argued. "I know, I grew up in church and everything and if there's anything I know, it's that church people are just as foul, if not fouler, than the rest of us. If there's anything I hate, it's a hypocrite. My main reason for not being in church is because I know I'm not living right. I need to get myself together first. I'm just not ready to give up Marcus or the rest of the things I'm doing in my life that don't abide by the so-called Christian way of living to start going around acting like a nun or something. Seriously, Joan, you know dang on well if I don't give up the booty to Marcus, somebody else will. And I ain't trying to lose my man. I just don't know if I can do this. I know I made a promise along with every other woman in that auditorium that day, but it was all so emotional and stuff. I think I was just caught up in the moment. When I got back home, everything changed. I don't know if I am strong enough for this."

"I know, Tisha, it's hard to change when you are used to doing things a certain way," Joan said, remembering the other day when Darren came to her hotel room. "I almost gave in to Darren. Can you believe his GQ, smooth-talking behind found his way right up to my hotel room, figuring he could have his way with me? Girl, I was like an addict who had just found her fix after looking all day. I couldn't believe how quickly I lost my self-control."

"That's what happened with Marcus," Tisha interrupted. "We started out watching TV, then a little kissing, and then touching. Before long, the feeling was so strong I was taking my panties off. I know they have places to go when you are experiencing alcohol withdrawal, but where is a girl to go when she is experiencing penis withdrawal?"

Joan laughed at the fear in her friend's voice. Tisha was as serious as ever with her last comment. "I wonder if they have a pill for that," Joan joked, then after thinking for a moment said, "Hey, why don't you come to the conference with me? Registration was only a hundred dollars. I got your back," Joan offered, knowing Tisha lived beyond her means and rarely had extra money.

"Is a conference going to make me stop jumping every time I hear a noise, fearing that woman is back to continue torturing me?" Tisha responded. "Is a bunch of preaching going to make me feel better about the fact that I'm routinely having conversations with a woman I can't see? Is sitting in the pew beside the same sister I saw in the club dropping it like it's hot one day and quoting Bible verses the next going to give me the strength to journal about my innermost thoughts? The only thing I need right now is twenty . . . no, make that thirty-five minutes of mind-bending sex. At least then maybe I could think straight!"

From the other end of the phone, Tisha started to cry fake tears and make loud noises as if she was blowing her nose into a tissue. Joan felt sorry for her, but laughed at her dramatics at the same time.

"Tisha, are you sure you don't want to go?" Joan asked her again, "because I need to start getting ready, and frankly, I don't know where the closest penis rehab center is located."

Tisha stopped wailing instantly. "Bye, holy roller!"

"I love you, too. Bye."

Chapter 8

Joan pulled into the parking lot of Miller Street Church bookstore one hour before the conference was scheduled to start. She wanted to make sure she could browse around the bookstore, get her ticket, and find a seat without having to rush.

She was determined to walk in this time with her head held high. "I wish I felt as good as I look," she whispered to herself as she looked in the rearview mirror. As soon as she spoke those words, a small pain shot through her stomach. "Oh right, I'm nothing but a ball of positive energy. Negativity will be allowed no place."

Not wanting to delay another second, she turned the ignition off, grabbed her purse, and locked the door while the entire time mouthing over and over, "I can do all things through Christ Jesus who strengthens me." As her anxiety slowly diminished, Joan entered the church, perused the bookstore, got her ticket, and then proceeded to high

step to the third row of the half-filled sanctuary like
she had a seat with her name engraved on it.

From the outside, the church looked like any
other church, but inside it looked as if it had been
decorated for kings and queens. The seats were
purple and oversized. The altar had touches of gold
on the pulpit and a beautiful stained-glass portrait
of Jesus graced the walls of the baptismal chamber.

Joan looked around to see if there was a person
who looked friendly enough for her to talk to.
Everyone seemed to have brought someone with
them and was already engaged in conversation,
except for the well-dressed pregnant woman seated
next to her.

"Hey, this place is starting to overflow," Joan
said, trying to spark a conversation.

"By the time they finish seating people, they will
have them in the choir stand, the aisle, and the
lobby," the woman responded eagerly. "That's why
I came early. Every time Makita speaks, people
want to listen."

Joan impulsively looked away so the woman
wouldn't realize she didn't know the reputation
of the woman who was scheduled to speak.

"Where are my manners? My name is Joan,"
she said.

The woman smiled and introduced herself as
Sage. Joan assumed she was probably married to
a doctor or athlete because she looked like a trophy wife . . . a Vanessa Williams look-alike with
long brown hair, blue-green eyes, expensive perfume, nine-thousand-dollar purse and teeth too
white to be natural. She appeared to be about five
months pregnant.

Joan's eyes habitually fell to Sage's left hand. Afraid Sage might have seen her, she quickly asked, "How many times have you heard her speak?"

Sage's smile convinced Joan she hadn't noticed, or just didn't care, that her finger was naked. In a whisper she said, "Ever since I got pregnant I've been searching for . . ." She paused. "I guess . . . the truth. You know, like why am I here? I can't believe it as I'm saying it to you, but I actually planned the pregnancy. Thirty-three years old and still stupid enough to think having a baby would help me keep a man. It was a bad night. I had been up all day crying and contemplating ending my life. I can remember crying out to God. 'Help if you are there. Help me because I've never needed you like I need you right now.' I had the pills in my hand and was ready to end it all when an overwhelming feeling of peace came over me." Sage slapped Joan on the thigh. "Girl, I could not do it!

"I went to my car and started driving, not knowing where I was going," Sage continued. "I ended up in Makita's office in this very building. She sat and talked with me for hours that day. She is a gifted teacher; she tells it like it is. I guarantee you're not going to leave here the same way you came." Sage paused for a second before continuing. "She reminds me of the woman in the experiment."

Joan looked into Sage's eyes intently, wondering if she had said what she thought she said. Sage's expression remained unchanged.

"She is just rawer and more intense, and not the least bit proper," Sage added.

Sage went on to say how she found out the church was near her house and how she had passed it before many times on her way back and forth from work, but for some reason had never noticed it. Sage said, "I guess if you are not looking for it you don't notice it." Sage went on to express how she had received Jesus Christ and was spending more time in the Word and was growing everyday.

Joan had so many emotions rushing though her body that she felt like she needed to run to relieve herself of some of the excess energy. Joan looked around the church and wondered if there was a water fountain she could use to hydrate her now dry throat, but decided against it when she saw how packed the church had become so quickly. She reached into her purse and retrieved a peppermint, hoping the distraction would calm her restless nerves.

It was minutes before the service was to start, and just like Sage said, the large church had to place folding chairs in the aisles, lobby, and in the choir section. With still not enough seating to accommodate the attendees, dozens of people were seated on the floor.

It spooked Joan to hear Sage say she had driven by the church many times and had not noticed it, just the same as she had. She was shocked by Sage's cavalier attitude. It was unsettling to hear someone mention the experiment so casually, as if it was commonplace for some force to zap up single women against their will.

Joan had not heard from the woman since she had written the letter to her mother, and she liked it that way. She was just too unnerving. Joan hoped that if she stayed on the right track, the woman would not make another appearance.

Picking up a discarded program from off the floor, Joan read how Minister Makita had endured all kinds of trials before surrendering her life to Jesus. Growing up in a small rural community, Minister Makita had overcome being fatherless and being raised by an abusive mother, along with a serious car accident she was involved in when she was in her twenties. The accident caused her intense back pain. She eventually became addicted to painkillers, and as a result of that, spent two years in jail, for writing fraudulent checks. While incarcerated she received Jesus during a church service and eventually overcame the addiction. Several years ago, she started Miller Street Church with her husband. She lead the women's ministry and he served as the senior pastor.

Joan looked down at her watch. It was exactly six-thirty, the time the conference was scheduled to start. A short slightly overweight man dressed in a sports coat and slacks walked to the front of the church and stood behind a waiting microphone. With a huge smile on his face he said, "Good evening, He has risen!"

Sage and some of the other women stood up and responded enthusiastically, "Good evening, Indeed He has!"

Joan was glad she was not the only that was still in her seat.

"It is such a blessing to be in the House of the Lord, this evening," the man stated. The women who had stood sat down as the man continued to speak. "I would like to welcome all of you to the Miller Street Women's Conference. For the visitors we have amongst us, I'm Benjamin Lawrence, aka Pastor Benji, the proud pastor of this church." The same women who had stood started cheering. Joan assumed all of them were members of this church.

"I welcome all of our members and visitors this evening. I pray that something will be said here tonight that will convict you if you need to be convicted, that will encourage you if you need to be encouraged, and that will comfort you if you need to be comforted.

"As many of you know, I have the pleasure of being married to Makita, the speaker of the hour." He smiled and backed away from the microphone. "Yes, pray for me, pray for me. Makita is a handful." He walked back to the microphone still smiling. "Don't be alarmed. I know as a man I am not supposed to be here. I just wanted to come by, read our opening scripture, and then I'm back to my office. Ladies, will you please stand for this evening's scripture reading?"

Sage and the other women reached for their Bibles. Joan shuffled through her oversized purse. She thought she had put her Bible and notebook in it. But she must have accidentally left it in the car.

Joan felt the tension building up in her body as she looked around and noticed everyone else seemed to have brought their Bibles. Joan stood and looked straight at the pastor.

"We'll be reading from the book of Romans chapter twelve verses one and two," the pastor said. Joan admired how Sage quickly found the scripture. Joan was glad when Sage put her Bible in between the two of them so they both could follow along.

After the pastor finished reading the scripture he waved and walked away. Joan almost took her seat before she realized the other women were continuing to stand. A group of five women in choir robes walked on to the pulpit.

"Please join us as we sing 'Make Me Over'," one of them said.

Joan was pleased to see the lyrics scrolling on two large screens on each side of the building. She sung along enthusiastically. Joan couldn't believe the energy at Miller Street Church. She remembered church as being quiet, subdued, and boring. But so far this church was anything but that.

The tempo slowed down momentarily as the women in choir robes exited after finishing the song. A group of four young women in long flowing skirts and leotards approached the pulpit. Sage and the other women sat down. Joan was glad because her new sandals were starting to hurt her feet.

The women appeared to be trained dancers executing each step with the precision of a ballerina. The song, "Journey to my Savior" was so moving, tears began to form in Joan's eyes. The song was about a young woman who led a sinful life. Due to her actions her family disowned her. She was on the streets and alone when somebody told her that God loved her. She was overjoyed to find the truth. When all four of the women leaped into the air at the same time, the congregation stood up and applauded. Joan did the same. Joan could tell Sage was crying. The woman in front of Joan had her hands in the air and was jumping up and down saying "Thank you, Lord" over and over again. She proceeded to do this until the dancers exited to loud applause.

On the right side of the pulpit three women, hand in hand, walked in slowly, as if they needed the support of each other to stand. Joan knew instantly the one in the middle was Minister Makita. She looked like an African queen; dark-skinned, dignified, bold, and beautiful.

The ladies walked her to the microphone, one placing her heavy, worn Bible down, and another placing a bottle of water at her feet. They stood there for a moment quietly praying before going to their seats in the front row. Makita, wearing a plain navy blue suit, stood tall staring straight ahead, but did not appear to be looking at anything in particular.

Instantly, all the anxiety that remained in Joan's body was removed. After seeing Minister Makita, she felt unexplained tears forming in her eyes. She looked around and noticed Sage and some of the other women already making use of their tissues even though Makita had not said a word.

Minister Makita grabbed the microphone from its stand, her deep melodic voice demanding everyone's attention. "I know ya'll have come here to hear me speak, and I had every intention of doing just that. But I have found it necessary to change my plans."

The women looked around at one another, excited with anticipation. Makita continued. "When you're a leader, you realize people will come searching for guidance. But this week, the things some of you have brought to me . . ." She stopped speaking and started to walk down the stairs into the congregation. "Well, ladies, what I'm trying to say is, can we just talk?"

The women nodded their heads, even though

Makita did not seem to be looking for her question to be answered.

Makita continued. "Church can be so pretentious sometimes, can't it? I find it unnecessary for people to walk around insisting that you call them doctor, reverend, or brother so and so. I just want to be a servant for the Lord. Amen?"

"Amen," the congregation repeated.

Joan could barely remain still. Something about Minister Makita's voice made her close, personal, and motherly. Joan drew in closer, staring and trying to decipher why she felt so intimate with a total stranger.

Makita shook her head from side to side, as if she was getting a silent message she didn't want to hear. She paced back and forth nervously. "So where do we start, ladies?"

The women stared in silence at Makita, who was now standing in the center aisle. Joan continued with her gaze on Minister Makita, afraid if she concentrated on anything else she would miss something.

Makita held the microphone tightly and walked across the aisles, making eye contact with each woman she passed. "Some of you have gutter self-esteem. You're just hurting and hurting, and instead of dealing with the issue you are choosing to drug your pain. You don't trust God. You believe you know what's best for you. Many of you are looking for somebody or something to make you happy. You're thinking *if only I get a husband* or *if only I get that job*. Well, I'm here to tell y'all no human or material possession will ever make you happy. Some of y'all are getting desperate, and you are starting to make stupid choices."

Sage and some of the other women stood up as a testament that they knew personally what the minister was saying was true.

"Some of you came into my office this week wanting to know why you keep attracting liars," Makita said. "Well, you attract what you are. Why else are you driving that car you can't afford? And why do you step through these church doors every week wearing suits you know cost you a whole week's salary? Oh, you're quick to tell your girlfriends how he showered you with flowers and an expensive designer watch on your birthday. However, you don't tell them the reason he bought you those things is because he was out creeping and you found out or that those gifts were to apologize for slapping you across the room. You leave that stuff out, don't you? Oh that's not you. Give me a second I'm about to knock on your door.

"Why are you always lying to your friends and yourselves about who you really are, what you really want, and how you really feel? Some of you come in here with your hair done, tailored suit with purse and shoes to match, your makeup done and eyebrows arched, your Bible in its case, strutting like Miss 'Got It Together' and hoping nobody realizes you're really Miss 'Don't Have the First Clue.' "

Joan released the tears she had been fighting back since the minister started speaking. Makita was unlike any speaker she had ever heard.

"Some of you are living to please your boyfriends more than you are living to please God. You are holding on to that little boyfriend of yours so tightly, like you truly believe without him you could not function. You come up in here singing songs and talking about you trust in the Lord. But you can't trust God if you are still holding on to what He had said let go of! If you trust the Lord, trust him completely. If you are single and the man you have in your life is not a man of God, you need to run, not walk, away from him."

Makita continued to stroll up and down the aisles, occasionally stopping to speak directly to those individuals who looked on intently.

"I have discovered that many of y'all are consumed with gossip. You are so concerned with the mess at somebody else's house because you don't want to deal with the mess at your own house. It's not amusing how some of you look down on a sister who has a couple of kids by different men; Acting as if you have never visited 'Dr. Make it go away,' 'Dr. I'm in my first year of college', or 'Dr. I'm just not ready yet.' I know all about that trip because I made it myself as a young lost woman.

"Don't act surprised. Before I started living the life of a saved woman, I was a woman, and a promiscuous one at that. I didn't discriminate. Whether a man or woman, white or black, all you had to do was make me feel good. I smoked a little of this and snorted a little of that. There's a lot I have done that would surprise you. And that includes traveling to a drug store miles from my neighborhood to purchase a pregnancy test or fill a prescription for a nasty infection I had caught."

Joan bowed her head, remembering a few days she had experienced like the ones Makita had described.

"We have all done stuff we regret. Don't ever

look down on another sister. Remember, she's going through the same stuff you're going through or have been through."

Joan cried openly like the other women as she thought about how she stood in judgment looking for a ring on Sage's finger.

Looking over at Joan, Sage grabbed her hand.

"We're all the same, sisters, and I'm about to lead you through an exercise to prove it," Makita said with conviction. "I want you to grab a sister . . . any sister." The women rushed to do what Makita instructed. Sage and Joan were already holding hands, so they looked to Makita for further instructions.

"I used to lie awake at night thinking about some of the horrible things I've done," Makita continued. "When you get lost in sin, it doesn't take long before it overtakes you. The devil will take your life on a road you thought you would never travel. But you see, I don't run around acting like I'm better than everybody else. I know I'm a sinner saved by grace.

"Now, that sister whose hand you're holding, I want you to tell her something you've never told anyone, and I want you to do it in spectacular detail. I want you to make her see it. It doesn't matter if you are holding your best friend's hand. I know there's something you haven't even told her. The Bible says we are to confess our sins to one another and that is what we are going to do today. I want you to realize there is nothing you have done that God does not know about and He cannot forgive."

Sage and Joan turned face-to-face, tightly holding hands. Instantly, each of them knew the story they would share.

"I was scared and crying so hard I could barely make out the numbers on the phone." Joan closed her eyes and started first. "I was locked in the bathroom with my younger brother, Travis."

"Nine-one-one, what's your emergency?" the nine-one-one operator asked.

"I was too scared to say anything at first. The nine-one-one operator repeated herself, "Hello, what's your emergency? Hello!"

Finally I responded in a whisper. "He's trying to kill my momma! Hurry! Please, don't let him kill her!"

"What's your address?" The operator's voice dropped. She could tell I was a frightened little girl.

"Twenty-three forty-five Juniper Valley. Hurry, he's going to kill her!"

"We have a unit in route. What's your name?"

"Joan."

"Joan, who's trying to kill your mother?"

Joan blinked away some tears and told Sage, "Jeffery, my mother's man at the time, was beating my brother, hitting him on his head with a broomstick. When my mother came to stop him, he started beating her. Travis and I ran upstairs, locked ourselves in the bathroom and hid in the laundry hamper.

"After the police came and took Jeffery away, I went downstairs. I saw my mother's tortured body spread across the living room sofa. My emotions felt like a hurricane in my stomach, threatening to blow me inside out. I felt sorry for her laying there in pain with bruises all over her body, but at the same time, I was experiencing an entirely different emotion . . . one I refused to acknowledge.

"Barely able to lift her head, my mother shouted, 'Why did you call the police? Now we got a bunch of trouble on our hands. If the people at his job find out, Jeffrey's going to be fired and it will be all your fault. What goes on in this house stays in this house, you understand? Now go get me some ice!'"

Joan smiled; it was the one thing she could do at the moment to combat the hurt she felt as she relayed her painful story.

"Joan, how did it make you feel when your mother said those words to you?"

Joan opened her eyes and looked at Sage. Sage looked back at her with an expression that let Joan know she had heard the voice too, but hadn't said the words. Joan started to speak.

"Stop, don't lie" the woman said. "I want to know how you really felt, not how you wished you would have felt. Speak to me through the thirteen-year-old girl. Tell me what she has to say."

Joan heard Makita praying for a woman several pews down. The church was loud with all the women having separate conversations.

While trembling, and with tears falling from her face, Joan closed her eyes again, waiting a full seven minutes before speaking again. "You stupid, dumb tramp!" shot out of Joan's mouth. "Only a fool would let a man beat her like a dog. If you had any sense, you would have left that pile of manure at the bus stop where you found him. I hate him. I hate what he did to us *and* what he's doing to us. I hate that you need him more than you love us. I hate listening while you have sex with him. How can a man who brings you so much pain have the opportunity to bring you pleasure? Why do we always have the police over here? Don't you know this ain't normal? We just wait for the next time he's going to kick your dumb tail, you good-for-nothing slut!"

Shocked by her own words, Joan opened her eyes. *Where did that come from? I would never talk to my mother in such a way.*

Sage continued holding onto Joan's hand, mentally preparing herself for her turn.

"There was a man in your life, Joan," the woman said, "a man much like Jeffery. His name was Nathan."

Now Joan was irritated. She had planned to tell Sage the story on her own and did not appreciate the woman pulling it out of her. "Yeah, but he beat me one time and I was out," Joan responded to the woman's voice.

"He beat you one time, yes, but how many times did you allow him to talk down to you?" the woman asked. "Words can hurt just as much as fists."

Joan heard Nathan's voice clearly in her ear. *"You're pathetic. You don't ever do anything right. Let me do that, 'cause you're too stupid to figure it out. How in the hell did you get a degree?"* Joan winced, feeling the embarrassment on her face.

"Can we agree that the time while you were with Nathan you were in an abusive relationship, just as your mother was?" the woman asked Joan.

"Yes, I suppose, but I never thought about it that way," Joan reasoned.

"Joan, when Nathan put you in the hospital, you didn't tell your mother or your friends. When they asked why you and Nathan had broken up, you lied. Your whole relationship was a lie," the woman reminded her.

Joan started to talk, hoping the woman would remain silent. "I would find myself thinking about Nathan all day and night during our relationship. He was different, very affectionate. He always wanted to hold hands and hug. He opened doors for me, sent flowers weekly, held my umbrella in the rain, or anything else I happened to be carrying at any given time. He was a tall, handsome, well-respected entrepreneur. He was good to my son. My girlfriends and family liked him a lot. I thought we might get married one day. I guess that's why when things started happening, I just let them go.

"A few months into our relationship the insults started. He would always apologize afterwards with roses, cards, and even diamonds a few times. I told myself it wasn't a big deal; that it was just words. Most of the time he treated me great, so why make a big deal out of the small stuff? I didn't believe I could find a man with Nathan's qualities twice in one lifetime and felt I would be crazy to let him go."

Sage listened intently as Joan continued.

"It would be weeks and sometimes months in between each episode, and during that period, Nathan was unbelievable to me. He was like a knight in shining armor. Whatever I wanted, he provided. I felt secure with him, like he could handle whatever problems arose. All my life I've had to be the smart one, the strong one, the one who made sure everything was okay. With Nathan, I could relax because I knew he had my back." Joan paused a moment, deep in thought. She wanted to find a way to end the story soon, but she knew she had to tell the entire story.

"I was spending the night at Nathan's house. We had gone to a restaurant and the food was upsetting my stomach. I was tossing and turning in bed, eventually waking up to vomit. When I got back from the bathroom, I expected Nathan to be up waiting for me, wondering if I was okay. Instead, he pretended to be asleep. I could tell he was faking, so I called out to him. I didn't understand what was going on and was too exhausted to try to figure it out. So, I attempted to go back to sleep, but eventually, the rest of the food demanded to come up." Joan inhaled a deep breath to calm herself before continuing.

"I was at the toilet when Nathan walked in furious. 'Heifer, you better not be pregnant,' he yelled. 'I'll kick that baby right out of you.' I couldn't believe him, talking to me like I was some trash on the street. When the vomiting stopped, I started to pack my things without saying a word.

"Repeatedly, he asked me if I was pregnant. I refused to answer, and the next thing I knew, I became his human punching bag. It went on for about twenty minutes. I was bloody, crying, and in a lot of pain mentally and physically. I was barely conscious when he picked me up, placed me in the car, and drove me to the hospital. After placing me on the sidewalk in front of the emergency room entrance, he got in his car and drove away. It was early in the morning, still dark, and no one was in sight. I had to make a painful crawl until I reached the door. I'd never felt so lonely, so defeated, and humiliated in my life. The doctors said I was lucky my injuries were not serious, but you couldn't tell from looking at me.

"I refused to talk to the police. The only person

I told was my boss, Dr. Wright, who took one look at me and offered to let me stay at her vacation home while my bruises healed. She seemed to understand why I wanted to keep things just between us. While recovering from my injuries, I told my friends and family I had been called to a last-minute extended business trip.

"What would they have thought of me? Joan—beat to the ground by Nathan, or any other man for that matter. I didn't know and didn't care. I felt bad about lying, but I believed it would feel worse to have them gossiping about me and feeling sorry for me."

Relieved she had made it through the telling of the story, Joan was glad the woman was silent. "I never thought I could admit to being an abused woman. I feel twenty pounds lighter," Joan sighed.

Taking in a deep breath, and determined not to need prodding from the woman, Sage began to share her experience. "It was supposed to be my wedding day," Sage half smiled. "I was twenty-eight years old and the highest paid rep at my agency. My maid of honor, Cheryl, and I had spent an entire year planning the perfect wedding. My fiancé was from Florida and the wedding was going to be on the beach right next to the beautiful, calming blue waters. It was a marvelous day; the sunlight was radiant and the wind was mild. Cheryl and I woke up and danced on the sand that morning. It was absolutely perfect.

"The wedding colors were red and gold. My bouquet was bright red Australian copper roses with prickly golden centers. I searched for the perfect dress and decided on a Nigerian dress designer. She designed an ivory-colored silk creation embroidered with crimson along with a fifteen-foot train. I convinced a local jeweler to allow me to borrow a dramatic princess diamond tiara."

Sage's voice dropped dramatically. "I was a sight to be seen, if I do say so myself. It was fifteen minutes before the wedding ceremony was to begin, and the two of us were putting the finishing touches on our makeup in the bridal suite of the resort when we heard a knock at the door.

"He yelled, 'Open the door! Open the door!' I thought of yelling to him that he was not supposed to see me before the wedding, but the urgency in his voice would not allow it. Cheryl ran to the door, and I followed behind as fast as the dress would allow me to walk.

"When he looked at me I could tell he was in awe. I was more beautiful than imaginable. I was so nervous. My heart was racing and sweat formed underneath my breasts and at the soles of my feet. He was not wearing his tux. He had bloodshot eyes and an unshaved face. The stench of alcohol was on his breath and he looked like a disheveled mess.

"He spoke softly, his eyes unable to meet my gaze. 'Last night after the dancers left my bachelor party . . .' He stopped as if in pain. I waited hoping whatever was wrong could be fixed. After a few moments of silence, he conjured up the strength to continue. 'This guy, Joseph, who works here at the bar said he had some videotapes he wanted us to watch.'

"He wanted to speak faster, but it was too hard laboring against his tears. Turning to Cheryl, he said, 'You are on one of those tapes.' He then turned to me and said, 'You too.' Cheryl and I looked up at one another, then back at him. 'The freakin' Texas beach party!' he yelled. 'He said he made and sold five thousand tapes with both of you on every single one of them.' He dropped to his knees and cried, 'Every last one!'"

Flashing back to the time her fiancé was referring to, Sage started to weep; her grip on Joan's hand softened.

"Cheryl, my other friend, Michelle, and I had made reservations for our beach house nine months prior to our Texas vacation to ensure we were on the seawall in the middle of the action. We rented a silver convertible, brought along plenty of film, and left at six in the morning to beat the infamous gridlock traffic that occurs when two hundred thousand young people converge on a small beach town all at once.

"I remember being really happy that day. Cheryl was celebrating her new dance teacher job and I was less than a month away from graduating. We were all twenty-one and just wanted to have fun.

"The energy was unbelievably high that Saturday. Music was coming from every direction. It was like everywhere I went someone was playing one of my favorite songs. Every single space for miles was occupied by something: a person, a vendor, a packed club, a slow-moving automobile or a restaurant with no available seating.

"After spending most of the day cruising around, taking pictures, and speaking to people we had not seen since the last beach party, we parked the convertible and pulled off our cover-ups to reveal our matching metallic gold bikinis. We stood around the car posing, drinking homemade margaritas, and waiting to see who would come by to speak.

"Several people did stop. We took pictures with them and they took pictures of us; the same old routine from every year, but then three good-looking guys on motorcycles stopped. All three of us stood at attention in front of our car. We had a weakness for a man on a bike. They were bald and had the bodies of seasoned athletes. They had ridden their bikes all the way from Georgia and were a little disappointed by the trip. We paired off, talked to one another privately, rode on their bikes, and drank way too much. When they complained they were hungry but didn't want to wait hours to get food at one of the congested restaurants, we invited them to have dinner at our beach house.

"It was our fifth consecutive beach party, so we knew enough to bring our own food and have some place to cook it. Enjoying the company of our new friends, we cooked fajitas with all the fixings. They couldn't stop complimenting us on the dinner. After dinner, we excused ourselves to take showers and told them they could do the same in the two guests' bedrooms, which they did.

"Cheryl, Michelle, and I were sitting in the living room sipping cognac when they rejoined us, dressed in nothing but their boxers. Cheryl got up, turned on the radio, and started yelling for them to dance for us, not just any dance, but a striptease. It was not long before things got out of hand. They were excellent dancers with chiseled six-packs and defined muscles. The sexual tension was off the Richter scale.

"After they finished dancing for us, they insisted we do the same for them. I never saw the camera. From looking at the tape, it had to be right in my face. I guess I was too drunk to notice it."

Sage spoke quickly, hoping to get through the difficult parts without breaking down. Joan squeezed her hand to let her know it was okay to continue. "All three of us were videotaped while bending down, grabbing body parts, and posing naked like we were doing a photo shoot for an adult magazine. We were on the tape rubbing all over one of the guy's crotch area while smiling and telling him he was the biggest, finest man we had ever seen. In the next scene, I was outside on the balcony having sex with the same guy. In the last scene, Michelle was laying on the bed while one of the guys directed her to touch herself. Cheryl was on the bed next to her completely naked and looking at the ceiling as if she was patiently waiting for her turn.

"It's amazing we didn't even know the tape existed until my wedding day. I'll never forget looking at the tape as I sat in my beautiful custom-made wedding gown. By then, I had a blossoming career, Michelle was an emergency-room nurse, and Cheryl was married with one child and four months pregnant with her second.

"To my dismay, my fiancé called off the wedding, claiming he could not marry a woman who all of his friends and family may have seen in that way. I worry because I don't know what I would do if one of my clients, or worse, somebody from my family, walks in one day and tells me they saw me on one of those tapes. I've blocked it out mostly to maintain my sanity. It's my, Cheryl, and Michelle's secret, and we don't even talk about it with each other."

"What bothers you the most about the tape?" the woman's voice chimed in and asked Sage.

"I looked like a whore on the tape," Sage tearfully replied.

"But you're not a whore. So why does that bother you?" the woman asked.

Sage didn't like the tone in the woman's voice. "I *know* I'm not a whore. Still, the tape is embarrassing. I don't want anybody to see me looking and acting like some cheap slut." Sage stopped to collect her thoughts. "I want people to see me as a strong, bright, confident woman; not some prostitute eager to please."

"Do you see yourself as a strong, bright, confident woman?" the woman asked.

"Are you psychoanalyzing me?" Sage responded defensively.

"No," the woman said. "I'm just not interested in how you want other people to see you. I want to know how you see yourself. You're the one who said you looked like a whore on the tape. Do you feel like a whore, or did you just look like one on the tape? Do you see yourself as a strong, bright, confident woman, or do you just appear to be one to the people around you?"

Joan sat listening, glad her turn at being scrutinized was over.

Sage sighed in defeat and then she whispered, "Frankly, I guess I should consider the facts. I have a tape floating around out there where I appear to be happy to show myself to anybody who has twenty-five dollars. Now, I'm carrying a baby."

Sage paused. "I'm thirty-three. I'm a highly paid executive with many employees underneath me and I own my home. I hold two college degrees and I'm almost seven months pregnant with a child from somebody else's husband."

Sage began to weep loudly and Joan joined in the tears while tightly holding her hand.

"Lady, if I'm not a whore, then who is?" Sage asked.

"No, Sage, you made a mistake," Joan said, unable to continue listening to Sage be so hard on herself.

"No, Joan, a mistake is setting your alarm clock for P.M. went you meant to set if for A.M.," Sage responded.

Joan embraced Sage while trying to hide her disbelief. Sage looked like the perfect "good girl" type, one Joan would have never suspected capable of doing the things she had mentioned. She looked around the room and wondered just how many other women in the room were like Sage— were like her.

Chapter 9

Joan looked around at the other women. Some were crying and others were shouting. Joan could tell she was not the only one who felt lighter. Relief was apparent on many of their faces.

"What do you think about your sister now?" Makita asked, finally speaking again from the pulpit. "Is she beneath you, or could she be you in the same circumstances? This exercise never ceases to amaze me." She shook her head and looked at the women. "Now, I want each of you to walk around the church, find three women you don't know and give them a hug and a word of encouragement. Hug her like you wish somebody would hug you. Encourage her like you wish somebody would encourage you. Give her the benefit of the doubt like you wish somebody had given you."

Joan opened her arms to hug the woman in the pew in front of her. She was crying and was too overcome with emotion from Makita's exercise to speak to Joan. She held on to Joan tightly and didn't let go until Makita started to speak. Joan didn't mind she only got to hug one woman out of the three she was supposed to hug because that hug felt so real it was like three hugs in one.

"Okay, now that we have that out the way, I got a few things I need to say to you single sweeties out there," Makita said, pointing. "After meeting with some of you in preparation for this event, it has become clear to me some of you just don't get it. I will not allow anybody to walk out of this church today confused about such important issues. I apologize in advance; I know many of you are not used to church being so real. But not addressing reality is what got us into this position in the first place.

"Those of you who are having sex outside of marriage need to stop. Those of you that are living with men you are not married to need to move away from him. Sex outside of marriage is, was, and will always be a sin. Sex is a gift to be shared exclusively between God and a married couple. Seventy percent of black children are born to single mothers. Yes, more black children are born to single women than married couples. This ought not be, my sisters. We can sit around all day and talk about how it happened and why it happened. I would rather discuss the plan to turn away from a worldly lifestyle to a godly lifestyle.

"I know it's hard, y'all. Once you've tasted a particular fruit, it's hard to give it up, but you can through the power of the Holy Spirit. Do you understand that you can't actively be participating in a sinful lifestyle and expect to get closer to

God?" Joan sat quietly admitting to herself what Makita said was true.

Makita slowly stepped from behind the pulpit. "I have grown more and more concerned with the overtly sexual music and images you are bombarded with all day long," Makita stated. "Just one lyric or one picture of people having sex could cause all kinds of desires to be reawakened. My sisters, you're going to have to do a whole lot to prevent evil from entering your lives in this new millennium. It might be something as big as packing up and moving, or something as small as finding a new radio and television station.

"You must be armed with prayer everyday, all day. You cannot put your job, your children, your friends, or family before God. You must make time with Him everyday. You must learn and live by His word. I urge you to memorize scriptures so that when you are faced with temptation you can recite them to yourselves. You must be on a twenty-four hour, seven-day-a-week war to avoid temptation and all its forms.

"If you have to move to avoid temptation, do so. If you have to change jobs, do so. If you have to stop watching your favorite television shows, do so. If you have to stop going to your favorite hangout spot, do so. If certain clothes cause men to look at you lustfully, stop wearing them. If your friends are leading you to do or think ungodly things, you must give your friends up too. You can't love the world and God too."

Half of the women were on their feet, loudly clapping and agreeing with Makita's every word. She took her position back behind the pulpit.

Joan knew if she wanted to successfully complete the experiment, she could not have any contact with her former lovers. If they showed up at her door, she would have to demand they leave immediately. If they called, she would not answer the phone.

"Ladies, you are in a war," Makita said in a powerful tone. "The only ammunition you need, the only ammunition that can save you, is the Word of God.

"I talked to two young women this week. One is living a successful Christian life. Yes, she has challenges as we all do, but she is growing in godly wisdom and in godly knowledge. She is not just reading the Bible, she is living it. Everyone around her has noticed the difference. She has made a commitment to come to Bible study at least twice a month and she wakes up at least thirty minutes before going to work to pray, read her Bible, and spend alone time with God.

"The other young woman I talked to has been a Christian for three years. She claims she would read her Bible and pray if she had more time, but right now she's going to college and working full-time. In the meantime she came to me for counseling. She wanted to know why her life is such a mess. She never has enough money even though over the past three years her income has increased drastically. She's in debt and getting deeper and deeper. She's obese; the doctors have told her she needs to get her weight together or else her health will start to fail. But despite all her efforts she has yet to lose the weight and keep it off. She hates her job but she doesn't know what type of job she should look for. She's dating and having sex with a man who treats her horribly but she can't seem to let him go. So she came to me looking for a quick fix." Makita stopped and looked straight ahead, "There isn't one."

The women nodded in agreement.

"I have a question for all of you." Makita continued speaking. "What do you have in your cup?" The women looked around puzzled then focused their attention on Makita. "Everyone was born with a cup that must be filled with something at all times. It's a desire beyond our control. In an ideal situation, as a child, this cup would have been filled with Jesus, unconditional love and appreciation, but as I stated, that would have been the ideal situation.

"In reality, many of you were brought up with deficient cups. One thing you need to remember about the cup is it must be filled at all times. If the cup is deficient of the things it needs, it will find something foreign to fill it.

"How many of you don't feel complete unless you have a man? How many of you are working in jobs because of the prestige, knowing God is calling you to another purpose? How many of you picked the cars you drive and the neighborhoods you live in because you wanted to impress people? I bet some of you have somebody's designer name on every piece of clothing you own and you couldn't be more proud.

"It does not matter how old you are and how much education you have, something is in your cup. Is it men in general or one man in particular? Is it that immaculate house with the immaculate Mercedes parked in your driveway? Is it the abundance of food you force down your throat when you are not hungry? Is it your designer clothes and shoes you have to match every outfit? Is it crack or speed or the bottle of wine you inconspicuously drink all day? You will not be satisfied until you fill your cup with what it was designed for—God and God alone.

"In a group this size, I can imagine we have a little bit of everything. I hear the rumblings of your heart. 'But, Makita, you don't know what I'm going through. You don't know my demons. You don't know what I've done, how many times I've done it, who I've done it with, and who saw me do it,'" she voiced in a sarcastic tone.

"I don't care if you were a crack prostitute that was working twenty minutes before you walked in here. It does not matter if you have ten babies with ten different fathers. It does not matter how many abortions you've had or how many people you have had sex with. God loves you. He wants you to know Him. He wants some of your time.

"If you refuse to make time for God, you will not grow. If you make time for God, you will. There is no quick fix. If you want to know what's wrong with your life, you need to spend time with the only One that knows. Don't come to my office with all your broken pieces and expect me to be able to put you back together again. I do not have that kind of power.

"It's funny the people who claim to not have time for God but they do have time to surf the net, shop for stuff they can't afford, go to the movies, and watch hours of TV. I urge you to put God on your schedule. The more you do it, the more natural it will become."

* * *

Makita nodded and a young girl came up to her with a large dry erase board. Makita spelled out the word MERCY.

Joan felt a chill; *mercy* was the word the woman from the auditorium told her to take special note of.

"Has anybody ever given you something wonderful knowing that you did not deserve it and even if you tried really hard there was no way you would be able to pay them back?" The women did not answer Makita.

Makita went on. "When I was a senior in college I stayed up late the night before my math final partying with my friends. I was so tired that I did not hear my alarm go off the next morning. By the time I woke up and walked into the classroom I was three hours late for the class. There was no one remaining in the class except the professor. Everyone else had completed the test and left. I knew what this meant. I would fail the class. I would have to repeat the class and I would not be graduating that semester.

"I walked up to my professor in tears. I expected him to rebuke me and send me on my way. Instead, he took a blank test and then he put my name on it. After that he filled in all the answers, and then he scribbled out *A plus* on the test, and then at the very top of the page he wrote this word, this word I have on the dry erase board, *mercy*. My professor then walked out of the classroom with my completed perfect test at the top of the stack.

"There are four things I want you to know about God's mercy before you leave here today." Makita began to write on the dry erase board.

1. You don't deserve it.
2. You can't work your way in to it.
3. You can't pay it back.
4. It's an amazing gift with no strings attached.

"How many of you believe you are worthy of going to heaven when you die?" Makita asked.

None of the women raised their hands; they only looked around at each other. "You are right; you are not worthy," Makita explained. "As a matter of fact, nobody is. But God does not give us what we deserve. He gives us mercy. Let me make this plain to you. Say I've just died. I'm in front of God. He is reading a list, or in my case, books of all the sins I have committed; you know the lies, evil thoughts, fornication, using God's name in vain—all of that. The Bible says the wages of sin is death. So based on my record, where do I deserve to spend eternity—heaven or hell?"

"Hell," one woman said.

"You are right. Based on my record I deserve to go to Hell. But I'm not going!" Makita almost looked as if she was about to start dancing. "Because back on September 16, 1979 I RSVP'd for my spot in heaven.

"How did I do that?" Makita looked at the women. "I turned to God in repentance and put my faith in Jesus Christ. Then God forgave me of all my sins and gave me a new heart. I believed that Jesus Christ bled and died for sins so that I don't have to. Now that my sins are erased I have a place in heaven. Because I deserve it?" Makita pointed to the board. "No! Because of God's mercy.

"I don't worry about dying anymore" Makita explained. "I know that Christ died for my sins. He was buried then he came back to life on the third day defeating death. Now He is at the right hand of the Father. I repented of my sins and put my faith in Jesus Christ. Now I'm on my way to heaven. It's that simple. I'm saved!" Makita exclaimed.

"Who out there has not made your reservations yet? The doors of the church are open," Makita said. The women who had escorted Minister Makita to the pulpit walked up to the altar. Facing the audience, they stood with their hands held out, ready to hug somebody.

Joan wondered why this was the first time Jesus on the Cross made any sense to her. She heard the story of Jesus dying on the cross every Easter, but it never quite came together until today. It was personal now; He died for her so that she could spend eternity in heaven!

A woman in the same pew as Joan jumped up suddenly, brushed past Joan and Sage, and joined the other dozen or so women who had begun to worship God on their knees in the aisles of the church.

Joan's legs and feet started to throb.

"Haven't you tried everything else? It's time to try the only one who can do anything but fail." Joan wondered why it felt like Makita was just talking to her. "I'm ready to follow you from this day forth, Jesus." Makita walked around the church with the microphone. "I'm tired and I'm ready. I'm ready to admit I am a sinner. I believe with all my heart Jesus died for my sins and rose again. I'm ready to call on Jesus to forgive my sins and make me clean. I'm ready to be baptized into the family of God."

Joan wanted to move, to join the others, but the pain in her legs would not allow her. Sage turned to face her. Sage sensed something was wrong. Forgetting her delicate condition, she grabbed Joan's right arm, wrapped it around her waist, maneuvered them out of the pew, and proceeded to help her to the altar. Two women in their row noticed how Joan was unable to move her legs. Each picked up one of her legs, and the three of them carried Joan to the altar.

Minister Makita stopped talking and knelt down and whispered in Joan's ear as she lay on the floor. "Welcome, my sister. We've been waiting for you."

Instantly, the pain in Joan's legs diminished. Tears of joy were flowing from her eyes. The devil had tried to keep her from the altar. But Joan had served the devil for the last day. Today was the first day of her new life, as a child of God.

Chapter 10

Joan rearranged the three oversized pillows underneath her body. It felt good to be out of the hotel and in her bed. A black currant candle was burning on the nightstand releasing its fruity aroma throughout the room. A gospel CD was playing so low she could barely hear the words.

Joan closed the Bible she was reading and placed it on her chest. She had just completed reading the Book of Romans in its entirety.

Her mind drifted off to the summers in high school she had spent with Aunt Alice in her bakery, making icing for cakes and measuring more flour on the floor than she did into the oversized bowls. She remembered how Aunt Alice always seemed grateful to get up to face the day, even at three in the morning. Even though it was never cold enough, she would light the fireplace because the flames relaxed her. The two of them would slowly drink peppermint tea while Aunt Alice read at least two Bible chapters out loud.

Then they would drive in silence to Aunt Alice's small shack-like bakery, which was nameless on the outside. It was originally surrounded by busy factories, and even though the factories were long gone, the legend of Aunt Alice remained. Alice had to start a sign-up list for the four broken-down tables in the bakery or else the retired workers who spent the day playing cards, reading the paper, and flirting with an oblivious Aunt Alice would fight over them.

Tomorrow would be Joan's first day back at work and she wanted to arrive at the office before everybody else did, so she set her alarm an hour earlier than normal. She turned off the lamp, blew out the candle, and turned off the CD. She lay on her back with her Bible still in her hands.

Aunt Alice never rushed while serving her customers, not even on Saturdays when dozens of people eager to have one of her pies for their Sunday dinner table lined up outside the door. In all her summers, Joan could not recall having heard one customer complain at the bakery.

Each evening, Joan and Aunt Alice would return to the back porch of Aunt Alice's spacious two-story house to drink too-sweet lemonade and eat tuna sandwiches cut in fours.

The rest of the family thought of Aunt Alice as an insane old maid with second-rate desserts. Alice never married nor had any children. She refused to gossip about anyone under any circumstances, which alienated her from her only sibling, Joan's grandmother, Betty, who gossiped constantly.

Aunt Alice went to at least two funerals a week whether she had known the person or not. She didn't own a TV and spent her spare time reading travel brochures of distant places, going to church functions, and making intricate quilts that sold for hundreds of dollars.

Growing up, Joan always knew something about Aunt Alice intrigued her. She could never put her finger on it. That was until tonight when she meditated on Romans 12:2.

Do not conform any longer to the pattern of this world, but be transformed by the renewing of your mind. Then you will be able to test and approve what God's will is—His good, pleasing, and perfect will.

She realized then what made Aunt Alice so different. She had not conformed to the world. She had not asked anybody but God how she should live.

The last summer before Joan's senior year in high school, Joan announced she was thinking of opening her own bakery. However, the moment she shared it with her family, all of her excitement was swiped away.

"Joan, please, Aunt Alice doesn't make any real money," her mother said, trying to dissuade Joan from her dream. "Besides, half of her cakes are old, stale, and nasty. Why don't you get yourself a nice office job? You don't want to have to work hard all your life, do you?"

Her grandmother responded the same way. She had taught Joan to make her first pie at the age of seven years old. "Joan, you've worked too hard to be a glorified cook. You can do better," her grandmother replied.

Joan decided to listen to her mother and grandmother. She enrolled in college and soon after declared her major as business management. The great look of pride on her mother and grandmother's faces the day she graduated from college was not to be forgotten. Aunt Alice didn't come to her graduation ceremony, but she sent Joan five crisp one-hundred-dollar bills and a note that read, "Jesus loves you, and my prayer is that you love Him too."

Joan enjoyed her current job. She liked the respect she had earned. When she walked in, everybody stood up straighter and tried to look busy. Her mother always found an excuse to bring her friends by the main office downtown to see Joan's large corner office with her assistant positioned outside her door.

Joan turned on the lamp. It was 12:00 A.M., past her bedtime but she wasn't sleepy. Between all Joan's thoughts back down memory lane and remembering what she had just read in the Bible, she found the urge to write. Climbing out of bed, Joan retrieved her journal so that she could write down her feelings.

I feel myself reevaluating success. To me, success has always been graduating from college, having enough money to do what you wanted to do when you wanted to do it, having your name on a business card, and having people work underneath you.

What is scaring me now is that at twenty-nine years old I've accomplished everything on that list, yet I'm still anxious, maybe even more anxious than I was before I accomplished anything. What if I have spent all this time and energy on the wrong road pursuing the wrong things?

This first week in the experiment has been as torturous as it has been uplifting. I've relived things I haven't

*thought about for many years; things I promised my-
self I would forget ever happened. I've also experienced
joy beyond my wildest dreams.*

*After my first week in the experiment, I have changed
more than I could have imagined. I wish I could say I'm
feeling better and more confident about the task before
me. In reality, I'm afraid because this is only the beginning. I'm afraid of failing in the experiment. I'm afraid
of failing my child. I'm afraid of sitting on a porch as
an old woman looking back at my life and realizing I
was successful in the world's eyes but a failure in God's
eyes. I don't want to miss what matters the most.*

*Can I give up trying to conform? Can I dare to be
different? What will it cost me to change? After all
this, would I dare go back to my old ways? Can I really
live in the world, but not conform to the world? I've
imagined the woman I could be in my head. I just don't
see how I, Joan Dallas, could ever become that woman.*

*My prayer for myself is that I take Romans 12:2
with me all day. Lord, I need you to make me into the
woman you have destined me to be.*

Chapter 11

Lila pulled up to her favorite soul food restaurant, Aunt Tammie's, stepped out of her black Escalade and watched as the women in the car parked next to her stared at the four-karat heart-shaped diamond on her ring finger. Everyone else had the same reaction when they saw the specially designed creation. There was a time when Lila would have been proud to sport her fifteen-thousand-dollar diamond, but ever since she had been taken away to that dark auditorium, her engagement ring reminded her of the promises she had made to God but had not kept.

She grew up in southwest Houston. Lila and her family, which included three older brothers, lived in a small trailer park. Her dad was a hard-working handyman and pastor of a thirty-member church. Lila's mother was a janitor at the elementary school where Lila attended.

As soon as Lila graduated high school she married Alonzo Fulton. At twenty he was living in his own house and driving his own car. When Lila married Alonzo she knew he was up to no good, but her strong need to get out of the trailer park and the almost daily prayer meetings her father had at their home caused her to ignore her suspicions.

The marriage was okay despite Alonzo's friends who were always there until all hours of the night. Lila didn't have to work and Alonzo kept her hair and nails done and clothed her body in the latest fashions. Within two years they had a baby girl, Jasmine. All was well with their young family until one day at three A.M. the cops came to raid the house. Alonzo and his friends had set up a scheme where they would buy credit card information from department store clerks. They would then purchase household appliances like refrigerators, dishwashers, and stoves. After purchasing the items online they had a contact that would sell them overseas. They thought none of this could be traced back to them.

When all the charges were handed down, Lila was facing a total of twenty-five years in prison, the exact same as Alonzo. Even though Lila had grown up in church she had not called on Jesus Christ personally until she was locked in a jail cell.

She made all kinds of promises to God if He would get her out this mess she was in. She promised to go to church every week. She promised to start a ministry to children. She would stop partying, cursing, drinking, and wearing revealing clothes. She would tell Tisha and Joan she couldn't hang out with them. She would get a job.

And she would never get involved with a man if he wasn't a man of God.

Lila dropped to her knees in praise to God right there in the courtroom when the judge looked at her and said he was dropping all charges against her due to a lack of evidence. Alonzo ended up being sentenced to all twenty-five years. Lila happily took her baby and moved back to the trailer park with her parents. She went to work at the church just like she had promised God. She refused to hang out with Joan and Tisha and she got a job at Elliot's, a men's clothing store in the mall.

Lila took a moment to check her reflection on the glass door before walking into the restaurant. She may be a big woman, but Lila refused to dress in boring attire. She was wearing a designer denim blazer with matching stretch jeans, forest-green handbag and matching high-heeled sandals. Her look was complete with bouncy shoulder-length spiral curls and a touch of makeup.

Aunt Tammie's was not a cafeteria like Lila expected the first time she visited it a year ago with Steve, her fiancé. They were coming from a play and decided they wanted to have dinner somewhere they had never been before. They passed Aunt Tammie's and decided to try it out. It became one of their favorite places. It was a trendy spot that played jazz as patrons munched on flavorful southern dishes served on fine china.

Lila met Steve when he came through her checkout line at Elliot's and handed her his business card. He was much older than her; short, unattractive, and badly dressed. Lila had no plans of giving him any of her attention. Lila put the business card in the trash without reading it. However, one of Lila's coworkers who witnessed Steve hand her the card insisted on reading it and took it out of the trash. The card read Dr. Steven Lennard, head of pediatrics at Bayou Glen Hospital. All of a sudden Lila got real interested.

She called Steve as soon as she got home from work that night. He picked her up in his Range Rover. Lila's hourglass figure, honey-brown complexion, and hazel eyes had caused many men that came through Elliot's to flirt with her. They offered to take her on dates to the movies, sports bars, and average family restaurants, but Steve lived according to a different set of rules.

For their first date, Steve took her to Sebastian's, Houston's premier steak house. Usually, in order to get a seat at this five-star restaurant one had to make reservations months in advance, but Steve was a regular and any time he walked in they found him a table. Lila was uncomfortable at first. She felt like the service was stuffy and she was going to make a fool out of herself by tripping on her way to the restroom or picking up the wrong fork when she was served her salad. But as the night wore on, Lila enjoyed the attentive service, impeccable food, and expensive champagne. After dinner Steve drove her downtown where he rented a horse and carriage to take them on an hour-long tour through the city. The evening ended at Café Renee where they shared a Grand Marnier chocolate soufflé delivered to the table by the chef himself. Lila had been introduced to the good life and promised herself she would not go back to the other side.

"Hello, Lila" the hostess said. "Will you be dining alone or will someone be joining you?"

"It's just me," Lila replied. "Let me get a table in the back." Lila followed the hostess to her table. Lila needed to think and that meant she needed a plate of delicious food.

Lila was going to church three to four times a week as well as working fifty hours a week at Elliot's when she met Steve. She was getting more and more burned out everyday. Every time she thought she was getting ready to get a promotion at work, somebody else got it. Every time she had a little money saved in the bank something major happened, and before she knew it her savings were gone.

Steve offered Lila everything she could have imagined: a massive two-story house, landscaped to perfection, five bedrooms, four full bathrooms, a three-car garage, winding staircase, fireplace, and a big backyard with a pool. There would be private schools for Jasmine, exotic trips, and money in the bank. And she could work if and when she wanted to.

Lila knew she was being disobedient, to what God wanted for her but she quit her job, packed her and Jasmine's stuff and moved in with Steve. Soon after she started planning the wedding of her dreams.

Lila started to feel self-conscious as she looked around the restaurant. It seemed as if she was the only one dining alone. She would have liked to ask Tisha to lunch with her, but lately Tisha was starting to ask too many questions about why she and Steve had not gotten married. Lila hated lying to Joan and Tisha, but she didn't know what else to do. Lila perused the menu out of habit. She already knew what she wanted to order.

Lila knew from the day Steve asked her to marry him that she wasn't in love with him. They were supposed to get married almost nine months ago but Lila called off the wedding two weeks before the wedding date.

The night she got engaged she had a dream of herself drowning. At first she would be sitting in a pond. Then it would turn to a lake. She would swim calmly in the lake. Then the lake would turn into an ocean. The ocean water would get bigger and bigger waves until finally it would take her under. Then Lila would wake up. She had that dream almost every night until the day she called off the wedding.

Lila told Steve the wedding planning was stressing her out and causing her blood pressure to rise. Steve hadn't appreciated her calling off the wedding that close to the date but was more concerned that she might leave him. They agreed to tell everyone that Steve called off the wedding to keep people from questioning her. He was better with words and could handle the questions better.

She knew right then she needed to pack up her bags and move away from Steve. But that meant the trailer park, public schools, and forty to fifty hours a week at the mall. There would be no more designer clothes, weekly hair appointments or gourmet lunches.

"Hi, Lila," Lila's favorite waitress, Pam, greeted her.

"What are you having today?"

"The usual plus a sweet tea," Lila said. "But for an appetizer I would like a side of fried sweet potatoes."

"All right," Pam said, taking the menu and then walking away.

Lila used to come in Aunt Tammie's once a week, but ever since the experiment started she had to have her fix of spicy jumbo lump crab cakes, seafood gumbo, and garlic mashed potatoes every day. She was stressed out and the decisions she had to make were blowing her mind.

Lila had not told anybody about the promises she made to God while she was in the jail cell. The guilt had driven her to find comfort in food, which is why she'd gone from a size fourteen to a twenty-four during the time she had been living with Steve.

She slowly stopped going to church after she canceled her wedding. Then she started going clubbing and partying with Joan and Tisha again. Lila would avoid the Christian television station, Bibles, or anything that would remind her of the vow she had made and broken to God.

But now that the experiment had started, Lila knew she could not avoid God anymore. He wasn't going to allow it.

She needed to leave Steve and go where? Back to the trailer park? Give up her Escalade and start riding the bus? Take her daughter out of private school where she was thriving and put her in the subpar crowded public school system? Go get a job at the mall where she would be lucky if she got paid eight dollars an hour?

Lila impatiently looked around for the waitress; she needed those fried sweet potatoes now!

Chapter 12

"Ms. Dallas, Tisha is on line one," Miriam said to Joan.

The last time Joan spoke to Tisha she had a negative reaction regarding the conference. How would she respond now that Joan had joined the church and was now a Christian?

"Ms. Dallas, would you like me to take a message?" Miriam asked after not getting a response from Joan.

"No, Miriam, I'll take the call." Joan stopped typing on her keyboard and picked up the phone, "Joan Dallas speaking."

"What's up, Ms. Dallas? You could have called your girl or something," Tisha responded.

"I know, Tisha, but things have been so crazy around here," Joan explained. "It's my first day back and stuff has piled up. I've had to handle three irate patients, two meetings, and answer eighteen e-mails. I was about to go to lunch when Dr. Wright called to say she needed two new medical assistants ASAP at the south office, and of course, she had to wait until I got back. You have no idea how hard it is to find good medical assistants. On top of all that, James didn't bring Jr. back when he said he would, and I've been calling his house all morning and not getting an answer."

"Don't panic. You know he didn't kidnap the boy or anything, so stop with the bull—"

Tisha's last word sent a pain through Joan's body, even though for as long as she could remember it had been a part of her vocabulary too.

"I'm not panicking. It's just when I tell him to bring my child home at a certain time, that's what I expect him to do."

"Joan, where do you get off calling James Jr. your child? I have news for you, sister. You did not make that boy by yourself . . . besides, the only reason you're tripping is because James married Raquel."

Joan wanted to know how Tisha learned this information, but she was too proud to ask. She resented how Tisha always found out everything before she did.

"Hey, I understand. I would be mad, too. After all the crap he put you through, I can't believe that sorry son of a b—had the nerve to marry somebody else. He is one lying mother—if I ever met one. But James Jr. didn't have anything to do with it, so he shouldn't have to suffer."

"Are you finished?" Joan asked. Tisha's language and attitude were irritating her.

"Almost, it's the summer, Joan. What's wrong with letting Jamie spend it with his dad?"

"Look, Tisha, I appreciate your input, but you

don't have any children, so you wouldn't understand."

"You don't have to have children to understand right from wrong. Anyway, I don't want to
argue with you about this. I was simply calling to
see if we're still on for Monday night at Eduardo's
and if you are still coming to the pool party. We
need to know how much food and drinks to tell
the caterer to prepare for. Oh, wait; let me guess.
Now that you're a church lady, you can't do stuff
like that."

"What?" Joan asked, wondering why Tisha
would refer to her as a church lady.

"Yeah, a couple of people I know were at that
conference and they told me how you're butt had
to be dragged to the altar." Tisha's tone sounded
almost as if she was mocking her. "I don't need all
that. I can read my Bible by myself. Besides, I got
enough people telling me what to do with my life,
you know what I mean?"

Joan was speechless. She contemplated hanging up the phone without saying good-bye.

Just then Miriam paged her, "Your son is on
line two," Miriam said.

"Tisha, I have another call, and yes, I will be
there. Why wouldn't I be? Surrendering your life
to God means a lot of things, but it does not mean
you don't get hungry, or that you have to stop
swimming," Joan said, then disconnected the call
with Tisha. "Joan Dallas speaking," Joan said after
taking the other call.

"Hey, Momma!" she heard the small voice
through the phone.

"Hey, baby, I miss you. I came to pick you up
last night from Grandma's but—"

"Momma, can I stay with Daddy, please?" James Jr. said, cutting Joan off. "Please, I'll be good, I promise." Joan was surprised at the excitement in her son's voice. "Yesterday, we went bike riding, and Daddy said if you let me stay, we could go camping." Joan wanted to cry thinking about the time James Sr. took her camping for the first time. She had hoped the three of them would go together as a family when Jr. went for the first time, but nothing concerning James Sr. had turned out as planned.

James Sr. grabbed the phone from his son. "Hey, Joan," he said into the receiver. She could sense the pretension in his voice. When they were dating he never called her Joan. He called her sweetie, sugar pudding, baby girl, but never Joan. "Jr. wants to stay with me. He's getting to know his brother and sister. Besides, I know you're busy with work and everything. Summer only lasts a few months. He'll be back with you before you know it."

"Don't you mean us?" Joan asked. "Jr. wants to stay with us. I understand congratulations are in order."

He ignored her, not wanting to get involved in a fight.

Joan knew she was wrong but she asked anyway. "Are you married, James?"

"Jr., go in the other room and watch TV, Daddy will be right there."

James Sr. waited until their son was out of the room before responding. "Look, let's not get into this right now."

"Let's not get into what?" Joan tried to keep her voice down. James always had a way of bringing out the worse in her. "You owe me that much. I should not have to hear this on the street. You act like I'm not supposed to be hurt. Look at the way you are talking to me like I'm some robot. Like you have never held me in your arms, like I don't matter, like I'm not the mother of your son."

"Joan, I didn't want to tell you because I didn't want to hurt you. I know I've done wrong by you. I've made a lot of mistakes. I'm sorry, I'm really sorry." Joan waited for him to answer her original question. "No, I'm not married, but I am engaged. The wedding will be—later."

Joan wanted to know when, but she knew he would not answer her if she asked.

"Does she live there with you?" Joan asked, then held her breath.

"Yes," James Sr. responded.

Joan could feel the tears forming in her eyelids but she refused to let James know she was on the verge of crying. She said in a strong voice, "I understand, James. I understand, just give me a heads-up next time, okay?"

"You're right. Joan, there is something else I need to tell you."

"What?" Joan hoped he didn't want their son to be in the wedding.

"Raquel and I will be at the pool party you and your friends are having."

"What do you mean?" Joan asked confused.

"Yeah, one of Raquel's clients is part of the book club. She invited Raquel and me. Raquel insists on going."

"Raquel knows I belong to that book club." Joan remembered punching the pillow in her hotel room like it was Raquel's head. "She only wants to make sure she can rub that rock you gave her in my face."

"I'm sorry about that, baby—I mean Joan. You know how she can be."

James Jr. came back into the room. Joan could hear him on the other end of the phone asking, "Daddy, what did Momma say?"

Joan knew she had no right to keep their son from his father. James Sr. could have, at any time gotten a lawyer, took her to court, and demanded time with his son. But he never did, believing the two of them should not have to ask a judge how they should raise their son.

She did not have to beg James Sr. to pay child support. He deposited the money into Joan's account regularly regardless of what was going on in their relationship. James Sr. had his faults, but he had always been a father to their son.

"Joan, I really need this time with Jr.," James Sr. pleaded. "He and his brother joined the soccer team in the neighborhood. I even changed my work schedule so I could help coach their teams. I want to take them to Louisiana to see their grandmother and camping. He's well taken care of; eating good and everything. He even has his own room."

A tear fell from the inner corner of Joan's eye. Last year James Sr. had given their son a birthday party at the bowling alley. He had come over a few days before to ask Joan what kind of cake she would be making, who he should invite, and what gifts he should buy their son.

They discussed the party, and afterwards he stayed to watch a movie. When they couldn't resist each other any longer, they laid on the floor moving slowly and quietly so as to not wake up their son in the next room. As he held her in the darkness that night, she felt an unmistakable closeness to him.

Therefore, when she showed up at the party in her brand-new outfit and freshly-done hair ready to be the perfect party mother and discovered Raquel had already beaten her to it, she lost it. Before making her exit, she yelled a few expletives about Raquel needing to ask her man where he was Thursday night. Then, she took Jr.'s hand and practically dragged him from his own party before it even had a chance to get started.

Now, she sat on the phone ashamed as she imagined her child on the other end of the phone having the same terrified look on his face as he did that day, awaiting her verdict of whether he could stay or not.

Since the experiment started, Joan was starting to deal with her true feelings about her mother. Joan's mother said she loved her but sometimes Joan didn't believe her because her actions did not match up with her words. Joan did not want James Jr. to say the same thing about her when he reached adulthood.

Joan tapped her fingers on the desk. "Put him on the phone," Joan said to James Sr. with no particular tone.

"Joan, come on now," James Sr. said, his voice pleading with her not to start trouble.

"Put him on the phone, James," Joan repeated.

Exhaling loudly, James Sr. did as she instructed.

"Yes, Momma," James Jr. said into the phone receiver.

Joan waited a few seconds. She wanted the

words that were about to come out of her mouth to be as soft as possible. "You can stay with your daddy as long as you want. I know in the past I've tried to keep the two of you apart, and I'm sorry for that. I promise you it will never happen again. Have fun, baby. I love you with all my heart and I'll talk to you later."

Excitedly, Jr. said, "I love you too, Momma."

She wanted to tell him to make sure he called her everyday, but she was interrupted by the sound of the dial tone.

Chapter 13

Eduardo's was bursting with energy and packed to capacity, as usual. The live mariachi band's music made the colorfully dressed waiters appear to be dancing as they carefully darted in between tables, serving huge platters of food and drinks to a boisterous happy hour crowd.

In contrast, Joan, Tisha, and Lila were sitting at their usual table in the center of the restaurant looking like a football team who had lost the game after having a twenty-point lead at halftime. Gone was the excessively loud laughter, idle chatter, and flirting with whatever businessmen happened to be within earshot.

The waiter, who had served them on many nights as they celebrated being single and sexy, thought someone had died as he served them their favorite type of margarita without being asked.

The waiter walked around the table. "And we have an extra-large strawberry with premium tequila for Joan, watermelon splash for Tisha, and mango-peach swirl for Lila." He placed bottles of water, chips, and salsa on the table and pulled out a notepad to take their food orders.

Joan opened her bottle of water and took a sip. She wondered why she was embarrassed as she looked at her margarita that was twice the size of her friends even though on a typical trip to Eduardo's she would down two of them the same size, without giving it a second thought. She almost wanted to tell the waiter to take it away and bring her a regular-sized drink or nothing at all. Deciding not to bring attention to herself, she kept quiet about the drink. She then ordered her food along with her friends and watched the waiter walk away.

Joan had been coming to Eduardo's with her coworkers or girlfriends during happy hour for years. Sometimes she came two or three times a week because of the fresh fruit margaritas, upbeat atmosphere, and legendary *tres leches* cake. But none of that mattered today. Joan noticed things she had never paid attention to before. The hostess's uniforms were too revealing. There were heavy clouds of cigarette smoke permeating throughout the restaurant and quite a few tables were ordering way too many tequila shots.

Joan, trying to act as if she were comfortable, causally took a chip out of the bowl on the table and looked at her friends. "It *is* good to see you both. This week has been a trip."

Tisha and Lila looked back at Joan but said nothing.

Joan put salsa on her chip and placed it her mouth. She chewed and swallowed then turned to Lila. "Me and Tisha already spoke about how strange this is, how frustrated we are, and how we are filled with anxiety about tomorrow and the days that will follow. Lila, I'm sorry I was so caught up in my own world to call you guys back last week. We should have been together."

Lila started to tear up as she pulled imaginary lint from her jeans. Once her glasses started to fog up, she took them off, revealing her smooth skin and pretty face.

Not wanting to follow her lead by crying, Joan and Tisha immediately looked down at their margaritas and swirled the thick liquid around with their straws.

Lila wiped her eyes with her napkin. "I don't know if I can do this. I just can't leave my man right now. I know I promised along with everyone else to commit to God's plan, but it's easier said than done." Joan and Tisha nodded in agreement. "He's good to me," Lila pleaded. "Look at all I would be giving up. Steve's practice is thriving and we have a nice home. I packed up my stuff three times last week, but I just couldn't walk out. I mean, it's not like he cheats on me or beats me."

"So, that's all you want? A man who does not cheat or beat on you? Is that all you deserve?" Joan responded.

"Joan, please, when was the last time you had a man, not to mention a good one. I heard about James and Raquel," Lila chimed in.

Joan looked across the room to avoid a sudden reflex to slap Lila. Tisha turned to Lila and spoke for the first time, "Now don't go sugarcoating your long-term fiancé, sweetie. I mean, he did call off the wedding two weeks before the date, leaving your bridesmaids stuck with those ugly three-hundred-dollar dresses."

Lila addressed Tisha. "I liked you better right after we came back from the meeting with the woman; when you were too dazed and confused to go off at the mouth."

Tisha rolled her eyes.

Having gained her composure, Joan said, looking at Lila, "And you know what? The funny thing about the whole ordeal was that you seemed not to care. Here you had spent thousands of dollars and many hours planning a wedding that didn't happen, and it was like you were more relieved than hurt."

"Yeah," Tisha interrupted through a mouthful of chips. "If Marcus had done me like that, I would have been ready to kill. But you just acted like it was next to nothing. Sometimes I think it was you who called off the wedding instead of him. You just lied to us and said he did."

"Why didn't you tell me you felt this way before?" Lila snapped.

"I don't know," Joan answered meekly. "I guess because we thought you would realize what we always knew."

Lila looked directly at Joan, and with contempt in her voice said, "And what might that be, my fellow experiment sister?"

Joan started to wonder if she had said too much. Joan looked away from Lila and filled her appetizer plate with chips and salsa.

Finally, Tisha said what Joan was afraid to say. "That you never loved Steve as much as you loved his résumé."

Shocked, Lila responded, making sure the people at nearby tables did not hear her. "How in the heck are you going to tell me I am not in love with Steve? He's a loving and compassionate man who also happens to be an excellent provider. I don't have to work like most women."

Tisha refused to let up. "If you're so in love with him, why do you avoid him?"

"Tisha, I don't know where you are getting your information," Lila spat.

"You!" Tisha replied. "I guess the fact that in the last two years you've spent more time at my house than your own sort of tipped me off," Tisha shot back. "I mean, right after you got released from prison, you didn't want to have anything to do with Joan or me. I would invite you out and you never showed up. I believe you said something about us dressing too sexy, hanging out to all hours of the night and cursing like sailors. Now, ever since you or whoever called off the wedding, we can't get rid you."

"What do you think, Joan?" said Lila. Feeling tense, Joan looked around for the waiter. "Joan, answer me," Lila repeated.

Joan drew closer to Lila and said, "Lila, um . . ."

"Just spit it out, Joan," Lila said.

"Well, if you insist, I'll answer you." Joan sat back in her seat and looked directly at Lila. "Your behavior has appeared to be somewhat strange. You went from being a good little church girl who was too caught up in Jesus to have anything to do with me or Tisha. Then Steve appeared on the scene. I don't understand your relationship with him. It's kind of strange that you never talk about him unless we bring up his name and you live with the man. You have what every woman wants. Steve adores you. He has a stable job with a stable income. Yet you're not married. I'm sorry, it just doesn't add up. You have to be leaving something out."

"Yeah, Lila," Tisha interjected, "what made you leave your holy lifestyle behind to hang out with us sinners? What's up with that?"

Joan continued, "Why did you pack your bags three times this week if you are so happy?"

With her curiosity piqued more than before, Tisha interjected, "And more importantly, why did you unpack?"

"Have you stopped seeing Marcus?" Lila responded vehemently.

Tisha glared at Lila. "We're talking about you, and no, I haven't stopped seeing Marcus. However, take this into consideration; Marcus loves me, and more importantly, I love him."

Lila counterattacked. "Steve is a good man. I've never known a man so caring, so dignified, and so trustworthy . . . not my daddy, not my brothers, nobody . . . and here this wonderful, amazing black man wants me, plain old Lila." She paused, looking down at her body. "I'm not exactly Halle Berry. He's more involved with Jasmine than I am. Isn't that what matters? My daughter's happiness? How many good brothers are out there anyway? I have one and I'm keeping him.

"I love the way he takes care of me," Lila continued. "It makes me feel good knowing I can depend on him. Am I wrong for trying to hold on to what I have? I'm so tired of this mess. You guys just don't know all the trials I've been through and what I'm still going through. I would do the right thing if I knew what the right thing to do was." Lila sighed and grabbed a handful of chips.

Joan spoke quietly. "You don't have it any worse than anybody else at this table. Every one of us is struggling with something."

"Yeah, we all have our own baggage." The three women directed their eyes toward the voice that interrupted their conversation. It was Janet, a woman who used to be in their clique. Janet continued talking as she stood beside their table. "Some of us carry it around everywhere we go, and some of us have enough sense to unload it so we can be free to prepare ourselves for something new."

Janet stood 5'11 and looked relaxed and elegant in a loose-fitted emerald cotton sundress and low-heeled gold sandals. Her long golden brown twists were slightly darker than her lightly freckled skin.

They stopped hanging out with Janet when she became a Christian two and half years ago and started acting differently. They tried to handle it at first, but one day the four of them along with a few other people were having movie night at Tisha's apartment. Halfway through the movie Tisha mentioned she had purchased the movie from a bootlegger. Janet went off on Tisha. She told her she was stealing and she should be ashamed of herself. Then Janet left refusing to watch the rest of the movie. After that scene they decided Janet was too holy for them and started to avoid her by changing their meeting times and places without notifying her. Janet quickly got the message and moved on.

"I hope you ladies don't mind if I join you?" Janet asked.

"It's okay with me," Lila said. She was sorry she had brought up Steve and welcomed the chance to change the subject.

Joan and Tisha nodded. Janet sat down in the only empty chair at the table.

"How's it going, Janet?" Lila asked, breaking the uncomfortable silence.

"Good, thank you for asking." Janet leaned her head forward, her voice almost dropped to a whisper. "I want all of you to know I've been praying for you in light of recent events."

Joan could see from the expression on Tisha's face that she was about to say something rude. Joan gently elbowed Tisha underneath the table hoping she would think twice before unleashing her tongue. It did not work.

Tisha blurted out. "What? So you think you're better than us now?"

"No that's not what I'm saying, Tisha," Janet said. "I just know that when I made the transition from a worldly woman to a godly one, it was the most difficult thing I had ever done. If any of you ever want to give me a call to talk or pray, my cell phone number has not changed."

Joan looked into Janet's eyes, moved her chair as close to the table as possible and asked in a voice so low that only the people at her table could hear her, "Were you there with the woman—in the auditorium?"

Without hesitation Janet responded, "Yes, and I saw all three of you."

Joan looked around the restaurant. "Was every single woman there?"

"No, I'm sure of that," Janet said.

Tisha asked suspiciously, "How do you know?"

Janet looked around to see if the waiter was coming to the table before she answered. "Because the woman in the white robe told me."

"Do you know how we were chosen?" Lila asked.

"She wouldn't tell me exactly," Janet said. "But from what I gather, there will be more meetings to come. We and the other thousands of women that were in the auditorium that day were simply in the first group. There will be meetings until every single woman has been there with the woman."

"If this really happened, why isn't it on TV, the newspaper, or Internet?" Joan asked.

Janet looked directly at Joan. "When you came back did you tell anyone?" Joan looked away. "Exactly, nobody in their right mind is going to give an interview. We have no way of proving the woman really exists or that she took us in the first place," Janet reasoned.

"What if we all got together and went to the authorities?" Tisha asked.

"What is that going to do?" Lila said as she sipped her margarita. "The woman does not operate in the human realm. What are they going to do, put her in jail?"

"So, what are we supposed to do then?" Tisha asked.

"Exactly what you guys are doing, being a part of a small cluster of women you can go through the experiment with," Janet said. "Crying on each other's shoulders, enduring the challenges, calling each other at four in the morning if you have to. It will probably get worse before it gets better. But remember, once you learn the lessons the woman is trying to teach you, she will no longer be a part of your life."

The waiter walked back to their table to refresh their chips and salsa. "Ladies, your food will be right out."

Joan, trying to appear as if they didn't stop talking because the waiter had arrived, looked at Janet and asked, "Still dating that guy?"

"Jerome, yes I am," Janet said.

To the dismay of her friends, Jerome was the postman Janet met at the detail shop right before they stopped talking to her. They said that with Janet being a computer programmer, she needed a man on her educational level and income bracket.

Looking at Janet the waiter asked, "Can I get you anything?"

"No, I already ordered my food. I'll be taking it with me," she replied before the waiter walked away.

"Jerome and me are just fine," Janet continued answering Joan's question. "In fact, I have something to tell all of you." Janet smiled and then flashed her left hand that had been resting under her right hand. She took a deep breath. "Jerome asked me to marry him!"

Lila spit out her margarita. Joan choked on a chip. Tisha enviously looked at the princess-cut diamond with the scrutiny of a gemologist.

"As soon as I got back home from work last Wednesday, I heard a knock on the door. There was a limousine driver with a huge bouquet of my favorite orchids." Janet took a deep breath and got a faraway look in her eyes like she was living the story as she was telling it. "The driver brought in the flowers plus an assortment of bags and boxes. He told me to get dressed and he would return for me in an hour. I peeked into the bags to find that they were gowns for me to choose from with shoes, purses, and jewelry to match. When I asked the driver where he was taking me, he only smiled and told me that Jerome had a place picked out that I would never forget. He then left and I hurried and got myself ready.

"Just as the limo driver said, he arrived back at my house in exactly an hour and escorted me to the limo. I thought I would find Jerome inside the limo waiting for me once I climbed inside, but all I saw was a bottle of champagne and three different rings with a note in his handwriting telling me to choose the one I liked best. About forty-five minutes later, I was boarding a plane first class with Jerome bound for Belize."

As Janet looked at each of them with their eyes bulging, she knew what they were all wondering. Therefore, she went on to explain.

"Jerome and one of his friends invested in an apartment complex downtown almost twenty years ago," she said, proceeding to explain where he got the money to create such a scene on his income. "It was already taking everything they had just to keep up the place. Jerome wanted to sell it many times, but he believed God was telling him to wait. Now that it's been decided to build the new huge convention hotel near it, the value of the property increased overnight.

"Well, anyway, one day some real estate guys called and said they wanted to buy it, and then a few days later some other guy called and said he was interested in purchasing it, and then several others showed an interest in the property as well. Soon, Jerome ended up having to get a lawyer to handle the negotiations. Well, to make a long story short, they went back and forth and it eventually sold for two million dollars!"

The women gasped as Janet continued her rags to riches tale.

"Anyway, on the airplane," Janet said, "Jerome got on his knees and made the sweetest official proposal. 'Janet,' he said, 'the day I met you I found a happiness I never knew existed.'" Janet stared off as if she was on cloud nine reciting Jerome's exact words. "'Everyday I find something different to thank God for in you: your beauty, your intellect, the way your voice squeaks when you get angry, the way your eyes slant when you smile, your infectious optimism, the way your fingernails gently poke my back when you hug me, your vibrant energy, the way you make my tea as if it's the most important thing you are going to do that day. Can we forget our days of "I" and "me" and become "us" for today, tomorrow, and always?'"

Just as Janet imagined when she had practiced telling her former friends the story, they were all silent.

The women played the proposal back in their heads, imagining what it would be like if it had been them.

Joan remembered the day she first met Janet. Joan was sitting on the floor in her dorm room talking on the phone when Janet walked in dressed in a long-sleeved black sweater and white wool pants in the middle of August. She had braces on her teeth and her natural hair was all over the place.

The only reason Joan agreed to hang out with her at first was because she felt sorry for Janet. Janet was very smart, but needed constant encouragement. Joan had to practically hold her hand in order to get her to complete the five presentations she had to do in order to graduate from college. When Janet walked across the stage to receive her diploma, Joan was just as happy as she was.

When Janet became a Christian she also took up swimming. Looking at her now, Joan could tell she had lost quite a bit of weight as a result of exercising. Along with swimming, Janet had joined a church where she was actively participating in the women's ministry.

It wasn't like Janet hadn't tried to share her insight with her friends, because she had repeatedly. However, they constantly made fun of her, often calling her names like Lil' Juanita Bynum and Paula White Jr.

As soon as Janet became a Christian she had vowed she would never have sex again until her wedding night. Joan and Tisha told her that was not possible and she would never get a man to marry her without sleeping with him first.

Joan finally asked Janet what she was dying to know. "Janet, you and Jerome have been together for what—a little over two years?"

Janet smiled. "I already know what you want to ask me. The first night me and Jerome make love it will be our wedding night."

"So it's possible?" Joan said.

"With God, all things are possible," Janet responded. "Don't get me wrong, it was hard, especially at first. You know during that time when you're just falling in love and you want to put your hands all over each other. We prayed together every night, sometimes on the phone, sometimes in person. We also fasted one day a week asking God to give us the strength to wait. We also limited the time we spent together without anyone else around, especially at night. And that's just the beginning, I could write a whole book about it."

Janet stared at her engagement ring with a huge smile on her face, leaving little suspicion as to how she answered Jerome. After searching but not finding a reason why they should not be happy for Janet, each of the women stood up from their seats and gave Janet a congratulatory hug before sitting back down.

"I'm so excited. I was worried y'all might be a little, well, indifferent," Janet said with tears in her eyes. "And another thing, we're getting married this Friday in St. Thomas, just the two of us. I know it's sudden, but it's taking everything we have to keep this relationship holy, if you know what I mean."

Afraid the envy might be evident in their voices, the women remained silent. Instead, they stared back at Janet with plastered smiles, searching for something to say.

To everyone's relief, the waiter came with their food. He handed Janet her to-go bag. When Janet reached for the bag her cell phone rang.

"Hello," Janet answered the phone. "Great! Everything is going so perfectly. God is truly with us."

Janet hung up the phone. "Guess what? My wedding is going to have its very own Web page! All of you will be able to watch it—live!" Janet got up from the table. "I wish I could stay, but I'm meeting Jerome for dinner. He loves the cheese enchiladas from this place. Then I need to go by the seamstress and pick up my dress. I haven't even chosen the flowers for my bouquet. Can you believe I don't know how I'm going to wear my hair?—I was thinking of wearing it down, but I don't know, Jerome likes it up."

Janet's cell phone rang again. She answered as she stood up to leave.

"Hey you!" Janet lit up. "Yeah, I got the food. Hold on, sweetie."

Janet walked around the table and gave each woman a good-bye hug. "Don't forget to check your e-mail . . . there'll be a link to the wedding."

Janet walked out the restaurant chatting with Jerome. Their eyes followed her.

Once getting over the initial shock of Janet's announcement, Joan was the first to speak. "So, Janet's pretty much out of the experiment. Who would have thought she would get married first?"

Still reeling over the way Tisha had spoken to her earlier, Lila said, "Yeah, I always thought it would be you and Marcus, Tisha. You guys have been together for a whole lot longer than Janet and Jerome."

"Why aren't you and Steve married? "Tisha shot back. "Aren't you the one who spent a whole year planning a wedding you didn't want to go to?"

"Quit with this nonsense," Joan said. "We are supposed to lean on each other and help support one another throughout the experiment. This dinner was a way for us to do just that, so let's start, shall we?"

Joan bit into her poblano chicken for the first time, hoping Lila and Tisha would start eating and stop bickering.

"Yeah, I hear you, Joan, but I'm not telling Lila any more of my business until she comes clean about Steve." Tisha pushed her food away and stared at Lila. "What's the point of us forming a sisterhood pact if one of the sisters is holding back info?"

Since Tisha insisted on talking about it, Joan gave up and joined in on the discussion. She put her fork down and pushed her food away. Joan turned to Lila. "Tisha's right, we need to know what's going on with you and Steve. I don't mean to be in your business or anything, but this whole experiment thing isn't going to work as long as you continue living with him. You're going to have to make up your mind; marry him or leave him."

"This is complicated," Lila responded. "I can't go into it right now."

"Why, Lila?" Joan asked. "Whatever the problem is, you have been running from it for a long time. Just go ahead and tell us. Maybe we can help you."

Joan stared back at Lila waiting for her to answer the question. Lila looked like she was about to cry. Joan didn't move her gaze.

"Joan, leave her alone," Tisha said sarcastically. "Lila's going to marry Steve when and if she happens to fall in love with him. Besides, she rarely gives him any anyway."

"Tisha, you really need to quit," Lila spat. Seizing the opportunity to get Joan off her back, Lila struck at Tisha. "Tisha, did you happen to tell Joan that you and Marcus are back doing the do?"

Joan's voice raised an octave. "Tisha, you're back to laying up with Marcus again?"

Tisha tried not to look embarrassed. "Yes," she voiced in defeat. "Look, I've tried that celibacy stuff and it's not for me. My man has needs, and after so many times, the scary woman gave up trying to stop me. I've decided Marcus and me aren't getting married anyway. Don't get me wrong, I'm still going to kick it with him and everything, just not long-term."

Looking at both of them in disbelief, Joan said, "What about the experiment? What about becoming a godly woman? We have barely gotten started. It hasn't even been two weeks and you two already want to quit."

"Look, Joan, you don't have a man and haven't had one in a really long time, so you can't possibly understand," Lila said.

"Exactly," Tisha agreed.

"Tisha, I just talked to you. You said you had tried to pray and mediate and read the Bible; well, keep trying. You can do all things with the Lord. You both need to pray for guidance. It will get better," Joan pleaded.

Joan could tell the conversation tone had suddenly changed when Tisha sat up tall in her chair. Joan wondered what she had said wrong.

"Look, I'm tired of this crap," Tisha said, followed by a long sigh. "When I was trying to do the right thing, that woman from the auditorium was always around telling me to journal, think, pray, and relive things I didn't want to relive. I had enough!"

Enough of what? Joan wondered. Tisha always had it good. She grew up in a well-kept large home with two parents who showered her with love and attention. Her mother died of breast cancer, but only after giving Tisha her best years. So far, she had only completed one semester in college, yet she lived in a plush apartment and worked when she wanted to thanks to her father and Marcus. Whenever they got tired of her begging and borrowing, she turned to Joan.

"You need to count your blessings," Joan said. "God has been very good to you. You would think you'd want to return the favor."

"Excuse me!" Tisha shouted, insulted by Joan's words.

The people at surrounding tables turned towards their table briefly, then resumed eating.

Joan tried to keep her voice low. "Tisha, come on. Any crap you've gotten yourself into was your own doing. Your parents have always been there for you. When my mother was too busy catering to her latest man to come to my school functions, your mother was right there with ice cream, cake, and a smile for yours. You need to be on your knees thanking God right now for the parents He blessed you to have in your life."

Tisha stood up from the table. Joan and Lila looked at each other wondering what Tisha was about to do or say.

"God? You mean the same God who took my mother away from me?" Tisha shouted. "Even after I prayed and prayed for him not to? The

God that has left my father to pick up the pieces after the only woman he has ever loved died? Yeah, we prayed and we went to church, but God still let us down, and apparently, He's going to keep doing it. My Aunt Yolanda called me this morning and it seems that God decided to strike her down with breast cancer too. She starts chemotherapy tomorrow. Now that she has it, it's almost certain—" Tisha paused in an attempt to control her emotions, but was unsuccessful, as her eyes watered. "It's only a matter of time before I get it too." Tisha burst into tears, her crying sending her body into spasmodic jerks.

Immediately Joan stood up, grabbed Tisha's hands, and tried to hug her. "Tisha, I'm sorry. I didn't know," Joan comforted her.

Tisha pushed her away. "So, Joan, that's why I'm through with the experiment. Being with Marcus is the one thing that brings me happiness, and I'm not about to give him up. Why should I be worried about God? He ain't worried about me. What am I supposed to do? Get married, have children, then die on them? What's the point?"

"Look, Joan," Tisha continued, "you have always thought my life was somehow better than yours. You've always acted that way from day one, and frankly, I'm tired of it! I got news for you; you are not the only one in the world with problems.

"What is it with you? My momma is dead! Even If I live to have a wedding, she won't be there. She will never be able to baby-sit my kids like your mother is able to baby-sit James Jr. I can't smell her. I can't touch her. I can't talk to her.

"You know, sometimes when I'm alone at night—when it's just me—whatever I do I can't seem to get her off my mind. I'm fine during the day when I'm busy, moving, working, existing, but at night I can't find any peace. The day she died something left me. It's like it flew away and no matter what I do I can't get it back. Joan, are you hurting so much that you can't acknowledge anyone else's pain?"

Tisha threw forty dollars on the table and walked out the restaurant's front door, not bothering to look back.

Joan and Lila finished their dinner in silence, too caught up in their own thoughts to care that most of the restaurant patrons and staff were busy discussing what had just happened at their table.

Chapter 14

Joan had given up finding the remote to the television and reluctantly moved her sore, tired body out of the bed. She walked to the television set and turned it on.

It was Saturday morning, and the night before, instead of going clubbing with her friends as she had done on Friday nights prior to the experiment, she had decided to spend the evening running on the treadmill she had purchased over eight months ago but never used.

Tisha and Lila were probably just waking up to their Saturday morning hangovers. She could not believe how they had barely tried to keep the promises they made after witnessing everything that had happened in the experiment. Then, she recalled how in the Bible the children of Israel saw the sea spread its waters and reveal dry land as well as numerous other miracles, yet they still questioned the power of God.

She clicked on the power button and slowly

got back in bed. The TV blasted louder than she expected.

"How did you contract HIV, Shannon?" the talk show host on the television asked the guest. Joan's sleepy eyes opened wide, inspecting the young woman on the screen to who the question was being addressed.

"I was so excited to be away at school and finally have my freedom," Shannon answered. "The first day of classes, my roommate and I went to this jazz bar."

No longer thinking about her weak muscles, Joan sat up in bed. Joan looked at the girl's flat chest, curve-less hips, light brown freckled skin, and conservative dress, convincing herself there was no way Shannon could have contracted HIV in a sexual way.

"I was so glad to finally be in a club. I met him there that night, the man who gave it to me," Shannon said.

Joan's knees started to tremble as she climbed out of bed and stood, not taking her eyes off the television.

"By the end of the night, I thought I was in love," Shannon said. "He had me believing I was prettier than Beyoncé and as smart as Condoleezza Rice. It was like I was brainwashed or something."

The tears started to form in Joan's eyes as she listened intensely.

"The next few weeks, we talked on the phone a lot and he took me to lunch a few times. About a month after we met, I had a fight with my roommate and called him. He picked me up and took me to his apartment. I had sex for the first time that night."

"Shannon, what about condoms?" the host asked.

"I insisted he wear condoms when we first started having sex, but as we dated longer and longer—" Shannon dropped her head.

Joan walked to the television and put her hand on the screen, as if she could touch Shannon and stroke away her pain.

"I should have never had sex with him in the first place," Shannon confessed. "I knew better. I was raised to know the value of my virtue. I have no excuses. I made a series of bad decisions. What can I say besides it all made sense at the time?"

"Why are you here, Shannon?" the host asked.

Shannon looked directly into the camera with determination she did not possess before. "I never thought anything like this could ever happen to me. Maybe because I didn't know anyone it had happened to. If I would have known of a nineteen-year-old from a happy two-parent home who got infected with HIV from the first man she had ever been with, I might have taken notice and been more careful."

"I admire your bravery," the host said. "We will be right back with more of Shannon's story after these messages."

The men Joan had been with flashed before her eyes so quickly that she got nauseous. She saw their bodies moving inside of hers without a condom in sight. She remembered the times the condoms broke, they didn't feel right, or how her and her lover had discarded them in the heat of passion. Like Shannon, Joan had insisted they wear condoms the first few times they were together, but later on was less demanding.

She remembered years ago when she and Tisha had gone to visit Tisha's grandmother in the hospital. They went to the front desk to ask for Patricia Carter's room, but the Patricia Carter in room 222 was not Tisha's grandmother. They had given them the wrong room number. However, Joan remembered how weak and frail the woman looked lying in the bed. She remembered how quiet it was and how lonely it felt in the room. She and Tisha practically ran back to the front desk.

Joan was frightened by what she was thinking. She wanted to know why it had never occurred to her that the woman might have been infected. Once again, she pictured Shannon in her mind. Joan couldn't understand how one person could be with twenty-eight men and not have HIV and another only slept with one and got infected.

She ran to the bathroom and looked at herself in the mirror. Her hair was disheveled and damp due to her perspiration. She removed all her clothes and looked at her naked body nervously as if lesions would suddenly appear. She moved her neck around and touched her toes as if flexibility was a sign of good health. All the time, the phone on the nightstand kept beckoning her to make the call.

Walking slowly to the nightstand, after giving into the urge, Joan picked up the phone. The number to her doctor's office was committed to memory, but she hung it up, telling herself she needed to verify it in her address book. She walked through the living room to the kitchen and picked up her purse, passing two phones on her way back to the bedroom. Number in hand, she paced the floor questioning if she really wanted to know.

She imagined what it might be like when she got her results. The ordinarily cheerful receptionist would be unable to make eye contact. The nurse with gold hair, who asked Joan about getting her a job every time she came in, would make it a point to ask nothing as she showed her to the doctor's private quarters. The doctor would gently grab her hand from across the desk and whisper the results. Joan saw herself crying as a nervous doctor tried to comfort her while making sure not to come in contact with her tears. She saw herself driving home, thinking how much easier it would be if she just accelerated as quickly as her car would take her and crash right into the tree on Ranger Street.

Joan had worked herself up so much that her head was pounding and drops of sweat were falling from her forehead. Unable to walk due to dizziness, she proceeded to crawl the few feet back to her nightstand. Noticing the Bible on top of it, she picked it up and opened it randomly to 2 Chronicles. Her eyes moved to a section she had highlighted one day while she was studying.

"Do not be afraid; do not be discouraged. Go out to face them tomorrow, and the Lord will be with you," 2 Chronicles 20:17.

Joan was in awe as she felt the words travel throughout her body like spiritual medicine. She repeated them over and over, each time feeling more peaceful.

Startling her, the phone rang. Habitually, she checked the caller ID. It was Dr. Wright.

"Hello," Joan answered.

"Hi, Joan, sorry to bother you at home, and on the weekend." Dr. Wright stated.

"Oh, that's okay. What's up?"

"You know Dr. Jones was supposed to cover me next week while I'm on vacation in New York? Well, something came up and now Dr. Furrow is covering me. I know, I know, Joan," she said empathetically. Dr. Furrow was notorious for being rude to his staff and taking long breaks in between patients.

"Don't worry. We can handle it. Maybe I can get Dr. Mitchell to handle some of the patients if he gets behind schedule. I know you need a break."

"Thanks, Joan. I don't know what I'd do without you."

Joan's heart jumped, but before she could change her mind and before Dr. Wright could hang up the phone she asked, "How long does it usually take to get the results of an HIV test?"

"No more than a week and a half. Why do you ask?" Dr. Wright said.

"I think I need to take one," Joan answered, trying not to sound anxious.

"I don't think so, Joan."

"Why?" Joan asked confused.

"Didn't you just take our annual physical like everybody else?"

"Yeah, but what does that have to do with being tested for HIV?" Joan responded.

"Well, they test the blood for a lot of common things, HIV being one of them," Dr. Wright explained. "They would have informed you immediately. They normally send out the results of your physical in the mail. Did you not receive it?"

"I'm not sure." Joan paused and tried to recall if she had gotten the information. "I guess you're right. I've worked at the office long enough where I should've known that, huh?" Joan let out a slight chuckle.

"Joan, what have you been thinking? You must be tired. I'll call you to check on things next week while I'm strolling down Fifth Avenue."

"Have fun," Joan said, trying to sound upbeat and unconcerned.

Joan hung up the phone, ran over to the drawer where she kept her old mail, and turned it upside down, dumping out its contents. She searched until she found the envelope she was looking for and tore it open. The results were three pages. The first page listed basic information regarding her blood type, blood pressure, height, weight, and whether or not she smoked. The next listed all the things she had been tested for, including tuberculosis, hepatitis, and every sexually transmitted disease she knew existed. The last page congratulated her on a healthy physical.

She dropped to her knees, joyful tears falling from her face.

"Welcome back, everyone!" Joan heard the talk show host say. She looked at the television in disbelief. The last few minutes that passed had seemed like days.

"Shannon, it is estimated that young black women like you are getting infected at an alarmingly high rate. Why do you think that is?" the host asked.

Shannon shook her head back and forth. "We just don't know what's really going on. Those who have it don't tell anybody, and a lot of people that have it don't know it."

"Shannon, some people say they would rather

not know if they're infected. What do you have to say about their decision?"

"That's ridiculous to me. Everybody should want to know so they don't spread the disease."

"But what about the—"

"I know what you are about to say . . . the loneliness, the ridicule, and the stares. Yes, when I first got diagnosed, I was scared to tell anybody. The day I told my parents, my mom picked up the phone and called every prayer warrior she knew. They met at our house and took turns interceding on my behalf for forty days straight. To this day, every single hour of the day somebody at my church is wrapping me in prayer.

"My father had not taken the time to seek a relationship with God his entire life. But after hearing my diagnosis, he fell to his knees, repented of his sins, and asked Jesus into his life. He has never been the same. He travels with me everywhere, witnessing constantly and asking people to intercede on my behalf. He's in the audience right now."

The camera moved to a man in the audience wearing blue jeans and a long-sleeved plaid flannel shirt. He stood, smiled, and blew a kiss at Shannon before taking his seat.

"We've lost count of how many men accepted Christ after they found out my daddy had converted," Shannon continued, " but the number is somewhere in the hundreds. My pastor started an AIDS ministry at our church, and at least seven churches started their own after hearing about ours. We meet up to support one another weekly. If somebody is looking for a job, we help them find one. If someone is in the hospital, we make sure somebody is there with them so they are not alone. If somebody needs a ride or needs help cleaning their house, we make ourselves available. We fellowship, pray, and educate others on this disease. Oh yes, what the devil meant for evil God used for good.

"My sister and I had not been enemies before my diagnosis, but we were not really close either. But now, we don't miss a day of talking to one another and we get together as much as our schedules allow. When some members of my family deserted me, God sent strangers to take their places.

"I'm in my second year of college, majoring in fashion design and merchandising, and I just purchased my first car. I love the mall and never have enough money to buy all the clothes I want. I love to praise dance, sew, and read poetry. I'd love to start a magazine for young godly women. My sanity is due to the Lord. I know who's in control. I recite the first six verses of Psalm one-oh-three all day, everyday to remind myself.

Shannon closed her eyes and began reciting the verses.

"Praise the Lord, O my soul;
    all my inmost being, praise his holy name.
Praise the Lord, O my soul,
    and forget not all his benefits—
who forgives all your sins
    and heals all your diseases,
who redeems your life from the pit
    and crowns you with love and compassion,
who satisfies your desires with good things
    so that your youth is renewed like the
    eagle's.

The Lord works righteousness
   and justice for all the oppressed."

Shannon opened her eyes. "I have accepted Jesus' death as payment for my sins, thereby, re-serving a space for me in heaven. Regardless of what I have to endure on earth I have the assur-ance of knowing I will spend eternity in the pres-ence of God. In heaven, there are no tears, no pain, no disease, and no heartache. Praise the Lord! I don't spend my days asking, 'why me?' Instead, I ask, 'now what?' "

Chapter 15

Joan went straight from work to church for a meeting with Minister Makita. Once Joan found out she would not be an official member of Miller Street Church until she completed all three of her new member orientation classes, she scheduled her appointments for three weeks in a row.

Makita said her husband wanted to make sure each member of Miller Street Church had a solid understanding on what the Bible teaches about salvation, evangelism, prayer, spiritual gifts, stewardship, and discipleship soon after they joined. He said it was sad to talk to the multitudes of people who claim to be Christians, but when asked, knew very little about Christianity.

Joan knocked on Makita's plain, white door. The first time she had knocked on this door she felt sort of weird, but not anymore. Today was her third and last new member session and experience had taught her that Makita was down-to-earth, easy to talk to, full of practical insight and godly wisdom.

"Come in, Joan, the door is open," Makita said from the other side of the door.

Joan walked in the door and handed Makita a workbook. "I completed all the assignments in the Bible handbook. I started out just doing the ones you told me, but then I was having so much fun and learning so much I completed them all. I also read all the gospels accounts and I finished reading Genesis." Joan took her seat across from Makita who was seated at her desk.

Makita took the workbook and placed it on her desk. "Of course you did. You know it has been a long time since I talked to someone who is as eager to learn about God as you are. I love to talk to new Christians. It's a lovely thing to be in the presence of someone who just wants to know God. Someone who is so busy soaking up God to argue about whether speaking in tongues is relevant for today or if women should preach."

Joan saw a *Radio-Active Magazine* on Makita's desk. Joan was surprised. The magazine was popular among young adults as it featured interviews with R&B, pop, and hip-hop artists.

"Is that your normal reading material?" Joan joked.

Makita looked down. "Oh no, one of our church members brought this to me along with a videotape. I read the article but I haven't seen the same tape yet."

Joan still looked puzzled. Makita explained. "I'm fifty-seven years old, Joan, and sometimes I get tired by this work the Lord has given me. On days when I'm really tired I'm tempted to retire so I can wake up when I get ready, spend as much time with my grandkids as I can stand, and work in my rose garden until my heart's content. So I have people that come around and give me things periodically to let me know that there is a whole lot of work to do for the kingdom of God and retiring is not an option.

"I'm not sure what's on this tape, let's look at it." Makita walked over to an armoire on the side wall of her office. She opened the wooden doors to a television with a DVD and VCR attached.

After she put the video in, Joan and Makita turned their chairs around so they could see it. It was Proxy Justice, an international pop superstar; she was Tisha's favorite artist. She had all of her CD's and even went to see her in concert twice. Proxy was known for her upbeat tracks, expert choreography, and flawless figure.

Proxy was walking on stage with several dancers at a packed concert. The massive crowd was jumping up and down. Proxy and her dancers were wearing short panty-like shorts with sequins bras and high-heeled shoes.

Proxy grabbed a microphone and said, "How are you feeling, New York. Proxy Justice in the house. Are you ready to feel me?"

Joan wondered if Makita was really ready for the lyrics she was about to hear. She knew the song Proxy was getting ready to sing. Tisha used to sing, "Are You Ready to Feel Me" all the time when the CD of the same name first came out earlier this year.

Proxy and her dancers turned around with their backs facing the crowd. The music came on and then they proceeded to squat down to the floor and begin vibrating their bottoms wildly. They turned back around to face the crowd. A group of men from offstage ran and placed chairs behind Proxy and her dancers. They sat on the chairs, then in a ripple, each dancer slowly spread their legs open. Proxy began to sing, "Do you want to feel me, taste me, come inside me, ride me, come on boy, jump-start my body."

Makita was looking for the remote to turn the VCR off when the video switched from Proxy's concert to Proxy making an acceptance speech. She was standing behind a glass podium holding some kind of statue. She looked completely innocent and elegant in a long pink satin baby-doll dress. Proxy looked overjoyed with emotion and was holding back tears as she accepted her award. "You don't know how much this means to me. I first of all want to thank my Lord and Savior, Jesus Christ, for making this all possible. I give God all the Glory. I would have never thought in a million years *Are You Ready to Feel Me* would have sold seven million copies. I want to say a big thank you to all of my fans. I want to thank . . ."

Makita turned the VCR off and turned towards Joan. "Now I see why somebody gave this to me."

Joan nodded in agreement. "They want you to know there are a lot of lost people out there and without a teacher they will not know the truth of the gospel.

"Before I started reading the Bible I had a real messed-up view of God too," Joan continued. "God is loving and merciful; all that I thought He was. But I'm also learning that God does not play.

You don't have to read very many chapters of the Bible to figure that out. If people would read the Bible, they would have an entirely different view of Him."

Makita looked surprised. "Are you reading the Bible from beginning to end?"

"Yes I am."

"You are going to mature more in three years than most Christians do in thirty. Keep at it. It's going to get difficult right around Leviticus; keep reading, it gets easier with practice." Makita crossed her arms and sat back in her chair.

"I'm interested to know what you think about that video we just saw."

Joan had grown used to Makita's intense stare. The first time she did it Joan wanted to run out of her office. She felt like Makita was looking right through her.

"I think we should have compassion on her," Joan explained. "It's really easy to get angry at her but I can't get angry at her, because just a few days ago I was her. I got baptized, I knew a few scriptures, a lot of the time I would pray, and if anybody would have asked me I would have told them I was a Christian. I didn't know that I wasn't one. I thought, hey, I'm a good person, and despite my faults, God loves me. It's not like I'm a rapist or child molester, so when I die I will go to heaven.

"God is loving and merciful, but He is also a God of justice. He punishes the wicked for their sin. Same as any upright human judge would punish a child molester for their sin. I deserved to go to hell, but because of God's grace and mercy through sending His son to die for my sins, I'm going to heaven.

"It wasn't until I came to this church and started reading my Bible at home that I got a clearer picture of what being a Christian really means. I had to stop looking at the people I knew who claimed to be Christians and read what the Bible says about being a Christian. And it is pretty clear to me that the two don't match and a whole lot of people are just as confused as I was.

"Now I have the truth. I can see clearly that I was deceived. How can I claim to love God if I refuse to obey Him? As they say, actions speak louder than words.

"If only somebody would have sat me down regularly when I was child and taught me the things I'm learning now," Joan stated. "I would have avoided so many mistakes. But I was simply in the world doing what I felt was right; making up stuff as I went along the same as Proxy Justice is doing now."

Makita stood up and walked up to Joan. "I've been praying for God to send me a speaker to present the gospel at our upcoming conference we're having for teenage girls next year. God just answered my prayers. I want you to speak."

Joan's mouth was wide open, but nothing came out. "Don't stop preaching now. The conference is not for months, in March, next year. I don't want the same ole style. I don't want a seasoned speaker. Instead, I want somebody like you who has truly met the living, true, and Holy God and is excited about it. Those girls are going to listen to you in a way they would never listen to me," Makita explained.

"We're going to have a few Christian bands, a fashion show, and a skit. At the end of the night you will speak. All I want you to do is take a few minutes to present the gospel in a way that would grab a teenager's attention. Then I want you to answer this question: what I wished somebody would have told me before I had sex for the first time. Joan, just like you I didn't have anybody living a godly life before me. So I didn't think it was possible. I want girls everywhere to know that they don't have to make the same mistakes we did. Maybe if we give them a glimpse of what it's really like to live outside of the will of god, they'll never bother to find out for themselves."

Joan was still speechless.

"Okay, you don't have to give me an answer right now," Makita told her. "I think we're done for the day. Come by my office regularly. Just because you've completed new member orientation does not mean I don't want to talk to you."

Joan grabbed her things and walked out the office feeling like she could scale a wall.

Chapter 16

After her final meeting with Makita, Joan went to the gym for aerobics class. The first four times she went to the class she had to stop because she had gotten so exhausted. But the last three times she was able to keep up from beginning to end. She had lost seven pounds since beginning her workouts and was slowly starting to change her diet; using beans instead of meat and eating fresh vegetables or fruit with every meal. Makita had suggested an exercise and nutrition regimen at their first meeting, saying as long as she was working on her mind and spirit, she might as well work on her body.

After leaving the gym, Joan sat at her kitchen table as she chopped vegetables for her salad. She was about to sit down to a dinner of spinach and tomato salad and the spicy black bean enchiladas she had made the night before. But then the telephone rang. She saw Tisha's number on her caller ID. She had hoped Tisha would call tonight to remind her that her birthday was coming up like she did every year. Joan had already made reservations at Tisha's favorite spa.

Since the incident at the restaurant, their conversations had been strained. She wanted to clear the air, but Tisha preferred to avoid it by quickly changing the subject whenever Joan brought it up.

It was two months into the experiment and Tisha seemed to be partying harder than she had before it started, as well as continuing to have sex with Marcus. Therefore, Joan thought a day at the spa would give her an opportunity to have a little talk with her best friend.

"Hello, Tisha," Joan answered the phone.

"Hey girl, guess what?" Tisha said, sounding like her old self. "I just got us tickets to the VIP room for tonight at Club Cleo."

"What?" Joan said in disbelief.

"Yeah, I just called this guy I know about having a party for my birthday on Saturday. He said it was all booked up, but if we came tonight, he would hook us up. Joan, these tickets cost almost three hundred dollars apiece. I'm talking food, champagne, celebrities, the works. We got to be there by ten, so hurry up. I'm going by to pick up Lila. I might as well pick you up too. I'll be there in about an hour." The call was disconnected without warning.

Joan felt a twinge in her stomach as she placed the phone back on the receiver. One of the scriptures she had meditated on that morning popped into her head.

"Be self-controlled and alert. Your enemy the devil prowls around like a roaring lion looking for someone to devour," 1 Peter 5:8.

She thought about calling Tisha back and telling her she couldn't go, but decided against it when she thought of how the two of them had always made a big deal about birthdays. And after the episode at Eduardo's, she didn't need to upset things any further.

Joan walked into her bedroom and made her way to the closet. She looked in the back of her closet where she stored her more revealing clothes so her son would not see them. Ever since the start of the experiment, she had avoided this section of her closet. The clothes that at one time had meant so much to her caused her stomach to turn when she thought of how much she had paid for such small pieces of fabric. She looked as if she were in someone else's space as she gasped at how seductive some of them were.

Joan picked up the phone to call Tisha. She thought about telling her she was sick, but didn't want to lie. She thought about telling her the truth, but didn't want to cause more trouble.

She put the phone down, grabbed a pair of black slacks and a short-sleeved red top and some black pumps. She would have normally only worn this type of outfit to work. Joan quickly dressed and after putting her makeup on and letting her braids fall over her shoulders, she admired herself in the mirror and smiled. She thought back to all the times she couldn't leave the house unless she had on a short uncomfortable dress, a pair of expensive pointed toe shoes, and a pre-club buzz. But tonight would be different.

Club Cleo had always been Joan's favorite place to dance, and Wednesday night was legendary. The VIP room would surely have a lot of people she knew in it. If Darren or any of her former lovers were there, she promised herself she would refuse to talk to them.

One of Makita's messages popped in her head. "If certain clothes cause men to look at you lustfully, stop wearing them. If your friends are leading you to do or think ungodly things, you must give them up too."

Joan went and found the latest addition to her scripture note cards and began to read them out loud. Before long, Tisha called to say she was downstairs.

Joan grabbed her purse and keys. Before walking out the door she stopped to look at her sofa. It never looked so comfortable. Sitting at home alone reading her Bible wrapped in a blanket on her sofa with a cup of tea was exactly how she wanted to spend the evening.

Joan knew she had no business in Club Cleo. Her spirit was telling her to stay home. But Joan had been friends with Tisha since she was twelve years old and she wasn't ready to let that go. So Joan slowly walked out of her condo and locked the door behind her.

Joan's plan was to act the way she always had when they went clubbing, ignoring the part of her that no longer had a desire to be in that kind of environment.

Once Joan made it outside, she climbed into the passenger's seat of Tisha's car with the same greeting she always had. "What's up, my sistas?" It came out of her mouth as if it was rehearsed, but nobody noticed.

Lila was in the backseat on her cell phone, lying to Steve and telling him she was going to spend the night at Tisha's since she was going to be up all night braiding her hair. She ended the conversation by telling him she loved him. Joan felt sad, realizing Lila had done nothing about resolving her issues with Steve.

Tisha was in the driver's seat changing the CD selection. Driving off and dancing in her seat, Tisha said, "Oh, y'all know we're about to have some fun. It's my thirtieth birthday! We are about to get this party started right! Do you feel me?" She turned to Joan for a quick high five.

Joan dropped her purse in the process of trying to get her hand up quickly. Nervous they may have noticed her uneasiness, she diverted their attention by enthusiastically asking, "Did y'all check out Janet's wedding on her Web site? I didn't log in for the actual wedding, but I did check out the pictures."

"No, I haven't gotten that bored. How do the pictures look?" Tisha asked.

Joan continued. "Janet was beautiful and the scenery was absolutely amazing. Jerome looked very handsome in his tuxedo. I e-mailed her and she said to tell everybody hello."

"When are they coming back?" Lila asked.

"Around the time they were supposed to return back home," Joan said, "it suddenly dawned on them that they were rich and didn't have a reason to rush back. Jerome quit his job and Janet took an extended leave of absence. She says they're going to travel for a while, going to places they've always wanted to go and leaving whenever they get ready. In other words, she makes me sick."

Tisha huffed. "The last thing I need is to see little Miss Janet and company. I did send her some real nice crystal glasses, though. She was always more your friend than she was mine anyway, and besides, I ain't even trying to lie—I'm jealous."

Joan was in agreement with Tisha's last statement. "I know that's right. What are the odds of meeting a postman who turns out to be loaded?"

Lila joined the conversation. "She's set. Next, they'll be buying a big house and raising a bunch of babies."

Joan instantly felt sad upon remembering a family may not be in Tisha's future. She knew Tisha still wasn't over the confusion about all the things she had discussed at Eduardo's. Joan hated the distance in their relationship. Joan wanted to grab Tisha, hug her, and tell her everything was going to be all right. She wanted to ask about her aunt and what the doctors said about her own chances of getting the disease. She had known two women at her job that had contracted breast cancer, and both had survived. She wanted to tell Tisha that getting breast cancer was not an automatic death sentence. She wanted to assure her God would be with her through it all, but Tisha never brought it up and she was too scared to.

Instead, in a voice just like her old self, she loudly said what she knew Tisha wanted to hear. "Where's our 'going out' music? Turn it up, turn it up. Turn it all the way up."

"Okay," Tisha and Lila responded in unison.

Tisha put Mary J. Blige on, and all three of them sang each lyric on the *Family Affair* CD until the twenty-minute ride to Club Cleo was over.

Singing with her friends had relaxed Joan. After being in Club Cleo for fifteen minutes, the lights, energy, and VIP treatment caused her relaxed state to turn into enthusiasm. Hearing one of her all-time favorite songs blasting from the main dance floor, she quickly made her way upstairs to the center of the empty dance floor. Lila and Tisha followed closely behind her.

Joan could feel the man on a stool in front of her staring as she moved her body to the beat of the music. She could see that he was at least six feet tall and the color of peanut butter. When he stood up to get a better look, she found herself moving faster and enjoying the attention. The song was about to end when he put his drink down and walked up to her and started dancing in front of her. He was wearing a tailored gray suit and an expensive silk tie. Joan got a glimpse of his shoes. They were perfectly polished and scuff free. He was fresh from the barber and his cologne smelled so good, Joan found herself getting closer and closer just so she could get a whiff of it.

Joan always loved a confident man, and the fact that this one risked embarrassment by coming up to a woman he didn't know in a crowded club had her taking notice. She could have walked away and left him standing there humiliated. Most men would have waited until she was out of the spotlight and nicely hidden at one of the tables to step to her.

With her friends having gone to their table, she continued to dance with the mystery man. Joan felt electric as she moved around the dance floor. He was able to follow her every move.

He whispered in Joan's ear in a deep melodious voice, "You are the most beautiful woman in this room."

Joan felt a sensation where she wasn't supposed to.

Eventually, Tisha and Lila retuned to the dance floor with dance partners of their own. It was like old times as they tried to out dance one another, bouncing up and down, turning around in circles, and dropping to the floor in front of their dance partners.

After a few songs, Joan's dance partner led her off the dance floor and to his table. Joan waved to her friends who were still dancing.

He wiped the chair with his handkerchief before he pulled out her seat. Now that they were both seated at the table he grabbed both of Joan's hands and looked into her eyes. Up close and personal Joan could see now that he was gorgeous. She felt a chill go down her spine.

"I'm Samuel Hawkins," he said. "I'm thirty-five. I just moved to Houston a month and half ago and this is my first time in this club. I'm an electrical engineer and I've been divorced for five years. I'm not on the down low now, neither have I been in the past. I have one son; he's nine, I have no pets."

Joan burst out laughing then said, "My name is Joan Dallas. I'm twenty-nine. I was born and raised in Houston and this is not my first time in this club. I manage the affairs of several doctors at three offices around the city. I never have been married. I'm not on the down low now, neither have I been in the past. I have one son; he's six. I have no pets."

They laughed together.

"I admire your creativity, Samuel." Joan blushed.

"I admire that smile of yours," Samuel said. Joan's scripture cards popped in her head, but she got distracted when Samuel continued speaking. "I had to come dance with you. You were having so much fun that I wanted to join you. I was sitting here by myself and I thought 'hey, why I should sit over here bored when I could be over there with her having fun?'"

Samuel looked around for a waitress. He found one and waved for her to come to their table.

Samuel turned to Joan and asked, "What will we be drinking tonight?"

"Sauvignon blanc?" Joan responded, trying to find out if Samuel knew anything about wine.

"Why Sauvignon blanc?" Samuel asked.

"Because, Samuel, you strike me as a man that would appreciate sipping a nice glass of summer white wine."

The waitress arrived at their table with her notepad.

Samuel stopped to think for a moment, then making sure Joan could hear him, he said, "We'll have the Chilean savignon blanc, Veramonte, Casablanca Valley. Because of the ripe grapefruit flavors, fresh-cut herbs, and the hint of citrus."

"My favorite part is the finish; it's both subtle and seductive." Joan smiled as the waitress walked off to get their bottle of wine.

"Sort of like you," Samuel responded. Joan pretended not to know what he was referring to.

"The wine is sort of like you." Samuel licked his lips, "Subtle and oh so—seductive."

Chapter 17

Terror gripped Joan's body when she realized the ceiling she had woken up to was not her own. She bolted up violently. In a state of panic, she looked left and then right, her eyes getting bigger and bigger as she inspected the silver canopy bed, the walls with no windows, the white leather sofa in the corner, and the big flat screen TV at the foot of the bed. She removed the soft red fabric from over her and looked down at her naked body as if she had never seen it before. Joan wanted to call out to him, the man she last remembered being with at the club, but she couldn't remember his name or if she ever had known his name. Her last memory of the night before was sitting at the table with him drinking wine.

Joan didn't bother to try to cover her body. She jumped out of the bed and flipped the sheets back and forth. Eventually she ripped them off the bed completely in a frantic search for a condom wrapper or box. A small trash can near the nightstand turned up nothing but an empty microwave popcorn bag. She walked out of that room and into the hallway. There were two doors and a staircase.

She knocked on the door closest to her. "Is anybody here?" she said in a voice laced with fear. Nobody responded.

She slowly opened the door. The room was eerily empty with sterile white paint on the walls.

She knocked on the other door. There was still no response. When she tried to open the door, she heard footsteps then a click like somebody was on the other side and they had just locked the door.

She took off down the staircase hoping there was a way she could get out of the house.

The first thing she saw was the front door. It was steel and didn't have a door knob. Repeatedly, she banged on it, trying to open it in vain.

She looked across the room to the back door. It appeared to be over ten feet tall and had an electronic keypad. She quickly punched in various numbers, but nothing changed. The door would not open.

She looked back at the staircase. Whoever was in the room was staying put for now.

She searched for some sort of window or opening, but didn't find one. The kitchen did not look lived in and was empty except for a stainless steel refrigerator and stove. The living room was clean and orderly but held no artwork or pictures on the walls. She looked for a phone but there wasn't one.

Exhausted, Joan grabbed her hair and fell to her knees in uncontrolled sobbing. There was no way out. Over and over she cried, "Oh my God, what have I done?"

She tried to imagine what it would be like for her mother and son when the police went to tell them they had found her cut up in pieces in a stranger's home. She thought of the people who would be at her funeral. She thought of her brother and each of her friends. She wondered if her father would come to her funeral and felt pleasure thinking he might blame himself for her death.

She thought of how she would miss all the important moments in her son's life, how she never learned to ski, and how she always wanted to take a trip to Africa. She imagined herself at the wedding she would never have and saw herself behind a counter at her own bakery. She thought of how she had never told Aunt Alice how much she loved her and how much she enjoyed those summer trips working in the bakery.

Frustrated, tired, and sweaty, Joan collapsed on the floor.

"What have I done? What have I done?" Joan cried out while beating her head harder and harder on the floor, trying to recall what had happened the night before.

"What if he gave me a disease? God, please tell me he didn't give me anything. Or what if I'm pregnant by a man I don't even know?"

Quietly, Samuel walked down the stairs. Seeing her naked body on the floor, he said nothing. Joan, sensing his presence, jumped up in fear.

"Please, don't kill me! Please don't kill me!" she pleaded. "Please, I'll give you anything, just don't kill me!"

Samuel kept moving forward, his face remaining expressionless.

Joan started to shake and gasp for air. As Samuel reached the bottom step he disappeared. Before she had a chance to react, Joan heard a voice and then a figure appeared before her.

"Good morning, Joan."

Ecstatic to see the woman again, Joan ran to her with open arms. "I'm sorry. I'm sorry. I'm so ashamed at what I have done. Please, can I have another chance?" Joan begged.

The woman gently took Joan's hands in hers and asked, "Do you even know what happened last night?"

Joan looked down at her naked body. "No, but . . ."

"Samuel was a decoy sent to teach you a lesson," the woman said. Joan looked at her with questioning eyes. "We know the type of men you're drawn to, so we created a man to those specifications to show you just how easy it is to get yourself in trouble. After a night of dancing and drinking with the tall, handsome gentleman, you eagerly went home with him, but he did not touch you," she informed Joan. Joan looked down at her naked body again. "We took off your clothes for effect."

Joan wanted to be mad, but she was too relieved after finding out she was not about to die at the hands of a crazed serial killer, be infected with a sexually transmitted disease, or end up pregnant. Joan put her head in her hands, shame written across her face.

"So now what?" Joan looked up and asked.

"I think you know the answer to that question, Joan."

Joan blinked her eyes and the woman disappeared. Looking around, she found herself standing in her living room, just as she had been standing in Samuel's a moment before. It was seven in the morning; time to start getting ready for work.

Chapter 18

Joan starred blankly at her computer screen. She had been working on the same memo for the last two hours. She could not stop thinking about what happened with Samuel. What if she would have actually had sex with him and had to start the experiment over? She understood maybe having to start over if she had a boyfriend like Tisha and Lila, but the thought of having to start over because she couldn't resist a man who was a stranger had been giving her chills all morning.

"Joan, Tisha's on line two," Miriam's voice interrupted Joan's daydreaming.

Joan had expected Tisha's call. She always called the morning after they had spent the evening at a club. The two of them would recap who came with whom, who left the club with whom, and their favorite subject—who was wearing what.

Joan knew that she did not need to wait to tell Tisha and Lila that she could no longer hang out with them so she picked up the phone and said "This is Joan Dallas."

"Hello, Joan," Tisha and Lila said in unison.

Lila chuckled. "Did you enjoy yourself last night?"

Joan ignored the question.

"What? He left you speechless? We looked around when it was time to go only to find out you had already left," Tisha said. "I don't blame you, girl, he was fine."

"You got that right," Lila agreed.

Joan looked at the clock on her desk. It was ten o'clock in the morning. Tisha should have been at work.

"You took off today, Tisha?" Joan asked.

"After me and Lila left the club we went to the Pancake Shack. By the time we left there it was four in the morning. Lila spent the night over here. We just woke up. I'm working the evening shift today, which is good because there's hardly any traffic coming through the dealership in the morning and afternoon anyway."

Since Tisha and Lila were in the same place Joan felt it was a sign she needed to talk to them today. "How long are y'all going to be at your house?" Joan asked.

"For a while," Tisha said.

"I'm coming over," Joan said.

"Now?" Tisha and Lila answered.

"Yes, now." Joan hung up the phone without explaining why she urgently needed to speak to them. She was afraid if she gave much thought to what she needed to say, she would end up not going to speak with them.

Joan cleared her schedule for a few hours and drove to Tisha's apartment.

"Hey, Joan," Lila said after answering the door and taking one of Joan's hands and practically pulling her inside. "Hurry up, we're watching *The Test* and the commercial break is almost over."

"What test?" Joan looked around confused.

Lila stopped dragging Joan and put her hands on her hips. "You never heard of *The Test*? Everybody's been talking about it every since it debuted a few weeks ago."

Joan recalled a conversation she overheard in the elevator last week. "Is that the show that somebody named Taylor is hosting and women go on it to find out who fathered their children?"

"Yeah." Lila got excited and continued pulling Joan until they made it to Tisha's bedroom. Tisha was sitting at the edge of the bed in front of the TV in her pajamas holding her cordless phone in one hand and her cell phone in the other.

Tisha looked up and saw Joan. "I know, I know, I should be ashamed of myself for watching this mess, but sit down and listen to this. This nasty heifer was with two brothers within the same week and—"

Lila cut Tisha off. "Shh—it's back on." Lila sat on the edge of the bed next to Tisha. Joan sat behind them on a chair Tisha had next to the bed.

The host looked into the camera with anguish on her face. "Nineteen-year-old Rhonda has come here to find out who fathered her eleven-month-old daughter, Kayla." The screen changed to an adorable little black girl with two pigtails and a white floral dress. She was smiling directly at the camera as if she knew she was on TV. The audience cooed in unison.

The screen then spilt in three parts. Kayla was in the middle with two men on either side of her. The host turned towards the audience and yelled, "Who's the baby's daddy? Calvin PD number one or his brother, Rico PD number two. "The two hundred people in the audience boisterously yelled out votes as they held up cards with either the number one or the number two written on them.

"What does *PD* mean?" Joan asked.

"Potential daddy," Lila answered without looking away from the screen.

The audience had calmed down and put their cards away. The host walked over to a man in the audience. "What do you think, sir? Is it Calvin PD number one or his brother Rico PD number two?"

The man stood up and spoke with perfect diction. "Well, it was a hard decision, because Kayla seems to have Calvin's nose and mouth, but it appears to me she has Rico's eyes and skin tone. In the past I've noticed that skin tone and eye shape say a great deal, so I'm going to have to go with Rico PD number two."

A woman behind him stood up abruptly waving her hands to get the host's attention. The host rushed to get the microphone to her. The woman took the microphone from the host and shouted, "That baby don't look nothing like Rico. That's Calvin's baby. They favor. They smile the same and everything."

The host took her microphone back and turned to the camera. "The audience seems stumped today. How about you? The phone lines are now open. You could win one thousand dollars. Stay tuned we will hear from the PD's after the break."

"One thousand dollars for what?" Joan asked.

Lila looked up to answer her. "Everybody who calls the show with the correct PD gets placed in a drawing. After every show, a computer randomly selects fifty people who each win one thousand dollars. It's free to call, but you have to get through before they announce the results of the paternity test."

Tisha had both her cell phone and her home phone to her ears. "Last night I ran into Gwen in the restroom, a lady I used to work with. She actually showed me a copy of the check. She said the day after she won a man called asking for her mailing information. He had it overnighted to her and the next day she was cashing the check." Tisha slammed the phones on the bed. "Shoot, I cannot get through."

"Let me try." Lila picked up her cell phone from out of her purse.

Tisha turned toward Joan. "What brings you by this morning? Did you have so much fun last night you couldn't stand the thought of being locked up in an office all day?"

Joan squirmed around in her chair suddenly remembering why she had been so determined to drop everything to come to talk to Tisha and Lila.

Lila started screaming, "I got through! I got through."

Tisha turned around. "Don't play games with me, are you for real?"

"Yes, but who do I want to vote for, one or two." Tisha looked at Joan then back at Lila. "Hurry up! My time is running out."

Tisha paced the floor for a few seconds then blurted out, "Two, vote for two. That baby looks like Rico."

Lila pressed number two then hung up the phone after keying in her callback number. "They said they would call me back if I get selected."

Tisha and Lila hugged and then turned back towards the TV just as the commercial break was over.

"Welcome back, everybody," the host said. "Our producers asked each of the PD's if they thought they were Kayla's father before the show. This is what Calvin had to say."

The screen switched to a prerecorded tape of Calvin. "Heck no, I ain't that baby's daddy. Yeah, I hit that a few times, but Rhonda is a slut. She's always been a slut and she will always be a slut."

The picture changed and revealed a cheering audience and Rhonda who was onstage with her arms folded looking down.

The host said, "We heard from Calvin; now let's hear from his brother, Rico, and Rico's fiancée Tiffany."

Rico said, "What kind of chick messes around with a dude and his brother? What kind of chick walks around the neighborhood with short skirts and no panties? It's sad to say, but Rhonda is like the city bus; everybody has ridden it at least once. Yes, I did take a few trips on the Rhonda express, but the last time was over three years ago."

Tiffany hugged and kissed Rico. Then she looked into the camera. "Rhonda, you know you need to quit. Rico is not the father of Kayla. We used to be girls, remember? I know how you bounce around from stick to stick."

The camera switched back to the host who was now seated next to Rhonda and said, "Do you want the baby to be Calvin's?"

"Calvin ain't all that. He already got four children with three baby mommas that he don't take care of now," Rhonda spat.

Tisha spoke to the screen, "Well why did you have sex with him then?"

Lila laughed. "I guess she thought her stuff was so good it was going to make him act right."

The host rubbed Rhonda's back motherly. "And what about Rico? Do you want him to be the father or do you think he will be too busy with Tiffany?"

Hearing Tiffany's name made Rhonda angry. "Rico claims he hasn't been with me in three years. Why don't you bring Tiffany out here so I can tell her what kind of lotion she has in her restroom and what kind of soda she got in her refrigerator and how good her green Egyptian cotton sheets feel next to my skin?"

The audience started jumping up and down and giving each other high fives. Then they started repeating, "Bring Tiffany out!" with their hands in fist like they were protesting a war.

The second Tiffany came from backstage, she and Rhonda started running towards each other. Right before they were about to meet, a group of security guards came and pulled them apart and directed them to their chairs on opposite sides of the stage.

As if nothing had just happened, the host said, "We have the results. Please send Calvin and Rico to the stage."

Calvin and Rico walked to the stage and then

slid their chairs away from Rhonda and close to Tiffany. Rhonda looked like she wanted to cry.

The host turned to Rico, who was now holding Tiffany's hand. "In my hand I have an envelope with the results of the paternity test. You said during your interview that you had not had sex with Rhonda in three years. Are you sure about that?"

Rico let go of Tiffany's hand and got a sad look in his eyes and said, "Baby sometimes when you go to work . . ." Before he could finish Tiffany ran off the stage crying.

The host watched her run off the stage. "I guess we have our answer."

The host opened the envelope, looked at the results, and looked back at the guests. Both of the men were anxiously stomping their feet. The audience was quiet. Rhonda had her eyes closed and her arms crossed.

The host spoke, "Calvin, you are not the father of Kayla."

Tisha and Lila gave each other a high five.

Calvin jumped out of his seat and ran into the audience shaking hands with the men on the first row. He turned around and pointed at Rhonda and shouted, "You lying slut."

Rico sat farther back in his seat trying to appear calm. The host said to Rico, "How are you feeling?"

"I'm chilling if it's mine it's mine," Rico replied.

"Rhonda, before the show you told our producers that you were absolutely certain that Kayla's father was either Calvin or Rico because you had not been with anyone else during the time you became pregnant with Kayla. Are you sure about that?

Rhonda was adamant as she looked at Rico. "I'm one-hundred percent sure. Get ready to pay child support, Rico."

Lila stood up and started dancing. "I'm about to get paid."

The host opened the envelope and pulled out Rico's test results. "Rico, you are not the father of Kayla."

Joan, Tisha, and Lila looked at each other then their mouths dropped opened. Then they turned back to the television. Rhonda was too embarrassed to face the cameras and ran offstage crying.

Rico fell to his knees relieved he was not Kayla's father.

Tisha turned off the television and looked at Joan. "We're sitting here watching this nonsense when we could be hearing all about what happened last night with you and ol' dude from the club."

Joan couldn't think about anything but Kayla. She said to Tisha, "What's going to happen to Kayla?"

"She'll probably be on *The Test* one day herself trying to find out who's her baby's daddy," Lila answered her. "Hopefully she'll have it narrowed down to two, unlike her mother. One time I saw a show and the girl had like eight dudes on there trying to find out who was her baby's daddy, and none of them tested positive."

Tisha blurted out. "Yuck! Moving right along, Joan, we're going to order a pizza before *My Teenager Daughter Tried to Kill Me* otherwise known as

The Mandy Carter Show comes on, do you want to split it with us? Then you can tell us all about last night."

"Yeah, Joan, are you going to need to know who your baby's daddy is?" Lila joked.

Joan could tell her friends were not in the frame of mind to hear her about her new lifestyle. "You know what? I gotta get back to work." Joan grabbed her purse and keys. "I'll talk to you ladies later."

Joan walked out the door feeling overwhelmed. She didn't know what emotion she was feeling the most. She was angry at the network for exploiting young women. She was shocked to know that so many women didn't know who had fathered their children that there could even be a daily talk show such as *The Test*. She hurt for Rhonda but at the same time she was angry with her. She wanted to be mad at Calvin and Rico, but it was clear they were just confused little boys in the bodies of grown men. She hurt the most for Kayla. *What would happen to Kayla?*

One thing was clear, Joan thought as she drove back to her office, *if Rhonda, Calvin, and Rico had lived under God's Word, they would have been completely different people. But how were they to know if nobody took the time to teach them?*

Chapter 19

Joan rolled over in bed. She had hoped she would have slept through the pool party so then she would have a legitimate excuse as to why she had missed the party when her friends called and asked what happened to her.

She had taken a nap right after she got home from church, and since this was the Sunday of her and her friends' annual pool party it was now time for her to get out of bed and get ready to go.

It had been three weeks and two days since the incident with Samuel, and Joan still had not told her friends that she couldn't hang out with them since they were continuing to live their lives outside of the will of God.

When Tisha or Lila called to make plans, Joan had been making excuses. She didn't even go to last month's book club meeting and she had never missed a meeting in the last five years since she and her friends established it. She had to work late or she didn't feel well were two of her favorite excuses. Joan decided that as soon as she arrived at the pool party she would have the talk she had been avoiding with her friends.

This evening was not just going to be difficult because she might lose her friendship with Tisha and Lila, but today she had to see James Sr. with his new fiancée, Raquel.

Joan got out of bed and walked into her bathroom. It was three o'clock. She had an hour and a half to prepare herself spiritually and physically for tonight.

Joan bent down over her garden-style tub and tested the water until she found the perfect combination of hot and cold water. She then opened and poured a few tablespoons of lavender bubble bath into the running water. After lighting five candles, she placed them around the tub.

She undressed and slowly lowered herself into the warm water now bursting with fragrant bubbles. This would be the first time she had arrived at the pool party alone. The delivery guy, Curtis Rodgers, she had asked to go with her the day she was taken to the auditorium had never called and another driver had taken over his route, so she had not ran into him at the office. Joan was glad Curtis never called, that way she didn't have to explain why she had to cancel.

She put her bath pillow underneath her head and closed her eyes. After the last pool party she and her date, Walter, had left early at his request. As they were driving home, Walter pulled into an hourly motel. Joan asked why he couldn't take her to his house. He said something about his brother spending the weekend with him. Joan thought he was lying but she had sex with him in the motel anyway. Three days later she saw him in a restaurant with a woman. She could tell then that the woman was his wife even though he had told her he wasn't married.

Walter randomly looked up from his food and saw Joan standing at the hostess stand. The fear on his face said it all.

Joan began to weep as she lay in her tub. That very same night she had seen Walter with his wife, he called her. Walter and Joan took a midnight drive to the beach in the same car he had used to drive his wife to dinner hours earlier. Joan had smelled her perfume lingering in the car as she and Walter had sex.

Joan cried happy and sad tears at the same time. The sad tears were for the woman she used to be; the woman who was so weak and broken that she thought it was okay to be the other woman. The happy tears were for the woman she was now; the woman who God took out of the darkness and brought into His light.

Joan got out of the bathtub and rubbed shea butter over her damp skin. She dried off her newly toned body. The aerobics classes had reshaped her muscles beautifully.

She pinned her hair up and made up her face. She put on big black hoop earrings and strappy high-heeled black sandals. Joan walked into her bedroom and then slid into her black bikini. She looked at herself in the full-length mirror.

Instantly she became convicted. She had no intentions of actually getting in the pool; she never did for the pool party. She mostly lounged around in an overpriced swimsuit admiring the lustful glances she received from the boyfriends and husbands of the ladies in her book club.

Joan took the bikini off. The next man to see that much of her body would have to go through God first. Yes, she was fierce. But it made no sense to advertise what was no longer on the market. She could sport her swimsuit another time when there were no impressionable minds around and she actually planned to swim. Joan put on a pair of shorts and a tank top, grabbed her sunglasses, keys, and purse, and walked out the door.

As soon as Joan pulled up to the recreation center where the pool party was being held, she saw James Sr. and Raquel get out of his shiny red pickup truck. Joan had hoped they would have brought James Jr. with them. Normally children were not allowed at their book club meetings, but the pool party was different. Members invited their friends and families and everyone spent the day eating barbecue, swimming, and playing games.

The fact that James and Raquel arrived on time and without James Jr. and his children from Raquel, Morris and Alexis, had Joan more convinced than ever that Raquel made her way to this meeting only to make sure Joan knew that she and James were officially engaged.

Joan hated seeing the two of them together. Raquel had on a long flowing red sundress with a matching hat. Joan had to admit the outfit was nice and flattering to Raquel's larger figure. James Sr. looked like he had been working out. Joan noticed his muscles appeared to be bigger. He had on a pair of khaki shorts and a blue short-sleeved shirt.

Joan was focused on telling her friends what she needed to say and was not about to let this sideshow get her off course. She decided the best thing to do was to meet it head-on.

She quickly parked her car so she could walk up to James Sr. and Raquel before they walked into the party.

She approached them from behind. "Hi James, hi Raquel."

They both stopped and turned around. "Hello, Joan," James said as he looked her up and down. Raquel starred back at her. "I was hoping y'all would have brought the kids with you."

Raquel said, "Their uncle from Louisiana is visiting us. . . ." She paused to get Joan's reaction. When Joan starred back with a blank expression on her face, Raquel continued. "The boys were playing a video game with him and didn't want to stop. Our daughter is spending the weekend with my sister."

Joan chuckled. "Oh I see. Jr.'s trying to beat Morris at that basketball game again."

James Sr. smiled. "Yes, they have been up for two days straight. I got to tell you, Joan, that son of ours is a fighter."

Raquel casually turned around and said, placing her diamond-laced finger on her face as she moved her head, "I wonder where Tamika is. She told us to meet her in the front."

"Oh, that's who invited you, Tamika? James told me one of your clients invited you to join us. I should have known it was Tamika; her hair is always so gorgeous. You should pass out some of your cards when you get inside," Joan said.

Joan could tell Raquel was annoyed. She grabbed

Raquel's finger and looked down at her engagement ring. "It's huge." Joan looked back up at James Sr. knowing full well he had not picked out the over-the-top diamond ring. He preferred simple jewelry.

"You did good, James."

"Oh I didn't pick it out. Raquel did," he said.

Raquel looked like she was going to slap him at any moment. "Regardless of who picked it out it's quite—memorable. Congratulations to you both." Joan looked around. "I got to go. I have some people I need to see. Then I'm leaving. I have a big bag of popcorn and a movie waiting for me. I hope you guys enjoy yourselves today." Joan walked off smiling.

James Sr. looked confused. Raquel looked angry. Joan felt like doing a cartwheel. She had not allowed Raquel and James Sr. to take her joy. Yes, she loved James, but she had to deal with the fact that his feelings were not the same about her. It was time for her to move on. Besides, he wasn't a man of God anyway, and if a man wasn't rolling with God then he couldn't roll with her.

Joan walked into the recreation center and immediately saw Tisha sitting down in the waiting area. She had on a yellow bikini with a short see-through Rodney Alana cover-up. Joan had seen that cover-up the last time she was in the mall. It was selling for four hundred and thirty-five dollars.

Joan could see other members of their book club and the people they had invited were in the back of the building and outside around the pool.

Joan took a deep breath. "Hey, why aren't you by the pool?" she asked Tisha.

Tisha looked up and smiled. "Hey, girl, I was

just trying to call your cell. This year's pool party is so weak. I did not get this cute for this. It's more Bebe's kids back there than there are men. They're everywhere! Picking all over the food. I was about to get me a chop beef sandwich when some kid sneezed all over the meat. I don't know who invited all these people this year, but they were dead wrong. I already talked to Lila. I'm searching the net trying to find out what's poppin' tonight." Joan was about to speak. Tisha interrupted her, "Wait I'm a getting message." Tisha starred at her BlackBerry screen. "They're having a Sunday night patio party at the Symposium. Ladies get in free all night and they're having drink specials too." Tisha started dancing in her seat. "I was afraid I was going to waste my new outfit."

Joan could not believe Tisha was thinking of wearing a bikini and a cover-up to a club. Joan asked, "Where's Marcus?"

Tisha, still staring at her BlackBerry screen replied, "Playing basketball, they're having some tournament he couldn't get out of." Joan had hoped she would say something about not talking to Marcus anymore.

"Hey," Lila said loudly as she walked into the recreation center. Joan and Tisha turned around. Lila was wearing what Tisha wished she could afford: Rodney Alana from head to toe. She had on a hand-painted mesh top, hat, full-length skirt, and sandals by the designer *Represent* magazine had announced as the world's next fashion design icon.

"You look amazing," Joan commented on Lila's stylish outfit.

"Just a little something I ordered from LA," Lila replied. Tisha mumbled something. Lila looked up at Tisha. "Did you have something to say, Tisha?"

Tisha said nothing. "That's what I thought," Lila snapped.

Tisha said meekly, "I just didn't know Rodney Alana made plus sizes."

"There's a lot you don't know, my dear," Lila said.

Joan felt like she had missed something.

"Tisha, did you tell Joan that we were thinking about ditching this party and going out tonight?" Lila asked her.

"Let's just go from here," Tisha said.

Lila looked Tisha up and down. "I suppose we need to stop back by your house since you left without your clothes."

Tisha stood up and faced Lila. "I'd rather be dressed like a whore than be one."

Joan walked in between them. "I know the experiment got us all tripping. Let's not start fighting each other. I came to tell you both I'm not going to club Symposium or any other clubs anymore."

"Why?" Tisha and Lila asked.

"Well, I'm a Christian now and being in that environment no longer matches with my beliefs; dancing next to men, listening to songs about sex, all while drinking, is a bad combination for me. I've had to reevaluate how I spend my time. I hope we can still talk and hang out. I just can't do the clubs and stuff. We can still have movie night and go shopping, you know, things like that."

Tisha yelled, "So what are we? A couple of heathens headed straight to hell?"

"No, Tisha, that's not what I'm saying," Joan moaned.

"Yeah, Tisha, calm down," Lila said. "God don't like ugly."

"But He likes hoochies? You may be Rodney Alana down, but that's only because you are using Steve's money," Tisha stated. "I should call him and tell him he should find him a cheaper whore."

"Like you? You know what I just noticed? Every time I wear something you can't afford, you start talking about Steve. Do you want my man, Tisha? That way you wouldn't have to settle for just half of the outfit."

Lila put her sunglasses on and then looked at Joan and Tisha. "You know, Joan, maybe you are right. Maybe we've been in each others' lives a season too long." Lila walked out the front door. Tisha walked out the back door. Joan took a deep breath. *It wasn't supposed to go like this.*

Chapter 20

Lila saw Steve sitting on the sofa reading a book as she opened the door and walked into the house. She had expected he would be sitting at the kitchen table with Jasmine. The two of them had planned to work on Jasmine's lines for the school play while Lila was at the pool party.

Lila had driven around for a while but when she couldn't figure out anywhere she could go where she would be comfortable going alone, she went home. She didn't know who she was angrier with: herself for allowing Tisha to get to her or Tisha for getting to her.

Lila put her purse and keys on the table in the foyer then plopped down next to Steve on the sofa.

"You won't believe what happened at the party." She bent down and took off her sandals.

Lila waited for Steve to look up at her. Instead, he continued to stare at the book.

"Babe, what are you reading?"

Steve did not respond to Lila.

Lila put her hand on Steve's thigh. "Babe, you think we could go by the video store? Maybe we could all watch a movie tonight. After everything that happened at the party I need a distraction." Steve moved her hand and placed it on the sofa.

"What's up? Did you have a bad day at the hospital?" Lila reclined on the sofa and put a pillow behind her back. "Tell me all about it."

Steve got up off the sofa and slammed the book on the coffee table. For the first time Lila could see the cover of the book he had been reading. It was plain, brown, thin, and leather just like her journal.

Lila sat up straight on the sofa. Steve's back was to her. He was wearing dark gray slacks that needed to be a size bigger, a wrinkled white business shirt, and worn black tennis shoes. Lila had tried to get him to dress more fashionably but he only did when she handpicked his clothes and she had grown bored of that soon after they started dating. So unless they were going out somewhere in public together, Steve dressed himself.

He walked over to a cordless phone that was on the bar in front of him. He dialed a number and waited then he said, "This is Steve. I called earlier. Send the cab now."

Lila could feel her stomach start to rumble as the liquids in her stomach began to circulate rapidly. Steve placed the phone back on the bar and slowly turned around. Now, Lila could see his eyes. If there was any question as to whether or not he had read her journal in its entirety it was now gone. She could tell he had been crying. Lila couldn't remember having ever seen him cry. She dropped her head down.

"You never loved me." Steve started to pace back and forth on the wooden floors; his shoes caused the floor to squeak. "My mother told me you were no good from the first day I brought you to meet her. I was such a fool. You played me for a fool," he yelled.

Lila's eyes filled with tears. She knew she should have never written the truth in that journal. Her grandmother had told her if she wanted to keep a secret she had to make sure there was no record of it. You couldn't write it down and you couldn't tell anybody.

"My sister called soon after you left today." Steve continued to pace the floor as he talked calmly. "She wanted that picture the whole family took over here at Christmas last year, said she wanted to have it printed on our T-shirts for the family reunion." Steve stopped pacing and looked at Lila. "If she hadn't of needed it right away it would have never occurred to me to look through your things. But she claimed she couldn't wait, she needed to have the picture or else the T-shirts wouldn't be ready in time. So I went into your closet and started looking through your things."

Lila had placed the journal at the very bottom of a big chest she kept in her closet. She placed boxes of shoes and old pictures she needed to place in photo albums on top of it. She felt safe keeping it there believing Steve would never have a reason to go through the chest and find it.

"I defended you to everybody. They told me you didn't love me, you just wanted me for my money." Steve dropped to his knees. Facing Lila he shouted, "how do you think it felt to read in your own handwriting, 'I knew from the day he asked me to marry him I didn't love him.' " Lila covered her face with her hands. Steve continued, " 'I hate having sex with him, but I've gotten it down to just three times a month, which is bearable and doesn't freak me out too much.' "

Lila did not know if she should be scared or not. She had never seen Steve this angry before. Steve got up off his knees and walked until he was right in front of Lila. He removed her hands from her face and said, "I guess I shouldn't feel too bad because you're a superb actress—or shall I say liar."

Steve tried to make contact with Lila but she avoided his eyes. She looked across the room; one of Jasmine's books was on the floor. Lila looked around. "Where's Jasmine?"

Steve said nothing. Lila was worried about Jasmine and looked into his eyes. Steve looked like he could suffocate her with his bare hands. "Take my ring off." Lila stood motionless. Steve grabbed Lila's finger and roughly maneuvered her engagement ring until it came off her finger.

He put the ring in his pocket. "Get out of my house." Lila couldn't believe what she was hearing. She couldn't get herself to get up. Steve took her hands and drug her into the foyer. "I said get out of my house!"

"Steve," Lila said in a whisper moving closer to him. "Baby, let's talk about this. Those are just words; you know me better than that."

Steve pushed her back slamming her into the wall. "Your daughter is at your mother's house. You know the trailer park you were so desperately trying to avoid. I dropped her off after I read your diary. I didn't want her to be here to see this."

"Steve, I know you are angry and you have a right to be so, but I need to pack our things" Lila pleaded.

"I'll have the stuff you brought with you sent over there. But everything I bought stays here. You're lucky I'm letting you leave with the clothes you have on now."

Lila rolled her eyes then grabbed her purse from off the table where she had placed it earlier.

Steve snatched it out of her hands, then he searched until he found her key chain. He took her car and house keys off of it before putting the key chain back in her purse. Steve gave the purse back to her and opened the door.

"Don't worry about using your debit or credit cards. I've canceled them all," Steve stated.

Lila looked into his eyes. She wanted to say something but she couldn't think of anything to say so she walked out the door he was holding for her. Lila could see the cabdriver he had called waiting in the driveway parked behind what used to be her Escalade. She turned around to take one last look at Steve. His eyes moved from her feet to her face. He shook his head from side to side. Then he slammed the door, locked it, and turned on the alarm.

Chapter 21

I had an amazing dream last night. I don't ever want to forget it. Joan wrote in her journal. *Tisha and I were riding along the freeway, simply talking and listening to the radio. I don't know where we were intending on going, but we seemed to be in no rush to get there. It was just the two of us laughing and joking, being the lifelong girlfriends we have been for years.*

Tisha was driving and I was in the passenger seat. As we were going along, she asked me something about what turn she should make next. I hesitated, leaving her to make the wrong turn. We didn't let it bother us, though. We just kept driving along, laughing and talking.

Then the freeway ended suddenly, and we were diving to the earth in slow motion. Looking down, it looked as if we had fallen from space. Everything was so small and so far away. I remember thinking we were going to die, yet I was completely without fear. I had this feeling of happiness I can't begin to describe. It was pure bliss. Bliss one cannot experience on earth.

The next moment, I was no longer in the car, but I was floating; no longer in my physical body. I was weightless. I was surrounded by colors so vibrant that they had personalities. I've never seen anything so intensely beautiful. I was relaxed and filled with a peace I didn't know existed. I looked around and noticed Tisha was still in her physical body falling downward. I yelled for her to hurry up and repent. I told her to accept Jesus as her Lord and Savior. She did as I said, and instantly, she too began to float. Two friends, Joan and Tisha, floating in heaven and looking around at the miraculous beauty of their new surroundings, as happy as can be.

Joan was getting in from her women's discipleship class at church when she reread the journal entry she had written that morning before leaving for work. She had thought about the dream the entire day, carrying the peaceful feeling throughout her hectic workday.

She checked the caller ID and the answering machine hoping one of her girlfriends had returned her phone calls, but there was nothing. Joan had tried to call her friends repeatedly but they had not returned her phone calls. Taking a seat on the sofa, Joan came to the conclusion that Tisha and Lila were deliberately avoiding her.

She replayed the conversation she had had with her friends over two weeks ago, telling them she wanted to continue their friendship but she could not go partying with them. The ordeal with Samuel after a night of clubbing with the girls still had her shaking in fear every time she thought of it.

Here it was, Thursday night, which meant Club Red's happy hour buffet. Joan hated the thought of Tisha or Lila sitting around in their designer clothes, drinking overpriced martinis, eating cocktail shrimp, and pretending to smoke flavored cigars while thinking about how crazy she was. Joan thought about calling Janet, just to talk to someone but decided not to, realizing she really did not want to hear about how great it was to be happily married and newly rich. Besides, Janet was probably on some exotic island with her new husband.

Joan was lonely inside. She felt alienated and hurt as tears fell from her face. On one hand, she felt proud of herself for starting a new beginning, and on the other hand, she felt sad her friendships were fading.

Joan was lying on the couch when the woman appeared in front of her in the same white, fine linen outfit she had been wearing the previous times she had seen her. Seeing the woman suddenly manifest on her couch did not startle Joan in the least. She was comforted by her presence. She placed Joan's head on her lap, caressing her hair gently as one would a small child.

"My dear Joan, you can't love the world and God too," the woman told her. "When the year ends, do you still want to be facing the same battles you were facing when the year started? Well, that's exactly the road Tisha and Lila are on. They have decided they don't want to try something different and would rather hold on to what is familiar than embrace something that is new."

"I know I'm on the right track," Joan replied. "I just have to adjust to the changes. I wish my friends would take the road I'm taking."

"So do we, Joan, but the best thing you can do for your friends is pray for them and continue to build your relationship with Jesus Christ. Some people are called to be leaders. They have to be the first person to step out on faith. You, Joan, are that person. As you develop yourself in Christ, you will be surprised at how many people will follow your lead. Don't concern yourself with your friends. Your friends are God's business and God always handles His business."

"I feel bad for them, though," Joan said. "They are out doing the same old things, which will only cause them grief and despair. I wish I could make them see, but I don't know what to say or how to say it. I'm really just getting serious about Jesus myself, and I really don't know how I'm supposed to minister to other people."

"That's what I'm telling you, Joan. Live your life, and if you must tell your friends something, tell them the truth of what you know."

"Like what?"

"What was your life like before you devoted it to Christ?"

"Really jacked up," Joan said with a chuckle.

"And what is it like now?"

"A whole lot less jacked up," Joan responded, chuckling even harder.

"So, in other words, you are not the woman you want to be, but you are not the woman you used to be."

"Exactly," Joan answered, more serious.

"That's all you need to tell them, Joan. You don't need to know every verse of scripture or walk around like you are holier than thou. Be yourself and tell it like it is. You will be surprised at how effective that is."

"Last week at church, my pastor was preaching

about how to share our faith. As I was trying to do just that the other day, I lost my train of thought. I was too embarrassed. Here I was about to minister to a sister who I knew needed it, and I choked. She, Melinda, is relatively new to our staff, and she's already gotten herself quite a reputation with the men in the building. I feel like God led her to me and I failed Him."

"Joan, I love your enthusiasm. Pray to God and ask him to give you another opportunity."

"I'll do that, but can I practice with you what I want to say to the girl and then you can tell me how I did?"

Joan lit up like a second grader whose mother just pinned her latest project on the refrigerator. The woman smiled, letting her know she was receptive to her idea.

"Okay, it went like this," Joan began. "I was walking to the restroom, but as soon as I reached the door, my assistant was walking down the hall after me. She said my boss was on the phone and needed to speak to me right away. So, I walked back and took the phone call." Joan looked at the woman, suddenly realizing she must have known the whole story like she knew everything else.

"Joan, go on. I want to hear the story from you," the woman instructed her.

Still eager to continue, Joan went on. "Well, by the time I got off the phone, I was jogging to the restroom. I violently swung the door open with Melinda behind me, and the impact hit her. I apologized the entire time we were walking to our stalls. As we were washing our hands, Melinda seemed to want to end the silence by asking me what I had done the night before. At first I thought it was a peculiar question since it was Tuesday. I mean, it's not like Monday is some big party night. Then it hit me. This was an opportunity to share with her how my life had changed."

"So, tell me what you wish you would have said when Melinda asked what you did the night before," the woman said.

"I wish I had told her that I went to a class at my church and learned about the wide, deep love Jesus has for me. Ever since I've learned that, I have been walking in a peace I never knew existed. I have accepted the fact that God loves me. I know it sounds cliché, but I began to walk in that love.

"I confessed Jesus Christ as my Lord and Savior. I believe in my heart He died on the cross just for me. I repented of my sins and I prayed for God to show me the plans he has for my life. Yes, I've had a casual relationship with Jesus most of my life, but now I am committed to fully giving my life to him. Now that I'm saved, when I leave this earth I'm going to spend eternity in Heaven where Jesus has prepared a place just for me.

"At first I had a hard time accepting Jesus died for *me*. I looked at my life and wondered why He would do that? I mean, I'm just not worthy. But we don't get to God by being worthy. The Bible says all men have sinned and fallen short of the glory of God. That means nobody is worthy. We can't be good enough for God. I can't pray enough or fast enough or give enough money away. God loves me just as I am, without conditions. I can't do anything to make him love me any more."

Joan looked pleased and comfortable with the response she had given, so the woman tested her.

"I think Melinda would have asked why God sent His son to die for your sins."

Joan smiled, remembering the scripture her pastor had told them to memorize in class. "Ephesians two: eight, nine says, 'For it is by grace you have been saved, through faith—and this not from yourselves, it is the gift of God—not by works, so that no one can boast.'

"And Jesus did not just die on that cross for me," Joan continued. "He died for you too. All you have to do is confess and believe in your heart that Jesus Christ died for your sins, and you too can be saved. I know it sounds too easy. But that's what I mean about the deep enduring love of Jesus.

"Then if she seemed really receptive, I would have led her in prayer right there in the restroom. If she was not as receptive, I would have simply tried to get her to come to church with me this Sunday."

"Joan, you did very well," the woman commended her. "However, I think you would have lost Melinda somewhere before you got a chance to express all of that. That's a little heavy for the restroom, don't you think?"

"Yeah, I kind of realized it as I was talking, but I had made such a big deal about it, I just kept rolling with it," Joan responded, laughing.

"You're going to be all right, Ms. Dallas."

"You think so?"

"Yes, I honestly do."

Chapter 22

Joan lay in her bed and began to write in her journal. *When the woman left me today, I was filled with the Spirit; excited about my future, and welcoming my new life. Three days later, I'm embarrassed to admit it, but I'm feeling more horny than Holy. Even on the days I manage to keep my thoughts pure, my nights are anything but that. All night long I had men in and out of my dreams. As soon as I woke up, I was repenting.*

I actually reached over this morning and thought someone was there. It's not like I long for the sex, but for the intimacy. Joan needs a hug.

I went to get the mail and found myself looking at the gardener who was trimming the bushes, the maintenance man who was cleaning the stairwell, and the UPS man who was walking out of my neighbor's condo as I was walking by. It didn't matter to me that he is probably twice my age. I'm longing for some kind of affection.

I tried burning off some of my sexual frustration by

exercising. I've tried power cycling, weight lifting, and tennis this week alone, and now my body is sore from the swimming class I took yesterday. From the way my body is feeling, swimming must be the best workout known to man.

I can hear my neighbor's children playing with their dog and smell the tamales the lady across the hall makes on the weekends when her relatives come to visit. I miss my son and my friends. It's hard being alone, especially on a beautiful Saturday like this. Sometimes I can't wait for Monday, just so I can get back to work and be around people.

I tried to watch TV, but it just made matters worse. Watching those half-dressed girls smiling on videos like whores, as if that's how their mothers raised them to be, makes me depressed. And the fact that before the experiment I didn't find anything wrong with it makes me even more depressed.

One of the videos starred a little boy who couldn't have been more than twelve years of age. There he was a puppet, made up with diamond chains and clothes three sizes too big with grown women gyrating next to him and singing lyrics that would've made me vomit if I had managed to stay out of bed long enough to eat anything.

I turned the channel to the news and a picture of an adorable four-year-old appeared. The reporter said his mother had sold him to her crack dealer, who in turn raped him repeatedly before murdering him. I can't get those eyes out of my head. What was the little boy thinking? Was he too young to know? Next, they reported on the violence in Israel. A masked gunman had opened fire in some small town in Sweden killing seven preschoolers. Afterwards, I had to endure a grandmother crying her heart out on television because all *the money she had in her savings account was stolen by someone claiming to be able to help her invest it. And if that wasn't enough, a whole college girls' basketball team died when the bus driver fell asleep behind the wheel.*

I thought all this praying, journaling, exercising, and studying on God's Word was going to help. It does most days, and I know I'm growing in the right direction. Yet, sometimes I have days like today when I'm just a ball of frustration. I opened the Bible this morning and tried to study, but my spirit was restless. I just kept reading the same passages over and over, unable to digest anything.

I looked through a bunch of cookbooks in search of things I could make, such as caramel brownie cups or my famous cheesecake, banana cream pie, or double fudge brownies. But then I realized I didn't have anyone to eat it with me. Jr. is still with his father.

I called my mom to see if she and my grandmother could come over, but she said they were catching the bus to Louisiana to gamble. She said Travis had called and told her he would be working a double shift this weekend. She went on to say how Travis finds the time to call her everyday even though he's a nurse and works much longer hours than I do. Then, she started rambling on and on about how I never call her and when I do it's only because I want to do something right then and there.

She was telling the truth, though. Ever since the experiment started, I've been distant with my family. It's not like I even have words to explain everything I'm going through. However, that is not the only reason I don't call as much as before. Another reason is whenever we are on the phone she starts with her gossiping, which I am not interested in hearing.

Why couldn't I see Aunt Alice had it right and my mother and grandmother had it wrong? Last Sunday my pastor said there are people in our lives who help us to discover our divine purpose, and then there are also people in our lives who are poisonous to us finding our divine purpose. They have their own limited expectations of God, and if allowed to, will poison everybody around them.

God sent me to Aunt Alice for a reason. Each day since deciding to abandon my own dream of opening a bakery, I have been rowing a boat traveling against the current. I should have followed my heart and did what I felt was right. Why did I have to go get buried in someone else's dream when I could have been creating my own?

Okay, so maybe it would have failed . . . a lot of new businesses do. But at least I would have tried. Now what? It's not like I can leave this job or something. Could I? And do what then? Open my own bakery? People would think I was crazy. I would have to be crazy. I have a son to take care of, not to mention the mortgage on this condo. I can't just go and gamble our futures on a dream. My mother and grandmother would definitely be traumatized. I can see the looks on their faces now.

Oh how I wish I had the bold spirit of Aunt Alice. I'm ashamed to say I haven't spoken to her in years. I suppose she's still alive or else I would have heard, I guess. I wonder how she's doing and if she could help me.

Hey, this journaling thing is really not that bad after all. Because now I know how I should be spending this weekend.

Chapter 23

Joan felt a sense of peace as she cruised the highway singing loudly to the radio. The frustration and loneliness she was feeling earlier was gone. She had prayed the Twenty-third Psalm over and over until she felt the anxiety leave her body.

With every song, she thanked God for contemporary Christian radio stations. Ever since she started her walk with God, she had all but stopped listening to her extensive CD collection because most of them were filled with sinful lyrics. She was grateful for a station that provided beats she wanted to move her feet to and lyrics that reminded her of the goodness of the Lord.

The uplifting music made her feel like she could do anything. Even the bakery idea didn't seem so crazy all of a sudden. She reminded herself she was not a total novice on running a business. She had found and leased out office space, planned and implemented budgets, worked in accounting processing payroll, and dealt with any number of human resource issues.

Joan thought of all the times people had told her she made the best desserts they had ever tasted. The recipes for some of her original desserts started to come to mind even though she had not made them in years.

She knew the community college near her house had a food certification class. She made a mental note to call them first thing Monday morning. Then she remembered her high school friend whose family had run a successful Caribbean restaurant for years. She almost ran into the car in front of her when she allowed her mind to wonder about how to ask him for help.

The four-hour trip seemed much shorter as Joan saw the gigantic hill that signaled to her that Alice's house was near. Suddenly she got nervous realizing she had driven all this way, and within minutes she may be face-to-face with her aunt or find out that her aunt had moved away. But something told her Alice was still there.

Everything seemed to move so slow in the town back when Joan was younger. Everybody seemed so old and content. For entertainment in the evening, they would walk out to their porches, drink tea or lemonade, and talk. When Joan was a teenager, this ritual seemed boring to her, but now the simplicity of the people who lived in those well-kept old brick homes spaced too close together had her wondering if that was true or not.

The white house with black shading looked as if it had recently been given a fresh coat of paint.

The dandelions were blooming neatly in one row as they always had. The yardman must have just left, because as Joan stepped out the car, she could smell the green in the grass. The garage was open and inside was Aunt Alice's old beaten-up Chevy. She smiled as she remembered her petite aunt driving the full-sized truck.

It was four in the afternoon and still hot. Joan was thankful none of Aunt Alice's old lady friends were sitting on their porches inspecting her every move as she gathered her strength and walked to the door. As soon as she held her hand up to knock on the door, it opened. Joan stumbled for something to say, but instead found herself, with a perplexed look on her face, starring at her Aunt Alice.

Alice's face held not a hint of surprise as she opened the screen door, grabbed Joan's hands, and led her inside. She looked younger than Joan had expected. Alice's soft, warm hand and the melodic spiritual music quietly coming from the back of the house relaxed Joan. Alice led her to an olive-colored sofa that felt like a bundle of feathers. She didn't realize how hot she had been outside until she felt the cold air blaring in her face from Aunt Alice's wall unit.

Once Joan appeared settled, Alice walked out of the living room saying nothing. Joan looked around the room and remembered those mornings of drinking peppermint tea and reading the Bible well before the sun came up. She wanted to cry. She didn't know why, but she could feel the tears welling up in her eyes. The joy she felt those mornings was coming back to her. The energy of

Aunt Alice's house was running through her, making her feel as if she was welcomed and loved.

Alice returned with lemonade Joan could taste before it was handed to her. Then, Alice sat directly across from Joan, still not uttering a word. Joan looked down and suddenly felt the need to explain her visit. She still didn't know where to start, what to say, and what not to say. However, once she looked into Alice's eyes and saw the compassion and concern they displayed, she was instantly calmed.

Mimicking Aunt Alice, Joan got comfortable, laid her head back, sipped her lemonade, enjoyed the cool air, and listened as the woman on the record told the story of how the Lord would make a way somehow.

When you call Him, He'll hear you
He will send you His peace
You'll wonder what's going on, but no
*   need*
Your father in Heaven will make a way every
*   time, every time*
The Lord meets you at your need. He'll never
*   leave you nor forsake you*
Because He loves you, really loves you
*   deeply*

The lyrics were sung with such fervor that Joan knew it wasn't just a song, but a testimony. The lady who was singing knew the Lord she was talking about intimately. Joan took a deep breath to ward off the tears, but was unsuccessful in doing so. Soon, they covered her face.

She waited for the words to come out naturally. Too embarrassed to look directly into her Aunt Alice's eyes, she stared at one of her prized hand-made quilts hanging on the wall behind her.

"I love you, Aunt Alice, and I loved the time I spent here with you. I can't apologize enough for allowing myself not to call you or come see you." Joan pulled a tissue from the box seated on the lamp stand and wiped her face while her Aunt Alice sat motionless. "Aunt Alice, do you remember when I graduated from college and you sent me a card that said, 'Jesus loves you, and my prayer is that you love him too?'"

Alice nodded in acknowledgement. Joan hoped she would say something, but instead, she just stared as if urging her to go on.

"I've been thinking about you a lot," Joan went on. "How do you do it? How do you manage to live in this world and not be of this world? You make it seem so easy. Sometimes I feel like I'm at war with my own body. I have a dream I would like to pursue, but I'm too scared to even try to make it a reality. My son is spending a lot of time with his father and his father's fiancée and I don't know how I should feel about that. Since I've became a Christian, I've all but lost my friends. It's just too much floating around in my head. How do I make sense of it all?"

Alice responded slowly in almost a whisper. "Matthew sixteen:twenty-six, 'What good will it be for a man if he gains the whole world, yet forfeits his soul.'" Joan repeated the Bible verse silently, wanting desperately to posses the same peace her aunt possessed and feeling that it was within her reach.

"I seek His approval and His only," Alice said.

"But how when everything seems to be working against you?" Joan shook her head back and forth, frustrated she could not grasp what her aunt was saying.

Aunt Alice got up, walked to the mantle, grabbed a picture of herself as a young woman, and handed it to Joan.

"I was only a few years younger than you when this photo was taken," Alice said.

Joan stared back at the young stoic woman. Upon careful inspection, she noticed how unhappy she looked. Then, she turned to her Aunt Alice, who had now turned away from her.

Alice turned back only long enough to grab a tissue from the box Joan was using, and then turned away again. Alice covered her face in an attempt to hide her tears. Joan got up quickly to comfort her. Joan had not meant to upset her aunt.

"What's wrong, Auntie?" Joan asked.

Alice pushed her old but strong arms back forcefully, causing Joan to fall back in her seat. Alice turned and saw the shocked look on Joan's face.

"I'm sorry, baby," Alice said, crying harder. "There's something I have to tell you."

"You don't have to, Auntie, not if it's causing you this kind of grief," Joan responded in a panic-stricken tone.

"Yes . . . yes, I do."

Joan had never imagined her aunt could be vulnerable like she was witnessing right before her eyes, and it had her nervous. Alice grabbed her picture from Joan and walked around the living room a few steps before stopping, staring at it, and quietly weeping.

Through the tears, she spoke. "You know, Joan, over the years I've gotten really good at making people think I am superior. I know I walk around like God has a special diamond engraved crown with my name on it."

Joan said nothing, but mentally agreed with what Alice had said so far.

Alice paced back and forth across the floor, still staring at the old picture and holding it tightly in her hands. "Looking at this picture reminds me of the woman I used to be. The two of us thought we were happy. We moved out to Memphis when we got tired of hiding around here."

By now, Joan displayed a look of surprise. She always heard Aunt Alice had never been in a relationship. Her mother used to make jokes about her being too holy for sex.

"We had it all worked out," Alice continued. "We could be together and no one would suspect anything. We both had good jobs and our own apartments. We didn't have to answer to anyone, or so we thought.

"At church functions, we were constantly trying not to smile at one another too much or sit too close together for fear someone may suspect what was going on between the two of us.

"We both knew it was wrong. I was doing things I never thought possible. I tried plenty of times to stop our relationship. It got to where I felt so guilty, but time after time, we found ourselves together again."

As Joan felt her heart pounding through her chest, she tried to remain motionless, but the anxiety in her body would not allow her to remain still. She shifted from side to side in her seat as Aunt Alice continued speaking.

"We volunteered to cook for a church conference in Atlanta where our pastor was the keynote speaker. The two of us were staying in a private residence. The people who were hosting the conference found families to open up their homes for the week. Realizing we were alone for the first time in days, we were burning with desire. We acted out on our lust right there in somebody else's living room.

"When the man of the house walked in and saw two ladies engaged in such an act, he assumed we were prostitutes who had been sent as some sort of sick, thank-you gift. In our shame, we did nothing to convince him otherwise. Neither of us had been with a man until that night."

Joan could not believe what she was hearing. She tried to conceal her shock.

"When it was over, I knew I had two choices. I could continue in my sin or I could do what the Word says. Choosing the latter, I came back to Texas and went into a period of fasting and praying. During that time I surrendered my life to the Lord.

"Before, I was just playing church; I was busy singing in the choir, teaching Sunday school, and hosting charity functions. But God was not real to me. I could talk about Him at length, teach about Him, but I didn't know Him.

"God revealed his long, deep, wide love to me.

It wasn't until I had gotten myself in water so deep, to the point where I was drowning in my own sins, that I knew who Jesus really was. His blood buried my sin into the sea of forgetfulness. His blood washes me and makes my slate white as snow. I just have to cry when I think about the goodness of the Lord. He did it because He loved me. We don't even have a word in existence to explain that kind of love."

Alice stopped pacing and sat down next to Joan.

"No one ever found out," Alice sniffed. "She moved to California and I haven't heard from her since." Alice paused a moment before asking, "Do you trust God, Joan?" Joan remained quiet, not wanting to answer the question. "It did not happen for me overnight. Sometimes, I think we have to try it our own way first, often times failing over and over again before realizing we don't know what we're doing and neither does anybody else. Only the Lord knows the plans He has for you, Joan. Yeah, we all do what we feel is right for us, but we will never have peace until we find peace in Jesus. He put it in my heart to turn that old shack into a bakery. People thought I was crazy. A young, single black woman just didn't do things like that. But He gave me the strength and wisdom to make it a success. I give him all the glory. He gave me a beautiful home and friends to share it with." Aunt Alice paused to glance at the clock that hung on the wall above the doorway to the kitchen. "Oh, look at the time, baby. Do you want something to eat?"

Joan nodded.

Alice walked to the kitchen as Joan followed closely behind her.

Not wanting to lose sight of her visit, Joan asked, "Do you ever miss your sister and my mother? I miss my best friend Tisha so much it hurts."

Alice pulled a bowl with a marinated steak out of the refrigerator. She put it on a cutting board. "This is a big steak. It will be more than enough for the both of us." Alice began to season the steak with salt and pepper.

"After we had that big argument about that thing with your father," Alice continued answering Joan's question, "I was too angry with them, and they felt the same way about me. It just seemed to make sense at the time for us to keep our distance from one another."

Joan wore a puzzled look on her face. She had no idea her father had anything to do with her mother and grandmother's separation from Aunt Alice. She had always assumed they didn't speak much because Aunt Alice was an outspoken godly woman and didn't want to be around worldly women.

"What big argument?" Joan casually asked, taking a seat at the table behind her Aunt Alice, who was now standing at the counter peeling potatoes.

"Joan, I know it was long ago, but you must remember all the commotion after the father-daughter dance. Your mother can be a tyrant. It wasn't enough she lied to him and told him you had the flu so you couldn't go to Disneyland, but afterward she told him to stop calling you period. That's when he called me. She was lying because of that man, Harrington, yeah—Montgomery Harrington. She thought he was getting ready to ask her to marry him and didn't want your father around. That's why she made up all of that nonsense; she was sure he was about to propose and she didn't want your father coming down spoiling the plan."

Joan was speechless.

Alice continued. "After the father-daughter dance, when she asked your dad to cut his planned two-week visit short, I expressed to her how wrong she was for trying to keep your father away from you. She said what she did with her children was none of my business, and that was the last real conversation we have had since. When your mother and grandmother came to drop you off during the summer, they barely said anything to me, and unfortunately, my pride caused me to do the same thing to them."

She put the potato skins in the garbage disposal, and then removed some fresh green beans from a brown paper bag and started to wash them.

"I suppose he decided it was just easier to part ways with you until you got to be eighteen. Larry always said he hoped you would go to college in New Mexico so then you two could start rebuilding your relationship. You want some more lemonade?"

Joan was glad she was not facing in the direction of her aunt. She didn't want her to see the pain on her face. She was learning more about her mother and father in one evening than she had in her entire life.

"Yes, please. Excuse me while I go to the bathroom. I'll be right back," Joan answered in a voice that came out stronger than she had expected.

Joan fell to the floor as soon as she locked the bathroom door behind her. Grabbing a towel off the rack, she held it up to her mouth and screamed into it, feeling the chicken sandwich she had on the way to Marshall rumbling in her stomach. She crawled over to the toilet and released it.

Influenced by the fact she had to get out of the restroom before Aunt Alice started to worry, she got up and looked at herself in the mirror.

"Hey, girl, we can't do this right now, so we're going out there and we're going to act like this never happened," Joan told her reflection. She wiped all traces of tears from her face before returning to the kitchen with a smile.

Upon returning, Joan looked out the kitchen window to see Alice placing the steak on the grill in the backyard. When Alice reentered, Joan was sitting at the table.

"Joan, I don't know all what your mother and grandmother told you," Alice started. Joan stared straight ahead, unable to make eye contact. "But there's one thing I know for sure; your mother and father love you very much. They made decisions that they thought made sense at the time. I thought it made sense to not communicate with my sister and niece. At the time, it made sense just to stay away from one another in order to keep the peace, but now that I'm closer to being with the Lord than I've ever been, I find myself praying things would be different. Most of my friends are gone to glory and things are a little lonely. I sold the bakery to a young couple a few years back. Ever since, I've been talking to God, asking him if he was through with me yet. Well, when I saw you at the door, I knew my prayers had been answered." Alice paused, hesitating for a few moments. "Your father still calls to check on me occasionally. I have his number. Why don't you call him?"

Chapter 24

Joan was oddly comfortable as she sat at the airport pickup area waiting for her father. She kept thinking there should have been a camera crew and a journalist whispering in the background, "Twenty-nine-year-old Joan Dallas is about to meet the father she has not seen since she was a child. What will her reaction be?"

After dinner with Aunt Alice, Joan had found the courage to pick up the phone and call him. She needed an answer to her questions. She needed to look at him face-to-face. What would she be like if she had grown up with her father in her life? Would she be the woman she was today? Did her mother actually tell her father to stay away from her so that she could keep a man? Was her mother capable of doing such a thing to her? If everything was true, why didn't her father fight for her? Wasn't she worth it?

During the two-hour drive to the airport and four-hour flight to New Mexico, Joan did not allow herself to think about these questions. But now that she was moments away from seeing him, she allowed the questions to ponder in her mind.

Both of the phone calls she made to her father were brief. Aunt Alice was watching her the entire time and Joan didn't want her to know the magnitude of the bomb she had dropped on her. When Joan's father answered the phone the first time, Joan simply told him who she was and that she would like to see him the next day if she could get a flight. He was extremely excited at the thought of meeting her. Joan ended the call and called the airport. She called him back and told him she would be on the Sunday afternoon flight and asked if he could meet her at the airport at three o'clock in the afternoon. Her flight was actually scheduled to land at two o'clock, but Joan told him three o'clock. She thought the extra hour might allow her time to get her emotions under control. Her father clearly seemed as if he wanted to say more. However, Joan cut the conversation short. She told him she looked forward to seeing him the following day.

Joan looked at her watch that read 2:23 P.M. She started get dizzy. She had not been able to eat anything that morning. A few moments later, Joan's stomach started to bubble with nervousness. When she got up to go get a drink to settle her stomach, Joan's path was blocked by the most handsome man she had ever seen. She knew who he was instantly. He said nothing; he simply opened his arms wide to hug her. Joan could see the tears in his eyes.

Her father held her close. Joan was so happy she felt like running around the airport when the hug was over. He released her and looked into her eyes. "Joan, you are beautiful. I'm so proud of the woman you have become. I love you and pray for you everyday." He then hugged Joan again and picked up her bags. Her father grabbed her hand and led her through the busy airport. She felt like a child again as he maneuvered through pedestrian traffic while looking periodically at her to make sure she was okay.

He was honestly the most handsome fifty-plus man she had ever seen. His dark skin, tall height, and fine clothes had more than a few women taking a second and third look. He seemed not to notice any of the attention he was receiving. His mission was to get Joan out of the airport and into his car, and he was as focused as a soldier on a military operation.

Joan didn't say anything. She couldn't speak. The feeling that circulated throughout her body was not completely foreign to her. She had felt it once before at the father-daughter dance. She was unable to identify with it back then, but now she knew what it was; it was happiness.

As soon as they were buckled up and in her father's car, he looked over to Joan and said, "How are Travis, James Jr., and your mother doing?"

Joan smiled and said, "They're fine." Joan knew this was the part where she was supposed to ask about his wife and children but she decided against it.

Joan knew his name was Larry, but she didn't feel comfortable calling him that. She felt just as uncomfortable calling him Daddy. So she decided not to call him anything as she asked, "Have you eaten?"

"Oh, so you do talk?" He smiled. "I love seafood; there's a really nice place up the road. Would you like to go?"

"Sounds perfect." Joan wanted to be witty and say something else, but she couldn't think of anything she wanted to say. She didn't want to ask about his family. She didn't want to ask about his job. She didn't want to ask why he had abandoned her. She just wanted to enjoy his company.

He reached over and grabbed her hand as he was driving. They remained hand in hand until they arrived at the restaurant, where they were seated in a nice little booth.

Joan looked at the menu then at her father, wondering why she was positively giddy. She had looked across a dinner table at many men, but not one of them had prepared her for the joy she was experiencing just by being in her father's presence.

"What do you recommend?" Joan asked.

He looked down at the menu and paused for a moment. "You look like a stuffed shrimp person."

"What kind of person are you?"

"I'm a seafood platter type of person."

Joan smiled and they soon ordered their food.

When the food arrived, Joan's father grabbed both her hands from across the table and blessed the food. "Father, thank you for answering my prayers and bringing my daughter back into my life. Father, I pray that she forgives me and realizes, despite my action, I never stopped loving her. Father, thank you for this food and for our time together. Amen."

"Amen," Joan said.

As they were eating their food, Joan's father said, "What do you want for dessert?"

"I don't know; something with chocolate sounds good."

A grin with a question mark crossed his lips. "But you haven't finished your dinner. How do you know you will want dessert?" her father asked.

"Oh, I always have room for dessert especially when I'm at a new restaurant." Joan grinned. "Sometimes I look at the dessert menu before I look at the main menu."

His grin now turned into a smile. "Me too. We just started talking and we already have something in common."

They ate their food mostly in silence but neither one of them minded.

When they left the restaurant Joan could tell the mood had changed. A sad look appeared in her father's eyes and he had stopped doing the little bit of talking he had been doing. Joan didn't bother to ask him where they were going once they were back in the car. She knew it would be a quiet place where they could talk.

Joan's spirit lifted a bit as they drove down a long circular street that led to a park. It was beautiful. There was a man-made lake with ducks quacking loudly, park benches, and swing sets. There were two other people who looked to be lovers taking an evening stroll.

Her father parked the car and walked to a park bench. Joan followed him. He stood next to the bench as Joan sat down.

He started walking back and forth on the grass before saying, "I can't believe some of the things I

did as a young man. I made mistakes, Joan, mistakes I will take to my grave. I am haunted by
what I did to you." Interested in knowing more,
Joan drew nearer.

"Every time I see my two other children together, I think about you and wonder where you
are and what you are doing."

Joan wanted to tell her father she was never
lost, but held her tongue.

"I cheated on my first wife with your mother. I
promised your mother I would leave my wife but
I never did. The job I had at the time caused me to
travel a lot. I met your mother while I was doing a
job in Houston. We begin a relationship and she
became pregnant. For the first three years after
you were born, I juggled my life between your
mother and my wife."

He stopped and started to cry. Joan looked
away.

"Then one day my wife killed herself while I
was spending time with your mother. My family,
as well as my wife's family, blamed me for her
death. Shortly after her death, I fell into a deep
depression and started using cocaine. Eventually,
I ended up in jail for stealing. I was in there for
three months."

He stopped crying. "It was the best thing that
ever happened to me. One day, a missionary visited the jail," Joan's father continued. "That same
day I accepted Jesus as my Lord and Savior. The
missionary encouraged me to spend time with
you, which led to the Disneyland trip idea when
you were eight years old. You remember that?"

Joan nodded.

"I called and spoke to your mother several

times regarding the trip, but as soon as she was sure I wanted to come to town only to see you, she started to cause trouble. Eventually, I gave up. I should not have done that."

He stopped pacing and looked at Joan. She avoided his eyes afraid she might begin to cry. "Years passed and my heart began to ache for you more and more. You were thirteen when I decided to fight for custody. I contacted Aunt Alice and she agreed to help. The father-daughter dance was an initiation of sorts. I wanted to see how well we would get along, and we got along beautifully. I was so excited."

Joan liked knowing her father had attempted to fight for her.

"By this time, I was married again and had bought a house. I was hoping to look like the ideal father. But my hopes were shattered when I went to visit a lawyer. He said trying to get full custody was far-fetched considering my criminal record and previous cocaine addiction. Therefore, I tried to negotiate with your mother for full custody. Knowing my past reputation of being unfaithful, my new wife started to get nervous about these conversations and feared that I may have been cheating on her with your mother. That's when the major battle with her ensued. Whenever I left the house, she accused me of cheating. Then she went on to say she wasn't sure she wanted to have a teenager living with us after all. With both women fighting the idea and the lawyers not giving me much hope, I relented."

Joan's father sat on the bench and started to cry deeply. "I'm so sorry for what I did to you."

Joan began to cry too. She used her hands to

cover her face. Her father understood how his absence had caused her great pain. After they had
both dried their eyes Joan looked at her father.
"Let's go to the movies." Joan had always dreamed
of going to the movies with her father.

They didn't talk as they drove to the nearest
theater. Joan was satisfied with her father's rea-
soning thus far and she didn't want to trigger him
into saying something that would change how
she was feeling by prying so she preserved the
moment in silence.

Joan forgot about all the drama as she shared a
box of extra large popcorn with her dad after arriving at the theater. She loved listening to him
laugh and talk to the movie screen. It was pure
fun just as she had always imagined it would be.

As they were walking out of the theater, her father's cell phone rang no sooner than he turned it
on. It was his wife. She had assembled their
daughters and was inviting Joan to join them for
dinner.

Joan did not want to have dinner with his wife
and their kids. For once, she had her father all to
herself and she didn't want to share him. But he
seemed overjoyed at the prospect of having his
three daughters together, so she pretended to be as
eager as he was.

While driving through the well-kept community, Joan's happiness started to turn to sadness.
She looked at the school she should have graduated from. She looked at the lovely house that
should have been hers as her father drove into his
driveway.

His wife greeted them outside. "Welcome to our

home. I'm Sarah." She smiled. Joan could tell she was pretending to be happy to see her. But it didn't matter because she could pretend too.

"Thank you, your home is lovely," Joan said politely as she was escorted to the door and into the house. Joan looked at her father. He looked like the happiest man alive. If only she knew what she should call him!

"Allow me to take you on a tour," Sarah said.

Joan smiled. "Thank you, that would be wonderful."

As Joan walked through the home, she kept thinking that she had been robbed. She saw pictures of his other children with him at the beach, park, and Little League games. She saw the bedroom that should have been hers. She saw the table she should have done her homework on. She saw the sofa she should have sat on while she watched TV.

After the tour their daughters walked in from the back door. Apparently, they had been picking flowers to give to their big sister.

As soon as they saw Joan sitting on the living room sofa, they each ran to her and hugged her and then gave her a handful of handpicked flowers. "It's so good to finally meet you," the fourteen-year-old, Reyna, said.

The fifteen-year-old, Paige, grabbed Joan's hair. "Your hair is so cute. Will you do mine like yours?"

Joan felt like she needed to throw up. Here she was sitting around with a perfect little family in their perfect little house yet she grew up in a home that was anything but perfect. She was glad

when his wife said dinner was ready. She was
starting to feel like she was on a set of a television
sitcom.

Joan waited while they all took their seats around
the table. She then sat down in the only empty
seat. She never remembered feeling so out of place.
He was just as much her father as he was Reyna
and Paige's but she would never know him like
they knew him. Joan had thought coming to his
house had been a bad idea. As she sat at the same
table where he had dinner every night with his
wife and children, she knew it was.

After everyone was seated around the table,
her father blessed the food and they started to
have dinner conversation. Joan couldn't remember a time when her mother and brother sat down
together at the table for dinner. They mostly ate in
front of the television.

Reyna asked her father if she could go on a date.
He refused, saying she was too young. When Joan
was around her age she was on her knees in front
of Jamal. Paige reminded them that she was giving a speech the next night at church and they
needed to get there early so they could sit on the
front row. They promised they would. Joan's
heart sank. She wasn't giving speeches at church
when she was teenager, she was in Todd's house
loosing her virginity.

After a while, the girls started to bombard Joan
with questions. "Where did you get your handbag? When is your birthday? Do you have pictures of our nephew?" They thought it was so
cool that they were somebody's aunt.

Joan answered their questions with enthusiasm. She was glad her true feelings didn't show on her face or in her voice. Her father seemed so pleased watching all of his daughters having a conversation. His wife said nothing.

After dinner and before dessert, Joan excused herself to the bathroom and called the airport on her cell phone. She had hoped to spend more time with her father. She had even thought of making arrangements with Dr. Wright so she could spend a few more days in New Mexico. But being with his family reminded her of everything she had missed out on and she had had about as much as she could take. She couldn't bother to hear Reyna or Paige say "Daddy," one more time. He was her daddy too, only he wasn't.

There was a flight leaving in two hours. After returning to the table she thanked Sarah for a fantastic dinner and told them she had to get back home. All of them except Sarah looked very disappointed.

Joan couldn't wait to get back in her father's car. It was such a pleasure to be with him. They both wiped tears from their eyes during the fifteen-minute ride to the airport. He held Joan's hand as they were driving. As he parked his car they both began to weep louder. Joan didn't know why he was crying but she was crying because he was much more than she thought he would be. As a little girl Joan had a lot of time to imagine what her father was like. But after meeting him as an adult he had exceeded all of her childhood expectations.

Hand in hand, they walked into the airport. Joan bought her ticket and went to sit with her father

in an empty corner. She kept taking deep breaths,
trying to prepare herself for what she knew she
needed to say.

They sat in silence, holding hands, for a long
time before Joan even parted her lips to speak.
But Joan realized time was running out. Looking
directly into her father's eyes, she said, "I can't
help but think how great it would have been to be
your daughter, but dinner at your house has
made me aware that I am not your daughter and I
never will be." Her father looked confused as
Joan continued, "When I was eighteen and you
contacted me, I couldn't find it in my heart to forgive you. However, now that I've done a little bit
of living I can forgive you. I have made more than
a few mistakes myself and I know personally
how good intentions can turn bad. I thank you for
praying for me. I thank you for meeting with
me."

Joan kissed him on his cheek, picked up her
bags and walked away. She resisted the urge to
turn back.

The pain I had been carrying around is subsiding,"
Joan wrote in her journal on the plane. *It's not
gone yet, but I'm healing. Yes, Jesus is healing me.
He's making me over. It wasn't long ago that I spent
my weekends partying with my friends and drugging
my pain so I wouldn't have to deal with it.*

*The whole time Jesus was knocking on the door try-
ing to tell me He had all the answers; I wanted to look
to people who didn't know any more than I did. It's
only been a short while ago since I've opened my door*

for Him to come into my life, and look at what He's already done!

I didn't think I could live without sex, but I am and have never felt more alive. I didn't think I would ever forgive my father or lay eyes on him again, yet in one weekend I have done both. I thought Aunt Alice was different and possessed something the rest of us never would. Now I know following behind Jesus is what makes her different, and left to her own diplomacy, she is just as flawed as I am. I know I should be angry at my mother, but I'm not. This is another reason why I know the Holy Spirit lives inside of me. Things I used to do, I don't have a desire to do anymore. The places I used to frequent, I cannot go to anymore. The words I used to say, I don't feel comfortable in saying anymore. The clothes I used to love wearing, I don't see myself wearing anymore.

Hallelujah! I'm already new and improved.

Chapter 25

Smiling, Joan looked at her completed schedule. She had hired two new people, had three meetings, and decided which software to purchase for the new computers. She felt like a piece of Aunt Alice had rubbed off on her. Each morning since leaving Marshall, Joan had started waking up an hour earlier so she could pray, journal, and study the Word of God just like Aunt Alice did.

She could tell her efforts were making a difference in how she handled situations. For instance, yesterday when all three of the copy machines crashed and everyone started yelling at her at the same time because the repair man had failed to show up, she closed her door and prayed to God for help. When she emerged from her office, she began to look up equipment rental places in the Yellow Pages, maintaining her calmness the entire time. In no time at all, a company delivered three replacements and they were back in business.

Another sign she was gaining better control over her life was when James Jr. called the night before to tell her how much fun he had on his camping trip with his father. He rambled on about Raquel rescuing him when he managed to tip over his canoe, how pretty his baby sister, Alexis, was, and how he wanted to spend the school year with his dad. She prayed God would get her through the conversation with nothing but love emitting from her voice.

When she hung up from talking with James Jr., she expected the tears to fall and the anger to rise. However, to her surprise, what she felt was happiness. Her son was happy, therefore, *she* was happy over the fact *he* was happy. God is good!

As Joan sat at her desk preparing to leave for the day, she stopped for a moment, bowed her head and silently prayed to God.

Before leaving the office, Joan reminisced about her phone conversation with Alice last night. They talked about James Sr., James Jr., her father, her girlfriends, the bakery she wanted to open, and the tension she knew it would cause with her mother and grandmother.

Aunt Alice's responses were biblical ones. "All things work for good for those who love the Lord and are called according to His purposes. The devil meant it for evil, but God can turn it into good."

When Joan talked about having committed too much sin to ever truly be clean, Aunt Alice reminded her, "God forgave you, now it's time for you to forgive yourself."

Joan expressed to her aunt how sometimes she got down and didn't believe her messed-up life was ever going to make any sense, for which Alice told her to pray without ceasing.

"I bet Jonah felt his life was a mighty big mess," Alice had said, "considering he was in the belly of a big fish for three days for disobeying God. Still, he did all he knew how to do and all he needed to do. He prayed, and God commanded that fish to place him on dry land."

Joan also shared with Alice the dream she had about Tisha and how she felt like God wanted her to step in and lead Tisha to the Lord. Alice then shared with her the story about Queen Esther and how God used her to save the Jewish people from death.

"Nothing is impossible with God, Joan. Pray you will learn to trust Him. And Joan, be patient. You can't rush the process," Alice had said.

Joan felt closer to her aunt than she ever had her own mother. She had hoped to learn more about Aunt Alice's personal life, but Alice offered nothing beyond that first dramatic story. Joan wanted to know if Aunt Alice ever wanted to marry or have a relationship, but she dared not ask. She consoled her curiosity by telling herself everyone deserved their secrets.

Joan felt like singing out loud as she practically skipped to the cafeteria for dinner before heading to the salon.

She was on the fourth day of a ten-day Daniel's fast where she drank only water and ate only fresh fruits, vegetables, and whole grains. She went through the buffet line passing the red meats, fried chicken, and other high-in-fat dishes. She opted for fresh steamed green beans, baby carrots, and a spinach salad with a whole wheat roll. Before, she would not have had the discipline to stick with a fast. She smiled as she thought of how God gets the glory in even the small things.

Since it was almost closing time, the cafeteria was quieting down. Joan loved it at this time of day. She could go to a corner table, pull out whatever Bible verses she had been memorizing, and know she was going to leave there more blessed than when she had first come in.

As she was finishing her dinner, Joan looked up and noticed three women laughing and talking across the room. She felt a moment of sadness as she thought of her friends who she hadn't spoken to or seen in quite a while. Joan gathered her things and threw her trash away. She needed to start making her way to the parking garage or else she would be late for her hair appointment.

Joan had plans to meet Rick Patrick of the famous Caribbean eatery, Blue, in the morning for coffee and to discuss the restaurant business. She had met Rick in high school. They didn't hang around together, but they were at least social. Rick's restaurant had been a hit ever since it opened, and she was hoping he could give her some helpful advice on picking a location and finding funding for her bakery. She was nervous when she called him to ask if they could meet, but then she remembered God did not give her the spirit of fear. Rick did not seem overly enthused, but he agreed to meet her the following morning.

Joan wanted to look professional and capable. She planned to wear her dark-blue pantsuit and blue lace blouse to match. She had been wearing her hair the same way for weeks and decided she wanted something different for the meeting.

When she arrived at Arlene's House of Style, she could see that it was packed with people like always. She parked in the vacant lot across the street. Before getting out the car, she did a quick lipstick check. In the rearview mirror, Joan noticed a car pulling up next to her. With a second glance, she realized it was Tisha, not in her car but her father's.

Joan could see that she was yelling at someone on her cell phone, but could not make out what she was saying.

Ignoring the butterflies in her stomach, Joan stepped out of the car and locked the door and turned towards Tisha's car. This was the first time she had seen Tisha since the pool party.

Tisha looked up, rolled her eyes, turned away, and started fussing some more into the phone. Joan could feel the warmth in her eyes. She quickly walked across the street, getting angry with herself for allowing this to bother her.

By the time Joan approached the salon, tears were falling down her face. She passed right by the receptionist desk and proceeded to walk straight to the restroom, not wanting to have to explain her tears. As she entered a stall, she began to cry even harder as she replayed the repulsive look Tisha had in her eyes when she looked up and saw Joan standing by her car.

Joan thought of all she and Tisha had been through together. Both of them had fell in love with the science teacher in eighth grade. They tried out for the cheerleading squad in high school together and cried for two weeks when neither made it. When Tisha's mother died, Joan helped her plan the funeral. Tisha was with Joan through all eleven hours of her labor with James Jr. and even stayed at her place with her for two months after he was born; cooking, cleaning, and watching the baby so Joan could rest.

Joan became angry when she thought of all the times she had helped Tisha financially. She had given her money toward her rent numerous times. She bought her books in college when she squandered all her money partying. *As a matter of fact,* Joan thought, *when Tisha had needed anything, she's called on me.* Each year, they went on vacation, and each year, Tisha needed money paying off the final balance.

Joan couldn't believe Tisha had the audacity not to talk to her. She felt frustrated and hurt and continued to weep loudly until she heard someone walk in the restroom. She dried her eyes, fixed her makeup, and walked out.

Arlene was busy with another client, so Joan sat down and grabbed a magazine. Tisha was nowhere in sight. She knew she needed to pray for Tisha and forgive her, but instead, she just became angrier and angrier. As the tears started to flow once again, she used the magazine to hide her face.

Arlene, Joan's stylist, had just greeted and called Joan to the shampoo bowl when Tisha walked into the salon almost fifteen minutes later. Joan instantly regretted not having had a chance to give Arlene a heads-up on the situation.

"What's up, Tisha?" Arlene said. "What do y'all have planned for this weekend?" The two of them had been going to Arlene for over ten years, often coming in together when they had something major planned.

"If you're referring to me and Joan," Tisha replied, "we won't be going anywhere this weekend or any other weekend."

Arlene glanced at the other two stylists, and then they all looked at Joan. Joan kept her eyes closed as she usually did when Arlene washed and conditioned her hair.

They turned their attention back to Tisha when she continued to speak. "I want to go to the party they are having at the Highlight Bar tonight, but those idiots at the insurance agency are giving me the runaround. I talked to somebody last week who said my check was in the mail. Now, there telling me it might be a couple of months before I can get it. I can't believe this crap. Did I ask that fool to run into me?"

"How long ago did you have the car accident?" Arlene asked while drying Joan's hair with a towel.

Joan couldn't help but look up at Tisha, noticing her right leg and both her elbows were wrapped in white gauze. She felt sympathy. Tisha saw her looking and turned away from her with abhorrence. After shampooing and putting a deep conditioner in Joan's hair, Arlene put a cap on it and signaled for her to sit under the dryer.

"You know one thing I can't stand, Arlene?" Tisha said, watching Joan pass by.

Arlene, feeling the tension in the air, decided not to answer Tisha until Joan was safely under the oldest, loudest dryer in the shop.

Walking back to the shampoo bowl, and glad to have the two former best friends at opposite ends of her newly remodeled salon, she called Tisha to her chair and asked, "What can't you stand, Tisha?"

At the exact moment Joan lifted up her dryer to grab a magazine from off the counter, she heard Tisha say, "I can't stand whores who all of sudden start acting holy."

Joan thought of the time Tisha was depressed because she could not find a stable job. Joan paid for Tisha to go to massage therapy school. Tisha said she would pay Joan back, but never did. As soon as Tisha completed school she got hired at a salon, within days she got fired. The sundress Tisha had on right now was one Joan bought on their trip last year to San Diego. They were all going to an outside concert and Tisha didn't have anything to wear. So, she asked Joan if she could borrow the money for the dress; money she had not paid back. She never paid money back, and then had the nerve to talk about her.

In a fit of rage, Joan forgot about the magazine, leaped up, walked over to the shampoo bowl, and stood in front of Tisha.

"You mooching heifer, I can't believe you're treating me this way after everything I have done for you. You just make sure the next time you get yourself in trouble, which will be sooner than later knowing how completely dense you are, you call on somebody else to help you."

Tisha stood up from the shampoo bowl, her wet braids dangling at her shoulders. "Forget you, trick. I don't need you or nothing you have. You know, you got a lot of nerve acting like you're better than everybody else. But don't forget one thing, miss high-and-mighty, those knees you praise the

Lord on are the same knees you sucked many a di—" Before Tisha could finish her sentence, Joan grabbed her by her braids and rammed her head into the shampoo bowl four times before Arlene pulled her off of her. Once free, Tisha took a cup of hot coffee, which was sitting on a nearby counter, and threw it at Joan. Missing its target, some of it splattered on Arlene. With the water scalding her, Arlene released her grip on Joan, and before any of the other women in the shop could come close to stopping them, Joan and Tisha lunged at one another like two male lions in a den, fighting over one female.

Joan grabbed a handful of Tisha's braids and pulled until they released into her hands. Tisha used her long fingernails to scratch Joan down the side of both her arms. At the sight of the blood and the onset of pain, Joan roared out before climbing on top of Tisha and punching her in the face. The rage burned in Joan as she continued to punch Tisha repeatedly in the face.

Then, as if someone had switched on a light, Joan suddenly stopped and looked around at the terrified faces. She looked down at Tisha and saw the fear in her eyes. Two little girls were crying as their mothers rocked them back and forward trying to calm them.

The shame that started at Joan's feet was quickly replaced with guilt and then fear. She hurried, grabbed her purse, ran to the car, and sped off quickly with her wet hair dripping down her back.

Chapter 26

All night and all the next morning, Joan cried. Her eyes were swollen and sore to the touch. She tried getting up so she could attend her meeting with Rick Patrick, but the task of dressing and showing her face in public when her heart was broken with shame was entirely too overwhelming.

When she called in to work, Dr. Wright tried to offer help, but Joan refused to elaborate, simply stating she needed a few days to get herself together.

The more she tried to motivate herself to get out of bed, the more she heard Tisha's words repeating in her head. *"Those knees you praise the Lord on are the same knees you sucked many—"*

Joan found herself thinking back to the time she was in Cancún during the jazz festival in a club where she and her friends spent all seven of their nights. She had chosen Cancún because she found out James Sr. was going to be there.

When she finally saw him the day before they were about to leave, he had a Jennifer Lopez look-alike hanging on his arm. Joan would not allow him the satisfaction of seeing her in pain. Instead, she took two shots of tequila, grabbed the bartender who had been flirting with her the entire time she was in Cancún, and led him to her rental car.

"Who did I think I was fooling anyway?" she spoke out loud.

Next, Joan thought about Robert, James's best friend, who had come over to drop off the CD's he had borrowed weeks before. He was having an eighties party and remembered Joan saying she had an extensive music selection. James and Joan were broken up at the time so Robert called her directly.

Joan was dressed and looking nice when he arrived. She was also sad because her date had stood her up. Being a gentleman, Robert offered to take her to dinner so she wouldn't consider the evening a total waste. Thinking it wouldn't hurt to have dinner with him, especially since she didn't look at him as anything more than James's friend, she went along.

Now she found herself staring at the ceiling, just as she had the night she realized she and James would never be together again since she had shared something with his best friend that best friends were not supposed to share.

Joan remembered the look in James's eyes and the satisfaction she felt when she blurted out she had been with Robert during one of their arguments about Raquel. He looked as if the wind had been knocked out of him.

The men in her life continued to dance in her head for hours and hours. She saw them going in and out of the revolving door in her mind. She couldn't remember their names, at least not all of them. It was as if somebody kept pushing the rewind button. She was exhausted and shame enveloped her entire body.

What kind of woman am I? she thought. She remembered Aunt Alice had told her that no one could out sin the cross. Joan took that to mean everybody except for her.

Tisha was right. She was nothing but a whore and then had the nerve to go around acting like the queen of Sheba. She knew Tisha and Lila put together had not been with half the number of the men she had been with.

"Why didn't somebody stop me?" Joan yelled. "Why didn't I have enough sense to stop myself?"

She pulled the covers over her face until the phone rang. Thinking it was Dr. Wright or Miriam calling about work, she answered it without looking at the caller ID. It was Rick Patrick wondering if she was okay since she had seemed to be so excited about the meeting but failed to show up. He had gone through the trouble to make special arrangements for somebody to run the restaurant while he was away, and when she did not show up or call, he got worried.

"I'm so sorry. I really do want to meet with you, however, a family emergency came up," Joan said through to the phone receiver.

"Oh, Joan, I'm sorry. I didn't realize you had an emergency," Rick stated.

"Oh, it's going to be okay. I just need a few

days to get things straight," Joan tried to assure him.

"All right, call me when you are ready to reschedule our meeting." The genuine concern in his voice intensified the pain in Joan's body.

She hung up the phone and then slammed her head on the headboard when she flopped back down in her bed. Numb to everything but her thoughts, she didn't wince at the pain.

"The only man I've ever loved is engaged to marry someone else," Joan began the pity party. "My only child does not even want to visit me on the weekends. I'm a liar. I am a slut. Oh, and by the way, I hate my cushy office job."

Joan knew if she called on the woman she would come. She knew that Aunt Alice had told her to call anytime and Makita said her door was always open, but still, she called on no one. She didn't pray. She didn't want to feel better. Joan felt she deserved to be in the slimiest of pits, so that is where she remained.

Chapter 27

I *need some help. Last night I thought about going in* *the medicine cabinet and taking every pill I had,* Joan wrote in her journal. *What am I going to do?* *I'm starting to scare myself. I hurt so badly. I've been* *crying for two days nonstop.*

It's Sunday morning. I forced myself to get out of *bed. I've spent the last few days and nights reliving* *every wrong thing I have ever done. The shame and* *embarrassment have not allowed me any peace of mind.* *I have not eaten and I haven't answered the phone or* *checked my voice mail since Rick called. The doorbell* *rang twice and I ignored it as well.*

What happened? Why did I lose my cool with Tisha *like that? I can't believe it was me who was pounding* *her face. What made me get up from the dryer in the* *first place? I just kept having flashbacks of the things I* *have done for her and started to get angrier and an-* *grier. Before I knew it, I was in her face.*

I feel like dying. How can I face anybody? Between *the gossiping at the salon and Tisha running her mouth, everybody probably knows by now. How can I ever show my face there again? Or anywhere?*

What is my mom going to say? My grandmother? I bet Raquel found out and has probably told James and James Jr. My son is never going to learn to trust me. I used to see a way out of things. But right now, I just don't see a way out of this. What will the people at work say? I bet even the people at the grocery store know about what happened. After all, everybody knows somebody that goes to Arlene's.

What am I going to do? How will I face them? What will they think of me? Maybe I should just move to an-other state. It's not like I have much going on here any-way.

Well, I'm going back to bed. When I wake up, maybe I'll know what to do next.

After drifting off into a deep sleep, Joan found herself back in the auditorium where it all began, only this time the room was illuminated. The women were not screaming and not scared like the last time, but held expressionless faces. Joan looked around and eventually saw Lila and Tisha staring straight ahead, both of them refusing to meet her gaze.

Joan became anxious and stared at the podium, hoping the woman would make her entrance quickly. As if reading her mind, the room dark-ened slightly and the woman began to speak.

"Happy Sunday, ladies," the woman said. "I had hoped we would never need to meet like this again, as I prefer to do my work one-on-one." The woman spoke cheerfully as she walked on to the stage.

"Our hearts pain for those of you who have not surrendered your lives to Jesus Christ." Joan instantly thought of Tisha and Lila.

"This meeting is designed for those of you who have surrendered your lives to Christ, and as a result, are going through a few changes."

Joan shook her head in agreement.

"I went to a woman recently who has three children by three different men, having had the first when she was only fifteen," the woman informed them. "She dropped out of school and has done many things in order to provide for her children, including exotic dancing. Eventually, she became a prostitute and participated in bisexual experiences. She has sold drugs and served time in jail. She's slept with more people than she cares to name and has been treated for two sexually transmitted diseases. She welcomed the change the experiment promised." The woman paused, allowing the women to digest what she had just said.

"She prayed for and received a job working as an activity director at a nursing home. The people there loved her smile, her enthusiasm, and looked forward to the days she brought her children by to cheer them up. Her aunt, having noticed her lifestyle change, agreed to rent her a house she owns for a third of what she usually gets for rent. She even gave her a car she wasn't using.

"She received Jesus Christ, joined church, regularly attended Bible study, and even joined the praise dancing ministry. Yes, instead of dancing for men in a strip club, she is dancing for the Lord; or at least she was until a week ago when she walked into work. No one could even look her in the face. She cornered one of the younger girls in the restroom about information as to why everyone was acting so strangely toward her.

"It turned out that one of the patient's sons recognized her as the dancer who had performed at his cousin's bachelor party. The staff and patients spent the morning watching the videotape. She was humiliated. She went into the cafeteria where she met the patients after they had their lunch, only to have them treat her badly. The women simply ignored her as she tried to get them ready for their craft lesson. As difficult as it was, she kept working until one of the old men grabbed her head and shoved it toward his crotch as she was trying to help him up out of his wheelchair. "

Joan gasped along with the other women.

"She got her purse and ran out of the building inconsolably crying," the woman said. "She's been that way for the last five days. Her children have been in and out of her room trying to wake her up, but their mommy is always sleeping. When she is not sleeping, she is lying in the dark, rotting and feeling silly for ever thinking she could really change her life.

"She was unaware of something many of you seem to be ignorant of, as well."

Joan opened her eyes wider, as if it was going to make her hear more clearly.

The woman stood up taller and spoke in a resounding voice. "Who is the devil? I know you're picturing a little red man in tights with big horns like you see on the cartoons, right? How many of you know you are in the middle of a war?"

Some of the women looked puzzled, while others nodded in agreement. "Many of you are losing this war, and that's why you came in here today brokenhearted, confused, and utterly exhausted from this journey.

"Do you ever wonder why the moment you started to live for Christ your world turned upside down? Do you ever wonder why the moment you started to think you could actually do this experiment something happened to make you feel like an idiot for even trying? The devil has had a hold on you for so long, and he is going to do anything and everything to keep you bound.

"Don't be fooled, my sisters. He is not some little red man in tights. He is a powerful fallen angel, and he is launching an all-out attack on you.

"But don't fear my sisters, just because you have a formidable foe does not mean you are helpless. The devil is powerful but he is no match for the living, the true, and the Holy God of this universe.

"Ephesians six: eleven reads, 'Put on the full armor of God so that you can take your stand against the devil's schemes.'

"Fighting the devil without the armor of God is like a soldier going to battle without his helmet, gun, and armor. In other words, you do not have a chance.

"Let me explain how this works. Its eleven o'clock Saturday night and it's Marie's normal bedtime, but she's not really sleepy, so she begins to get her clothes ready for church the next day. She's growing in the things of God and can hardly wait to hear the message her pastor will preach the next day.

"As she is ironing her blouse, Marie's home phone rings. She's alarmed because it's so late. She checks the caller ID. It's a man that she used to participate with in an ungodly relationship. The devil just threw out the bait. Marie goes back to ironing her blouse.

"After she finishes ironing her blouse she gets into the bed. Before she can go to sleep the phone rings again. She didn't take the bait the first time so the devil is trying again.

"Marie starts thinking that a single conversation with her old boyfriend can't be that big of a deal. Right? And besides, she's strong enough not to fall into temptation. It's not like they can have sex through the phone. Marie picks up the phone. When Marie makes the decision to pick up the phone and talk to her old boyfriend, she takes the bait the devil laid out for her.

"Before Marie realizes it, the two of them have been on the phone for two hours. Everything about Marie's old boyfriend seems to have changed. He started a new position he loves and just bought a new car.

"He invites Marie to have dinner with him at one of those twenty-four-hour restaurants. At this time it's around one o'clock in the morning. Marie enjoyed talking to him a lot and wants to continue so she accepts the date.

"The moment Marie puts the phone down, she knows she's made a mistake. I mean, this is the guy she promised herself she could not see during the experiment, especially since he has a way of pushing her sexual buttons. Marie decides that she will only eat with him, then afterward she will leave so everything will be okay. She gets in her car and drives to the restaurant to meet him.

"It's been a long time since Marie had the attention of a man and she's really enjoying his company. They are laughing about old times in between delicious bites of food. When he reaches over to kiss Marie the first time, she pushes him back. The second time, she waits to push him back until after he has gotten close enough to brush her face with his lips.

"Marie and her old boyfriend stay at the restaurant talking until four in the morning. Marie's not worried she'll be late for church because instead of going to the early service like she had planned, she will go home sleep for a few hours and go to the late church service. Even if she's a little late it's okay because after all, everybody knows they stay in the late service all day anyway.

"He walks Marie to her car and she allows him to kiss her. She tells herself it's okay to let him kiss her just one time because the date is almost over. That one kiss turns into several. Marie was never one for public displays of affection, but it's been a long time since she's been in a man's arms, so the fact that she can hear people around her does not stop her from allowing him to touch her right there in the restaurant's parking lot.

"Marie starts telling herself that her body is acting this way for a reason. She needs this. After all, she is a flesh-and-blood woman and every woman needs to be held sometimes, right?

"He takes Marie's hands and walks her to his car without saying a word. She gets into his car. She knows she should get into her car and leave, but then he lands one of those kisses on her before he drives off so Marie decides to stay. The two of them give in to their passion at every red light. Marie can no longer hear the voice in her head that's telling her to stop. All she can hear is, 'Go! Go! Go!'

"Twenty-seven minutes later, the party is over. They drove back to the restaurant to get Marie's car in silence. He parks next to Marie's car and smiles, signaling to her it was time for her to get out. She gets out of his car and into hers.

"During the drive back to her apartment Marie is angry at herself. She feels so stupid. All she can think about is how many times she had promised herself she would never allow that to happen again. She walks to her apartment quickly, practically running over somebody, not wanting anyone to see her looking a mess this early in the morning.

"As soon as Marie walks into her apartment she sees her Bible and notepad in the kitchen. She usually read her Bible first thing in the morning with her coffee. Today, she walked past. Once she reaches her bedroom, she sees the church clothes she laid out the night before.

"Suddenly, Marie's mind flashes like a movie in her head, replaying all the things she had just done with her old boyfriend in his bedroom. She knows she has messed up and needs to go to God in prayer, but she feels like a total failure and is ashamed of what she has done. Marie decides to take a bath and go to sleep. She does not belong in church after what she just spent the night doing. It'll be better next week she tells herself.

"Do all of you understand what happened?" the woman asked, not waiting for an answer.

"First, Marie was tempted to sin. Then she made the choice to sin. After she sinned, instead of confessing her sin to God and asking for forgiveness, she decided to go to sleep and canceled her plans to go to church, therefore getting further and further away from God.

"This is what happens when you go to battle with the devil without the armor of God. You lose. The devil is a liar, a destroyer, and a thief. The devil is not after your money, your man, or your job. He is after—your mind! Don't ever underestimate the devil and his team of demons."

Joan was speechless. Could it have been the devil that provoked her to lose control in the salon all of a sudden? Was it him who kept reminding her of what happened at the salon each time she had tried to get out of the bed?

"The devil will try to make you think you done too much dirt to be forgiven and that change is just too hard," the woman said. "He will make you doubt the truth. He will make you think that fornicating is okay, because he knows if you are actively in sin, your relationship with God will be severely hindered. He will keep you focused on your difficult circumstances. Why? Because he knows if you stay focused on the problem, you will forget the problem solver. He wants to keep you bound in sin so you can't live the abundant life God has promised you.

"You need to know that you are no match for the devil. You cannot fight him by yourself. He will always win."

Joan sat back in her seat, wishing she had a paper and pen to take notes.

One lady from New York jumped up and yelled, "So what should Marie have done?"

"When Jesus was tempted by the devil, what did he do that she did not?" the woman answered the question with a question.

An older woman from Louisiana stood up and shouted, "He used the Word of God."

"Exactly! The devil told Jesus after fasting for forty days to turn stones into bread. The devil knew he was hungry. Jesus quoted scripture. 'Man does not live on bread alone, but on every word that comes from the mouth of God.'

"The devil took Jesus to a very high mountain. He showed Jesus the entire world and told him to worship him and that it all would be his. Jesus didn't have a conversation with him. He quoted scripture again. 'Away from me, Satan! For it is written, worship the Lord your God, and serve him only.'

"So when our young woman saw the telephone call was from her ex-lover calling out of the blue late at night, what should she have done?"

A young lady from Kansas stood up proudly. "She should have dropped to her knees and asked God to give her the strength to not answer the phone. She could have meditated on first Peter, chapter five, verse eight because it says, 'Be self-controlled and alert. Your enemy the devil prowls around like a roaring lion looking for someone to devour.'"

Next, a woman from Nebraska spoke. "She could have begun to pray One Corinthians six: eighteen–twenty, putting her name in the scripture so it would have gone like this, 'Lord, I pray to flee from sexual immorality. All other sins *Marie* commits are outside her body, but when *Marie* sins sexually she sins against her own body. Does *Marie* not know her body is a temple of the Holy Spirit, who is in her, whom she received from God? *Marie* is not her own; She was bought at a price. Therefore *Marie* honors God with her body.'"

"Praise the Lord, I like that. Make it personal," the woman said. "Anyone else?"

A woman from Indiana stood. "One Peter one: thirteen–sixteen, 'Therefore, prepare your minds for action; be self-controlled; set your hope fully on the grace to be given you when Jesus Christ is revealed. As obedient children, do not conform to the evil desires you had when you lived in ignorance. But just as He who called you is holy, so be holy in all you do; for it is written: Be holy, because I am holy.'"

Joan stood up next. "Hebrews thirteen: four, 'Marriage should be honored by all, and the marriage bed kept pure, for God will judge the adulterer and all the sexually immoral.'"

"Great job, ladies," the woman praised them. "Do not ever underestimate the power of scripture. Remember, you are in a battle with the devil everyday of your life. A gun and bullets will not help you win this battle. You cannot fight supernatural battles with natural strength. Your bullets are the Word of God. The scriptures say if you submit yourselves to God, the devil will flee.

"The devil is going to try to distract you from your alone time with God. He's going to use people, your job, your children, television shows, phone calls etc. . . . to keep you too busy to pray and study the Word of God. Because he knows that the Bible holds the truth and when you know the truth you will no longer believe the devil's lies.

"Now, repeat these words after me. I cannot fight supernatural battles with natural weapons. I must use the weapons God has provided me. Anything less will render me defeated."

The women did as they were told.

"If the young lady would have used scripture to combat the lies of the devil, she would not have found herself in that predicament," the woman added. "And remember, you have to know scripture in order to use it. In other words, stay in the Word. "

A young woman from California stood up and said, "So now what does the woman in the scenario do now that she has committed the sin and she's all depressed and stuff?"

"When she messed up, she should not have run away from God, she should have run to Him," the woman answered. "Marie should have admitted that she was wrong and asked for forgiveness. One John one: nine says, 'If we confess our sins, he is faithful and just and will forgive us our sins and purify us from all unrighteousness.'"

One lady from South Carolina added, "She should have read Philippians four: six–seven. 'Do not be anxious about anything, but in everything, by prayer and petition, with thanksgiving, present your request to God. And the peace of God, which transcends all understanding, will guard your hearts and your minds in Christ Jesus.' That's what I read over and over whenever I've done something I know I should not have done.

Eventually, the anxiety goes away and I find myself repenting. Just like the scripture says, I get a peace that transcends all understanding."

Joan stood up, thinking more of herself than the woman in the scenario and said, "She could make up her mind to submit herself to the Holy scriptures more than ever, relying on God and not herself. She should have meditated on Proverbs three: five–six instead of participating in a conversation with the devil."

Taking a deep breath, Joan continued, "The scripture proclaims that we are to bless the Lord at all times in every situation. If I may paraphrase, I will bless the Lord even when I've spent the night fornicating. I will bless the Lord when I lose my cool at the salon and embarrass myself shamelessly. I will bless the Lord when I walk into work and find out all my coworkers are looking at me doing things that are beneath me.

"I will thank the Lord for his grace and his compassion, and I will seek his forgiveness. I will trust in the Lord with all my heart and lean not on my own understanding. In all my ways, I will acknowledge Him and trust that He will make my paths straight."

Suddenly, Joan woke up. She looked at the clock and jumped out of bed. She would be late for church, but it didn't matter because they stay in the late service all day anyway.

Chapter 28

Joan comforted herself by listening to her favorite Christian radio show throughout the drive to church. But now that she had reached her destination, her enthusiasm dwindled and was replaced with anxiety. As much as she tried to stop it, her heart started to race the closer she walked from the parking lot to the sanctuary. It had only been a few days, but it felt like she had been locked in her room for weeks.

The two ladies in front of her were laughing and talking. Suddenly, Joan pictured herself pounding into her best friend's face. She thanked God for 1 John 1:9. She had been forgiven.

A little girl a few years older than James Jr. held the church entrance door open as she approached. She smiled and said, "Thank you." Another little girl and a woman Joan assumed was their mother waited by the door. Joan could feel the woman staring, but did not make eye contact.

Joan took a deep breath, comforted by the fact

that the lobby was empty and the choir was singing one of those upbeat songs where everybody was standing, shouting, and clapping. She could find a seat in the sanctuary without everybody breaking his or her neck to find out who had walked in late.

Two steps from the usher, Joan heard one of the little girls say to her mother, "That's the lady who was acting crazy at the beauty shop, huh, Momma? She almost killed that hurt lady."

Her mother quickly hushed her, grabbed her hand, and walked in the opposite direction. But not before Joan heard the last thing the other little girl said. "What's she doing in church? I thought church was for good people."

The tears formed in Joan's eyes as she grabbed a service program from the waiting usher. Instead of walking in the door he was holding open for her, she turned completely around and walked to the restroom. The tears were coming down fast as she rushed into a stall another lady was rushing out of.

"Girl, what's up? For God's sake, why are those tears falling?" It was Sage, the woman who had practically carried her to the altar the day she joined church.

Joan's tension subsided. Finding they were the only two in the restroom, she began to speak. "I don't know if anything has ever bothered me more than what I'm going through right now. I know God is going to make a way, but this is hard, real hard. Some little girls and their mom were just discussing a humiliating incident I took part in."

Sage looked puzzled. So, Joan went on to tell her about the incident at the salon.

"I can't believe I did something like that." Joan continued. "And the fact so many people know just makes it worse." Trying to reassure Sage that she would be okay, she said, "I'm going to be fine, girl. I just need to take a moment to myself and pray before I walk in there."

Sage looked sympathetic as she walked to the sink to wash her hands. "I've been there and done that. You kind of get used to it when you've had a baby by somebody else's husband."

Joan looked down at Sage's flat stomach and remembered she had been pregnant when she first met her.

Before Joan could say anything else, Sage said, "I gave my baby up for adoption."

Joan looked up stunned.

Sage turned to the mirror and began touching up her makeup nonchalantly. "I grew up without a father, which is probably why I got so messed up about men in the first place. Sometimes, I cry myself to sleep at night thinking that my father is somewhere alive and well and wants nothing to do with me. I wasn't going to put my child through something so painful. Contrary to what others may think, girl, a mother's love just ain't enough. Children need fathers."

Joan nodded her head in agreement, remembering how happy her son seemed each time he had called from his father's house.

"As I was walking out of the doctor's office one day, a couple was walking hand in hand out another doctor's office across the hall," Sage told her. "The woman was crying uncontrollably. The man was so caring. He held her tight and said encouraging words, even quoting scripture. I just kept thinking I wish my baby could have a father like him. Just then, I felt something tell me that man *was* my child's father."

Joan had a shocked look on her face.

Sage continued. "That's exactly what I was thinking," she said, referring to the look on Joan's face. "Part of me wanted to run, but it was so real, I surrendered. I can't explain it. I just knew.

"The moment I walked into their home, I felt the love. I spent the last month of my pregnancy living with them. He is a high school principal and she was an English teacher until she stopped working so she could take care of the baby full-time." Sage smiled. "They met at the University of Houston their freshman year and have been to-gether ever since. They have spent the last five years trying to have a baby. The last attempt had failed, which is why she was crying that day at the doctor's office.

"They both came from large families and both sets of their parents are still married! My daughter has aunts and uncles and cousins and a com-fortable house with trees in the back. Her adoptive father started building her a swing set and a tree house before she was born."

Sage turned away from the mirror and towards Joan. "I don't even want to tell you about her bio-logical father. I prayed and I prayed for God to show me what to do. I certainly did not think it would be for me to give my baby up for adoption. I prayed to God for His will and not my own." Sage could no longer hold back her tears. "I love waking up in the morning knowing my baby has something I never had: two loving, caring, happily married Christian parents." Sage dried her eyes. "I know you don't understand."

"I do understand," Joan whispered. "I understand more than you know."

Joan grabbed Sage and the two of them hugged. Then, Joan pulled her away and looked her straight in the eye. "You are one brave woman, Miss Sage. Glory to God for giving you the strength. I feel so silly crying over this crap when you have so much more on your plate."

"You should bring your friend tonight for the foot-washing ceremony."

"I heard about it, but I wasn't planning on coming. What exactly is it anyway?"

"What's your friend's name and number?"

The one who I got into the altercation with?"

"Yeah."

"Her name is Tisha, and trying to get her to come here would be a waste of time. She ain't ready."

"Okay, just give me the number," Sage insisted.

Joan wrote it down on a paper towel and asked Sage if she needed to get a pedicure for the foot-washing ceremony if she did decide to come.

Sage wanted to laugh but didn't. "I felt like you the first time I went to one. All I'm going to say is whatever you have to do to make sure you're right back here tonight, do it."

Chapter 29

Tisha glanced over at Marcus from across the table. He had invited her over and prepared his famous vegetable lasagna. They ate mostly in silence. Tisha didn't have to ask why Marcus was so quiet. She knew what he was thinking. At least he had the decency to do it face-to-face, Tisha thought.

After they finished eating Tisha took their plates and put them in the dishwasher. This was the day she knew was coming but she hated to see it just the same. Tisha sat back down at the table. She could now see tears forming in Marcus's eyes.

"Tisha, you know I love you and I would do anything for you," Marcus explained. "But for a while now you haven't been yourself. You barely want to make love and then when we do I can tell your heart's not in it. I got needs, baby. What happened? We used to be so good together. You remember that time at the movie theater? When we were the only two in the back? That's was the best sex ever! What happened to that, Tisha?"

Tisha starred at him blankly. "I'm sorry, Tisha, I can't live like this."

"I understand, Marcus." Tisha grabbed her belongings and gave Marcus a kiss on the cheek without putting up a fight. She no longer had the energy to fight with him or anybody else. She walked to the door.

"It's like that, Tisha. You're just going to walk out? Don't I deserve an explanation of what happened to you?"

Tisha left him standing at the door looking confused. She opened her car door and drove away. Tisha's cell phone rang.

"Hello," she answered the phone.

"Hello, baby girl," Tisha's father said. Tisha suddenly became ashamed she had been in such a daze for the last few months she couldn't remember the last time she spoke to him.

"Hey, Daddy. I was just on my way over there," Tisha lied.

"Tisha, I just called to tell you that I moved into those apartment homes on Shelby Street."

"You mean you moved into a nursing home?"

"No, Tisha, it's not a nursing home. It's an apartment complex for elderly people. I thought we already discussed this. I was getting so lonely in that big ole house by myself. This will be good for me. They have somebody to cook and clean, and I don't have to worry about cutting the yard or changing lightbulbs. You know I'm just getting too old for that kind of stuff."

"Daddy, why didn't you call me? I could have helped you move or something?"

"Tisha, I did call you. I told you I was moving. What is going on with you, baby girl?"

Tisha started crying. "Nothing Daddy, I've just been busy. How about I come over and see you in your new apartment? I'm driving near Shelby Street now."

"I'm going to need to take a rain check, sweetie. The widow across the hall asked me to accompany her to dinner." Tisha was silent. "Tisha?"

"Yes, Daddy. I'm still here."

"Get some rest, okay baby girl; I'll call you in the morning."

Tisha hung up the phone. It was starting to rain softly, the same as it had the day of the car accident where she should have died. A pizza delivery guy lost control of his car and hit her head-on. She didn't have time to react. The delivery guy died on the scene. Tisha escaped with a few bruises. The cops couldn't get over how two cars involved in the same major accident could have such different results. Tisha had been so shaken up since the accident that she was having trouble sleeping through the night and couldn't function at work. Eventually, her boss let her go, which also meant she had to give up the Lexus she had been driving. She could only drive it as long as she worked on the lot. Now she was driving what used to be her mother's Toyota Tercel. It had been locked in the garage for years and was barely working when Marcus had it towed to a mechanic for repairs.

Tisha hadn't remembered feeling more alone in her life. She didn't have Marcus. She didn't have Joan and she didn't have Lila.

Tisha drove into her apartment complex and as soon as she got out of the car and up the stairs, she saw the envelope sticking up from under her door. She didn't have to open it. She knew it was an eviction notice. After losing her job her already stretched finances had reached the breaking point. Marcus had paid her bills last month but had made it clear if she wasn't meeting his needs he would have to stop meeting hers.

Tisha was banking on her settlement check arriving before her rent was due again, but that had not happened. The electric, telephone, and insurance bills would be due soon too, and she had no idea how she was going to pay any of them. She bent down and picked up the envelope, unlocked the door and walked inside her apartment. Tisha threw the eviction notice on her coffee table along with her purse and keys. Falling face-down on her sofa she began to cry deeply. Tisha heard her telephone ring four different times while she was on the sofa crying, she didn't think about answering it, believing it was probably somebody she owed or a telemarketer, seeing that she didn't have any friends. Tisha was half asleep when she heard her phone ring for the fifth time. Immediately, she answered it without thinking.

Chapter 30

Joan drove up to the parking lot of her church five minutes before the ceremony was to start, later than she expected because she decided to get a last-minute pedicure before allowing some-one to touch her feet.

She walked inside the room where it was being held. It was only half full. She was a little nervous about not knowing the protocol for a foot-washing ceremony. Just in case she felt the need to leave, she grabbed an aisle seat in the back so she could slip out unnoticed.

Minister Makita and the other women leaders in the church were hugging as they greeted one another. Sage was on the second row talking to another woman. They seemed really happy to see each other. Joan looked around pleased, noticing she was not the only one who had come alone. The perimeter of the room was lined with folding chairs and water-filled basins.

Spotting Joan, Sage walked down the aisle and

gave her a quick hug. Joan wanted to ask about Tisha but didn't.

Sage said nothing besides, "I'm glad you came," and then returned to her seat.

As they were about to start, Joan went through great pains to take a leisurely look around the room. No Tisha.

Minister Makita walked to the front of the room and said, "Greetings, my fellow Christian sisters. I want to thank all of you for coming. The staff and I have been fasting for the last three days in preparation for this ceremony. We believe lives will be changed in the place tonight." Joan stood and clapped with the rest of the women. "How many of you have been to a foot-washing ceremony?" Looking around once again, Joan took a count of hands and learned most of the women had not. "Well, let me tell you, you are in for an event, my sisters.

"I don't know how many women have approached me in the last few days saying, 'Makita, I would love to go to the foot-washing ceremony, but my feet are not in any shape to be touched. I have bunions and corns and rough, dry skin. I would just be too embarrassed.'"

There was nervous laughter in the room.

"Can I get you to just stop being frivolous for a moment?" Makita asked. "Don't be concerned with if your pedicure is fresh or not, or if your feet are sweaty or larger than the sister's next to you. You've spent all this time worrying about your feet, but, sister, how much time did you spend worrying about your heart? What condition is it in, my sister? Is it hurt? Is it broken? Does it crave for forgiveness and a second chance?"

Joan looked down at her freshly pedicured feet and sat back in her seat, grateful Sage had made her come.

"In the Book of John chapter thirteen," Makita said. "Jesus washed his disciple's feet. In Bible times, slaves would wash the feet of their master's and those visiting their master's homes. It was one of the lowest jobs one could have. However, Jesus took a towel, wrapped it around his waist, poured water into a basin, knelt down before his disciples, and began to wash their feet and dry them with the towel he had around his waist."

Minister Makita wrapped a towel around her waist and knelt down as she was speaking. "If there is anyone in this room I have hurt, I want to apologize. All I am is a servant of the Lord. Sometimes I get concerned with my outer appearance. I look down on some of my sisters because they don't do things the way I would have done them. I get caught up in my position and the way people react when I walk into the room. How dare I walk around like I'm better than somebody else when Jesus, the Son of God, dressed like a slave and washed His disciples' feet?

"I want you to grab her feet as if you were holding her heart." Makita grabbed the feet of one of the women in the first row and placed them in a basin of water. Then Makita started to gently wash the woman's feet.

"While you are washing them, pray for that sister." Makita said. "Pray she does not give into temptation. Pray for her strength. Pray God guides her. Pray she knows her spiritual gifts and uses them. Pray for her children. Pray she studies the

Word of God and understands it. Pray for her health. Pray that if she is holding a grudge or has unforgetfulness rotting in her heart, it will be removed. Pray she lets go of her past and embraces her future. Pray that any relationship the enemy has destroyed be restored in the name of Jesus.

"After you have finished praying, get up and hug that sister real tight. Tell her you love her and that you're praying for her and her family." Makita hugged the woman whose feet she had washed, tightly. She looked at the congregation. "Oh, don't you want to be like Jesus? Sisters, let's love, encourage, and serve one another."Makita instructed half of the women, including Joan, to sit on one of the folding chairs and take off their shoes. Joan nervously walked to the folding chair closest to her.

The other half of the women lined up behind Makita. Makita handed each one of them full-sized white towels. Then she said something to them Joan could not hear. The next thing Joan knew the women who had been talking to Makita were walking to the women seated in the folding chairs. A woman who looked to be about thirty-five with gray slacks and white blouse knelt before Joan.

She carefully placed Joan's feet one by one into the water. Then she started to pray as she gently washed and dried Joan's feet. The next woman to kneel before Joan was a young woman around eighteen with blond hair and blue eyes.

Sage was washing someone's feet a few chairs away from Joan. She was singing a song without music Joan had never heard before. "Take me, Father. Rearrange me, Father. Make me into who you want me to be. I need you, Father. I'm ready to let go. I want to be free. I know that you are the one, the only one that can rescue me."

Joan believed she would never be able to explain fully what is was like to have strangers humble themselves to wash her feet while praying heartfelt words for her with tears coming down their faces and Sage singing that song with what Joan knew was her pain.

The atmosphere was like nothing she had ever experienced. She thought church ladies were happy all the time, but sitting there watching them grieve as she was grieving had her taking notice.

It didn't take long before Joan was overcome with emotion. She tried to hold it in but she could not. She started to cry about everything that had happened since the experiment started. Tears began to fall down her face so hard she could not see.

The woman who was before her walked away and an elder woman of the church knelt down before Joan. Joan didn't know her name, but she knew she was well respected around the church. She looked to be eighty or ninety years old. Joan's first reaction was to get up and let the woman have her seat, but the woman shook her head no.

As soon as the elder woman knelt before Joan she said softly, "It's over, Father, and I thank you for it. Whatever it is, my sister, God just said it's over," then she sprinkled water on Joan's feet and began to silently pray for her.

Joan had been crying before, but now she reached an entirely new level. She screamed, yelled, and shook her hands in the air long and hard. A part of Joan wanted to be embarrassed because she had never cried like this in public before.

She was shaking and crying so hard she didn't realize that the elder woman left and another woman had come to kneel before her. Joan heard a whispery voice say, "I love her. I need her. I thank God you brought her to me. Father, I pray she forgives me. I pray she allows me back in her heart. I pray nothing tears us apart again.

"Father, I ask that you forgive me because I know you have been calling me and my best friend, Joan, to help me," she pleaded. "I'm sorry, Father. I know you only want what's best for me. I'm tired of running from you. I want to be free. I'm ready, Father. Please guide me, and whatever you do, give me my best friend back."

After she spoke those words, Joan jumped out of her chair, grabbed the woman, and hugged her tightly. That woman was Tisha. When they finished holding one another, and after the ceremony, Joan and Tisha walked out of the church hand in hand.

Upon returning to my home, Joan wrote in her journal, *Tisha and I went into the kitchen to get a bag of potato chips, pulled out the convertible sofa bed, and spent the whole night talking the way we did when we were young girls.*

Tisha told me about the car accident and how almost dying had affected her. She got to the point where she could barely sleep. Because she couldn't sleep soundly she couldn't function. It was like she was always in a daze and working was not an option. Having sex with Marcus started to make her feel guiltier and guiltier. Eventually, Marcus broke up with her. She was sad when he broke up with her but a part of her was relieved. She knew that with him in her life she could not completely surrender to God. Her aunt's finished with chemo for now and is doing okay. Her doctor is watching her closely, so if something comes up, he can detect it early. Her father is living in an assisted living facility and has a new lady friend.

Tisha had just gotten an eviction notice and was feeling lost and didn't know what her next move should be when Sage called. It was like God was saying, "You've tried everything else, now it's time to try Me." She couldn't do anything but surrender.

She seems timid and scared, not like the "loud, say anything to anybody" Tisha I used to know. Tisha has a lot to deal with. She will not admit it, but I can tell she still has some anger towards God regarding her mother. She didn't build up that anger overnight and it's not going to go away overnight. I'm looking forward to keeping an eye on her. She's going to live with me in my extra bedroom until she gets on her feet.

It felt good to talk about everything with her: James Jr., James Sr., my bakery dream, grandmother, mother, father, and the wisdom of Aunt Alice.

Alice and I speak on the phone almost daily. She is such a blessing. I wish every woman had an Aunt Alice when they first gave their lives to the Lord. I understand my mother more as a result of speaking with Alice. I know that my mother realizes that she made a mistake by keeping me from my father and didn't want me to do the same with my son. That's why she insisted that Jr. spend time with his father. I pray she doesn't feel guilty. As mothers, we all make mistakes. I know that better than anybody.

Alice told me to allow my father back into my life. She said the only reason I shut him out is because I'm afraid he will hurt me again. I know she's right. I've spent so much time hating him, I can't imagine loving him. I have his phone number programmed in my cell *phone. I pray one day soon I will have the strength to make the call.*

James Jr. called and said he missed me. His dad is dropping him off so he can spend time with me. I want my son to know he has two homes. I'm not allowing anything to come between Jr. and his father again . . . especially not me.

I feel so blessed right now, and I have God to thank for making it all happen.

Chapter 31

"Wake up, Joan!" Tisha shouted. Joan shuffled her blanket so she could see the clock.

"It's eight A.M. What exactly are you doing waking me up this early on a Saturday morning? You know I like to sleep late." Joan asked her.

"I have an idea," Tisha replied enthusiastically. "Actually I've been praying about and planning this idea for a while now. I just had to wait for something to come to pass."

"Okay, Tisha, I'm listening," Joan replied, sounding more frustrated than she was, but happy to see the spark in her friend's eyes.

"You need to get up, get dressed, and get to baking those lemon pastries you make, and the chocolate ones with the caramel and raspberry, and those delicious cherry cream cheese tarts that are my favorite."

"What?"

"Girl, look, I'm tired of you talking about your

business. It's time we did something," Tisha said, snatching the covers off Joan.

"I'm taking a culinary class at night starting in the fall and a food certification class on Saturdays. I was going to wait until I completed the classes before I did anything," Joan said.

"I've been praying about what I could do to show you how much I appreciate everything you've done for me. I know you told me not to worry about anything, Joan, but I really want to do this. Therefore, since I finally received my settlement from the accident, I've got an idea." Joan looked unimpressed and Tisha was not fazed the least. "You need to get up. I found your recipe box and I've bought all the stuff," she said, grabbing Joan's hand and pulling her toward the kitchen.

Once inside the kitchen, Joan noticed at least five ten-pound bags of flour and sugar, twelve grocery-sized crates each of fresh lemons, cherries, and raspberries, two paper bags filled with butter and cream cheese, and ten cartons of eggs sitting on the countertop.

"Tisha, girl, you know you are crazy! Even if I do bake them, where are we going to sell them? Don't we need a permit or something?"

"Look at this, boss." Tisha had been busy working on the computer.

Joan still had her mouth open when Tisha walked over with a flyer and a template for business cards that read:

When was the last time you ate something that made your toes curl?
Never?

Well, you haven't tried Joan's flaky lemon butter
pastries, cherry cream cheese tarts, or choco-
late caramel raspberry mini soufflés.
This one is free.
Next time, you'll have to pay to have the earth
move.
Coming Soon!
Happy Endings by Joan
2345 Justine Lake Square

As soon as Joan looked up from the paper, Tisha snatched it away.

"No, we don't need a permit," Tisha said, "because we're not selling anything yet, just giving samples. I'm going over to Copy Mart. You get started baking. I want to hit the beauty shops, barber shops, and the Little League games this afternoon."

Joan appeared to be incoherent. Tisha spoke loud and slow, as if Joan was hard of hearing. "Joan, we've started your bakery; the one you've been dreaming about for years. I'm Tisha, your director of marketing, advertising, and promotions. You are Joan, the owner, operator, and culinary extraordinaire. Aunt Alice, your mother, and grandmother should be here in a second. They are your bakery assistants.

"I've looked into a space for the operation, but it will not be ready for a few months. But I placed good faith money down so the place is as good as yours. In the meantime, we are going to spend our weekends getting the word out. So when we open, people will be lined up outside."

With Joan still not responding, Tisha grabbed Joan's hand, and she began to pray.

"Father, Heavenly Father, I thank you for this day. I thank you for the dream you put in my friend's heart many years ago and the precious gift of creativity you have blessed her with. I ask that you walk with us today. I ask that you guide us. Father, take the spirit of fear away from us and give us a spirit of triumph. Father, we claim victory in the name of Jesus."

Joan started crying in disbelief.

"Firstly, where did you learn to pray like that?" Joan asked, wiping her eyes. "Secondly, how did you get my mother, grandmother, and aunt to agree to do *anything* together? And thirdly, you bought *me* a bakery?"

"Ask Jesus." Tisha smiled.

"Jesus?"

"That's right, Jesus. It's amazing what He will do for you when you allow him," Tisha responded as she practically flew out the back door.

Joan went to the CD player and put *Worthy to Be Praised* on repeat while she stared at the abundance of groceries in her kitchen. She turned around just in time to see Tisha drive out of the complex and her mother's car drive in, complete with Aunt Alice and her grandmother.

"God, you are truly worthy to be praised," Joan said.

She stood back in amazement when her mother, grandmother, and Aunt Alice entered with each of their arms filled with groceries. Joan was near tears at the sight of the three of them together, smiling like they actually liked one another.

Alice walked in, placed her bags on what little space was left on the counter, and started unpacking. Joan's grandmother and mother walked in and casually tasted a few raspberries.

Noticing the perplexed look on Joan's face, Alice said, "Tisha called us. I drove up here a couple of days ago."

Joan knew there was more to the story than what she was telling, but considering the results, she really didn't need to know the details . . . right now anyway.

"Let's get to work," Joan's mother piped in. "I'll start measuring the flour for the lemon pastries."

"I'll start cracking the eggs," Alice said.

"I will start squeezing the lemons," Joan's grandmother offered, "if that's okay with you?"

They all looked at Joan. She smiled and nodded yes. Just then, the phone rang. It was Tisha calling from her cell phone.

"Hello," Joan answered.

"Hey, girl, we might need to move the bakery date up. I have everybody at the copy store already wanting to buy your desserts and I just got started," Tisha said.

"Really?" Joan asked.

"What can I say, girl? God gave me this mouth for a reason. Anyway, I'm calling because I flew out of the house so fast I forgot to tell you the good news. Guess who I saw at the grocery store this morning?"

"Who?"

"Lila and Jasmine."

"For real?"

"You will never believe what happened. After the pool party she came home and Steve told her to leave his house. Apparently, he found some stuff she had written about him and went through the roof. She and Jasmine have been living with her parents ever since."

"I didn't think Steve had it in him," Joan replied.

"She cut off her hair. I almost didn't recognize her."

"Really?"

"She started walking around the track everyday. Which means she's sweating a lot. Her hair was starting to get damaged, so she cut the relaxed ends off. Who would have thought Lila would have gone natural? She even has a job."

"Where?"

"She's a receptionist at Jasmine's new school. She went to the school to register and got to talking to the assistant principal about how she was committed to Jasmine getting the best education possible. The principal said he needed more parents like her to make the public schools everything that they should be. Days later Lila found out the school needed a receptionist. She filled out the application and ended up interviewing with the same man who she had talked to about Jasmine. She was offered the position the next day."

"Wow."

"You don't know the half of it. She enrolled at Houston Community College. I would have never thought it, but it turns out Lila has always wanted to be a nurse. As we were saying our good-byes, I offered to take her home since she doesn't have a car and she and Jasmine rode the bus to the store. She turned me down saying bus trips were good for her and her daughter because it allowed them to spend quality time together. But the last thing she said took the cake."

"What?"

"She wants to come to church with us this Sunday."

"Yes! God is good!" Joan sighed. "Talking about Lila reminds me of somebody I've been meaning to call but I'm embarrassed to admit that I haven't got around to it yet."

"I know . . . Janet. We should call her."

"But how do we explain ourselves?" Joan asked. "I feel bad about the way we treated her."

"We'll say 'hey Janet, remember us? We're your former friends who dropped you when you needed us the most because you were convicting us with your godly lifestyle. When we saw you living for Jesus it made us feel bad for refusing to do the same. It wasn't you we were running away from. It was the God you boldly represented. We never meant to hurt you. We're sorry. Will you please forgive us?' "

"It's that simple, huh?" Joan said. "Let's invite her and Lila to meet us this Monday like we used to, just not Eduardo's. How about we meet at a coffeehouse?"

"That sounds good, Joan. Oh yes, we're back representing in that SSE!"

"SSE?" Joan said in a puzzled tone.

"Yes, that Single Sister Experiment."

Tisha began rapping.

"From the clubs to the pews,
From dropping it like it's hot to I think not,
From lifting up 'make you holla' hands to lifting
*   up 'Holy' hands,*

From being focused on a man to being focused on
    'the Man,'
You better catch that SSE train as fast as you
    can,
So you can get on with your life and God's won-
    derful plan."

"Praise the Lord! She's back! I know the people
in the store think you're crazy;" Joan laughed.

"I am crazy. I used to be crazy for Marcus. I
used to be crazy for money. I used to run myself
crazy thinking if I just had a certain car I would
be okay, or if I just had some designer clothes I
would be okay."

"And now, Tisha?"

"I'm falling crazy in love with the only one
who will ever be crazy in love with me. He is the
final piece to my puzzle. He completes me."

"Jesus," said Joan.

"Yes, Joan, Jesus. Don't you just love the sound
of His name? He loves me all the time, everyday.
And you know what I love about him the most?"

"What, Tisha?"

"He loves a work in progress."

"I feel you, girl. We're growing everyday."

"Joan, do you think you will ever get married?"

"I don't know, but I would like to. Only God
knows the plans He has for me. In Philippians,
Paul said he had learned to be content in whatever circumstances he was in. My prayer for myself is that I learn to be content. If poor, content. If
rich, content. If single, content. If married, content. I want whatever God wants. He made me
and knows what's best for me. Now that I have

given my life to the Lord, I know I can trust him to make my path straight."

"Well said, Joan. I second that."

The woman whispered to each of them. "You know what this means, ladies?"

"What?" they answered in unison.

"Joan Dallas and Tisha Lewis, you have completed the first phase of the Single Sister Experiment. Congratulations, ladies! Mission accomplished!"

Reader's Group Guide

1. Minister Makita asked Joan to give a speech entitled "What I wished somebody would have told me before I had sex for the first time." If this applies to you, name something you wish somebody had told you before you had sex.

2. Minister Makita told the women about her drug addiction, jail time, and promiscuous lifestyle as a younger woman. She was also blunt in explaining how sex outside of marriage is a sin. How did Makita's style of teaching relate to her effectiveness as a speaker? Would you have been drawn into the message like Joan or would you have found Makita's presentation insensitive and ineffective? Do more ministers of the gospel need to adopt her style or was Makita's message hindered by her outspokenness?

3. Joan was compassionate when she saw Proxy Justice's music video. How do you

feel about celebrities who claim to be Christians yet their music and videos do not reflect Jesus Christ? How have celebrities, talk show hosts, or professional athletes influenced you?

4. Sage gave her baby up for adoption because she didn't want her child to grow up without a father. In Sage's position, what would you have done and why?

5. Joan didn't think she could live without sex. What have you overcome/accomplished with God's help that previously seemed impossible?

6. Joan confronted her father over his absence in her life but she never confronted her mother with the letter she wrote her or the information Aunt Alice had told her. Why do you think Joan chose not to confront her mother?

7. Joan wrote about her hopes, failures, and unresolved pain in a journal. What were the benefits of journaling? Have you ever kept a journal? Why or why not? Imagine Joan rereading her journal from the beginning of the experiment years later. Do you think she would be surprised by some of her entries? Why or why not?

8. When Minister Makita found out Joan was reading the Bible in its entirety she made this statement, "You are going to mature more in three years than most Christians do in thirty." Do you agree or disagree with Makita? Why or why not?

9. Janet had previously had sex outside of marriage, yet when she became a Christian

she stopped. She met and dated Jerome two and half years and they didn't have sex until their wedding night. Do you believe this is possible? Why or why not?

10. Joan, Tisha, and Lila avoided Janet after Janet became a Christian, yet when Joan became a Christian she still could not get herself to contact Janet. Would you have called Janet or would you have responded the same way Joan did? Why?

11. Joan understood Jesus Christ had died for her sins yet she was still plagued with guilt. What would you say to Joan about her guilt over past failures?

12. The Single Sister Experiment is fiction, but what do you think would happen if all single women really did stop having sex? Would men change? How would our children be affected? Would marriages increase?

Brothers Trilogy

Danny

ZOE ZIMMERMAN

BANTAM BOOKS

NEW YORK · TORONTO · LONDON · SYDNEY · AUCKLAND

RL: 6, AGES 012 AND UP

DANNY

A Bantam Book / May 2000

Cover photography by Michael Segal.

Produced by 17th Street Productions,
an Alloy Online, Inc. company.
33 West 17th Street
New York, NY 10011.

ISBN: 0-553-49322-1

Visit us on the Web! www.randomhouse.com/teens

Published simultaneously in the United States and Canada

PRINTED IN THE UNITED STATES OF AMERICA

OPM   0 9 8 7 6 5 4 3 2 1

One

"LET SUMMER BEGIN!" Kevin Ford declared as he hurled his backpack across the living room. It hit the torn couch against the wall with a poof of dust, then landed on the old carpet with a thud.

"Guess it's the cleaning lady's year off," Johnny Ford commented, waving dust motes from the air in front of his face.

"Cleanliness is for the weak," Kevin scoffed.

Danny Ford rolled his eyes. It was hard to believe: Two days ago he was in a classroom at Spring Valley High. Now he was at the beach.

This is it, he thought, surveying the apartment and letting his duffel bag hit the floor. *This is where I'm going to spend the summer. The wet, wild . . . widiculous summer before my junior year. Shouldn't I be just a little more psyched?*

It was a bittersweet deal, he figured. Sweet in

1

that his parents were letting him and his brothers spend their summer in Surf City, one of the hottest beach towns on the southern California coast. Bitter in that he had to live *with* his two brothers in a rattrap apartment. Wasn't it bad enough that he spent his whole life sandwiched between seventeen-year-old Johnny and fifteen-year-old Kevin like some sixteen-year-old cold cut? And now he had to share his space with them during his summer vacation.

Ha, he thought, *this ain't no va-cay. I'll be working at the restaurant every day just to break even on this little money pit.*

Pit was a generous term. The door of the apartment opened into a small, dank living room with a couch, a lounge chair, and a coffee table that looked ready to collapse under the weight of a soda bottle. To the left was the kitchen, a space marked off by stained, peeling linoleum and another precarious table. The stove had two gas burners and probably couldn't reheat a pizza. The refrigerator was small, squat, and rattled and hummed louder than U2.

The whole place was done up in an early seventies paneling the color of stale caramel. The meager decorations consisted of a painting of an old man in a dinghy and three crookedly hung sand dollars, each mounted and framed on red felt.

"Cool, cozy, comfortable," Kevin declared. He jumped over the duct-taped arm of the Barca-lounger that was so rat eaten, it made the chair in Frasier Crane's living room look positively chic. In midair Kevin crossed his feet and assumed a relaxation position. The springs squealed on impact, sending up a mushroom cloud of mildew as thick as a feather pillow. "Ahhh . . . I do believe I can live here."

"You could live in a hollowed-out pumpkin," Johnny said, rubbing the dust out of his brown eyes.

"Nah, too humid," Kevin replied as he looked through his framed fingers at a space in the corner—no doubt plotting where the TV should go. "But give me a shoe box, a burlap sack, and some blank paper, and I'm good to go."

"Artists have to suffer, Kev," Danny said. He stretched muscles, cramped from the four-hour Jeep ride. "You're too enthusiastic."

"Suffering's in the eye of the sufferer," Kevin stated, now framing the front window. He leaned forward, gazing more intently at the world through the glass. "Hey . . . not a bad view. You can see the water."

Johnny dumped his bag on the kitchen table a few feet away. Somehow it didn't collapse. "That's why we're paying for 'ocean view,' brainiac. You get this close to the boardwalk, they can charge you seven bills a week for a wet shoe box." He ran his hand along the kitchen countertop, scowled, and quickly wiped his fingers on his shorts. "Man, it smells like Dad's bowling-ball bag in here."

Danny smirked. His brother wasn't that far off. In one breath you could smell the clean salt air, the french fries off the boardwalk, and coconut suntan oil (hopefully smeared on tan female limbs). In the next breath you got old sweat dried into couch cushions and leftover lobster.

"I'm just glad we found a place," Danny pointed out. "We were lucky. We waited way too long."

"Hey, you were the one who wasn't sure if he wanted to come," Kevin shot back. He yanked the handle on the side of the lounge chair and reclined it with a loud creak and thud. "Are you ever sure of anything, Danny?"

"Gee, I'm not sure," Danny replied, though he felt his face growing red. The truth really did hurt sometimes. Danny truly wasn't sure about a lot of things.

He felt pressure mounting from all sides. He was sixteen. He had to start "getting serious" . . . "thinking about the future" . . . "deciding what he wanted to do with his life." Name your cliché, he heard them all—and from all directions. Parents. Teachers. Friends. And older brother, of course.

Johnny was the example everyone used. He worked hard. He had been accepted at a great college. And he'd probably go on to make lots of money and make everyone proud. Which was great for Johnny. There was just one problem. Since Johnny was doing it, everyone naturally expected Danny to do the same thing.

But he didn't know what he wanted.

Nope, not a clue.

He hoped that this summer would show him

4

something. Anything. Actually, he knew that was asking too much. But his life was such a gray area. His brothers knew exactly what they wanted to do with their lives. Johnny was a numbers whiz. He loved money. Well, everyone loved money, but Johnny truly *loved* it. He knew how to make it and, better yet, how to keep it. He was all set to attend Allman College in the fall for, you guessed it, finance.

Kevin, on the other hand, was a one-eighty spin. At fifteen he could draw, and that was about it. But, man, *what* he could draw with pen, pencil, charcoal, and occasionally paint. Anything and everything, as long as it fit his strange world-view. And if it didn't fit? Kevin made it fit. And he was great at it. He could create whole comic strips or serious portraits—yet his signature style always shone through. Danny figured if Kevin could use his titanic charm to get the Kate Winslets of the world to take off their robes and pose for him, he had a pretty bright future. Might even make some money.

There's that word again, Danny thought. Money. *The word that brought on all those other words:* future, college, career, direction.

Danny knew what those words meant, but they didn't apply to him. At least not yet.

What did he like, after all? He'd rolled it through his head countless times. The likes-dislikes. The pros-cons. The possibilities that seemed oh so impossible.

Music. That was it. He liked music. But he

couldn't play it. He'd tried both the guitar and piano and lasted maybe two weeks on both. Playing music had to be in the soul. You were supposed to feel something magical when you picked up an instrument. Danny felt nothing.

But when he listened to music? Danny was moved. His heart raced, his spine tingled. He felt alive. It didn't matter what kind of music: metal, punk, ska, hip-hop, and good old rock and roll. He loved the purer forms as well: blues, jazz, and classical.

His CD collection was in the triple digits. He'd have bought more if he had the money (that word again), but he also maintained an extensive bootleg collection that he taped from friends and the public library. All those cost him were a few bucks' worth of blank cassettes.

But what good did it do him? To enter the musical realm in college, you had to play. You couldn't major in "listening." And even if you could, what kind of a job could you get?

DJ.

Great, Danny thought. *I'll play weddings and bar mitzvahs for the rest of my life, one step below Adam Sandler because at least he could sing. What would that make me? The Wedding Jockey?*

Danny's day-mare was broken by Johnny clapping. "Okay, bros, let's get the Jeep unpacked and set this joint up. We can draw straws on who gets the couch."

Danny and Kevin just stared at their older brother.

Johnny clapped again. "Come on, bums, stop acting homeless, and let's get to work. We have a lot to do, and tomorrow's no holiday."

Kevin turned to Danny with a quizzical look. "Who invited Dad?"

"Not me," Danny replied, not budging.

"Don't start this again," Johnny grumbled, folding his arms across his chest. "Mom and Dad never would have let you two come if I wasn't here to watch over you." He shook his head. "Besides, you think all our stuff is just going to walk itself up here? Someone has to kick your butts, or nothing would ever get done."

"Another Dad-ism," Kevin muttered, wearily rising from the lounge chair. "You really need some new material, John Boy."

Johnny shrugged. "Fine. I'm hauling my stuff up here, and I'm taking the back bedroom."

"You are not," Kevin growled. "We draw straws, just like you said."

"Hey, bud, you snooze, you lose on the sleeping quarters," Johnny told him. "I'm not playing nurse-maid to you guys. Your gear can sit in the parking lot all summer for all I care. But it is *not* sitting in my Jeep. Get it?"

Kevin glowered. "Yeah, you never know when Mr. Happy here might get a visit from the Ice Princess."

Danny smiled. "Hope the Jeep has fresh antifreeze, John Boy."

Johnny's face darkened, and Danny immediately

saw the old familiar "madman" Johnny face. He knew his brothers' facial tics like veteran actors in a long-running TV show. The "madman" showed up anytime anyone criticized Johnny's girlfriend of three years, Jane.

"I'm not biting, Kevin," Johnny said coolly. "The ride was too long, and the summer's just starting. You just have to deal with the fact that Jane's gonna be around. I love her, and that's the way it is."

"Awwww," Kevin cooed. "How sweet. Have some insulin with that sugar?"

Johnny's face hardened, and he took a step toward Kevin. Danny moved between them, bumping chests with his older brother. "I think what my younger brother, Kevin, is trying to say is that Jane is perfectly welcome here anytime, Johnny. But just because you have a steady girl doesn't mean you get automatic dibs on a bedroom."

"Says who?" Johnny challenged.

"Says the unsilent majority, pal," Kevin shot back. "Two bedrooms. Three guys. We draw straws just like we agreed three months ago."

"Hold it, hold it, hold it." Danny held up his hands. His brothers glared at him as if he had changed the channel in the middle of the Super Bowl. "This is ridiculous. It's the first day. I'm sick of you guys already. I'll take the couch for the first month of the summer. Okay? Then I get a bedroom, and you two can fight over the last two months. Does that work for you knuckleheads?"

They chewed on it for a moment. Finally Kevin spoke. "We should draw straws."

"Forget the straws," Johnny replied, turning toward the door. "Danny, if you want the couch, great, man. I don't care. Whatever the two of you decide is fine by me. I'm not wasting my time on this kiddie turf war anymore. All I know is that two months out of three, I get a bed."

"Just like we all do, Johnny," Danny replied.

Johnny nodded, kicked open the apartment door, and disappeared.

Kevin sidled up to Danny, smiling. "Nice to have him along, don't you think?"

"What did you expect?" Danny asked.

Kevin clapped a hand on Danny's shoulder and mock hugged his brother. "You know what I expect, Dan-o? I'll tell you what I expect. I expect nothing less than the summer of my life. I expect to meet and fall in love with four to five beautiful older women per month. I expect to eat leftover pizza and have garlic breath. I expect to fill countless sketch pads with the bikini-clad forms of nubile beach beauties. I expect parties, romance, and endless intrigue—you know, as seen on TV. But most of all, and I think you'll agree with me on this one, I expect to bring home a big, fat volleyball trophy and a check for ten thousand dollars."

Danny smiled at his younger brother.

"Yeah," Danny replied, punching Kevin's fist with his own. "That sounds about right."

★   ★   ★

The Surf City 3-on-3 Beach Volleyball Tournament was the Ford brothers' primary reason for existing. *If we don't kill each other first,* Danny thought.

As Johnny and Kevin carted their stuff up the three flights of steps from the Jeep, Danny unpacked his gear in the living room (as much as he dared unpack clothing in that "public" space. Who needed his boxers paraded in front of guests?). He hadn't packed much: one duffel bag, a CD boom box, a CD Walkman, a cassette Walkman, and a large plastic crate full of CDs and tapes. Danny had brought roughly one-third of his collection because of space. This had meant boiling down his music stash into the bare essentials: greatest-hits collections and live albums, which gave him the most music in the least amount of space. There were some classics that he couldn't live without, of course, but the three days it took him to pack his music was an endless torture of indecision and sacrifice.

Let's not talk about indecision anymore, Danny told himself. Living in a constant gray area was bad enough. He didn't need to torture himself with it.

He forced himself to think about something important. Something that raised the stakes and got his adrenaline pumping: volleyball.

Johnny was the one who had suggested it. Danny remembered the day six months ago when his older bro assembled them at the local burger joint and presented them with a daring idea. "Dudes, listen up. You remember how we always

10

talked about playing v-ball for something meaning-ful? Well, listen to this. . . ."

Johnny had gone on to describe the mother of all beach-volleyball tournaments: the Surf City War. The official name was the Fizz Cola Surf City 3-on-3 Beach Volleyball Tournament, but v-ballers up and down the California coast referred to it sim-ply as The War. Anyone who ever spiked one into another guy's face knew the significance of this tournament. If you won, you took home a five-foot trophy, a lifetime supply of Fizz Cola, and ten thou-sand dollars in cash.

But that was just the hardware.

What you really won was the undisputed bragging rights to the most coveted amateur-beach-volleyball championship on the West Coast. Danny liked to put it this way: Pretend the World Series is a kaiser roll. Slice it in half, pile on some Stanley Cup mustard, a few slices of Olympic gold medal, and a generous helping of Super Bowl, and that sweet-tasting sand-wich would be eaten in one sitting by the Surf City War trophy.

"Heads up!" Johnny screamed.

Danny heard the familiar slap of skin on ball be-fore the cry and instinctively turned, hands up. He caught the volleyball on the fly.

"You're gonna have to do better than that, bro." Danny laughed. "Your serve needs work."

"So, show me the mustard, hot dog," Johnny jeered, gesturing for Danny to bring it on.

Danny did.

11

He tossed the ball lightly and popped it with his palm, cutting across the axis with his fingers. The ball sprang from his hand, firing toward Johnny like a comet. But halfway there, it began to fade away from him toward the kitchen. By the time the ball reached Johnny, it had curled a good two feet to the right, losing none of its velocity.

Johnny lunged for it but missed. The ball caromed off the kitchen cabinets and floor like a wayward bullet.

"Ace, dude," Danny declared. "You lose."

Johnny snagged the ball and palmed it. "I still don't know how you do that, Danny. You serve like that in the tournament, and we're golden."

Danny shrugged. "The tourney's two months away. We'll go crazy between now and then."

"No way," Johnny replied. "Between practice and pickup games on the beach, we'll be sharper than ever. I guarantee it."

"You're George Foreman now?" Kevin asked, emerging from his bedroom. "You could use a muffler."

Johnny tossed him the ball. "Just getting psyched. I can taste that ten-grand check already."

"Forget the money, man," Kevin replied, dribbling the ball through his legs. "I'll be the youngest v-ball champ on the West Coast. I'll be Velcro, and chicks'll be felt."

"Pun intended, right?" Johnny said with a smirk.

"Of course," Kevin replied, wiggling his eyebrows.

Danny was grateful for the moment of peace. They were rare. Volleyball was the glue that held the Ford brothers together. If that fell apart, they would probably kill each other. They were so different. The championship was a prime example. Johnny wanted the cash. Kevin wanted the fame. What did that leave for Danny? The lifetime supply of Fizz Cola.

Not bloody likely.

No, Danny clung to volleyball because it gave his life direction. When the money talk, the college chat, or the future fantasies got too intense, there was music. And there was volleyball. In a way, the Surf City championship was the ultimate goal for him. But on the other hand, winning it scared him. Not because he was intimidated by the competition or afraid of failure.

He was scared of winning because after that there would be nothing in his life left for him to shoot for.

Soon the day grew long, and the sun set over the water outside their front window. It was then that the Ford brothers took advantage of the one civilized perk of their rattrap apartment: the balcony. It was tiny, no more than three feet by ten feet, but it was still a balcony that faced the ocean.

Danny took a deep breath of salt air and sighed. Not bad. He could see the whitecaps now turning crimson in the glare. The waves crashed, devouring the dusk surfers like predinner snacks. On the sand the last of the shriveled sun worshipers folded their chairs for the night.

And three stories below the brothers, rolling off in either direction like a spool of toy railroad, was the Surf City boardwalk. The flashing lights were just winking on. The pizza and fries hit the counters and filled the air with the thick scent of grease. People trundled along, moms wheeling their jogger strollers, tourists slurping down ice cream cones, kids tugging the parents' arms for more, more, more. In-line skaters click-clacked along, weaving in and out of all of them.

"I love the beach," Kevin said wistfully, watching a gorgeous redhead in a black bikini top and cutoff shorts skate her way toward Mexico.

"Yeah, well, we'll see how much you like it after a couple of weeks of cleaning up after the snobby slobs at the hotel, Kev," Danny replied, leaning on the rail and sipping a soda.

Kevin shrugged, as if his job as a cabana boy at the ritzy Surf City Resort Hotel was no sweat off his back. "At least I won't be schlepping buffalo wings for ten-percent tips at Jabba's Palace."

Danny chuckled. Because that's exactly what he was going to be doing. Jabba's Palace was a greasy spoon disguised as fine dining about twenty blocks down the boardwalk. It was named after its owner, an overfed monster of a man who was known only as Jabba. Danny had met him just once, when the brothers came to Surf City in the spring to secure summer jobs. But Jabba wasn't the kind of man you forgot.

"Remember, guys," Johnny cautioned. "It's not about the jobs. It's about the money. We have to pay for this palace."

"That's easy for you to say," Danny replied. "You're a lifeguard at the poshest hotel in town. You get to do the *Baywatch* thing in front of rich, lonely women in bathing suits."

Johnny was set to work the Surf City Resort Hotel's private beach and pool, a cushy summer job if there ever was one.

"Hey, all you had to do was get certified," Johnny shot back. "I put in a lot of hours for that. It's no picnic."

Kevin grinned. "All I have to say is that if I hear, 'Oh, cabana boy, get me a towel,' from your mouth just one time, you're toast. Got me?"

Johnny laughed, shoving his smaller but wiry little brother. "Okay, shrimp. Do your worst."

Kevin held up his hands in surrender. "Just getting it out in the open right now. Just because we work at the same place doesn't mean you can boss me around."

"Whatever you say, Kev," Johnny snapped sarcastically. "Whatever you say."

"If you guys are through barking at each other," Danny interrupted, "I'd like to propose a toast." He raised his plastic twenty ouncer of Fizz Cola. "To The War. Here's hoping we survive each other long enough to win it."

His brothers nodded and raised their own sodas. "To The War," they said in unison.

15

They drank. And for a moment Danny felt like he truly belonged to something special, something beyond even brotherhood. They were united in a single purpose—something that was bigger than anything they'd ever done by themselves. They needed each other like never before.

Danny enjoyed the feeling. But it was going to be a long, hot summer. And none of them really knew what would happen. Still, Danny savored the moment and the first sunset in their new home.

Because for that moment the possibilities really were endless.

TWO

"GIMME A CHEESY fish, a side of waffle fries, and three blue heart attacks!" bellowed Archie, a hippie wanna-be with a long, red ponytail and grease stains on his apron.

Danny tried to do the translation in his head: *Cheesy fish . . . That's a tuna melt. . . . Waffle fries are, well, waffle fries . . . and three blue heart attacks are three half-pound burgers stuffed with blue-cheese dressing.* There were also gold (cheddar) heart attacks, red (chili) heart attacks, Italian (alfredo sauce) heart attacks, and, believe it or not, canine (hot-dog) heart attacks. Leave it to Jabba to stuff a hamburger with a hot dog.

If all of that was too much, you could order from Jabba's "light" menu: Caesar salad with anchovies.

"I *do* cook light," Danny had overheard Jabba say earlier to a customer. "I use butter instead of lard!"

Jabba's Palace was basically a hole-in-the-wall.

17

But on the Surf City boardwalk, that didn't matter. Several sets of peeling shutter doors opened onto the boards, providing some relief from the heavy air. Ceiling fans spun overhead, the blades coated with greasy dust. The tables were ancient, made of thick wood and covered with paper tablecloths that were crumpled up and tossed in the garbage when each feeding frenzy was through.

At lunch and dinner people lined up out the door, waiting for a table. Grease was popular, after all, and Jabba's heart attacks were renowned up and down the boards. If you came to Surf City, you ate at Jabba's. It was that simple.

Jabba roamed his restaurant like a tank, cracking jokes and cracking cholesterol records. He didn't really resemble the *Star Wars* Jabba, but he was in a physical league of his own. He stood about five-seven and had to weigh at least four hundred pounds. His whole body was involved with each step. The lower half of his face was covered with black-gray hair, which made his crew cut even more strange. His cackle could be heard out on the boardwalk. And his jokes were terrible.

Danny just tried to keep his head down and his orders straight. The wait staff had a language all its own, and he found himself having to learn on the fly. Burgers were heart attacks (because Jabba marinated the meat in a garlic butter sauce before grilling), hot dogs were canines, buffalo wings were lipstick, and nachos were junk piles because of the size of the servings.

18

He sidled up to table six. The couple there ordered two heart attacks, blue and gold, a dozen lipsticks, and fries. Easy one.

Table four was a family of five. Three heart attacks, a cheesy fish, and four canines. Fries and Fizz all around.

Danny posted his orders as fast as he could. Jabba liked turnover, turnover, turnover.

Table seven, seven attacks and seven pitchers of beer. "Seven pitchers?" Danny asked, glancing up from his notepad.

The table was filled with little old ladies in sun hats.

"Seven pitchers, kid," one old lady grumbled in a voice that sounded like a dirt road. "You heard right."

Danny grinned. "No problem."

The day rolled on like that. He was scheduled to work from noon to ten, with one half-hour break for dinner. At minimum wage plus tips Danny figured to break even after rent and living expenses. *Ha,* he thought. *You have to have a life to have living expenses.* His one day off a week, Monday, left him with minimal free time.

I didn't want a tan anyway, he reasoned.

"Yo, kid, where's my burger?" barked a customer to his left.

Uh-oh. "You ordered a tuna melt, sir."

The guy, an overweight father of two, rolled his eyes and glared at his family as if to say: What kind of moron am I dealing with? "No, kid," he replied

19

with mock patience. "I ordered a hot-dog burger ten minutes ago. The rest of my family has their food. I got squat. You wanna check your little notebook again?"

Danny frantically flipped pages. His face grew hot.

The guy cursed. "Can you believe this? Yo, kid. Forget the notebook. Just bring me my burger."

"Hot-dog burger?" Danny confirmed. "Not a tuna melt?"

The guy balled up a napkin in his fist and forced a smile. "Very good, kid. There may be a future for you in food service yet."

"What's the problem here?" came a loud voice.

Danny felt Jabba's presence before the man spoke. *Like a disturbance in the Force,* he thought glumly. *Great. Now I'm in for it.*

"Your boy here," the guy growled, gesturing at Danny with contempt, "is trying to cover his butt. I'm waitin' on a hot-dog burger for half an hour now."

"Half an hour?" Danny blurted out. "More like ten minutes!"

Jabba turned full bore on Danny. "I don't know how they wait tables in Pleasantville or wherever you came from, kid, but here in the big leagues we don't usually refer to our customers as liars."

Rage churned in Danny's belly. The guy at the table smirked in triumph. Jabba folded his arms across his thick chest, breathing through his mouth like an idling freight train. "Well?" he asked impatiently.

Danny took a deep breath and swallowed his anger. "I'll get the burger."

Jabba grabbed his sleeve. "Hold it, kid. Don't you have something else to say to these nice people?"

Boy, do I, Danny thought. He glared at the guy and his smug little family and tried not to lose it. "I'm sorry, sir. I'll bring your burger right out."

"Hurry it up, will you?" the guy replied. "My kids want to hit the Spiral Terror before the line gets too long."

The Spiral Terror. The killer roller coaster on the amusement pier. *Hope they lose their lunches,* Danny thought. "Right away, sir," he said snappily, and headed for the kitchen. As he moved away, he clearly heard Jabba's comment to the man:

"That's what you get for minimum wage these days. . . ."

Danny was allowed to take his break at four-thirty, before the hard-core dinner rush. Jabba allowed his employees to have a free soda and fries. Anything else had to be paid for.

Danny had to get out of there. In four and a half hours he'd served something like fifty heart attacks, which he figured was illegal in some states. He needed air and space and sunlight. Danny poured himself a tall Fizz and snagged some waffle fries in a plastic basket lined with wax paper. He drowned them in ketchup to cover the grease and slipped between two tables and out a door to the boardwalk.

21

He took a deep breath and sighed, picturing thick wafts of steam floating out of his clothes. Jabba's Palace was like a chamber of bad breath. Danny hadn't realized just how bad it was until he smelled the clean salt air.

Finally, he thought. *Peace . . .*

He took a step toward a bench on the other side of the boardwalk.

Then someone slammed into him at what felt like sixty miles an hour. The air whooshed out of Danny's lungs. The boardwalk felt like concrete on his shoulder and hip. And the french fries, soda, and ketchup felt like a hot blanket of slime on his face.

Aw, man . . .

"Dude!" screamed a deep, enraged voice. "Scumbag! Moron! Dog! Get up!"

Danny stared up into the face of a freak. His head was shaved clean on the sides, leaving a bristly blue patch up on top. His eyes were wide and angry. His front teeth were crooked, and his eye-teeth were long and vampiric. A shark-tooth ear-ring dangled from one ear. He wore a torn Marilyn Manson T-shirt and canvas shorts low on his waist. The shirt was stained with ketchup. His arms were flexed and ready. Veins ran up his forearms like thick phone wiring.

"I said get up!" he repeated.

Danny slowly rose, trying hard to figure out what had just happened. Then he saw the upside-down skateboard stained with ketchup. This guy had been motoring down the boardwalk and slammed into him. Danny's dinner was spread out in a ten-foot radius. And this guy now wanted a piece of him.

Danny straightened up to his full height. The skateboarder was still a good three inches taller. His teeth looked even worse close up.

"Why you in my way, pretty boy?" the guy demanded, his face closing in on Danny's. "You got ketchup all over my shirt! I *hate* ketchup!"

"Smear him, Doberman," came another male voice.

Three more skate rats skidded to a halt around the pair. All of them were dressed in various versions of Doberman, though they were smaller and skinnier. One rat hauled a boom box cranked up to distortion.

Finally a fourth skate rat clattered up. A girl. She stomped on the fin of her board, popping it vertical and grabbing it in midair. She had pink streaks running through her shoulder-length brown hair. Her ears were loaded down with rings of varying shapes and sizes. Her shredded jeans revealed flashes of smooth leg underneath. She wore a black spaghetti-string tank top that hugged her form like a second skin.

It was a real nice form, Danny thought.

But what drew Danny's stare was the girl's eyes. Smoky gray eyes, wide and clear. Full of casual amusement at Danny.

"Hey, cupcake," Doberman grunted, smacking Danny's shoulder. "I'm talkin' to you."

23

Danny broke away from the girl. "So? What's the problem? You weren't looking where you were going."

Doberman's eyes widened. "Me? *Me?* Moron boy, you are about three seconds away from instant death."

Danny smiled and wiped his face with a crumpled napkin. "If it takes three seconds, it's not very instant, is it?"

The skate rats surrounding them ooohed as if Danny had just smacked Doberman in the face with a white glove. And maybe he had.

Danny had never considered himself a fighter. But he wasn't one to back down either. Right now he was tired, frustrated, and still facing more than five hours of work. All he wanted to do was have a soda and fries. But surveying the overturned basket and crushed soda cup, he knew that wasn't happening.

Doberman grinned his nasty teeth and flexed. "Okay, pretty boy. Prepare to eat your tongue."

"Dobie, don't," the girl interrupted.

Doberman scowled but didn't take his eyes off Danny. "Shut up, Raven. You know I hate ketchup."

Raven laughed sarcastically. "What I know is you're acting like a jerk again. This guy didn't mean it. Leave him alone."

The frustration grew in Doberman. Whatever hold this Raven had on him—call it a leash for Doberman—was working. Danny hoped so anyway.

24

There was no way he could take this guy . . . and he couldn't back down now.

"Okay, pretty boy," Doberman said, massaging a fist, his restraint obvious. "I have a better idea. We'll play a little game. If you win, you walk. If you lose, you go down. *Comprende?*"

Danny shook his head and looked back at Jabba's Palace. "I don't have time for this—"

Doberman yanked Danny back by the shirt. "Make time, pretty boy."

Rage overflowed in Danny. He batted Doberman's hand away and got in his face. "Okay, pal, what's it gonna be?"

Doberman yanked the boom box from his bud and brandished it like a weapon. "Simple game, pretty boy." He put his ear to the thudding speaker. "You hear that?"

Danny shrugged. "The whole block can hear it. So what?"

"So, pretty boy . . ." Doberman grinned devilishly. "Name that tune."

Danny glanced at the boom box. The speakers were shot. The sound getting through barely resembled music at all.

One of the skate rats giggled. "He's toast, dude."

Danny surveyed the circle surrounding him. They all looked the same: badly dyed and shaved hair, torn concert shirts, ripped jeans slung low. Their eyes were playful and indignant. They seemed smug in the knowledge that there was no chance

Danny could possibly recognize this little musical slice of their rebellious life. No chance at all.

The girl, Raven, smirked the worst of them all. She rocked back and forth on her heels to the beat, fingering a skull ring on her left hand. Her smoky gray eyes regarded Danny with pure amusement—and a hint of boredom. As if she enjoyed his challenge of Doberman but knew that it would all be over in a few seconds.

They all figured Danny was played.

That's when he blurted out, "'Chainsaw Perfume,' by the Dustmites."

Doberman blinked. "Say what?"

Danny smiled. "You heard me."

"Wrong, pretty boy." Doberman shook his head. "Not even close. It's 'CIA Is for Apple,' by Ball Peen Hammer." He flexed his forearms. "You lose. Prepare to die."

"Dobie—," one of the rats began.

"Shut up, Skunk," Doberman growled.

"He's *right,* Dobe," another rat argued.

Doberman whirled on the guy named Skunk. "He is *not* right, dude. That's Ball Peen Hammer. I gave you the tape myself."

"Yeah." Skunk nodded. "And I switched it a half hour ago to the Dustmites. I was sick of the noise."

"He's right, Dobe," the other rat repeated.

Doberman was really frustrated now. "So what if he's right? He got ketchup all over me."

Doberman balled a fist . . .

26

Here we go, Danny thought.

He prepared to dodge it, but before anything could happen, the punk girl stepped between him and Doberman. In the process she brushed against Danny. He could smell her hair, a combination of fragrant shampoo and mousse. She had a small mole on the back of her neck.

"Fair's fair, Dobie," she said to the big guy, gently pushing him away. "He knew the song. You didn't even know the band."

Doberman bristled. "I don't care about right or wrong. Pretty boy was *in my way*."

Raven smirked. "Everyone's in your way. That's why you're Doberman." Then she turned and stared right into Danny's eyes. "But maybe pretty boy's a cooler cat than anyone thinks."

Danny gulped. This girl had enough ear piercings to hang laundry, and her hair was a rainbow of fruit flavors. But she was gorgeous beyond the hardware. He could see her face so much better close-up. Some black eyeliner around those smoky grays. A beautiful smile. He couldn't help the butterflies in his belly. They fluttered even worse when she stared at him . . . like she was doing right now. He didn't say a word.

"Let's roll, dude," Skunk suggested. "This scene's played out."

"I agree," Raven replied, still staring at Danny. "Don't you agree, Doberman?"

Doberman kicked over his skateboard and stepped on it. "Yeah. Right. Whatever. Fine."

Raven smiled at him. "Thought so."

Doberman leveled a deadly stare at Danny. "Watch yourself, pretty boy. Next time there won't be any games. Next time it's just me and you and the black 'n' blue. *Comprende?*"

Danny shrugged. "Sure, why not?"

Doberman pushed off and rolled down the boardwalk. Skunk and the other two guys followed suit. But Raven didn't move from her spot next to Danny. She was only inches away.

"Thanks for holding him off," Danny said, trying to catch her gray eyes again. But she was gazing down the boards after her friends.

"De nada," she replied.

Danny didn't say anything right away. Neither did Raven. She didn't budge either.

What's her deal? he wondered. Not that he minded her staying . . .

Finally she turned and met his gaze. "So . . . just how cool a cat are you?"

Danny smiled. "How cool can anyone be when they're covered with ketchup?"

Raven laughed.

"Yo, Raven!" Doberman called from down the boardwalk. "Let's roll!"

Raven dropped her board and stepped onto it. Her eyes never left Danny's.

She's leaving, he thought. *Say something. Say anything. Pull a John Cusack.* But nothing came to mind. All Danny could do was watch her push off and slowly roll away.

She smirked and gave a mocking buh-bye wave.

"Later, pretty boy," she said. "If you're lucky."

All Danny could do was stand there, struck dumb. In seconds Raven pushed off for real and disappeared into the crowd. She was gone.

Danny blinked stupidly, smelling like Fizz and fries.

Who *was* that girl?

What I Look for in a Guy
by Raven

1. Attitude. 'Nuf said.

2. Skating ability. I mean, a guy's gotta be able to keep up with me.

3. A sense of humor. It's a cliché, but hey, it's a cliché for a reason, right? Being able to laugh with someone is the best.

4. Intelligence. He doesn't have to be a brain, but I need someone to make me think.

5. Piercings. (Okay, I can overlook this.)

6. Eyes. I don't know—something about the eyes always grabs me. They're honest, I guess.

Three

THE NEXT MORNING Danny, Johnny, and Kevin hit the beach for a quick hour of volleyball practice. They found a deserted beach court several blocks away—not many people played beach volleyball at nine in the morning. They warmed up by casually knocking the ball around. Johnny and Kevin stood on one side, setting and spiking. Danny took the other side, serving.

"I think I'm going to have the smell of towel detergent on me permanently," Kevin complained, referring to his first day on the job. "Do you know how many towels I delivered yesterday? In one day? Guess."

"I'm not going to guess," Johnny replied, making a V with his arms and expertly setting up the ball so Kevin could spike it. "Besides, no matter how rotten your day was, it couldn't beat mine. My new lifeguard partner is Kylie Smith."

31

"And that's supposed to mean something?" Danny asked.

"Guess!" Kevin demanded, simultaneously slamming the ball over the net and into the sand.

"Dude, just guess," Danny grumbled, fetching the ball.

"One hundred eighty-two," Kevin declared, clapping sand off his hands. "That's one-eight-two. In one day. I didn't know there were that many wet rich people in the world."

Danny tossed up the ball and slapped it across the net, a straight serve with no English. "You make any tips, cabana boy?"

"Yeah," Kevin scoffed, shaking his head. He took a step back, lined up Danny's serve, and popped it straight up for Johnny. "Ten bucks and one practice-safe-sex tip from old Mr. Moran. That guy's like two hundred years old, and he needs five towels to dry off after being in the pool. What a gig."

Johnny timed Kevin's set perfectly, leaving the ground and stretching his body to its full length. His muscles worked in poetic unison as he walloped the volleyball across the net and into the sand at the speed of sound. That was Johnny's strength—his height and form allowed him to generate incredible spikes.

"Kylie Smith is Jane's total enemy. Can you believe that? We come all the way to Surf City, and I end up working with someone that not only does my girlfriend know, she hates." Johnny sighed.

"But, hey. I'll deal. The cash is great, and that's what I'm in it for." He turned to Danny. "How about you? Make any money?"

That word again. Danny chuckled. "Yeah, lots. Ten hours. Twenty-two in tips. And a faceful of ketchup."

"What do you mean?" Kevin asked, laughing.

Danny told them about his close encounter with Doberman and friends. He included the fries, ketchup, and music test. But he didn't mention Raven.

Kevin laughed even harder. "Cool, Dan-o. Very smooth."

Johnny scooped up the volleyball from the sand and eyed his younger bro skeptically. "You faced this skinhead down all by yourself?"

Danny shrugged. "I wouldn't call him a skinhead. He was just a skate rat. But yeah, I faced him down. All by myself." Then he thought of Raven. "Basically."

"Aha," Johnny said, nodding as he tossed the ball from hand to hand. "What's basically?"

Danny felt himself blushing. Luckily he was on the other side of the net, where they couldn't see.

"Speak up, Dan-o," Kevin called, folding his arms across his chest. "I didn't hear you."

Danny shrugged. "Well . . . I sort of met a chick."

Johnny and Kevin shared a look and burst out laughing. "You *sort* of met a chick?" Johnny asked. "How do you *sort* of meet a chick?"

33

"We weren't formally introduced," Danny replied with forced impatience, as if he didn't want to talk about Raven, even though he really did. "I caught her name when the rats talked to her."

"What, she was walking down the boardwalk?" Kevin inquired.

Danny shook his head. "She was with them. She stepped between me and Doberman just before the first swing."

Johnny looked quizzically at Danny, then casually bumped the ball over the net at him. "The chick's a skate rat?"

"Basically," Danny replied again. He caught the volleyball and held it, grateful to have something to do with his hands. "She doesn't look like a rat, though."

"She hot?" Kevin asked expectantly.

Danny nodded, thinking of Raven's gray eyes. "Smokin'."

"Of course she is," Johnny said. "Except for the shaved head, right?"

"You wish," Danny shot back. "The girl's totally hot. Why's that so hard to believe?"

Johnny shrugged. "I've never seen a hot skate rat."

"Oh, I get it," Danny replied. "If a girl isn't fit for the J. Crew catalog, she couldn't possibly be hot. Is that it?"

Johnny moved forward to the net, spidering his fingers through it and letting his weight pull it down slightly. He hung there. "Are you dating this girl, Danny?"

"Nope," Danny replied, coolly twirling the volleyball on his finger.

Kevin laughed. "Then why are you so sensitive about her?"

The ball spun on Danny's finger for two seconds and fell to the sand. "The girl helped me out. I said she happened to be hot. You guys seem to disagree even though you weren't there and didn't see her. You assume since she owns a skateboard that she must have pepperoni pizza for a face."

"I think he likes her, Kev," Johnny announced.

"I think you're right, John Boy," Kevin agreed.

Danny bristled, pressing his hands into the volleyball—hard. "So what if I do?"

Johnny's grin was a challenge. "Does she have a shaved head?"

"Nope."

"Dyed hair?"

Danny paused. "Yep."

"Green?"

"Streaks of pink."

"How nice. Multiple body piercings?"

"Yep."

Johnny's grin widened. "A tattoo?"

"I didn't see one."

"Ah." Johnny sighed dramatically. "Well . . . she's a real departure from your usual dating specimens, bro."

Danny knew Johnny was right, but he wasn't going to let him know that he knew. Letting Johnny win an argument was like letting Saddam

35

Hussein win the Gulf War. "What do you mean?"

Johnny let go of the volleyball net and ducked underneath to Danny's side. "Let's take a nice sample group. Say, the last three girls you dated. Who were they?" Johnny tapped his chin, remembering. "Oh yeah. Julie Horn . . . Carol Smith . . . and who was the other girl . . ."

"Kathy Hughes," Kevin added.

"That's the one," Johnny agreed.

Danny tucked the ball under his arm, trying to stay calm. "What's your point?"

"All those girls are really cute, and really nice, and really *normal*," Johnny said, rattling off their traits on his fingers with a special emphasis on the last one. "I'm just saying that I'm surprised you'd find a skate rat attractive, that's all. Don't be so defensive."

Danny shrugged. "I find hot chicks hot. She could be an alien. I'd still think she's hot."

"That alien chick on *Roswell* is pretty hot," Kevin offered.

Johnny chuckled. "All I'm saying is that it's our third day here. There are ten thousand sorority babes in bikinis concentrated in a thirty-block radius. And you want to date Wednesday Addams."

Danny tossed the ball at Johnny, maybe harder than he intended. Maybe not. "You're forgetting one thing, dude."

Johnny caught the ball with a smack. He smiled at the force of the throw. "What's that?"

"Wednesday Addams grew up to be Christina Ricci."

Kevin burst out laughing and high-fived Danny. "The man has a point, Johnny. Maybe we should meet this girl."

Danny grinned himself. "That might prove difficult."

"Why?" Kevin asked.

"Because," Danny said with a sigh, "I don't know if I'll ever see her again."

They finished up their practice session and headed back to the apartment. As Danny fixed himself some eggs on the Scary Stove, he ran over the beach conversation in his head.

His brothers were right. All the girls he'd dated last year were nice, nice, nice. The kind of girls you bring home to Mom with diamonds on their fingers. Nice was nice, he supposed.

Was it that simple? Was he attracted to Raven because she was "bad"? Because she had piercings and dyed hair and torn jeans? Or maybe because of the way she called him a "cool cat"?

Well . . . maybe it *was* that simple.

She seemed so *together*. Confident. Sexy. A girl with direction. All she had to do was point her skateboard and roll. So smooth.

Those eyes. That beautiful face. And yeah, that body. She wore that tight tank top real well.

But the eyes sealed it for him. Danny was drawn into them like a ship into a reef. Bottom line, he simply couldn't get Raven out of his head.

And the best part about that? He didn't want to.

*   *   *

37

Danny got off work close to eleven that night. It had been a long day, over ten hours schlepping heart attacks around the restaurant. He'd done better, however, in all areas. He messed up only one order and bagged nearly thirty bucks in tips. Plus he didn't get run over by oversized skate rats.

He walked down the boardwalk toward the apartment. It wasn't a bad walk. It would take him less than twenty minutes. After a day trapped in the Palace, the fresh air smelled positively wonderful.

The boards were growing deserted at this time of night. Danny could hear the surf pounding the shore, the breeze in his ears. Peaceful.

Then he heard something else. Behind him.

The clatter of small wheels on the boardwalk.

Skateboard wheels.

Before he could turn around, they were all around him. Screaming, laughing, slapping their boards against the planks beneath them. Danny recognized Doberman before the big guy slapped him playfully on the back.

"Hey, it's the punk-rock pretty boy!" he jeered. Doberman slowed down and turned a semicircle around Danny. "What, no ketchup tonight?"

Danny smirked coolly, but adrenaline pumped through his insides. Would Doberman be itching for another fight? And where was Raven? Danny looked around. He didn't see her. Just Doberman, Skunk, and the other two.

"So what's up, pretty boy?" Doberman asked sarcastically.

"Nothing," Danny replied. "You have another quiz for me?"

Doberman cackled, his shark-tooth earring dancing below his earlobe. "Not tonight, buddy. We have things to do. We're—"

"Very bored," came a familiar voice from behind them. Just then Raven skated between the pair, smoothly dragging her finger along Danny's jaw.

"C'mon, Raven." Doberman grunted. "We've got places to be." Doberman flashed his vampiric grin at Danny. "Later, pretty boy. Don't hurt yourself."

Doberman kicked away from him, his wheels rattling. The others followed him down the boardwalk, continuing their barking and catcalling over again. Danny sighed. Looked like they'd forgot about him. Which was just fine.

"Want some?"

Danny blinked. Raven was still there, slowly circling him on her board. She held out a half-gone lollipop, offering. And did she look fantastic. Her hair was pulled into spiky little pigtails, giving her a cool, girlish look. She wore the same torn jeans but with a tight, Lycra tie-dyed shirt that showed off her belly. A ring glinted in her navel.

"Hel-lo?" Raven called, waving the lollipop in front of Danny's face.

Danny blinked. "Sorry. It's been a long day. And night."

Be cool, he told himself. *Don't act like a dork. And don't sound nervous.*

Yeah, right.

"You work all day and all night?" she probed, returning the lollipop to her mouth. Her lips were bright red from it.

"Have to pay the rent," Danny said with a shrug.

She smiled, talking through the pop. "How did you know that song yesterday?"

Danny smiled back. Again he shrugged. "I don't know. I just did."

"You like punk music?" Raven gently pushed her board along as they walked. Danny noticed she was barefoot. Her toes were painted crimson. The soles of her feet were black with soot.

"I like every kind of music," Danny replied. "You name it, I probably have it."

"Calypso," Raven said immediately.

"Huh?"

"Calypso," she repeated, chuckling. "Harry Belafonte. It's a kind of music."

Danny laughed as well. "I guess I missed that kind."

Raven shook her head, tsking. "And you said you had it all."

Danny noticed Raven sizing him up. A wave of nervousness gripped him. He felt like a dork in his work clothes: black trousers and white button-down. He looked like, well, like an off-duty waiter. Raven didn't seem to care.

"I do . . . mostly," Danny replied, clearing his throat. *I sound like a moron!* "I listen to the Dustmites sometimes when I'm warming up for volleyball."

Raven's grin was incandescent. "Aha!" she said, holding up the lollipop as if to point to a lightbulb above her head. "I get it now. It's a bad-man, super-jock thing."

"I look like a jock to you?" Danny asked. He never thought of himself as a jock.

"Nope," Raven confirmed. "But guys who listen to punk music—or heavy metal, or grunge, or rap-metal; you name it—before they do something physical are usually trying to be meaner and more macho than they really are."

Danny chuckled. "I get it. I'm basically this clean-cut but wildly insecure jock wanna-be. Right?"

"You said it, not me," Raven replied. She offered the lollipop again. "Sure you don't want some? I'm gonna toss it."

Danny hesitated, and she met his eyes. Her gaze didn't waver. Which meant he couldn't let his waver either. A smirk slowly played across her face. "I don't have cooties."

Danny smiled and took the lollipop. He casually—extremely casually, he thought—put it in his mouth. It was warm and wet but tasted like a strawberry lollipop should taste. The stick just below the pop was frayed and wet. He swirled it around his mouth and pulled it out.

"Nope," he said. "No cooties."

Raven reached out and took the pop back. She returned it to her mouth. "So what's your name?" she asked.

"Danny," he replied, licking the strawberry from his lips. "Danny Ford. You're Raven, right?"

"No, just Raven," she said playfully.

Up ahead of them the sound of clattering wheels grew louder. Danny's heart sank. *Great,* he thought. *Here comes the Charm Squad again.*

Doberman, Skunk, and the other, unknown punks skated out of the dark. Doberman eyed Danny suspiciously, as if he was trespassing on private property.

"C'mon, Raven," Doberman ordered. "Let's jam. It's getting late."

"Past your bedtime?" Danny asked, hoping the comment didn't get him killed. But he wanted Doberman to know that he wasn't intimidated . . . even though he was.

"Watch it, pretty boy," Doberman said gravely. "You haven't earned the right to bust my chops." He nodded at Raven. "She's the only thing keeping you alive right now."

Danny looked at her. She didn't say a word.

What does that mean? he wondered.

"Leave the geek alone, Rave," Skunk said in disgust.

"Yeah, he's tired," Doberman added, looking Danny over from head to toe. "Like, *really* tired."

Danny rolled his eyes. "Yeah, I'm just a frat-boy-in-waiting."

"Gotta go, Danny," Raven said, stepping on her board and waving her little buh-bye wave.

Danny waved back. "Thanks for the lollipop."

"Anytime," Raven replied, but she was already turning away, pumping her bare foot against the boardwalk, picking up speed.

Soon the sound of clattering wheels faded away, and Danny was by himself. He let out a long sigh.

"Wow," he whispered, tasting sweet strawberry.

Four

THE NEXT DAY Danny floated through work. Heart attacks and lipsticks flew to the tables almost on their own . . . which was bad since several of the orders went to tables they weren't supposed to.

Danny shook himself out of his stupor, apologized, set things right, then drifted back into his own little world. Luckily none of the customers turned out to be jerks. All they wanted was their food, not a fight.

Danny couldn't help it. He couldn't stop thinking about Raven.

This is amazing, he thought. *I've never felt like this about anyone before. Especially someone I don't really know.*

When he'd returned home last night, he slipped a Dustmites CD into the boom box just to see if he could read something into the music and learn more about Raven. But it was useless. The Dustmites were loud and illogical. A guy's band. They spoke of rebellion and anger and angst. That was the stuff that every punk rocker spoke of. There was nothing really unique that seemed to apply to Raven.

After a few songs, however, Johnny got so PO'd about the noise that he yanked the plug on the boom box.

Danny didn't care. He wasn't sure why he was so drawn to Raven. Well, duh, she was gorgeous. Of course. That helped. But there was something else. He couldn't put his finger on it. A connection between them somehow. She wasn't like other girls. But that went even beyond the color streaks in her hair. She wasn't even like other punks.

Doberman was your typical punk, Danny figured. He yelled, he screamed, he bullied. But there wasn't much more going on there.

Raven was playful. Or at least, she was playful last night. The lollipop thing was something Danny wouldn't soon forget.

So what was it? He'd had his crushes over the years, like any guy. And the girls he'd dated had something going. Enough that he found them both attractive and interesting. But none of them stuck.

What are you talking about, "stuck"? he berated himself. *You've crossed paths with this girl twice, both times by chance. You're not dating her, you don't know her last name, and you never will. So stop thinking about her like she's someone you've been with for three years!*

Danny knew better. This wasn't some random obsession. He didn't have them. Except for his music, he didn't obsess about anything. Now that Raven had come home to roost in his mind, he knew she wouldn't be leaving anytime soon. He was all too aware of what she gave him: direction. He knew which way to go. He knew what he wanted. No wandering. No waffling. Raven was a magnetic north as true as anything he'd ever felt. And it felt good.

He had to talk to her again. But how? Even if he could find her, what was he going to do—take her to a movie? *Lame*. Plus her friends didn't exactly make her accessible. They thought Danny was a total preppy geek fool frat boy. Or something like that.

So how did he make this happen?

Maybe I'm not supposed to, he thought dejectedly as he picked up two more plates full of food. *Maybe I should just forget about Raven and stick to the nice, bland girls I'm used to.*

He served the food to table four. He reversed the plates between the two customers—a guy and girl about his age—but at least all the right food made it to the right table.

Danny looked at the girl he'd just served. She was cute. Brown eyes, blond ponytail, smooth tan legs, a hot pink beach pullover. That was the kind of girl he was used to. And the guy with her? Not that far from himself. Clean-cut. Calm. Courteous. The guy didn't flinch when Danny mixed up their food.

47

What's wrong with a girl like that? he asked himself. Nothing. She was cute. And probably a lot of fun.

There were hundreds of girls just like her, sunning themselves on the beach. Riding the merry-go-round on the pier. Strolling up and down the boardwalk. All he had to do was walk up and say, "Hi!"

But Danny didn't want to. He'd taken out girls like that his whole dating career (if you could call what he had a career). It was time to follow his heart.

He wanted to be with Raven.

Somehow. Someway.

He would make it happen.

Danny got off work close to ten-thirty. After three days he was starting to get into the routine. And he was getting better at the waiter stuff. Jabba didn't say a word to him all day, which he took to be a good sign.

Now it was time to go home. He wanted to watch the last few innings of the Dodgers game, then sleep.

But when he stepped out onto the boardwalk, he saw her immediately.

Raven.

She leaned against the railing on the far side. She had laid her skateboard on the railing, chassis up. She idly spun the wheels, as if waiting for something. Or someone.

Me? Danny wondered . . . but didn't dare hope.

She smiled when she spotted him, offering one of her playful little waves.

Now's your chance, he told himself. *Get moving. Talk to her. You may never see her again.* He paused. *But above all, be cool, dude.*

Danny smiled back and crossed the boardwalk. Raven looked as hot as ever. Her hair hung down straight tonight, the pink streaks fading into the light brown like disappearing ink.

It was really her. No Doberman, no Skunk, no skate rats hovering. Just her.

"Hi," Danny said casually, trying not to seem too happy or too blasé.

"What's up, Danny," she replied, spinning a skateboard wheel. "Fancy meeting you here."

"I'm always here," he said, nodding at the Jabba's Palace sign. "There's no escaping Jabba."

"I know—his burgers are killer."

"Literally," Danny muttered. Was he trying too hard? He couldn't stop staring at her eyes.

"Can you get me a discount sometime?"

"Anytime," he promised. "Three percent."

"Three percent?" Raven rolled her eyes. "What's the point?"

Danny shrugged. "Jabba doesn't like to give up the pennies. I get free fries and Fizz, but everything else is cash-and-carry. But if you ever come in, I can get you a good table. And guarantee good service."

Raven smiled and nodded. "Yeah, it's good to

49

know people on the inside. Maybe I'll stop in. But Doberman and Skunk will have to wait outside. They got booted from that place last week. They're banned for the summer."

Good, Danny thought. "What did they do?"

"Nothing," Raven replied, her voice growing angry. "They were just themselves. Jabba kicked them out because of the way they dressed. How they looked. That jerk should talk."

"Yeah, Jabba's lots of laughs," Danny said.

Raven looked him over. "You on your way home?"

Danny nodded. "I was."

Raven paused, then asked, "You want company?"

Danny blinked. His stomach flip-flopped. *Are you kidding? Are you nuts? Are you serious?*

"Sure," he said, trying to sound calm.

"Cool." Raven dropped her board and slowly pushed it along as Danny walked.

Danny eyed her. "No parties tonight?"

Raven shrugged. "I dunno. Why do you ask?"

"Where's the rest of the pack? Doberman get his shots today or something?"

Raven snickered. "Very funny. No, they're off doing some macho thing somewhere. I don't really know. Actually, they're the reason I wanted to see you tonight."

"Really?"

"I wanted to apologize for them," she continued. "Especially Doberman. They can be real jerks."

"No problem," Danny replied, shrugging. "I've seen worse." But Danny actually felt like saying, *I'd use a word so much nastier than* jerks *that I'd have to be bleeped.*

"They can *be* worse," Raven countered. "The song thing really threw Doberman. Not many people stand up to His Alpha Maleness, but you did."

Danny met her gaze. "Is that why you talk to me?"

Raven smiled. "Don't you want to talk to me?"

"It's about the only thing I want to do these days," he replied, instantly regretting his honesty. *Idiot, moron, dweeb!*

Raven only laughed, pushing her board along with her bare feet. "I don't know why I talk to you. I mean, we're both thinking the same thing: totally different people, totally nothing in common, totally useless."

"I guess," Danny answered. "Or not."

"I'll take not," Raven replied. "I don't know. Maybe it's because you stood up to Doberman. Maybe I think you're brave. Or reckless. Maybe I like your taste in music. Or . . . maybe I just think you're cute."

Danny's heart skipped a beat. She actually thought he was cute? Unbe-freakin'-lievable. He struggled to keep his voice from cracking. "I'm cute?"

"For a frat-boy-in-waiting," Raven replied, smiling.

"I'm kind of shocked," Danny said cautiously. "I

51

mean, I never would have guessed. I mean, I hoped. I mean, I never figured a girl like you would ever like a guy like me."

Raven chuckled. "That's three I-means. I think I see what you mean."

"You do?"

"Well . . ." Raven stroked her chin. "What exactly is a girl like me?"

Watch yourself, dude, he thought. Just be cool. Speak the truth. How bad could it be? "You seem like you have it together. Like you know exactly what you like. I'm like a thousand other guys here for the summer. I figured you'd like a guy who's different." *Say it,* he told himself. *Say what you're really thinking.* "I figured you'd like a guy like Doberman. I figured you were with him."

Her expression darkened. "That was seven 'likes.' And no," she added curtly. "But I guess what you see is what you get."

Uh-oh. Was she mad? Had he said something wrong? "What do you mean by that?"

"You see my hair, my earrings, my tattoo, and you automatically think I must be with Doberman."

Danny nodded. "He sure acted like you were together."

"Looks can be deceiving, Danny," she replied, staring him down.

"You have a tattoo?" Danny asked.

Raven nodded.

"Where? Or aren't I allowed to ask?"

She looked at him slyly. "You can ask. Who

52

knows if I'll tell? I wouldn't want you to get the wrong idea about me."

"What idea is that?" Danny asked, kicking a crumpled paper cup and trying to appear nonchalant. He didn't know what to do with himself. *Just walk, dude.*

"You're obviously looking at me and assuming I am how I look." She popped a wheelie with her board and slammed the front end down with a loud *whap*. "I must be a drug-doing, class-cutting, draft-dodging, mosh-pitting sleaze who likes to hang out in the backs of vans at Nine Inch Nails concerts."

"You mean you aren't?" Danny chuckled. "Darn."

Raven tried to keep a straight face, but a smirk crept through.

"What are you, then?" Danny probed. "And I'm not asking to patronize you. I'm asking because I really want to know. I'm actually relieved that you aren't a draft-dodging whatever. I'm not interested in that girl."

Raven shrugged. "My guess is I'm just like you. I hate school, but I get straight As. I hate the idea of college, but I want to go. And I consider myself to be the most stable person in my family even though I'm the only one with multiple body piercings and a tattoo."

"And dyed hair," Danny added.

Raven shook her head. "Nope. Both my mom and my older sister dye their hair. I'm just the one who chose streaks of dark pink."

"If you're so normal, why do you dress the way you do?" Danny asked.

"Because I like it," she said, as if it was the most logical thing in the world. "I like my friends. I like messing with people's heads. But only the people who think they're better than me because of the way I dress. I mean, I get looks of contempt from all the bottle bikini blondes my age because their boyfriends are checking me out. But because I ride a board and wear tight tops, I must be a slut. Meanwhile they aren't within a hundred slots of my class rank."

Danny nodded. "I get it. But you're wrong too. You assume by the way I look—"

"Neo–frat boy?" she interjected.

"Exactly," Danny continued. "You assume that since I have this look, I must be a college-bound-and-gagged brownnoser from the right side of the tracks."

"You're not?" Raven asked, eyeing him suspiciously.

"I could go to college," Danny said, shrugging. "But I don't know if it's in the cards. My grades are so-so. I have absolutely no interest in anything whatsoever except listening to music. I can't play an instrument. I can't do calculus. I can't write a coherent sentence. My dad's blue-collar, so I don't have any guarantees to fall back on. No family business to inherit. Basically I'm taking things one day at a time, hoping to be inspired by something. Anything." Danny sighed. "I guess the bottom line is that we're not the people we think we are."

"Looks can be deceiving," Raven echoed.

"Exactly," he replied flatly.

Neither of them spoke for a moment. They soaked up the finality of what they'd just said. Finally Raven turned to Danny. Her smirk had returned. "Even long, lingering looks?"

"What do you—," Danny began, but he stopped when he saw her. Really saw her.

Raven stared at him. Openly. Blatantly. Her eyes opened up and took him in, offering him a glimpse at the real person underneath all the hardware and color. She was like him, tender and vulnerable and fragile and, bottom line, just looking for the right person to open up to.

Danny couldn't speak. He didn't know how. After all, how did you respond when you got something you really wanted? When something turned out exactly the way you wanted it? Words could wreck the moment.

"You want a ride home?" Raven asked finally.

Danny blinked himself out of his trance. "What do you mean?"

Raven gestured at her skateboard.

"On that?" he asked, skeptical.

Raven slid her bare feet forward, offering Danny half of the board. "Hop on," she said. "But you have to get close."

Danny smiled. "I dunno. . . ."

Raven held up her hands. "Hey, if you want to walk, that's cool. I'm just trying to be nice."

"Okay, okay," Danny replied quickly. "I'm not one to turn down charity."

He awkwardly stepped up onto the board, first

one foot, then adjusting for the other foot when he realized just how close he would have to get to her.

"Closer," she urged.

Danny slipped in behind her, balancing precariously on the narrow skateboard. It was so awkward, but so nice. And so close.

"You have to put your arms around me, Danny," she said, her voice suddenly soft. "Otherwise you'll fall off. I promise I won't take it personally."

Danny did as he was told. He could smell the sweet shampoo in her hair. The faint scent of perfume on her neck, brand unknown. It was maddening. He tentatively slipped his hands around her waist. She grabbed them and pulled him closer, planting his palms flat on her belly.

Danny's heart pounded. His ears felt red-hot. Her body was so soft, the fabric of her top so smooth and warm.

"So, uh . . . how does this work?" he asked lamely.

"Just give us a push," Raven whispered, looking over her shoulder at him.

That move brought their lips within inches of each other. All Danny had to do was bend forward the slightest bit, and he would be kissing her. Her lips were moist, her smirk obvious. It was as if she was waiting for him to do it.

He couldn't.

Not yet, he thought numbly. *I'll blow it. I'll do or say something stupid, and she'll totally lose interest in me. She'll see what a dork I really am.*

Then another voice piped up in his head.

Dude, be cool. You're standing on a skateboard with a beautiful girl. She's giving you the go-ahead to plant a sweet one on her. But you shouldn't. Take your time. Don't let her make the play. Just be yourself, and she'll be back.

Who was *that?* Danny wondered. Obviously he knew it was himself, but it was a side of himself he'd never heard before. A side that was mostly instinct. And totally calm under fire. He was glad to hear it.

"You have to make the first move, Danny," Raven prodded. "Or we'll be here all night."

Danny slowly nodded. He dipped one foot off the board and pushed. They started moving down the sidewalk. It was a slow ride, but one of the most intense thrills Danny had ever experienced.

Maybe this is the kind of social stupidity that has been holding me back for so long, he thought. *Letting appearances dictate my actions.* If so, this was a good start, he figured. Why? Because riding that skateboard down the boardwalk felt so right.

It wasn't long before Danny's apartment building came into view. Not nearly long enough, if you asked him.

He spotted two feet sticking over the railing of their balcony, three floors above the boardwalk. Johnny.

Ignore him, Danny told himself.

"This is me," he said into Raven's ear.

They came to a halt. Danny reluctantly stepped

57

off the skateboard. "Thanks for the ride, Raven."

"Anytime." She smiled playfully.

They were silent for a moment, fidgeting. Should he do something more? Danny wondered. Kiss her good night? Shake her hand?

"Well . . . good night," he finally said.

"Later," she replied. Then quickly added, "Say . . ."

"Yeah?"

Her tone was back to all business. "There's a bonfire party on the beach this Saturday night, off Wayfarer Avenue. Starts around nine. The whole world will be there. Wanna come?"

Danny smiled—then paused. His two friends from home, Scott Walsh and Charlie McCay, were coming to hang for the weekend. Crashing on the floor. Sleeping on the beach. Napping in the late afternoon. Guy stuff. "I have friends visiting this weekend. They're coming Saturday afternoon."

"Bring them," Raven said simply.

Danny smiled. "I'll try."

"Try harder." Raven smacked him on the rear end, giggled, and skated off into the darkness.

Wow, he thought. Nice. In all, Danny couldn't have imagined a finer ending to a better night. Until . . .

From above him on the balcony came the humiliating echo of Johnny's and Kevin's hootchy-kootchy kissing sounds.

What I Found in a Guy!
by Raven

1. Beneath the guise of a preppy lurks . . . a rebel! Danny's a little square around the edges, but he's totally cool.

2. Hair that looks good without gel, mousse, and/or gelatin.

3. Someone who I can really talk to.

4. A great listener.

5. An even better kisser (I can tell).

6. Beautiful deep green eyes that turn me to mush.

Five

"GEE, SHE LOOKS like a very nice girl, Dan-o," Johnny commented as Danny shut the apartment door. The odor of stale garlic hit his nose. An open pizza box sat on the kitchen table, surrounded by empty Fizz bottles.

"You always spy on people, Johnny?" Danny replied angrily. He tossed his wallet and keys on the table. Wasn't it enough that he had to smell grease all day at work?

"Not spying, dude," Johnny countered from the ratty couch. He and Kevin were munching pizza while watching the Dodgers game on TV. "I was taking in the night surf on the balcony, and you just happened to cross my path."

Danny nodded. "You must have gotten a real good look at Raven from three stories up in the dark."

Johnny and Kevin glanced at each other. *"Raven?"* they blurted out simultaneously.

A wave of rage coursed through Danny. "Yeah. That's her name. Do you have a problem with it?"

"Oooh, do I have a problem with it?" Johnny repeated in a mock-afraid voice. "What is this, dialogue by De Niro?"

"You talkin' to me?" Kevin asked, snickering. He tore off a piece of pizza and tossed the crust across the room at the open box. It ricocheted off the kitchen table and landed in the far corner. Kevin made no effort to retrieve it.

"At least her name has style," Danny muttered, slumping into a kitchen chair. The ancient metal frame of the seat groaned with the effort. "Unlike, say, Danny or Kevin or John . . . or *Jane*."

"So what's your point?" Kevin asked, returning his gaze to the TV.

"The point is, I like this girl," Danny said. "Hopefully I'll be seeing a lot more of her. I don't need to hear hootchy-kootchy noises every time I say good night to her."

"So sensitive," Johnny teased. "You won't have any time to see her anyway. Aren't Tweedledee and Tweedledum coming up this weekend?"

"Yeah, *Scott* and *Charlie* are coming. I'm gonna take them to a bonfire party Saturday night. I'll see Raven there too. What's the big deal?"

"Bonfire?" Kevin asked, sitting up. "What bonfire?"

"On the beach, down by Wayfarer Avenue," Danny replied smugly. "What? Weren't you studs invited? The nerve!"

"Oh, man," Johnny said, his voice tight. "We

have to listen to this attitude all summer? No way. No way, man."

"I'm just giving what I'm getting, John Boy," Danny said. "You want to bust my chops about Raven and my friends, fine. But I'm not gonna just sit and take it."

"Can anyone go to this bonfire?" Kevin asked, ignoring his brothers' conversation. "It sounds cool."

"You can both go if you want," Danny said with a shrug. "You've been doing the monk thing so far. You won't meet anyone that way."

Johnny laughed in that annoying, older-brother way. "You meet one skate rat named after a demon bird with earrings all over her face, and suddenly you're Social Sally?"

Rage boiled in Danny once again. "She doesn't have any face piercings, Johnny. She's just as normal as you or me."

Johnny laughed again. "Yeah, I bet. Just wait until Scott and Charlie meet her. That'll be real cool. Their laces are so straight, their mothers probably iron them. They'll really like your new rebel friend."

Danny couldn't take it anymore. He stood up and savagely pointed a finger at his older brother. "That's just like you. Make a stupid remark like that when you haven't even met the girl. Scott and Charlie will be fine with her. You know why? Because Raven isn't like you. She'll talk to anyone, regardless of how they dress."

Johnny eyed Danny's grease-stained work clothes. "Obviously."

Danny left his brothers to their baseball game—a game he would've liked to watch. But he couldn't stand being around Johnny anymore. Sure, brothers fought, he reasoned, but Johnny had crossed the line.

No one ever busts his chops about Jane, Danny thought. *She and Johnny have been together for years. And she's as cold as ice to everyone but him. I don't know how he puts up with her.*

He wondered if that was why Johnny was acting the way he was. Maybe Johnny realized it was his turn to bust on the girlfriend for once.

Danny exited the apartment building and crossed the boardwalk to the beach entrance ramp. He kicked off his shoes and carried them. The sand felt cool and soft against his skin. His feet ached from the day's work. Danny curled his toes and flexed them in the sand, letting the stress flow out of them.

Stress, Danny thought glumly. *I'm at the hottest beach on the West Coast. I just met an even hotter girl who seems to like me. And I have stress. Ha. Some vacation.*

Remember the volleyball tournament, he told himself. That's why he was here. Things like his job, the beach, and Raven had to be secondary to the tournament.

Yeah, right.

Raven was a part of every thought.

The surf pounded the sand in reply. A cool Pacific breeze fluttered through his hair. The stars were bright in the sky. The beach was quiet. Peaceful. He wished Raven was with him.

Enjoy it now, he thought. *Once the weekend rolls around, it's all over.*

Danny had lied to Johnny. He truly wasn't sure how Scott and Charlie would react to Raven. Johnny was right about one thing: His friends were straitlaced tighter than an old lady's girdle.

What if they acted like Johnny? What if they wouldn't accept Raven?

Then, Danny thought grimly, *this bonfire party could get very, very ugly. . . .*

Six

THE BONFIRE RAGED eight feet into the night air. The coals at the base of the fire crackled with waves of yellow-red heat. Embers and smoke floated into the star-filled sky. No one could get within five feet because it was so hot. And there was no sign of the fire dying since a huge stack of firewood (and some old wooden deck furniture) was stacked nearby. It was a disco inferno if there ever was one.

Danny would've been shocked to hear any disco music, however. A roofless Land Rover was parked several yards away on the sand. Its muscular stereo blasted what Danny recognized immediately as the Farm Animals' rap-metal version of Led Zeppelin's "Ramble On." All bass, no prisoners.

A hundred kids of various ages, sizes, and appearance jostled back and forth around the fire, from skate rats to trust-fund brats. Danny, his brothers, and Scott and Charlie had arrived just after nine o'clock. The scene was red-hot in all ways.

"Nice," Kevin commented, surveying the party carnage. "This is my kind of beach."

Just then a long-haired, gray-bearded guy in a tie-dyed T-shirt and brown shorts shuffled up to them. "Dudes . . . free Fizz over in those coolers." He giggled, showing crooked teeth. "If you're into that sort of thing."

He tee-hee-heed away.

"That guy had to be in his sixties," Johnny said, staring after him.

"I think there's a lot about that guy that screams sixties," Kevin replied, laughing. He took a few steps in the direction of the coolers, then turned. "I'm going. Who needs one?"

"I'll go with you," Johnny replied, shrugging. "Better than standing here like a wallflower."

The two Ford brothers crossed the sand, entered the crowd, and disappeared.

"This is pretty cool," Scott Walsh observed. His curly brown hair was cut close to his scalp. His blue eyes glistened in the firelight. Danny thought his Polo shirt and Abercrombie & Fitch shorts seemed more suited to a tennis club than a beach party. "Not a bad way to spend the summer, Dan."

"No kidding," Charlie McKay added. His tousled blond hair and blue eyes were very California-beachy-keen casual, but his shorts were pressed, and his Teva sandals were brand-new.

His friends had arrived on schedule that evening. Danny was glad to see them, though they had only a couple of hours to catch up before it was time to go to the bonfire. Danny was able to scam a couple of free hours from Jabba's. It was Saturday night, after all, and his friends were in town. His overdressed, underrelaxed friends. But hey, nobody was perfect.

Danny slipped a casual hand in his own beat-up cargo shorts. He couldn't imagine dressing up for a beach party. Thus his Dustmites concert shirt and bare feet. It was the beach, not the club.

Which has nothing to do with trying to impress/charm/dazzle Raven, he told himself. *Absolutely not. No way. I'm not one to judge a person by their appearance. You own a few Polo shirts yourself, buddy boy,* he reminded himself.

Danny quickly forgot his hypocrisy before it could put a serious crimp in his party-go-nuts attitude. He was there to have a good time, after all. And see Raven.

And that's just what he was doing at that moment.

She was on the other side of the bonfire, near the Land Rover. A dozen skate rats surrounded her. Doberman, Skunk, and the others he'd run into were there, plus a platoon of others that he'd never seen before.

Raven spotted him. Smiled. Waved him over. She swayed with the music and continued her conversation with another girl.

Uh-oh.

69

She wanted him to come over. Her friends, Doberman in particular, wouldn't like that.

Dude, the girl you're totally hot for just invited you over, a voice in his head piped up. *Don't be a dweeb. Go!*

"I have to go check on something, guys," Danny said to Scott and Charlie, his gaze never leaving Raven. "I'll be right back."

"Is that her?" Scott asked, squinting through the fire's glare.

"Which one?" piped Charlie. "They all look the same."

Danny sighed. Oh, well. Of course they would want to meet Raven. Johnny and Kevin had made sure earlier that his friends knew all about Danny's new main squeeze-to-be. Anything to make his life difficult.

"That's her on the right," Danny relented, pointing her out. "The one with the tank top and torn jeans."

"And the belly-button ring," Scott added, his smirk growing by the second. "Verrrry nice."

Danny spun on his friend. "So she has a navel piercing. So what? You have Yoda boxer shorts."

Charlie cackled. "Yeah, but Scott doesn't hang them from his belly button."

"So that's it," Danny muttered, shaking his head in frustration. "You guys are going to be just like Johnny. I really like this girl. Can't you just be cool for ten minutes?"

Scott and Charlie shared a look. Then Charlie glanced at his watch. "Gee, Danny, I don't know. That's a tall order."

"You can do better than her," Scott said, glancing at Raven. "Why go for the most radical girl on the beach?"

Charlie laughed. "She looks kind of scary, dude."

"That's it," Danny snapped. "I'm going over to see her. You want to come, come. I'll introduce you. If not, I'm sure Johnny'll be back in a few minutes with more funny things to say about me. What's it going to be?"

Charlie sighed and crossed his arms. "Whatever."

Scott shrugged. "Go, then."

Danny turned away from his friends. He imagined their stares burning into his back as he crossed the sand to Raven, but that was just the heat from the bonfire.

They think I'm ditching them, Danny thought glumly. *Fine. Let them think that. I'm just going to say hello to Raven. Five minutes. Then I'll go back to them.*

Danny even believed it.

"Hey," she said.

"Hey, back," he said.

Raven looked amazing in the fire's glow. Her features were cast in flickering shadows. Her hair hung straight along her cheeks. Her eyes seemed to dance as she sized him up. Through it all she never stopped her rhythmic swaying to the music.

Danny gulped. *Be cool,* the voice told him. *You're just a regular guy, and she's your garden-variety gorgeous amazing wonderful unattainable girl. And she wants to talk to you.*

71

No sweat.

"Cool party," he said calmly, offering a slight smile.

"Not really," she replied, shrugging. "Want to go for a walk?"

Danny blinked. "Um . . . sure."

"Come on," she muttered, grabbing his hand and pulling him toward the dark surf.

"Yo, Raven!" came a familiar bellow.

Uh-oh. Danny closed his eyes and whispered a curse. *Here we go again.*

Raven turned impatiently at the voice. *"What?"*

It was indeed Doberman. He held a bottle of something in his hand. Danny couldn't tell what from the angle. He and his spiked hair, shark-tooth earring, and ripped clothes were silhouetted in the firelight. Danny could also see the muscles and veins flexing in Doberman's arms. He didn't have to see his face to know the big guy's vampiric teeth were flashing too.

"What's with punk-rock boy?" Doberman asked indignantly. "Suddenly we're all second-class citizens?"

Raven sighed wearily and shook her head. "Nothing so melodramatic, Dobie. Just plain old boring."

Doberman's head tilted as if he hadn't heard her right. *"Boring?* Raven, you're holding hands with *boring.* That guy represents everything stompable in this whole world. You hate guys like him for breakfast."

Adrenaline rose in Danny. He felt Raven's hand tighten around his own.

"Times change, Dobie," she replied haughtily. "And looks can be deceiving."

Doberman chuckled bitterly. "You're right, Rave. A Dustmites T-shirt doesn't make him worth even one of your glances."

Raven laughed. "Keep it up, Doberman. You'll be a poet yet." She tugged on Danny's arm. "Come on, let's go."

"Where are we going?" Danny asked lamely, trotting to keep up as she headed down the beach.

Raven led him along the fringe of the surf line, the sand growing wet and cold under Danny's feet. "Destination unknown, Danny. Let's make it up as we go, okay?"

Danny smiled. "I've been doing that my whole life."

The bonfire quickly became a faint glow. The sound of the heavy bass was replaced by the pounding surf. Raven never let go of his hand, and Danny had no plans to argue.

Soon they came to a jetty—an outcropping of rocks and massive concrete pilings that ran so far out into the ocean, it was swallowed up. The waves slammed against the man-made barrier, sending up dramatic sprays of foam.

Finally Raven let go of his hand and scrambled to the top of one of the concrete pilings, perching there like a gargoyle. Danny followed suit on one of the rocks, careful not to cut his bare feet on the rough, slick surface.

"Why did you leave your friends?" he asked. He could see her profile against the starlit sky, a perfect black outline of beauty. *We're all the same in the dark,* he thought happily.

"I'm with them all the time," Raven said. "They're my friends, but they all talk about the same things day after day. Skateboarding, partying, making out, whatever. My girlfriends are even worse. Sometimes I just have to get away."

"Am I different enough for you?" Danny asked carefully.

Raven chuckled. "You're not all that different, Danny. Just a change of speed."

Danny felt a wave of warmth flow through him, and he wished Raven wasn't so far away on her concrete piling. "Speed has never been my problem," he said softly. "It's direction that I have trouble with."

"Me too," Raven replied, nodding. "Sometimes I feel like I'm floating out there on the ocean. My friends spin around me at a hundred miles an hour. But it's all random. There's no land to shoot for."

Danny couldn't help smiling. She'd nailed it right on the head. That was his life to a T. "Seems like everyone I know is shooting by, but they all have places to go. My brother Kevin has art. Johnny has college. What do I have?"

"Freedom," Raven said firmly.

"I don't know about that," Danny replied with a

sigh. "I don't feel very free slinging burgers at Jabba's. I don't feel free when my parents and relatives ask me what I want to do with my life. An answer like 'be free' doesn't cut it with them."

"People can't tell you how to live," Raven said, her voice gaining a momentary edge. "It's hard enough just being yourself. You think my family likes the torn jeans and hot tops I wear? The earrings? But there comes a point where you have to say, 'I don't care what you think. This is me.' "

"Even if you don't know who you are?" Danny replied.

"You can't force direction, Danny," Raven countered, slipping off the piling and silently hitting the sand. She took a step toward him, and her voice grew tender. "It's a little bit like falling for someone. It just comes out of nowhere, and all you can do is go with it."

Danny's stomach fluttered. Maybe it was Raven's tone. Maybe it was the beautiful shape of her silhouette. Maybe it was her words. But Danny had never felt so right with anyone. She knew what was burrowing inside him, eating away. She knew how to feed it. Suddenly Danny didn't feel so alone about the future because out here, among the random waves of the ocean, the future didn't matter. He wasn't the only one floating through life's gray areas. The irony of it all was that this beautiful randomness, this great discovery, now gave him a sense of direction. And everything pointed to Raven.

Without thinking, Danny stood from his rock, stepped forward, and kissed her.

He expected her to pull away. Smack him. Bite his lip and tell him to get lost.

But she didn't.

She grabbed handfuls of his T-shirt and pulled him closer. He wrapped his arms around her, feeling the warmth of her skin through tight fabric. Her lips were firm and alive against his own, and Danny realized that Raven was not only letting him kiss her, but she was kissing him back.

He never dreamed she would.

It was a long shot.

But she was.

And the whole world fell away until it was just him and her . . . and an amazing moment that he never wanted to end.

They didn't talk on their way back to the party. Their kiss simply broke, mutually, and they took each other's hand once again and walked.

It made sense. No one had to say anything.

Danny's head was swimming, pounding along like the endless surf. What did this mean? Were they a couple now? Danny hated words like that, the window dressing of relationships: couples, dating, communicating, all that.

Don't make a big deal of it, the inner voice told him. *You guys kissed, that's all. You connected.* People did it on first dates all the time. He watched TV. People did it in fifteen-second commercials. *We're a kissing society, and one kiss does not a destiny make.*

Danny knew he was downplaying it. He had to, for his own sanity. If he acknowledged his true feelings, he'd be hanging out in the wind. The sun had a funny way of rising and making people suddenly feel strange about what they did the night before. Who knew how Raven would treat him later? Was the kiss as amazing for her as it was for him?

Could she possibly feel as good as I do right now? he wondered.

No way. No chance. Impossible.

So Danny took it one step at a time. And buried all of his feelings under a bed of cool denial thick enough to sleep on.

Soon the bonfire came into view. The heavy bass thumped into his chest. The party was still rocking well. Danny spotted his brothers and friends talking to a group of girls near the Fizz coolers. Out of the corner of his eye he caught Raven staring at them.

"You want to meet them?" he asked.

Raven shrugged. "Okay. If you want to introduce me, that is . . ."

Careful, he warned himself. *That sounds like a verbal trap if I ever heard one.* "Sure. Come on."

They walked over to the group. Kevin caught Danny's eye and grinned. He then nudged Johnny and pointed at them. Johnny wore a bemused smile.

Just before they reached the group, Raven let go of Danny's hand. His palm felt cold without hers.

"Hey, everyone," Danny announced. "This is Raven."

"Hey," everyone replied.

Danny ran down the names for her, Johnny, Kevin, Scott, Charlie. The three girls they were talking to were Angie, Katherine, and Jean Marie. They all wore designer summer wear, makeup, and perfume. And they looked at Raven like she might pull a knife on them at any time.

After the intros there was an uncomfortable moment of silence.

Finally Kevin stepped forward and smiled. "So, Raven, why are you hanging out with my loser brother?"

"I dig charity cases," Raven replied, smiling herself.

"Hey—," Danny protested, but Raven nudged him.

The others turned back to their conversations, but Danny noticed a distinct air of resentment coming from his friends. Scott and Charlie made no effort to speak to Raven, even though the girls they were with were less than scintillating conversationalists.

Is it about how Raven looks? Danny wondered. *Or is it about the fact that I'd rather spend time with her than with them?*

A little of both, he figured.

It didn't matter. All Danny had to do was look at Raven and think about their kiss. When he did that, nothing else mattered.

"I hear you're an artist," Raven commented to Kevin. "What do you draw?"

Kevin spread his arms wide, grinning. "Everything. The world is my oyster, and I'm the grain of sand that becomes the pearl."

Raven giggled. Danny rolled his eyes. "I forgot to warn you about Kevin's uncanny ability to lay it on thick."

"With a shovel," Kevin added, nodding. He gestured at Raven's legs. "Those jeans are perfect. How long did it take you to get them to look like that?"

Raven glanced at the shreds of denim and shrugged. "Forever, I guess. I didn't tear any of those holes. They grew naturally and decayed rapidly. All I had to do was wear them a lot. And fall off my skateboard a lot."

"Cool," Kevin replied. "Air-conditioned, even."

Raven smiled. "Saves money on the designer labels."

Danny felt relief that Kevin seemed to be warming toward Raven. At least one of his brothers would give her the time of day. That it was Kevin didn't surprise him, though. His younger brother ran a little on the ragged edge himself, or at least he liked to think he did. The artist in him kept his mind open. And his wit sharp. It was a combination that Raven no doubt found easy to relate to.

Just as Danny started to relax, a racket erupted from the other side of the bonfire.

Loud voices. Laughter. Cursing. A new group of people had arrived at the party, coming up the beach from the pier. Danny didn't get a good look at them until they neared the fire, but he caught the expression on Doberman's face over by the Land Rover: disgust.

I guess I'm not the only one who makes Dobie sick, Danny thought.

There were thirteen of them, all of them obviously older, all of them obviously drunk. By their clothes and general attitude Danny could tell they were rich. But it was the leader of the pack who drew Danny's eye. He had to be about six-four in bare feet. His T-shirt and shorts hung easy on his massive, muscular frame, adding to his entire air of confidence. His shaggy, styled blond hair fell to his shoulders, and his perfect grin never wavered, staying bright and magnetic even as he insulted the lameness of the party. And he looked very familiar . . .

"Danger, everyone," the guy announced to his friends as he surveyed the crowd. "Looks like we've gone back in time to the tenth grade."

His friends laughed.

"How witty," Raven muttered. "Let's tap another keg."

Danny suddenly noticed Johnny at his side. His older brother glared at the pack leader, almost willing the guy to look at him.

"You recognize him?" Johnny whispered.

"He does look familiar," Danny replied, confirming his suspicions. "Who is he?"

"Tanner St. John," Kevin replied, giving the name all the reverence of a cockroach.

Recognition flooded Danny. Of course. Tanner

St. John, all-American and captain of the national-champion California University men's volleyball team. Six-four, two-ten, known for his three-foot vertical leap, a spike that could crack your skull, and an ego the size of southern California.

Johnny pointed out two other guys in Tanner's group. Arliss Neeson, a dark-haired, lantern-jawed guy who stared nails through you from under his thick black eyebrows. He was second-team all-American and once put an opposing player in the hospital for coming too far over the volleyball net. When the guy went up near the net, Arliss swept the guy's feet. He came down on his head.

The other was Shooter Ridge. He wore a ribbed tank top to show off the definition of his arms and chest. His jet black hair was parted at the side and molded into place by lots of hair spray. Every few minutes he absently ran a hand along each arm, as if to make sure the muscles there hadn't deteriorated.

"The team to beat in this summer's tournament," Kevin said grimly.

Danny took a deep breath. All of them were over six feet tall. All of them were lean and muscular, the classic volleyball build. And all of them played on a national-champion team.

"It's a cakewalk," Johnny scoffed, watching every move Tanner St. John made.

Sure, it is, Danny thought. *My brother, the optimist.*

Then Tanner St. John looked right at Johnny. Danny saw a flicker of recognition in the rowdy guy's eyes. Tanner nudged his teammates and gestured at Johnny. Then they marched toward the Fords. Danny stuck out his chest. He didn't have a real idea of the opposing players' size until they stopped a few feet in front of him. Johnny was the closest, at six-one. But Danny and Kevin hadn't topped out at six feet yet.

"I know you," Tanner said, his eyes smoldering. He brushed his long hair out of his face and smirked.

"Yeah," Johnny said, his voice even and confident. He glared right back.

Tanner stroked his chin, thinking. "Your name's Chevy, or Pontiac, or something."

"Ford." Johnny took a deep, agitated breath.

Tanner smiled and snapped his fingers. "Ford. That's the one. Yeah, CU tried to recruit you last spring. You choked at the tryout."

Danny saw the blood rise in his brother's face. Johnny bristled but kept his cool. "Funny. That's not how I remember it."

"It's a shame that you're in such denial," Tanner said, to the tittering delight of his friends. "I mean, it's never you, right? Let me guess. The balls were half flat, and the net was six inches higher than normal. Does that explain your pathetic excuse for a spike?"

"Nothing wrong with my spike, pal," Johnny replied. The muscles in his jaw flexed.

Tanner shrugged, as if to grant Johnny his opinion. "Sure. Not if you're going to play for East Podunk University. But the program at CU is a little more demanding." Tanner held his hand a few inches over Johnny's head, as if measuring. "You don't quite make the grade."

Johnny batted Tanner's hand away. A ripple of excitement went through the crowd.

Tanner's eyes went wide. He held up his struck hand as if it were a prize. His perfect teeth shone dully in the firelight. "He touched me. Did you see that? Did you see this guy touch me?"

"He definitely touched you," Arliss Neeson agreed, smiling savagely. He crossed his massive arms over his chest.

"You gonna stand for that, Tanner?" Shooter Ridge demanded, taking up station at Tanner's left shoulder. He looked like he wanted to drool.

"Do you know what happened to the last guy to touch me?" Tanner asked, his voice out of a bad Western.

"He got your phone number?" Kevin blurted out. He'd snuck in next to Johnny, which was easy since he only came up to his brother's shoulder.

The crowd burst out laughing, which only made Tanner angrier.

"You must be the little Ford," he said, sizing up Kevin with a mocking stare. "A Festiva, right?"

The crowd laughed at that too. Kevin just rolled his eyes. "Good one."

Danny glanced at Raven. She never took her eyes off him. He wasn't sure what her face was saying. Hang tough? Cut and run? All he knew was that he wanted to lose himself in those smoky gray eyes. But he couldn't. Not now.

"I could bust chops with you little guys all night," Tanner was saying. "But I've got a better idea. I say you choked at your tryout. You say you didn't. Well, prince that I am, I'm going to let you prove me wrong. We can play a game."

Uh-oh. Another wave of anticipation went through the crowd. They seemed to know what was at stake.

Johnny's eyes narrowed. "What do you mean?"

"Volleyball, my man," Tanner replied impatiently, tossing his hair back over his shoulder. "Here's your shot. You get to play the national champs three on three. Right here. Right now. In the dark for all to see."

Johnny glanced at Danny, then at Kevin. Danny knew what that meant. Johnny wanted to do it. No question. The line had been drawn.

Danny met eyes with Kevin. His younger brother's body was as tight as a wire. He gave Danny a subtle nod.

Johnny caught it. And that was all it took. He looked Tanner St. John right in the eye. "Sounds good."

Seven

THERE WAS A public volleyball court about fifty yards down the beach. When the Fords and the UC team marched toward it, virtually the entire bonfire party followed. It figured, Danny thought. Bloodbaths always drew a crowd.

"Just be cool and play your game," Johnny warned as they walked down the beach.

"That's great," Danny said under his breath, "but I thought we were supposed to play our game when the tournament started."

"The tourney's two months away," Johnny replied impatiently. "This is the perfect tune-up. We'll know what kind of a game these guys have. Plus we get some full-contact action. Like I said, perfect."

"Perfect except for one thing," Kevin muttered. "It's nighttime. I usually like to see what I'm hitting."

Johnny's voice was tense, as if his brother's comments were tiny annoyances. "They can't see either, Kev. Just be cool—"

"—And play my game. Yeah, I know," Kevin replied, shaking his head.

Someone produced a volleyball. The two teams batted it around to loosen up and adjust to the night. It wasn't as bad as Danny thought. There was a streetlight not far away, and the boardwalk provided a lot of residual illumination. Danny could see the ball well enough.

"Volley for serve," Tanner declared, punching the ball across the net.

Danny didn't mind. They were as ready as they were going to be in these alien conditions. He decided he would take Chevy Chase's Zen-like advice from *Caddyshack: Be the ball, Danny.*

He scanned the sidelines for Raven. At first he couldn't find her, and panic gripped him. Did she leave? She wouldn't leave without saying good-bye, would she? Or at least good luck? Not after the night they'd had. Volleyball meant a lot to him— Danny really wanted her to watch him do the only thing he could do well. Then he spotted her. Off to the left with Doberman and the others. Raven's expression was tense. Was she worried about him? A ripple of excitement ran through him at the thought.

Concentrate, he warned himself, stretching his cold muscles. *She's watching, so be cool, play your game, and don't worry about what she thinks. Just win.*

86

Wise words, he figured.

The UC team flubbed the volley. Arliss set up Tanner for a spike but totally misjudged the distance to the net. Johnny went up and pounded the ball into the sand on their side. The sound brought up ooohs and ahhs from the spectators.

"Our serve," Johnny said, puffing with pride.

"Don't get too excited," Tanner muttered, kicking sand.

Johnny retrieved the ball and flipped it to Danny for the serve. "Shove it down their throats," he whispered harshly.

Danny gripped the ball, squeezed it, got a feel for it. It felt cold in his hand from the night sand. The surface gave just enough for him to palm it.

"Okay, Fords," Tanner taunted, dancing back and forth on his feet. "School is now in session."

Don't think about it, Danny told himself. *Just be the ball.*

He tossed the ball up like he had a million times before, watched the light shape spin against the black sky, and slapped it toward the net. He made solid contact in the darkness, a straight serve. He would save his fancier serves for when he was warmed up.

The ball shot across the net toward the far corner of the court. At first Danny thought he might have an ace, but Shooter Ridge dove and popped the ball into the air for the save. Arliss Neeson moved in expertly for the set. Then Tanner stepped up and prepared to spike it.

He mishit the ball, sending it off the side of his hand. He cursed for the whole beach to hear.

Kevin picked up on the lame hit, letting it bounce up from his folded hands. Danny stepped in and set up Johnny, a move they had performed over and over again during practice. He didn't even have to think about it.

Johnny timed the ball, glided up to the net, and leaped into the air as if taking off. His long arm snaked out and hammered the volleyball straight down into the sand on the UC side. Arliss dove for it but never had a chance.

Point for the Fords!

Johnny pumped his fist. Danny and Kevin high-fived him. "See, they aren't so tough," Johnny whispered, breathing hard.

Few people in the crowd applauded since no one knew who the Fords were. But Danny distinctly saw Raven clapping, which pumped him up even harder. He paced back and forth, flexing his hands, waiting for the ball.

"One–nothing," Johnny declared, rolling the ball to Danny.

"Savor it," Tanner grumbled back. "'Cause it's the only point you're getting off us the whole summer."

Danny smiled and served again. This time he spun the ball. But he didn't get his best stuff on it, and it floated. Shooter picked up on it right away. He sent it to Arliss, who popped it to Tanner, who sent a rocket into the sand between Kevin and Johnny.

"Our serve, hotshot," Tanner said, demanding the ball.

Danny stared at him, wondering where he generated such power on his spikes. The ball had been a blur on that last one. He would've had trouble picking it up in daylight, let alone at night. He'd actually heard the ball sizzling through the air before it hit the sand.

That's why he's an all-American, Danny figured. *They were just playing with us on that first point. We could be in trouble.*

Danny was right.

The next ten points were an object lesson in guerilla-rules beach volleyball. The UC team worked like teammates should, setting and backing each other up and landing spike after spike into the Fords' sand. Johnny grew angrier with each passing failure.

Inside fifteen minutes the score was twelve to one.

The UC group clapped and cheered their friends and taunted the brothers on every point. They knew they were pasting the Fords. And they knew they were getting to Johnny. Everyone knew they were getting to Johnny.

He cursed, kicked sand, or silently stewed whenever the ball was tossed back to Shooter Ridge for the next serve.

Shooter announced the score and sent a frozen rope over the net. Johnny had to step back to save it, diving into the sand and popping it up in the air. Danny moved up and set the spike for Kevin.

Kevin timed it, went up against Tanner at the net, and tried to pound it. But Tanner charged in hard, sending an elbow into the net. It caught Kevin in the chest and sent him to the sand. The ball dropped on the Ford side of the beach.

"Our point," Tanner said coldly, staring down at Kevin.

Kevin didn't move.

Johnny and Danny ran to their brother's side. Kevin lay there, heaving. He'd had the wind knocked out of him, but he seemed okay otherwise. Johnny charged the net.

"What kind of a cheap shot was that, St. John?" he bellowed.

"It was a clean hit," Tanner shot back. "If the little boy can't take the hit, he shouldn't be on the court. And you know it."

Johnny pointed an angry finger through the net. "All I know is you have a reputation for this garbage. If we were in the tournament, you'd be penalized."

Tanner stepped up to the net, his long hair wild, a dark gleam in his eye. "Look around, pal. You see any judges?"

Johnny fumed. Danny could see he wanted to charge Tanner, but he held back. "You're scum, St. John."

"Scum with a loaded trophy case," Tanner replied with a snicker. "And I'll have your amateur little head on my wall in a few minutes."

Danny helped Kevin stand up. "You okay?"

Kevin nodded, shaking Danny off and rubbing his chest. "He caught me . . . right in the solar plexus. I feel . . . ugh . . . like you look."

Danny chuckled. Kevin limped to his position and signaled for the serve.

And the massacre continued.

At one point Danny glanced at Raven. Her friends had left the game to return to the bonfire. But she sat by herself on the sand, watching.

I must be real impressive, Danny thought, the pit in his stomach growing deeper.

Just then the ball sailed toward him. He hadn't seen it coming. He dove for it, but the ball skipped off his hand and hit the ground.

Johnny roared. "Come *on!* At least make the *easy* ones!"

Danny's cheeks grew hot. He knew he should've had it. And he knew why he hadn't. He tried to force Raven out of his head. Tried not to look at her.

Have to concentrate, he told himself. But he knew it was a lost cause. He could forget about Raven about as easily as he could even the score of the game.

In a few minutes it was over. The final score? Twenty-one to one.

They'd scored one lousy point against Tanner St. John and his all-American goons.

"Good luck in the tournament, kiddies," Tanner called to them as he rejoined his group. "If you're lucky, maybe they'll let you use the playground while the real men play for the money."

"Just try your cheap shots at that tourney," Johnny warned. "We'll see who the real men are."

"You talk like a volleyball player," Tanner said. "Shame you don't play like one. Now the whole beach knows why you didn't make the cut at CU."

Johnny was livid. Danny could see the veins and muscles working in his brother's neck and jaw. His fists were balled at his sides, and his breath came through gritted teeth. All they could do was watch Tanner and his cohorts make their way back to the bonfire, hooting and laughing the whole time.

Scott and Charlie approached from the sidelines and offered their condolences, for what they were worth. "How could you play in the dark like that?" Scott asked. "I can hardly see my hand in front of my face."

"The dark didn't beat us," Kevin replied grimly. "They just plain stomped us."

Johnny kicked the volleyball across the sand.

"Let's go," he ordered.

"Go where?" Danny asked.

Johnny gestured at the empty beach around them. "Home, moron! In case you didn't notice, we just had our butts handed to us. I'm not going back to any party after that."

Danny blinked. Not going back to the party had never occurred to him. Raven leaned against the far pole of the volleyball net, casually tracing circles in the sand with her toe. She looked great, and Danny felt terrible, and he couldn't think of anyone he'd rather be with right then.

Certainly not Johnny. Not now.

Danny knew what it would be like back at the apartment. They would sit up until all hours listening to Johnny overanalyze why they lost. Whether or not they had what it took to play with the big boys. Whether or not this whole summer tournament plan was a waste of time. Danny couldn't bear the thought. Getting creamed was enough. He didn't need his brother rubbing his face in it all night.

"Come on," Johnny growled, marching toward the boardwalk and home. Kevin, Scott, and Charlie filed in behind him.

But Danny stood his ground. He glanced over at Raven. He saw a smile grow on her face. He walked over.

"Yo, Danny," came Johnny's voice. "Where do you think you're going?"

"Nowhere," Danny replied. He looked at Raven and smiled back. "I'm staying."

"You have to be kidding," Johnny called. "You played like it was gym class in fourth grade. Your head was ten miles away. The fun's over—it's time to go home."

"We *all* played badly," Danny replied, resenting the implication that the loss was his fault. "Now I'm going back to the party to forget about it. I don't need to break down each point to know how bad we stunk."

"Maybe you need a brain transplant to get your head back in the game," Johnny suggested bitterly.

He gestured at Raven. "You were staring at the sidelines the whole time. It's time to show some team loyalty and get back to the apartment. Now. We have a lot to talk about."

Rage boiled up in Danny. He wasn't a dog to be ordered around. "No. I'm staying. Scott, Charlie, why not come with me? It'll be cool."

Danny's friends glanced at each other. "No, man," Scott replied. "We've had enough for one night. Why don't you come back with us?" Scott shared another look with Charlie. "It'd be cool to actually hang out with you, you know?"

More anger churned in Danny. Now his friends were giving him guilt trips? No. Correction. They weren't so much interested in spending time with him as they were in *not* spending time with *Raven*. He looked at her, waiting. Then back at his family and friends. If Raven was any other girl, Scott and Charlie would go back to the party. Danny knew it. "I'm staying," he said after a moment.

"I don't believe you!" Johnny cried. "Get your butt back to the apartment now!"

The anger in Danny finally spilled over. He couldn't take it anymore. "No! If you're going to go all major general on us now, John Boy, don't waste your breath. I'm not thirteen anymore. I don't take orders from you or anyone else."

Johnny took a deep, steadying breath. He looked like he wanted to pounce on Danny. But then he simply turned and walked toward the boardwalk without another word.

Kevin only shook his head at Danny and followed.

Scott and Charlie stood there, as if they weren't quite sure what to do. "Come on, Dan," Charlie said. "Let's go hang out at your place."

Danny walked over to his friends and spoke in a low, careful voice. "Guys, I really, really like this girl. I wish you two were at least interested in hanging out with her, but you're not. I know you drove all the way up here, but you have to understand."

"We do?" Scott asked, barely masking the anger in his voice.

"I'm asking as a friend, dude," Danny replied, meeting Scott's stare. "You don't have to like Raven. Not that either of you bothered to get to know her. But you have to understand that I want to be with her. That I want my two best friends to want to hang out with us." Danny gestured in Johnny's direction. "I'm not listening to him bark at me all night."

"So we have to do it for you," Charlie pointed out, folding his arms across his chest.

"No, you don't," Danny replied simply. "You can come back to the party with me and Raven."

Scott and Charlie looked at each other. Then Scott said, "No thanks."

He turned away and walked toward the receding figures of Johnny and Kevin.

"What about you, Charlie?" Danny asked.

Charlie shrugged. "Have a good time."

And Danny was left alone on the volleyball-court

sand. He watched his friends disappear into the night. He knew he should feel guilt, or remorse, or something negative. Maybe staying was the wrong thing to do. Maybe he should remain loyal to his brothers and teammates and friends. Maybe he should go sulk with them. But he couldn't.

Something else was driving him now. Something he'd never quite felt before.

Passion. Deep-in-his-gut passion. In the *I'm-dying-to-make-out-with-you* sense, yes . . . but more important, in the *I'm-dying-to-be-with-you, get-to-know-you, listen-to-your-thoughts, learn-your-dreams, share-my-own* sense.

Passion. The kind of feeling that gives you direction, that makes you *you*.

He turned back toward the party. The bonfire still burned.

And Raven was waiting . . .

Eight

D ANNY AND RAVEN never made it back to the
bonfire.

They ambled off down the beach in the opposite
direction, toward the distant shimmer of the pier
and amusement-park rides. The echoes of the
boardwalk swirled around them. Music. Laughter.
Bells ringing. It seemed a million miles away. The
party still raged behind them, the bonfire reaching
with orange fingers into the sky.

"Will your brother be mad?" Raven wondered,
slipping her warm hand into his once again. "The
older one, I mean."

Danny shrugged, liking the perfect fit of her
palm. "Yeah. Probably. He gets like that whenever his ego is on the line. Or a lot of money. In
this case it's both. He's banking on winning that
tournament."

Raven searched his face. "Aren't you?"

"I guess so," Danny replied, kicking a clump of seaweed. "But honestly, I'm not thinking too far past tonight."

"Me neither," Raven said with a smile. "But sometimes you have to."

"There's that old worrying-about-the-future thing again," Danny declared, sighing. "I thought direction didn't matter."

"It doesn't, figuratively," Raven pointed out. "But you still need to prepare for the things that you can see coming."

"Such as?"

Raven shrugged. "Such as the fact that I'm transferring to a new school this fall and won't know a soul."

He squeezed her hand. "Why do you have to transfer?"

"My dad got a new job," she answered. "So we're moving." She looked at him forlornly. "I'm a little worried about fitting in and making friends—all that kind of stuff. You know how strangers act when they see someone who dresses like me."

Danny smiled. "Moving and going to a new school is a lot to deal with, Raven, but you'll do fine. I'd bet anything on it. And anyone who can't get past the look just has to talk to you for three seconds. You'll have no problem at a new school. Anyone would like you."

She looked into his eyes. "Your friends don't."

Danny dug the toe of his sneaker into the sand. He'd been hoping she hadn't caught that weird exchange between him and his friends. Or at least that the subject wouldn't come up. But he'd been stupid for thinking she'd avoid the issue. Raven wasn't the type to avoid talking about something just because it was difficult. She faced things head-on, uncomfortable or not.

And that was something he needed to learn from her. "That's exactly what I'm talking about," he said. "My friends didn't *talk* to you—they made a judgment based on the way you look, based on what they think they know of your crowd. It's wrong, Raven."

"Yeah, it's wrong," she agreed, running her hands through that silky brown hair. "But that doesn't mean anyone will give me a chance at my new school either. I'm okay with that—this is definitely who I am. And I don't go around worrying what people think of me—*obviously*. I just wish people would save their judgments till after they actually know me. Just because I'm comfortable with who I am and what I put out there doesn't mean it doesn't bother me when people judge me unfairly."

They were silent for a few moments. Danny had never had a conversation like this with anyone before. He'd talked music with girls. Television shows. Movies. He'd talked about classes, teachers, what kind of toppings he liked on his hamburgers. But he'd never talked about this. About life. Real life. Thoughts. Issues. He wouldn't have thought he'd be able to, let alone want to. But he seemed to be doing fine.

"You know, Raven," he said, brushing a strand of hair away from her eyes, "I have to admit something. I made a judgment on you based on how you look, based on you whizzing around on that skateboard. Maybe it's a similar thing to what you're saying, even if my judgment was a positive one. Maybe it's all superficial."

She tilted her head. "What do you mean?"

"I mean . . . the minute I saw you, I was sort of—" Danny paused, feeling his cheeks suddenly turn hot. He was grateful it was too dark for her to see him blushing.

"Sort of what?" she asked, a smile tugging at her lips.

Danny looked down at the sand, suddenly feeling shy. Raven gently tipped up his chin with her hand, her eyes questioning.

"Mesmerized," he finally said, his blush fading. "The second I saw you. I thought you were so pretty and so interesting. Just by the way you look, just by the way you dress, I decided you were this free spirit who knew exactly who you were, what you wanted, what you thought, and where you were going. I was attracted to all that. Everything I *assumed* you were just by looking at you. I couldn't get you out of my mind after that first night."

Raven smiled and knelt down to collect a palmful of sand. She stood up and let it sift through her fingers. *She's feeling shy right now too,* he realized, his heart pinging a little at that knowledge.

"And did the reality live up to the fantasy?" she

asked, letting the last of the sand flutter away in the night air. "*Am* I all that?"

He laughed. "You certainly are."

Raven froze. "Wait! I didn't mean it that way!"

They both laughed, and he took her hand. They continued walking down the beach, looking out at the water, up at the moon. Never before had silence felt so comfortable.

What is this strange connection I have with this girl? Danny wondered. *Why can I talk to her like this? Why do I feel so confident around her? Why do I feel like it's okay to be myself around her? She's nothing like me.*

Maybe you're asking yourself too many questions, Danny boy, he told himself as a perfect breeze swirled around them.

He squeezed her hand, and she squeezed back. *It's weird how much that says,* he thought. *A hand squeeze.*

He couldn't imagine anyone not liking Raven. Not wanting to be around her. Hear her thoughts. Hear her laughter.

But he wanted to be the only one who got to hold her hand.

"I'll bet every school has a rebel contingent," he told her. "Mine does, and the school you were going to obviously does. You'll find a new group of skateboarders to hang with. And you'll make friends in other crowds too."

"You're probably right," she replied. "I guess I'm just feeling a little nervous about changing schools. You probably didn't expect me to be Ms. Vulnerable, huh?"

Danny grinned. "Hey, just because you've got a friend named Doberman doesn't mean you don't have feelings."

Raven cracked up, and Danny couldn't help but laugh too.

"So where is this new school anyway?" Danny asked, sobering up at the thought of the summer ending. Of saying good-bye to Raven.

"The town's called Spring Valley," Raven replied. "It's about four hours from here. I don't know the name of the high school."

Danny stopped dead in his tracks. "Spring Valley High," he blurted out. He couldn't believe it. It couldn't be possible. Could it?

"How do you know that?" Raven asked.

Danny stared at her. "Because there's only one high school in Spring Valley. I should know. I go there!"

Raven stared back, her mouth slightly open.

"Are you sure that's the name of the town?" Danny asked, eyes narrowing. "You're not just messing with me?"

Raven shook her head. "How could I make that up? I didn't know where you were from."

"That is so weird," Danny said, his voice full of awe. "I mean, weird that we should meet now, the summer before."

Raven nodded. "It's a good thing. Because we probably wouldn't have met in the fall."

"What do you mean?"

"I mean what we've been talking about," she

replied. "Our crowds don't exactly mix. This is summer, Danny. And here, away from home, away from your friends, away from everything you're *supposed* to be, you can do stuff you wouldn't normally do. If we'd seen each other for the first time in Spring Valley, you probably wouldn't have looked twice at me."

Danny's expression said, *Yeah, right.*

"Well, okay, maybe twice," she agreed, surveying her clothes and rings. "But I don't think we'd be walking on any beaches in Spring Valley."

"There are no beaches in Spring Valley," Danny deadpanned.

"You know what I mean," Raven said, playfully punching his shoulder.

"Yeah, I do." Danny paused. "Maybe meeting you here and now is destiny."

"Maybe you're right." Raven met his stare head-on. "And maybe it's teaching us both some kind of lesson about appearances. If anyone had told me I'd be walking down some moonlit beach with a guy who shops at J. Crew, I'd never have believed it."

Danny laughed. "And Eddie Bauer."

Raven smiled. "Doberman's asked me why I like you. And when I tried to articulate it for him, I found it hard. I mean, I could say all the regular things, like that you're smart, you're sensitive, you think before you speak . . . you're really, really cute"—she glanced at him with a devilish smile—"but the actual feeling of why I'm drawn to you, why I want to get to know everything about you, is what I can't seem to put into words. It's just a feeling."

"A powerful feeling," Danny agreed, holding her gaze. He knew exactly what she meant.

In that moment he understood that stupid cliché about no words being needed. The feeling of understanding between them was so intense, it felt bigger than him.

Danny could hardly concentrate as he stared into those amazing gray eyes. This time it was he who tipped her chin up to him. She tilted her face, just slightly, and parted her lips, just as slightly.

And then he kissed her. Her lips were so soft and tasted faintly of cherries. Her smooth skin smelled deliciously like cocoa-butter suntan lotion. He wrapped his arms around her shoulders and pulled her closer to him.

Oh my God, he thought. *This has got to be what people mean when they talk about being in love.*

The very idea sent a shiver up his spine, and he pulled back. He felt nervous all of a sudden. Raw. Vulnerable. Exposed. Love?

Whoa.

He and Raven had something major going on between them, but Raven was right. This was summertime. This wasn't real life.

And she was transferring to his school in the fall.

"What's wrong?" she asked, looking at him. "Didn't like the kiss?"

Danny smiled. "Oh, I liked it. Big time. I guess

I was just thinking something. *At a really stupid time,* he realized. *Couldn't you have waited till after the most intense kiss you've ever had?*

"What?" she asked. "A kiss like that is supposed to be mind numbing. Whatever's on your mind has got to be big stuff."

Danny nodded. "Do you think . . . ," he began, but faltered.

"What?"

He shook his head, regretting that he'd opened his mouth. "Nothing. Forget it."

"What?" Raven asked again. She nudged him. "Tell me."

Go ahead, say it, he told himself. *Say it, and let the crumbs fall where they may.*

"Do you think we'll still be together then?" he asked carefully. "In the fall, I mean. When you come to my school."

Raven didn't answer at first, and Danny was sure he'd stepped in a hole. Then Raven shrugged. "Are we together now?"

"I hope so," Danny replied.

Raven smiled. "So do I."

Danny felt the butterflies in his stomach again, felt as light as the sea breeze in his hair. Not a bad feeling to have one week into the summer, he figured.

This time Raven kissed him.

They stood in the golden glare of the pier, arms entwined, Danny feeling nothing but the electric attraction between them.

He didn't have a thought in his head as she

105

deepened the kiss. Well, except for how beautiful she was. How amazing she felt in his arms. How comfortable he was.

She pulled away slightly, resting her head on his chest as he held her. "I have to get going," she told him. "I was supposed to be back a half hour ago. My brother's expecting me."

Danny nodded and held her tighter. They kissed again, and then he watched her jog away.

The loss of her presence hit him hard. Suddenly he felt chilly.

And this is the way it's gonna feel without Raven in your life, Danny told himself, shivering as he started back toward the apartment.

Despite how they felt now, Danny knew it wasn't a given that they would be together that fall when Raven joined him at his school.

He hoped so. But he wondered just how realistic that was. The crowd she'd fall in with at Spring Valley High would never let them live. There were Dobermans at his school, and that crew went around snarling down the halls at the Charlies, Scotts, and Dannys of the world. *Her crowd will never accept you or the two of you as a couple, Dan-o. So face facts.*

He crossed his arms over his chest as he continued on toward the apartment. *Or maybe it's your own crowd you're worrying about,* an inner voice challenged. *You know what your school is like. You know what your friends are like. You saw it tonight.*

So be truthful with what you're worried about, he

ordered himself. Which was: Could Raven be accepted by his crowd, by his family? And if not, was he willing to stay with her?

For the first time in his life Danny Ford went home with a twisting ache in his gut.

Danny awoke late the next morning. The other denizens of the rapidly deteriorating apartment had already risen, feasting on Pop-Tarts and handfuls of cornflakes. Danny blinked the sleep from his eyes, focusing on Scott and Charlie watching Bugs Bunny on the tube.

"Morning," he croaked.

Scott looked around as if a fly were dive bombing his head. "Did you hear something?"

"Nope," Charlie replied, stuffing pastry in his mouth, not taking his eyes off the screen.

Danny rolled his eyes and extricated himself from his blanket on the couch. He spotted Johnny and Kevin in the kitchen, improving on the mess of crumpled food boxes and milk cartons. He avoided their eyes. "Knock it off, you guys."

"What do you expect, Danny?" Scott demanded, finally tearing himself away from Bugs. "We drove four hours this weekend to see you. And we get maybe two minutes with you, a lame bonfire party, and a volleyball massacre. I mean, *yippee*."

"If you wanted to spend time with your skate-rat girlfriend, fine," Charlie added. "But you could've told us so we didn't waste our time coming. Mike and Sherry were having a party this weekend, and we could have gone to that. We could have been meeting Sherry's cute friends and hooking up. But no, we drove four hours to see our supposed best friend, and then he blows us off for some really weird-looking girl he's known, like, a week."

Danny rubbed his face with his hands, hardly believing his ears. Yeah, this is what he needed first thing in the morning. "Oh, I get it," he retorted. "It's about Raven. My so-called girlfriend. Look, guys, the word *girlfriend* didn't even enter into the equation until after last night. I didn't expect for this to happen. And you shouldn't expect me to stop it. I told you that I really like this girl. Can't you be happy for me?"

Johnny made no effort to suppress his snort from the kitchen.

"I'm ecstatic for you," Charlie muttered. "Overjoyed. Elated. Hysterical. Look at me."

"Yeah," Scott added blissfully. "Maybe you and *Raven* can get matching tongue studs."

Johnny snickered from the kitchen. Danny then heard Kevin grumble, "Lay off him."

"You guys are hilarious," Danny declared, stretching and picking up a cereal box. Empty. He crumpled it up and tossed it in a random corner. "But I think I get the picture. You guys were great with the sorority types at the bonfire. But add a few earrings and some hair dye and a pair of tattered jeans, and suddenly a girl becomes too freaky for

108

you. And I guess your bottle-blond dates from last year's Spring Fling dance—you know, the ones with more jewelry than the Home Shopping Network—they don't count, right? They're different, right?"

Scott and Charlie didn't answer. They just munched their food and watched Bugs.

"I don't know why you guys are being so weird," Kevin piped up from the kitchen table. "I talked to Raven last night. She seems like a cool girl."

Danny shook his head indignantly. "The problem with them is that they think *cool* and *girl* don't belong in the same sentence."

Scott snorted. "No, actually the problem is with *you,* Dan, and the fact that you've flipped over some freak. Can you imagine *Raven* at Mike's party? You'd walk in with her, and everyone would stop dead and stare. Sherry would probably watch her like a hawk to make sure she wasn't stealing anything. And everyone would probably be nervous she'd pull a knife or something or maybe that the rest of her freaky friends would crash the party—"

Danny had felt the blood draining from his face the minute Scott started on his little speech. "You're talking about someone I like a lot. So shut the hell up, okay?"

"Look, man," Charlie cut in, eyeing Danny. "He's being a little harsh. *Maybe.* But maybe you'd better wake up and face facts. Raven might be a nice person. *Might be.* But she looks scary, and so do

109

her friends. You want to hang out with her, fine. But don't expect us to."

"You know what?" Scott said, looking from Charlie to Danny. "It doesn't even matter. It's a summer fling. She's different; you're attracted to her. Who cares? Once school starts, you'll be back home and you'll be into normal girls again, like Sherry and her friends. You'll forget all about your summer fling with the skate rat real fast."

Danny stared at Scott. Then at Charlie. Then at Kevin, who had one eyebrow raised at him.

Kevin's wondering if I'm man enough to deal with the fact that I like Raven despite all this bull, Danny realized. *If I'm man enough to stand up for the girl I like and admit to myself and everyone that it's not a summer fling.*

Suddenly Danny felt very uncomfortable. Very *examined.* He'd always thought it was Johnny who was testing him, pushing him, demanding stuff from him. But here was Kevin, his younger brother, expecting something too. Looking at Danny to do the right thing according to *Kevin's* standards.

Who do my brothers think they are anyway? Danny wondered angrily. *Why do I have to live up to anyone? Johnny wants to date an ice-queen cheerleader, fine with me. And let Kevin go out with a skate rat if he's so fine with it.*

"Let's get back to the point," Charlie said. "It's just a summer fling. And you've got the whole summer to have fun with your little skater chick. We're here one weekend. Hang with us like you know you're supposed to."

110

Danny let out a deep sigh. His brain was fried.

He realized he hadn't mentioned the interesting little fact that Raven would be going to Spring Valley High in September. Danny had enough trouble dealing with his own thoughts about that. He didn't need everyone else's opinion.

And he didn't want to have this conversation right now. What he needed was some breakfast.

Danny stepped over the floor debris—sleeping bags, pillows, tortilla chips, Fizz bottles—to get to the kitchen table. He found the box of Pop-Tarts—empty. He moved to the kitchen proper to search for more food. Johnny scowled, bumped his shoulder, and shoved past him on his way back to the bedrooms.

"Top o' the mornin', ol' bro of mine," Danny muttered, tossing another empty cereal box aside.

"Dude, that really is the point," Scott added from the living room. "We came to Surf City to see you, and we *haven't*. If you want to see Raven, fine. But tell us so we can pack up and go. End of conversation."

End of conversation. That was exactly what Danny wanted. To end this whole mind-twisting discussion and veg out. He was tired of talking about it, tired of thinking about it. Tired of wondering what the hell he was going to do.

Danny turned around and looked at his friends. On the one hand, they were right. He'd invited them up to the beach, then ignored them in favor of a girl. Which was pretty bad behavior.

111

"I'm sorry, guys," Danny said softly. "I did invite you up, and I have been ignoring you. So, how about we hit the beach for the day? Prowl the boardwalk. Hang out like always, and give this whole talk a rest."

Scott and Charlie eyed each other, as if deciding whether or not to forgive Danny. Finally they nodded. Relief flooded him.

Until he glanced at Kevin, who gave him a *whatever* look back before he turned his attention to his bowl of cereal.

Danny closed his eyes, let out a deep breath, and then quickly prepared for a day at the beach. Which pretty much consisted of changing into swim trunks.

As the three of them headed out, a single thought plagued Danny: *Raven's coming to my school in the fall.*

Had he let his friends off the hook because he was sick and tired of talking about it? Or was he using their objections as a way to put some emotional distance between him and Raven?

Come September, there won't be any distance, he reminded himself. *She'll be walking down the halls of Spring Valley High. Skating down the streets of your town.*

Danny sighed again as he closed the door behind him and his buds. These questions were way too heavy for the summer.

It was a beautiful day. The sun blared down on them, warming the boards and the sand. They soaked up the rays for a while and then wandered down the boardwalk to the pier, playing the occasional video game, eating some fries, and shooting the breeze. It was like old times between Danny and his friends. He even managed to push Raven from his thoughts briefly. Very briefly.

Until he saw her.

She skated up to them as they played a BB-gun game for baseball hats. She looked amazing in a black bikini top and beat-up sweat shorts that were spotted with paint. A towel hung around her neck, and her hair was wet.

"Hey," Raven greeted.

"Hey," Danny replied, watching Scott and Charlie for a reaction to her. They simply nodded, then stared at Danny expectantly.

Here we go, Danny thought. *Just say hi. That's all. I'm here with Scott and Charlie.*

"Where were you?" he asked.

Her cheeks were ruddy with sun and activity, and her smile just about pinned Danny to the wall. But he had to be cool. "We were on the water slide," she said, pointing at the massive coil of snakelike tubes that ran several hundred feet into a big blue pool. "You want to come? Doberman and the others want to get another hour."

Danny's smile evaporated. Of course he wanted to go. Right? But there were Scott and Charlie, BB guns in hand, their expressions asking him, *What's it gonna be?*

"I can't," Danny replied, hoping he didn't sound

angry. "The three of us have some stuff to do today."

"So why don't all three of you come for the hour?" Raven suggested. "It'd be really fun to get to know you guys," she added, looking at Charlie and Scott. "It'll be great. The water is perfect."

Danny quickly shook his head. "I don't think so, Raven. We really have some stuff to do."

Raven nodded. "So how about later? We could all get burgers or something for lunch, then go swimming."

Danny squinted up at her. "That sounds great, but I don't think we'll be able to."

She tilted her head and looked at him for a moment. "Oh. Okay." She took a step back, gripping the towel around her neck and bowing as if leaving a camera frame. "Sorry to bother you."

Something squeezed inside Danny's chest. He felt horrible but paralyzed.

No, Danny corrected. *Not paralyzed. You have a choice. And you're making it. Your friends came up to visit you, and you're going to hang out with them. That's the right thing to do, period.*

Isn't it? he wondered as he noticed the slight pink flush creep up Raven's cheeks.

"Look, Raven, it's just that Scott and Charlie drove all this way to hang with me, and . . ." He let the sentence trail off in the way he'd heard people do on television. He hated the way he sounded, like he couldn't just say what he really wanted. Like he had to imply what he meant.

"No, it's okay, Danny," she reassured him while simultaneously backing away. "I understand. Really. You have things to do." She dropped her board and stepped on. She offered Danny one last hurtful glare. "See you around. Maybe."

She pushed off and disappeared into the crowd.

"Raven—," Danny began, but she was gone. He cursed.

"What was her problem?" Scott asked, plinking a BB at his target.

"All you said was you were busy," Charlie replied, pulling another dollar bill from his pocket. "Chicks are weird, man."

Danny sighed.

What had he just done? Had he just ruined the greatest thing that had ever happened to him? Or had he done what was realistic for him? Sensible.

Johnny would be proud.

Kevin would shake his head in disappointment.

And Danny . . . what would he be?

Miserable, he told himself. *Because that's exactly how you feel right now.*

What I Will Now Look for in a Guy, Revised

by Raven

1. Honesty.

2. Integrity.

3. Someone willing to stand up for what he believes in despite what his narrow-minded, jerky friends think.

4. Someone who doesn't think what I look like represents who I truly am inside.

5. Someone who doesn't blow me off because he's embarrassed.

6. Someone who . . . Oh, who am I kidding? I don't want to look for anyone new. It's those darn eyes.

Nine

THE WEEKEND PASSED, and Danny saw no more of Raven.

Scott and Charlie left Sunday night, seemingly satisfied that their friendship was not only still intact, but maybe even stronger than ever. Yet Danny sensed an underlying suspicion that they somehow knew Raven wasn't out of the picture. And that maybe Danny somehow resented them for what had happened between them that afternoon on the boardwalk.

Either way, his friends hit the road, and Danny returned to work Monday afternoon.

Not seeing Raven ate at him. He delivered his orders robotically, scribbling and serving and clearing without thinking. Strangely enough, he got none of them wrong.

But everything seemed hollow. He wished he could talk to Raven, try to explain what was going on in his head. Why he'd acted that way on Sunday afternoon. Why he hadn't been around the rest of the weekend.

So just call her, man. Call her, make a date like normal people do.

I've never even taken her out on a date, he realized. *Why is that?*

Danny stuffed his order pad in his apron pocket and headed for the kitchen, where the employee phone was. He picked up the receiver and prepared to dial Raven's number.

And that's when he realized he didn't know it.

He didn't know her telephone number.

He didn't know where she lived.

He didn't even know her last name.

Frustrated, Danny hung up the phone. *I've been so focused on how she affects me that I ignored who she actually is,* he thought regretfully. *I don't know anything about Raven. I don't know how it feels to look different from everyone else. How it feels to want to look different. How it feels to be moving from your town, from your friends, your school. How it feels to start over somewhere else.*

How it feels to have your maybe-boyfriend's friends judge you as unworthy just because of the way you look.

How it feels to have your maybe-boyfriend be too much of a wuss to deal with it.

But I do know what it's like to be judged based on how I look. And it's crap.

I'm such an idiot, he told himself. *I am superficial.*

"Hey, Dan man. Your tables are freakin'."

118

He glanced up to see The Skipster, another waiter, eyeing him as he wrote out a bill. Danny nodded, took a deep breath, and placed his orders, then headed back out to the floor.

Around five he took his break. He grabbed some fries and a Fizz and walked out of Jabba's to his usual spot on the bench across the boardwalk.

He never got there.

Doberman skated up and batted the food out of Danny's hands. It scattered across the boardwalk, forcing passersby to dodge. Rage boiled up in Danny. This was the last thing he needed. He was miserable, tired, and hungry and wasn't about to play déjà vu games with a psychotic skate rat.

"What is with you and fries, man?" Danny demanded, surveying his spilled dinner.

Then Doberman grabbed Danny by the collar, slamming him against the railing of the boardwalk. And Danny knew he was in trouble. At this section the beach was a dozen feet below.

Doberman's biceps bulged. Veins popped in his forehead. His teeth glinted in the sunlight. "Forget the fries, cupcake," he growled. "You're about to have a very bad day."

Danny gulped. "I'm already having one."

Doberman bent him back farther on the railing. The wood bit into his back, rubbing angrily against his vertebrae. Danny smelled day-old pizza and body odor. Beads of sweat broke out on his forehead. He blinked involuntarily when a drop ran into his eye. Terror gripped him when he looked

119

into Doberman's eyes; he truly had no idea how far the big guy would take things.

"What are you doing?" Danny asked, his voice tight with panic. People gave them a wide berth, trying to ignore them. He was on his own.

"Normally I'd flatten you on principle just because you're such a dork," Doberman said viciously, shaking Danny. "But since you broke Raven's heart too, well . . . now I have an even better reason." He lifted Danny higher on the rail, pushed him out farther. He could see the beach below—and it wasn't soft enough. "Prepare to die, pretty boy."

"Wait a minute!" Danny pleaded. "How could I have broken her heart? We had one night together! I hardly know her!"

"Tell it to the crabs!" Doberman replied bitterly.

Danny struggled, but Doberman had several inches and a couple dozen pounds on him. If he didn't think of something fast, next stop was the sand below.

"Are you nuts?" Danny asked frantically. "You don't just toss people over railings, Doberman! I didn't do anything!"

"Oh no?" the big guy declared. "So why is she so miserable? Why is she crying? *Why is she even into such a monumental loser like you?*"

"How am I supposed to know?" Danny replied helplessly. "I didn't mean to hurt her. I swear. I didn't even know I hurt her until now." That was a lie, Danny knew, but he was about to get tossed off the boardwalk if he didn't come up with something.

"Come on, Doberman. You know the score. Why would I hurt her?"

Doberman paused, clearly frustrated. He obviously knew that tossing Danny over the rail wasn't really an option. And since his threats were no longer really frightening Danny, Doberman's options had dried up. But his rage had not.

Doberman let go of Danny. His feet clunked back to the boards. He sighed and straightened his shirt and apron.

"You make me sick," Doberman said, his voice lethally serious.

"Why?" Danny demanded, his own anger surfacing now that the danger was passed. "What did I ever do to you?"

"Nothing, stupid," Doberman replied, dismissing his comment with a scowl. "But she's, like, in love with you, man. And you're too dense to see it. Or you do see it, and you're too much of a loser to deal with it."

Danny froze. Raven was in love with him? *Me?* he wondered. He'd realized just a little while ago that he'd thought about Raven only in terms of how she affected him. He'd never even given a thought to how *he* affected *her*.

He'd never thought he had much effect on anyone, especially not an amazing girl like Raven.

Could she feel the same way about him? Was she feeling the same misery he was now—the same twisting stomachache, the moody tension, the need to be alone and miserable? . . . No way. There was

121

no way Raven could feel so much for him. Be in love with him. "That's impossible," he whispered.

Doberman sneered. "I thought so too. I personally don't get it. I mean, *look* at you."

Danny ignored the comment. He was too fixated on the *L* word. "She actually told you that?"

"Of course not," Doberman replied, as if Danny had just made the dumbest comment in the world. "She'd never say it to me. But she does, Danny. Even if she won't admit it. I know her really well."

Danny was dumbfounded. His mind raced. He didn't know what to say. It was all happening so fast, so out of his control.

All he knew was how he felt. Deep down. No filters. Exactly how he felt. And he said so. "I think I love her too."

Doberman laughed in his face. "You're a moron."

Danny blinked. "What do you mean? Now what did I do?"

Doberman shook his head in disbelief. "What are you telling *me* for?"

Ten

AFTER WORK DANNY combed the boardwalk for her.

It was a useless gesture, he knew. It was now dark, closing in on ten at night. Surf City was huge and packed to the gills with people. If Raven didn't want to be found, she wouldn't be. It wasn't until Danny wandered down near Wayfarer Avenue that he had an idea.

He found the site of the bonfire party. Much of the burned wood had been cleared and the ashes plowed under the sand by cleanup crews. But it didn't take long to reach the jetty where he and Raven walked that night. And it seemed so simple to find her perched on the same concrete piling.

Yet there she was, almost as if she was waiting for him.

"Get lost, Danny," she ordered.

Or not, he thought.

Now that he'd actually found her, he realized he didn't even know what he was going to say. *I love you too?* Suddenly he didn't know *how* he felt.

Why is this so confusing? he wondered. When he'd held her in his arms, when he'd kissed her so intensely, he thought he'd pass out, when he'd looked into her eyes, it had all seemed so simple. There was just feeling. Now there was almost too *much* feeling. His, hers, and everyone else's.

"Can we talk?" he asked gently.

"I have nothing to say."

A wave pounded the rocks in front of them. Sea spray fell across Danny's cheek. He wasn't going to give up that easily. "Well, I do. Your friend Doberman came to see me."

"So I heard," she said with a shrug.

"He's pretty subtle," Danny said, attempting a lame joke. "But he led me to believe that I've hurt you somehow. If I did, I'm sorry. I didn't mean to. But I needed to spend time with my friends. They drove all the way up here to see me—"

I'm lying through my teeth, he realized. He *had* meant to hurt her. He'd meant to drive her away so that he wouldn't have to deal with it. Her, his brothers, his friends, and the thought of September.

"—and you were spending all your time with some freak girl," Raven finished, her tone bitter.

Danny paused. "That's not right. I was spending time with a girl I really like. But I had to spend time with them too. I mean, a guy needs to spend time with his friends."

Where is this bull coming from? he wondered. *Why aren't I saying what I really mean?*

Because you don't know what you mean.

But this is Raven. The only girl I've ever been able to really talk to. And here I am, saying the kind of crap I'd say to a girl I don't even like. Just tell her how confused you are. Then the both of you can talk it out.

"Then why didn't you just tell me that?" Raven demanded. "Why'd you act like you'd never seen me before? Like I was just some girl bothering you? Your friends don't like me, so *you* won't like me anymore—is that it?"

Danny looked down at the sand. "Raven, I . . ." He trailed off, unsure what to say. What *could* he say? She was right. But that wouldn't make either of them feel better.

"You made me feel like—" Raven stopped talking. Danny could feel her eyes on him. "You know what? Forget it. You can't handle it, Danny."

He glanced up at her. "Can't handle what?" he asked.

He knew exactly what she was talking about. But he needed to hear her say it. Needed her to let him off the hook.

Raven crossed her arms over her chest. "Can't handle direction after all."

Huh? he thought. *What's that supposed to mean?*

"What does direction have to do with this?" he asked. "This is about you and me and our friends getting in the way. My friends can't deal with you; your friends can't deal with me. And once we're in

125

the same school, forget it. No one will be able to deal with us as a couple."

Raven glared at him. "First of all, Danny, this has *everything* to do with direction. It has to do with you feeling something and letting yourself feel it, no matter how wrong or right someone else tells you it is. That's called believing in yourself, following your own heart. But like you said, that's something you know nothing about."

Danny felt himself stiffen. He didn't want to deal with this right now. First he had everyone on his case about Raven, and now she was on his case about his shortcomings. Great.

"Oh, like you know me so well," he shot back. "We barely know anything about each other, Raven. I don't even know your last name. Did you realize that? I couldn't even call you because I don't even know your phone number or where you live."

"Gee, Danny," she said. "Maybe you could have asked. Or maybe it doesn't matter. Maybe all that matters is how we feel when we're together. You didn't need my phone number or last name to know exactly where to find me tonight, did you?"

She had him on that one. Danny stood there, his hands shoved in his shorts pockets. All he'd wanted was to make up, but . . .

Raven stared at him for a moment. "And second of all, we're obviously *not* a couple, so I guess you don't have to worry about what your friends think or how anyone will react to us in September."

Danny felt a stabbing pain in his gut. He *did* want

126

them to be a couple. Instead of fighting right now, all he wanted was to grab her in his arms and hold her. But what about tomorrow? What about September?

"Forget it, Danny." Raven shook her head and slid down to the sand. She scooped up her skateboard and brushed past him. "Let's just forget the whole thing."

Danny marched after her. "Yeah, well, maybe we should."

Raven kept walking. "I guess I was wrong about you. We *are* too different. You proved it yesterday. Your friends made you brush me off. And my friends helped. But you caved. You couldn't handle it. It's better we know that now before . . ."

Before we fall in love, he finished silently for her.

As if we're not already there.

Wait a minute. This is really happening, he realized. *She's really dumping you. And you're letting her.*

"Raven, wait!" he shouted after her. "I don't care about our friends. I just want you."

Raven whirled on him, causing him to stutter step to a halt. "You're not listening to me, Danny." Her eyes glistened in the dim light. Her voice was desperate, as if she was forcing herself to speak the words. "You've already proved that what *you* want doesn't matter. It's over between us."

"Raven, come on," Danny pleaded, the lump in his throat making it hard to speak. "Maybe we just need some time to figure all this out." Just when he'd met the coolest girl ever, she was going to tell him good-bye?

Raven turned one last time. "No. *You* need to grow up." Her lips were quaking as she added, "Leave. Me. Alone."

She spun on her sandal and was gone.

Danny wandered the boardwalk for hours. It became very late. Finally he made his way back to the apartment. When he opened the door, he saw both Johnny and Kevin sitting in front of the TV. They looked about as happy as he felt.

"Are you dead?" Johnny asked.

"Huh?" Danny replied, hardly hearing him.

Johnny crossed his arms over his chest. "You better be dead because that's the only excuse for missing practice."

Practice. What was he talking about? Then Danny remembered. Volleyball practice. They had agreed to meet at the lighted courts on the King Street beach after Danny got off work. But Danny had totally forgotten it. He'd left work and immediately begun his quest to find Raven.

"Sorry, guys," he said, his brain still fuzzy. "I had a . . . well, it was a rough night."

"What happened?" Kevin asked, absently scribbling on a sketch pad. He hardly seemed interested in the answer.

"Raven dumped me."

There. He'd said it. Now maybe it could actually sink in. But Johnny's reply was like a bee stinging him awake.

"Good," he said.

Danny scowled. "Good? Good for you, maybe. It's what you wanted since the day I met her."

"Don't give yourself a hernia lifting the weight of the world, bro," Johnny replied. "You only knew the girl a week."

"Shut up, Johnny," Danny growled, slumping into a kitchen chair. "You don't know anything about it."

Johnny rose from his chair. "Oh, I think I do. I think I know how badly we tanked out in that volleyball game. I think I know how badly we need to practice. I think I know how this Rave chick has turned your spine to jelly. You're forgetting why you came here in the first place."

Danny nodded wearily. "The tournament."

"The tournament!" Johnny echoed. "Hallelujah, Kevin! He remembers."

"Your precious little tournament," Danny continued. "Your precious little trophy. Your precious little king-of-the-beach crown."

"Hey, dude," Kevin said, angrily tossing aside his sketch pad. "Get it straight. Your actions affect all of us. Johnny won't admit it, but we can't win that tournament without you. That is not meant as a compliment. It's a fact. And if you go off the deep end with some girl, then you better be prepared to deal with us."

Danny chuckled. "I've been dealing with you two since the beginning of time. What's another summer?"

Kevin stood up and approached his brother.

"I'm serious, Dan. Raven might be a nice girl. A great girl, even. I'm no idiot. I see through the pink streaks and the belly-button ring. But when it comes to playing and winning that volleyball tournament, all bets are off. There is way too much at stake, and I won't let you mess it up for us."

"So much at stake," Danny grumbled. "Gee, sorry. I wouldn't want you to miss out on that lifetime supply of Fizz Cola."

Johnny paced back and forth. "You know exactly what we're talking about. The money! The ten grand! We *need* that money, Dan."

"Ah, yes," Danny said, holding up a finger as if remembering an old joke. "Johnny's legendary greed rears its ugly head once again, dictating what everyone else must do to satisfy his quest for the almighty buck."

"Stop talking stupid," Johnny shot back. "You know the score. That money's a big key to all our futures. College isn't just a dream for me anymore. It's a fact. It's happening. I'm not going to work in a factory my whole life like Dad. My share of that prize money is a big start toward something. And I'm not going to let you screw it up over a girl." He paused, letting out a massive sigh. "I mean . . . I know you don't care about me or Kevin—"

"That's not true," Danny said, but Johnny spoke right over him.

"—and you don't have any real ambition toward anything else. But I know that you love the game. Don't you care about volleyball? About winning?

Don't you want to crush those all–American morons out there?"

If there was anything Johnny could've said to reach Danny, that was it. Danny knew it. Johnny and Kevin evidently knew it. But his brother might be too late. Because Danny heard the words, understood them, but felt nothing but the old ache in the center of his being. The heartbreak.

And that had nothing to do with money, v–ball, or victory.

Danny gazed at his brother. Johnny expected an answer. Danny wanted to give him one. The right one. He felt he owed his brothers that. But there was nothing there.

In the end all Danny could say in response was, "I don't know."

Eleven

THE NEXT DAY at work Danny's luck didn't improve. He messed up three orders and dumped a bushel of hot wings on the floor. It was as if every planet was aligned against him. Every move he made backfired in some way. Everything he did ended badly, whether it was giving someone a hamburger instead of a cheeseburger or mopping up hot sauce with white linen napkins.

After Jabba chewed him out for that mishap, Danny just shook his head, sighed, and thought, *It's official. Everyone hates me. My brothers. Raven. And now even Jabba.* Though Danny doubted that Jabba liked anyone at all, so he didn't take it personally.

Then, to top off his day, Doberman sauntered into the restaurant.

Uh-oh.

Doberman was in his full glory. Ripped sleeves. Skater shirt. Torn cargo pants cut off at the knees.

The usual shark-tooth earring and evil look. His board in one hand and some cash in the other.

When he saw Danny, he grinned maliciously and shook his head as if to say, *You're a lost cause, pretty boy.*

Danny tried to ignore him.

The cashier-hostess, a pretty girl named Louisa (and the kind of girl Danny figured everyone would want him to date), met Doberman at the door, asking if she could help him.

"Two dozen wings to go," Doberman ordered, no doubt savoring the look of fear he brought to Louisa's face.

"One moment, please," Louisa replied, shuffling off to the kitchen to put the order in as quickly as possible.

Probably to get Doberman out the door fast rather than a concern for quick service, Danny figured.

Doberman leaned against the wall near the exit, admiring the looks he got from the other customers as if he didn't have a care in the world.

That's when Danny spotted Jabba.

The big man had seen Doberman come in and was moving toward him, slipping his big belly between tables. Danny immediately remembered Raven telling him how Jabba had banned Doberman, Skunk, and the others from his restaurant.

And now they were on a collision course.

Danny thought of warning Doberman, but there was no need. He caught a whiff of Jabba and rose to his full height as the owner closed in.

Doberman's eyes grew livelier by the moment. Jabba might as well have had steam whistling out of his ears.

"I thought I told you to stay out of my place!" Jabba bellowed, apparently not caring that his scream brought the entire restaurant to a screeching halt. Everyone—customers, cooks, and waiters—stopped what they were doing and watched.

"But I just ordered some wings," Doberman said simply.

"I don't care if you ordered filet mignon or franks and beans," Jabba said, jabbing a plump finger on Doberman's chest. "I don't want you punks in here, making the place look like a halfway house for junior-high dropouts and ex-cons-to-be. Out! Now!"

"But I just ordered some wings," Doberman repeated, same tone of voice, same delivery.

"Consider it canceled!" Jabba hollered. "You're banned. You don't scare me, kid. You're a loser, and I don't want you stinking up my place."

Doberman took mock offense, flashing his vampiric smile. "I'm insulted. It costs a lot of money to look this good."

"You got surfboard wax in those pierced ears of yours, punk?" Jabba asked, incredulous. He poked Doberman harder on the chest. And from the look on his face, Doberman didn't like it. "I said get out!"

"No," Doberman said, all mirth gone from his voice.

Jabba's eyes widened in their paunchy little sockets. "What did you say to me?"

"I said no," Doberman repeated, stepping into Jabba's face, staring him down. "I ordered hot wings. I have cash." He held up the money. "And I want what I came here to buy."

Jabba snatched the bills from Doberman's hand and threw them back in his face. "Your money's no good here. I'm not serving you a thing. I don't care if you have a hundred dollars. I want you *out*."

The arguing escalated, each one yelling louder than the other. Danny hung on every word until something shook his attention free, and he scanned the crowd in the restaurant. They were riveted. And they were clearly rooting for Jabba.

That figures, Danny thought. *Kick around the skate punk. He dresses mean, he looks mean, he acts mean. He's worthless, and he deserves to be tossed out on his ear.*

Danny had no love for Doberman, but he knew what was going on was wrong. Doberman just wanted some wings and had the money in his hands. And Jabba wasn't going to serve him simply because he didn't like the way Doberman looked.

I'll toss out any punk who comes through the door just on principle, Jabba once bragged. And he was making good on that promise.

But what galled Danny the most were the patrons. The restaurant was nearly full. Dozens of people stared in rapt anticipation at the heroic Jabba chasing off the evil skate punk polluting his establishment. Ugh, the looks on all their faces. Superiority. Contempt.

They're just a bunch of greased-up, sunburned piles of self-loving ego, feeding hungrily on heart attacks and fries, Danny thought in disgust. *And they have the audacity to ridicule Doberman for the way he looks.*

It was so wrong. Everyone judging everyone on how they looked. It had destroyed his relationship with Raven. It had destroyed his relationship with his brothers. And now it was happening again right in front of him. It made him sick. It made him angry. It brought every last vestige of rage to the surface in Danny.

Enough was enough.

Danny marched over to the counter where he picked up people's meals to be served. An unclaimed basket of hot wings was waiting there, steaming. Danny grabbed the plastic basket and headed for the front of the restaurant.

When he got to the arguing pair, he shoved the food between them. "Your wings, sir."

Doberman and Jabba froze in midsentence. At first Doberman blinked. Then a smile broke out over his face. He grabbed the basket of wings and stepped away from Jabba. "Much obliged," he said, laughing.

Jabba's face turned as red as a cooked lobster. He whirled on Danny. "What do you think you're doing?" he roared.

Danny didn't back away. He got right in Jabba's face and opened the floodgates to all of his anger.

"No, what do *you* think you're doing? This is a restaurant. This guy wants some wings. We serve them. He came in here and politely ordered some, and for no good reason, you tell him his money's no good. That he was already banned. And for what? For looking like a freak."

Jabba's eyes narrowed. He raised a porky finger at Danny. "How dare you tell me my business, you little twerp?"

"How dare me?" Danny asked. "How dare you! I stand in this restaurant every day, listening to you ridicule people. Like *you're* perfect. You ought to take a look in the mirror sometime. Does ragging on people make you feel good? Does it make up for something? Some personal lack?" Danny pointed at Doberman, who was happily munching on a hot wing and listening to every word. "What did he ever do to you, Jabba? I'm so sick and tired of people judging people by how they look."

Jabba's jaw was hanging open, and his jowls quivered with rage. "Get out. You're fired. Both of you punks get out of my restaurant right now, or I'll call the cops."

Danny quickly untied his apron and threw it to the floor. He took a deep breath, held it, and walked out of a restaurant that was so quiet, you could hear a french fry drop.

"Not bad," Doberman declared as he chomped on a chicken wing. "Not bad at all."

Danny glanced over his shoulder, pausing when

138

he saw the big guy behind him. The air smelled fresher outside the restaurant, mostly because of the greasy Jabba food but also because of the insane adrenaline pumping through his system. "That guy makes me sick," Danny muttered, for lack of anything more clever to say to Doberman.

The big skate rat rode his board slowly alongside Danny. Danny just marched along the semicrowded boardwalk, fuming. He didn't feel much like talking to Doberman, but he also figured he didn't have much of a choice at this point.

"I owe you one, Danny," Doberman declared, licking his fingers. "No one ever stood up for me like that before, especially not for a basket of wings." He smacked his lips. "Say what you want about Jabba. But his wings are the best in southern California."

Danny was still wired. He felt the words spilling over without his really thinking about what came out. "Unbelievable. I lost my job. And for what? I'm so sick of people and how they look. I'm sick of how I look. I'm sick of having no direction. Of having to *have* a direction. Everything is do this, work that, practice this, stay away from that. Auuugggh!" He gestured at the ocean, the sand, the girls in skimpy bikinis. *"I've had it with this place!"*

"That's the way," Doberman encouraged him. "Let it all out. You'll feel much better."

Danny stopped dead in his tracks. He glared at Doberman with no fear because he was beyond caring what anyone thought about him. He was a man with nothing to lose.

"You know what, Doberman?" Danny replied bitterly. "Why don't you just leave me alone? You do it too. You took one look at me and saw a loser. You did everything you could to discourage Raven from hanging out with me. Remember 'pretty boy' and 'punk-rock boy' and 'frat-boy-in-waiting'?"

Doberman nodded and smiled. "That one was my favorite."

Danny scowled. "Just get away from me."

Doberman pushed his board and caught up to Danny. "Hey, don't hand me that, man. Everyone does it. It's human nature. Believe me, I've ranted this rant a hundred times before, and I've gotten nowhere with it. All you can do is be yourself and let everything else take care of itself."

"That's a crock," Danny returned, walking faster. "I've always been myself, and just when I think it's getting me somewhere, Raven yanks the rug out from under me."

"Raven?" Doberman asked skeptically, the early evening sun glinting off his spiky hair. "Dude, Raven didn't do anything to you. You did it to yourself."

Danny whirled on Doberman. "No. That's not it. I was always myself with her. I never tried to be something I wasn't. But when you and your friends and my brothers and my friends started seeing things they didn't like, bam, Raven suddenly doesn't like me very much."

Doberman didn't answer him. He only shredded the last wing and dumped the basket in a trash barrel.

"Tell me I'm wrong," Danny challenged.

Doberman shrugged. "You're dead wrong. She filled me in a little on the convo you two had. You *let* her go, man. You couldn't deal with everyone being on your case. You probably figured what was going on now was nothing compared to how bad it would get in September, when she transfers to your school."

Danny swallowed. Doberman was right. He *had* been wondering what it would be like to have Raven at Spring Valley High. To see her walking down the halls—to see her in the cafeteria . . . maybe even to sit next to her in math class! And even though he didn't consider himself to be conservative, he was by association.

In Spring Valley, Danny palled around with guys who wore Tommy Hilfiger and Gap, who had short hair and no piercings and dated girls named Lauren and Jessica. Raven was the complete opposite of anyone he'd ever known, let alone dated.

Besides, his friends had showed their true colors—if he showed that he was still interested in Raven come September, who knew what would happen to his social status? He knew it was pretty disgusting of him to worry about something like that, but he was just being honest. And besides, how would Raven enjoy being raked over the coals every day simply because she wanted to be with him?

Danny sighed. "What am I supposed to do, man? Let everyone make us both so miserable that we end up making each other miserable?"

Doberman rolled his eyes. "You're an idiot."

Danny scowled at Doberman. "Now what?"

"Man, I hear a whole lot of whining," Doberman said. "But I ain't seeing a whole lot of fighting for what you want."

"Yeah, right," Danny said. "Raven doesn't want anything to do with me anyway."

"Let me tell you something about Raven, Danny." Doberman stepped on the end of his board and popped it up into his hand. He leaned it against a bench and hopped onto a railing, swinging his bare feet as if he didn't have a care in the world. "I've known her a long time. And she talks a good game, but she's a marshmallow inside, just like you and me."

"You?" Danny asked, smirking. "A marshmallow? Yeah, right."

Doberman spread his arms wide. "There you go again. Judging away on stuff you don't know. Just because I could rip your head off with my pinkie doesn't mean I don't get all choked up watching Hallmark commercials." He laughed at Danny's expression. "My point is this. Raven's a girl. And maybe she chased you in the beginning. But she isn't going to chase you anymore. You're going to have to do some chasing yourself now."

Danny sighed, watching the sunset over Doberman's shoulder. "I don't know, man. She chased me off pretty good last night. She made it pretty clear that I wasn't welcome. That I was a big loser for not being able to deal."

Doberman was quiet for a moment. Then he cleared his throat. "You said before that you were in love with her. Is that true?"

Danny didn't answer right away. He wasn't expecting to have a conversation like this with Doberman. *But Doberman isn't the guy you thought he was, is he?* Danny reminded himself. *He asked you an honest question, and the least you can do is give him an honest answer.*

"Yeah," Danny replied. "I am."

Doberman sighed and slipped off the railing. His bare feet hit the boards without a sound. "So do something about it," he said, flipping his skateboard onto its wheels.

Danny figured that was the highest compliment Doberman could ever pay him. The skate rat was giving his version of a blessing. "Thanks."

"*De nada,*" Doberman replied.

"Do you really think I have a chance to get her back?" Danny asked.

Doberman offered a sly smile and clapped Danny on the shoulder. "Well, pretty boy . . . I'll see what I can do."

Twelve

"**Y**OU GOTTA BE kidding," Johnny said as he rose from his chair in front of the TV. An empty tortilla-chip bag fluttered to the floor. "Is this a joke?"

Danny had arrived at the apartment just after midnight. He and Doberman had roamed the boardwalk and beaches of Surf City all night. Danny felt like a huge weight had been lifted from his shoulders. He felt free, liberated. Doberman understood everything he was going through because the guy went through it all himself with his friends and family. In the end, Doberman was right. All you could do was be yourself.

Kevin's jaw dropped, revealing a half-eaten chip.

Danny chuckled and ran his hands along the bristly hair that remained on the sides of his head. Then he touched the field of angry spikes up on top. His new haircut would take some getting used to. Apparently Johnny and Kevin agreed.

"What, now I'm not allowed to get my hair cut the way I want to?" Danny asked, rolling his eyes.

"Yeah, if you want to look like a moron," Johnny replied angrily.

"Easy, Johnny," Kevin said, scowling. "It doesn't look that bad."

"What's with you anyway, Johnny?" Danny demanded. "It's more than just the volleyball. It has to be. Is it the late nights? Is it that I don't listen to you like you're Dad?"

Johnny didn't answer him. He just pointed to the fresh white bandage on Danny's bicep. "What gives?"

Danny grinned and gently tugged at the adhesive tape, peeling back the bandage to reveal a still-sore tattoo of a volleyball hurtling across his arm, streaking flames like a meteor.

"Whoa!" Kevin exclaimed, diving in for a closer look. "Cool!"

"Yeah, I like it," Danny said, beaming.

"Who drew it?" Kevin asked excitedly.

"The guy at the tattoo parlor," Danny replied. "You should see some of the stuff he did. He has pictures hanging all over the shop. It's incredible."

Kevin poked him on the chest. "Dude, why didn't you tell me you were going to do this? I could've drawn it for you."

"Sorry, Kev," Danny answered. "It was a spur-of-the-moment kind of thing."

Johnny only laughed, pinching the bridge of his

nose. "Well, now I can die happy because I've seen everything."

Danny let out a sigh, nodding. He'd expected this reaction from Johnny. In fact, he'd almost hoped for it. "Relax, Johnny. It's not your arm. You're still Mr. Clean-cut around here as far as I'm concerned." He'd tell Johnny when he was good and ready that the tattoo was a good fake. Doberman's friend at the tattoo parlor had drawn and colored it, and it did look like the real thing. He hadn't really wanted to do something that extreme—and besides, he wasn't old enough.

"Hey, heaven forbid if I offend," Johnny replied in mock terror. "I think it's really you, Danny. It looks great. Honest and truly. But I was just wondering when you had time to have all this art performed on you. After work?"

Here was the hard part, Danny knew.

He nodded, smiling. "Actually, yeah, it was after work."

"Did you leave early again?" Johnny wanted to know.

Danny smiled even wider, meeting his brother's stare head-on. "Actually, yeah, I did."

Danny could tell Johnny was running a slow boil now. "I see. And your boss just lets you come and go as you please? I thought that restaurant was superbusy."

At last, the moment of truth. "Actually, no, he doesn't. I quit. Or I was fired. It depends who you ask."

Johnny went absolutely ballistic. "I knew it! I

147

knew it! You idiot! You let all this rebel crap go to your stupid spiked little head!"

"Oh, relax," Danny said. "You'll pop a blood vessel."

Johnny's eyes went wide at the comment. His face grew more livid. "Relax? Are you kidding? Inside two weeks you've taken any trust we had in you, and you stomped it. What are you going to do now? Where are you going to work?"

Danny shrugged. "I haven't decided yet."

Kevin's face darkened. "Danny, that's not cool, man. How are we supposed to make rent?"

"Exactamundo!" Johnny cried. "Did you think about that when you staged your great walkout? Did you think about what you might be putting the rest of us through?"

"Yeah, I've thought about it," Danny said, nodding. "And I have a solution."

"Oh, I'm *all* ears," Johnny muttered.

Danny watched his brothers' faces carefully as he spoke. "It's easy." He paused for effect. "We win the volleyball tournament."

Johnny threw his hands into the air. "That's rich. You hear that, Kev? Suddenly Sid Vicious here is Joe Volleyball again. Uh, Dan-o? I have some news for you. You have to *practice* to be good at volleyball. To practice, you have to show up. You seem to be having a problem with that lately."

"Not anymore," Danny replied, confident.

Johnny blinked. "Not anymore. Okay. Good answer. I'm just supposed to take 'not anymore' and

148

run with it after you shaved your head, stuck ink needles in your arm, and quit your job. Is that what you're saying?"

Danny shook his head. "What I'm saying is that I'm willing to do what it takes to win this thing."

Johnny straightened up, eyeing him skeptically. "Really?"

"Really," Danny confirmed.

Johnny took a step closer, focusing hard. "Are you willing to give up Raven to win?"

Danny's eyes narrowed. This was the challenge he'd expected. "Not a chance, Johnny. I don't see you giving up Jane or any of the things you're into. All I'm saying is that I'm ready to bleed to play ball. Just like you are."

"It's about time," Kevin replied, high fiving his older bro. "Good to have you back."

But Johnny shook his head angrily. "No, that's not good enough, Danny. All it took was one look from that girl to send you packing. She and her striped hair and Sex Pistols wardrobe have to go."

Danny had had it. Where did Johnny get off? Had Danny ever told him that his girlfriend, Jane, with her perfect hair and smile, her coordinated wardrobe, and superachieving GPA, had to go?

Danny looked Johnny straight in the eye. "Don't you see what you are? You dis people because of how they look. Are you so much better? Raven's grade-point average is near perfect. She reads books and listens to music you don't even know exists. And I'm through taking this garbage silently. From you. From the world." Danny took a deep breath and sighed. "Maybe I need to try something different for a while. Maybe I need to see someone different for a while. I didn't realize how dead I was until I met Raven."

Johnny's scowl remained. But the savage tone left his voice. It wasn't a conciliatory manner, but almost exhausted. "Maybe you're right, Dan. Maybe I do make fun of people because of how they look. But people dress for that reaction. You could put a bone through your nose, but all you'd be is ridiculous. Different is inside, not outside. If punks and skate rats are so different, how come they all look alike?" Johnny slumped into a kitchen chair and crossed his arms. "The bottom line is, I don't need a brother with an identity crisis. What I need is a teammate who wants to play volleyball."

Danny smiled at the words and nodded slowly. He'd stood up to Johnny. In doing so, he'd stood up for himself. "Okay, brother. You got that. If you need proof, just check out my boss tattoo."

Johnny cracked a smile at that. Then laughed outright.

Danny grinned as well and offered his hand. Johnny shook it.

"It's always been the volleyball anyway," Kevin said, meeting his brothers' gazes. "It's what makes us brothers. We remember that, and nothing else matters."

Kevin put out his hand, palm down. Danny understood and was filled with relief that the three of them finally had it out. Danny was doing his own thing, and it didn't matter if Johnny and Kevin liked it or not. What mattered was that he didn't let them down in ways that did matter. Like the tourney.

But Danny knew nothing had changed between him and his brothers except the fact that they agreed to disagree. Which was fine with him. It was the best he could expect. He put his hand on top of Kevin's without hesitation. Johnny followed suit.

Now all he had to do was make things right between him and Raven.

But he had to find her first.

Thirteen

THE FORDS PRACTICED hard the next morning, slamming the ball around as if their lives depended on it. And in a way, they did.

Danny remained true to his vow. He concentrated. He dove. He was there in every sense of the word.

It was easier than he'd thought it would be. Raven remained in his thoughts, of course, but now he possessed a new focus. Danny had reached a turning point. It had happened when he'd stood up for Doberman in Jabba's. He'd realized that he believed in something quite strongly: acceptance. And that he had an appreciation for people's differences. Maybe that was why he'd gotten that haircut and the tattoo. To show himself and maybe everyone else that a spiky do and some ink didn't turn a clean-cut guy into a violent criminal. And the game mattered to him again. And that made it fun.

After their killer practice he showered the sweat and sand away at the apartment, then took to the boardwalk after his brothers left for their jobs at the Surf City Resort Hotel. He'd promised his brothers he'd look for another job—it wasn't fair to watch Kevin trudging off in his cabana-boy uniform and Johnny heading off to suffer with his annoying life-guard partner for yet another baking day in the sun while he was free to roam the beach and practice his volleyball serve. But he didn't want to fill out applications just yet. Right now he had more important things to worry about.

Correction: a more important *person*.

Morning sunlight flooded the beach. Instead of the loud children and parents dressed in even louder clothing who would be crowding the board-walk by midday, joggers pounded by. Walkers. Runners of every shape and size. They gave Danny and his haircut a wide berth.

He had to laugh.

Looks will always matter, he figured. *Fitting in is the hard part. A lot of people can't get past appearance. Look at Doberman. He's a real sweetheart once you get past the nasty shell. And Raven too. Well, I already know about Raven.*

That is, everything she wanted him to know. Danny knew plenty of things that mattered: like who her favorite bands were, what she really thought about life, how she liked eating cotton candy while skating the boardwalk. But he didn't know plenty of things that really mattered *now:* like where she lived, what her last name was, and her phone number.

"Duh!" Danny exclaimed out loud, causing the woman in front of him to turn around, startled. How could he have been so stupid?

I have to get Raven back, he thought.

It was that simple. Somehow. Someway. He had to do it.

As if on cue, Doberman rolled up beside him on his skateboard. Their eyes locked, a new understanding there.

"Dude," Doberman greeted.

"Dude," Danny replied, nodding.

"Nice hair."

"You too."

Doberman held up a crumpled piece of paper between his long fingers. Danny could see scribbling on it.

All Doberman said was: "Be there. Tonight at nine. The rest is up to you."

Danny snatched the paper from his fingers. Doberman skated off into the crowd. Danny uncrumpled the paper and read what was on it.

58 Arlington St. *An address,* Danny realized.

Raven's?

He'd find out soon enough.

Fourteen

THAT NIGHT DANNY had work to do. He figured it would take him about twenty minutes to walk to the address on the scrap of paper. Around eight he started to prepare.

He was still unused to hair maintenance. Spiking his hair was easy with hair gel; deciding whether or not he liked it was another matter. His hair wasn't that radical by some standards. He'd seen worse on some male models. He finally just left it alone, trusting what the barber—or rather *stylist* did to him.

The fake tattoo still looked great despite some tiny smudges from his sweat and the shower. The volleyball had been done in blue ink, the flames in red, orange, and yellow. Nice.

He chose a beat-up concert shirt from the Funeral Homeys, a thrash-rap group he'd seen live last year. The sleeves were short enough to show off the whole tattoo.

Now it was time to work on the jeans. . . .

Danny took them into the kitchen for surgery. He swept the crumpled fast-food bags and torn snack wrappers off the table to the floor. Then he spread out the jeans and took a dull butcher knife to them. A nip here. A tuck there.

Kevin wandered over and watched. "You want some artwork on those jeans?" he asked. "It'll take me ten minutes with a felt-tip pen. Might look cool."

"Nah, thanks anyway," Danny replied, focusing on his cuts. "I don't have time."

"Those holes won't look right until you wash the jeans," Kevin pointed out. "You should've thought about that."

Danny shrugged. "I didn't have time. I didn't know I was going anywhere until this afternoon."

"Where *are* you going?" Johnny asked from the living-room couch. "You look like you're dressing for the skate-rat prom."

Kevin laughed. Again Danny shrugged, taking the insult in stride. "I don't know. I was just given an address and a time. No other details."

"Sounds screwy to me," Johnny said. "You sure it's not a setup?"

"Setup for what?" Danny asked, eyeing his brother.

"Who knows?" Johnny answered. "Didn't this Doberman cat have it in for you?"

Danny shook his head, refusing to consider it. "No, this guy's totally cool. We made peace. My guess is Raven's going to be there tonight. This is my one last shot."

Johnny rose from the couch and joined them in the kitchen. He playfully tested the spikes of Danny's hair on his palm. "You sure that this makeover will help? She liked you before, didn't she?"

Danny knocked away Johnny's hand. "Maybe the makeover's not just for her."

Kevin smirked. "You mean it's for Doberman? Dan, I never knew. . . ."

"You're hilarious, Kev," Danny muttered. He flipped the jeans over his shoulder and tossed the dull knife into the pile of moldy dishes in the sink. Several fruit flies rose from the disturbance. "I meant me. Like I said, it's time to try something different. Maybe I'll like it. Maybe I won't. But I'll never know until I try."

"What about Raven?" Johnny asked. "What if she doesn't go for this whole punk-rebel thing? Then what?"

Danny shook his head. "I don't know, Johnny. I'll jump off that bridge when I come to it."

Johnny held up a hand and continued. "What I mean is, you made a promise to Kevin and me about the volleyball championship. It's the whole reason we came to Surf City in the first place."

Danny bristled. "Yeah, I know. So?"

"So . . . we need you to be a hundred percent into it," Johnny warned, obviously trying to word his remark carefully.

"What are you trying to say?" Danny asked, motioning for him to get to the point.

"A broken heart sucks the life out of you," Kevin blurted out. "If this chick stomps you, you have to remain human. That's what he means."

"Exactly," Johnny said, nodding. "No disappearances. No psychotic behavior. None of the stuff we saw all last week. *Comprende?*"

"Is that an order?"

Johnny chuckled. "No. We're just holding you to your word."

Danny nodded. Maybe Johnny had finally got the message about all the major-general-Dad stuff. Just like Danny got the message about the volleyball. "No problem, bro," he replied, walking toward the bedroom to get dressed. Then he turned back.

"I wouldn't worry, guys," Danny said. "My heart won't be broken for long."

"How do you figure?" Johnny asked.

Danny grinned. "'Cause I'm gonna win her back."

Fifteen

THE ADDRESS WAS south. Danny walked as far as he could on the boardwalk, enjoying the last of the dying day out over the water—a postnuclear glow of deep red where the sun went into the sea. The air was cool and breezy, the kind of wind that used to shuffle Danny's hair. Now his spikes just stood in the breeze like a petrified forest.

This will definitely take some getting used to, he thought, patting the crunchy gelled creation.

The boardwalk ended before he reached his destination. He took the street the rest of the way. As he walked, the houses got larger and more opulent. Huge postmodern structures with multiple levels, decks, and garages.

This is some big money, he thought. *Where is Doberman sending me?*

He got his answer soon enough.

The address matched that of the last house on

a dead end—right on the beach. The place was massive—a fantastic, slate-colored wood mansion with tall windows and decks of every size up and down the four-story frame. Danny could see dark figures on the decks. The pounding of a deep bass and voices filtered out the open windows.

"Big bucks," he whispered.

Danny made his way up a plank boardwalk to the front door. The house loomed even larger as he approached. The music grew in intensity. The laughter floated down from the glowing windows like an invitation.

Who lives here? he wondered, spotting a private-access path to the beach. *Someone's superrich parents, no doubt. This is a million-dollar joint.*

The front of the house faced the ocean. The double doors of the main entrance were wide open. A few kids near his age hovered there, soaking up the night air and laughing, talking. They ignored Danny as he walked right in.

He climbed a wide staircase to the main floor, a massive living room of expensive furniture and high-end stereo speakers built into the wall. He recognized the song immediately: "Miss Fickle's Pickle," a country spoof by the band Smog, a one-hit-wonder-to-be.

There had to be more than two hundred kids at the party. The crowd was mixed—girls in khaki shorts danced next to guys in shreds; guys in surf wear lounged next to girls in leather and studs.

Danny spotted Doberman chatting with two

gorgeous girls, preppies by the look of them. Maybe opposites really *did* attract, Danny thought.

When Doberman saw Danny, he immediately excused himself from the girls. He crossed the living room and bumped fists with him in greeting.

"How goes the battle, dude?" Doberman asked.

"This is pretty amazing," Danny replied, gesturing at the room, his eyes scanning for Raven.

"Thanks," Doberman replied casually. "I just put the word out, and people come. It's sort of like *Field of Dreams*. Kind of creepy sometimes. I'm thinking I should close the doors before things get out of hand."

Danny gaped at Doberman. "You live here?"

Doberman nodded.

"What does your dad do?" Danny asked, marveling at the cathedral ceiling and its huge skylights.

"He's retired now," Doberman replied. "But he used to be a plumber."

Danny blinked. "A plumber? How does a plumber afford a place like this?"

Doberman laughed heartily, clapping a hand on Danny's shoulder and pulling him close. "Dude . . . it's not my dad's house. It's *my* house."

Danny paused. "Say what?"

"You heard me."

Danny didn't know what to say. Could it be true? Was Doberman messing with him? "I don't believe it. . . . I mean . . ."

Doberman grinned. "Relax, dude. It's no big deal. I had to do something with my money.

Figured I might as well have a good time. I'm not really a yacht guy."

"How did you . . . ," Danny continued, still trying to make sense of it.

"You know the computer game Slob?" Doberman asked.

Danny nodded. Of course he knew it. Slob was the hottest PC game going last year. It was funny, disgusting, and superviolent like a great PC game should be. He owned a copy himself.

"I designed it," Doberman said matter-of-factly.

"You did?"

Doberman laughed. "What did you think I was, some kind of bum? I'm nineteen, for crying out loud. I have to have some kind of a life."

"I guess so." Danny chuckled, still dazed by the news. So Doberman was a multimillionaire computer-game designer. Unbelievable. "I guess looks really are deceiving, aren't they?"

Doberman winked at Danny. "Do tell, dude." Then he nudged him. "Don't look now, but I think your whole reason for existence is staring at you."

"Huh?"

Doberman pointed toward a corner. Danny followed his finger.

It was Raven. She was standing across the room, a look of disbelief and anger on her face. She stared right at him.

"Like I said before, Danny," Doberman said. "The rest is up to you."

Raven shot Doberman a look of death and disappeared into the crowd.

"Hurry up, dude," Doberman urged. "She walks real fast when she's mad."

"I know," Danny replied, taking off into the crowd after her.

He followed her down a twisting staircase to the lower floor. A massive sliding-glass door opened onto an elaborately decorated patio. Tiki torches burned at varying intervals, casting the whole area in a surreal island light. Raven was about to escape down a narrow path that led over a sand dune to the beach. Danny heard the pounding surf over the faded music from above.

"Raven, wait!" he called.

He didn't think she would. In fact, he anticipated another beach chase. But Raven actually stopped, whirling on him like the fabled woman scorned.

"When are you going to get the hint, Danny?" she growled, her eyes wild. "I don't want to talk to you." Then her eyes widened a little more as she took in his wardrobe and hair. A look of confusion crossed her face. "What did you do to yourself?"

"Do you like it?" Danny asked, feeling his cheeks get warm.

Raven sighed. "I liked you the way you were. Now go, Danny. Just go."

"No, Raven," he said, his voice rising. "I didn't just do this for you. I did it for me. Maybe you were the inspiration for it. But I realized I wasn't happy with who I was. I needed to change."

"You still don't get it, Danny." Raven shook her head, her voice weary. Even upset she looked totally hot: wild hair, smoky eyes, tight torn jeans, red tank top. Danny was just glad to see her . . . even if the feeling obviously wasn't mutual. "All you did was change your look. You can't change who you are with a haircut and arm art."

Danny nodded. "If that's true, then I'm still the same guy you rode the skateboard with that night on the boardwalk." He smiled. "Now I just have a killer tattoo."

Raven tried to suppress a chuckle but failed. This made Danny laugh as well—a breakthrough.

Go for it, the inner voice told him. *That little chuckle is your last hope.*

"I love you, Raven," he said, wording that momentous phrase with every ounce of sincerity in his body.

Raven shook her head, her voice cracking. "Don't do this, Danny. Just don't. It's too hard. We're too different."

Danny took a few steps toward her. He felt a floodgate open in his head. Words were flowing out in his mind before he even knew he was thinking them. But it didn't matter now. He had to say them. Because he didn't have anything to lose.

"Not anymore, Raven. I don't care what anyone thinks. It feels right. It *is* right. I'm not denying it anymore. I've been sitting around feeling sorry for myself too long. You're coming to my school in the fall, and I want to be with you. I'm asking you, please, if you feel anything at all for me . . . give me another chance."

A tear rolled down Raven's cheek. And it wasn't dyed pink or strange in any way just because it came from her. It was just a tear.

"What about your friends?" she choked out, wiping the tear from her cheek. "Your brothers?"

Danny shrugged. "They can find their own girls."

This made Raven laugh again. He smiled and risked a couple more steps toward her. She didn't back away.

"This is it, Raven," he said. "I can't put it any better. I'm putting it all on the line here. I need you. And I'm in love with you. I want to be with you and no one else. The rest of the world will just have to deal."

Her eyes finally locked on his. They glistened in the torchlight as she tried to blink back any more wayward tears. Then she stared at him. Shamelessly searching his eyes for something. *The truth?* he wondered.

After a few seconds she turned away, gazing at the beach, listening for something.

His mind raced. *Did I just lose her? Is she going to answer me? Or is she just going to take off again? I can't do this anymore. It's too much. I can't just spill my guts, tell her how I feel, and then hope that she says—*

"I love you too."

Danny blinked. Raven was looking right at him.

"You—You do?" he stammered, suddenly feeling woozy.

Raven nodded, a grin spilling across her face. She ran to him and wrapped her arms around his neck. Danny met her head-on, kissing her like he'd never kissed anyone before in his life.

All thought and sound fell away. There was just him, her, and the moment. He felt his heart pounding in his chest, in his ears, in their locked lips. It was a sensation he didn't want to end or to ever forget.

Then a gruff voice came from behind Raven from the beach.

"Awww, ain't that cute. It must be the tattoo."

Sixteen

THEIR KISS BROKE. Danny and Raven whirled at the voice.

A group of guys was coming down the narrow sand path in the dune grass. Some of them carried beer cans or smoked butts. But it was the guy in front who Danny recognized immediately: Tanner St. John.

His long hair was yanked back in a sloppy ponytail. His massive, lean frame was covered by a cotton sweater that hung loose from his broad shoulders. His tan feet sank into the sand with every step.

Then Danny noticed Arliss Neeson and Shooter Ridge behind him. Along with a dozen other guys who were obviously on a quest for a party.

"Well, well, well," Tanner said, grinning. "The freaks are out in force tonight." He leered at Raven. "You know, you'd be pretty hot if you took some of that dye out of your hair."

"Take a hike, frat boy," Raven muttered.

"Oooh, frat boy," Tanner replied in mock offense. "I'm touched by the poking finger of ridicule. Maybe you oughta get some staples for your lips too. Can anyone kiss you, or is it just Loser Appreciation Night?"

Danny felt adrenaline run through his system like molten steel. Rage built within him, bypassing every caution alarm that normally would have held him back.

But he was sick of holding back.

"Back off," he ordered, stepping between Raven and Tanner. "Take your act up the beach to the fun house. I hear they're short a clown."

Tanner and his friends burst out laughing. Tanner slapped his knee and staggered slightly. A few drops spilled from his beer can. "Oh, now that's a fresh one. You've been watching a lot of *Saved by the Bell,* haven't you?"

"Have another beer, frat boy," Raven scoffed, eyeing the half-crumpled can in Tanner's fist.

Tanner grinned. "You know what? You're absolutely right. Yo, beer dude!"

A can flew out of the darkness and landed squarely in Tanner's free hand. He popped the top and took a long gurgle. A tiny stream squirted down his cheeks. "Ahhh! The pause that refreshes. Okay, boys, let's paint this town battlefield red."

Tanner belched and marched toward the sliding-glass door. His posse followed like well-trained soldiers.

Danny stepped in front of him and planted a hand on Tanner's chest.

"I don't think you heard me the first time, dude," Danny warned. "I said get lost."

Tanner batted away his hand as if it were a fly. He stood to his full height—a good five inches over Danny—and glared down at him like he was now a serious nuisance. "I heard you, spiky," Tanner said angrily. "I chose to ignore you. Now get out of my way before something really bad happens to you. I mean *really* bad."

Danny smirked. "How bad is that?"

"Worse than your haircut," Tanner replied, sneering. "Now step aside. Or you'll find out what it's like to be danced on." He turned to Raven. "And *you* can be my partner."

The group fanned out behind Tanner, each of them larger than Danny, each of them primed and eyeing him like a fresh steak. Suddenly the high of winning Raven cooled off. The invincibility he'd felt was gone. Now Danny knew that it was just him against fourteen college guys who collectively outweighed him by one pickup truck.

He tried to remember everything he knew about fighting, which was very little.

Raven tugged his elbow. "Let's go, Danny. It's not worth it."

Danny knew it. Boy, did he know it. But something kept him rooted to his spot in front of Tanner. His mind said run. His feet said no.

If I back down, it's just one more victory for these

morons, the inner voice said. *Every time I see them, I'll know they got the best of me. I'll know that they can beat me. And I won't be able to do a thing about it. I can't back down. Not now. No way.*

"I'm not moving," Danny said flatly, staring right into Tanner's face.

"This isn't the volleyball court, little Ford," Tanner warned. "If you think it was bad out there, wait until I'm through with you. You'll think you dropped into the devil's backyard on laundry day."

Danny blinked and glanced at Raven, who shrugged. "What does that mean?" she asked, confused.

"It means I'm going to put you through a wringer and hang you out to dry," Tanner replied with a cocky smile.

"You make that one up yourself?" Raven asked in disbelief.

Danny refocused on Tanner. "If it takes fourteen of you to stomp my guts out, then fine, go to it. I can't stop fourteen guys. But remember what happens tonight because it'll all be squared on the volleyball court come tournament time."

Tanner roared with laughter. "Are you kidding? We beat you by twenty points in the dark when we were half wasted. What do you think is going to happen when we show up at that tournament with our game faces on?"

"We'll have to wait and see, won't we?" Danny replied, not a trace of fear in his voice.

Tanner shook his head. "Such a confident

young lad. Mama must be so proud." He flipped his wrist, spraying Danny with droplets of beer. "So what's it gonna be, tough guy?" He flicked more beer. "Are you going to move, or are you going to be moved?"

Danny ignored the drops of beer on his face and in his hair. He just took a deep breath and smiled. "Eat it, Tanner."

Danny batted the bottom of Tanner's can with his fingers, launching a healthy spray of beer right into Tanner's face. Tanner gasped, blinking as warm beer washed across him. A ripple of anger went through his friends as they waited for his reaction.

Tanner was livid. He tossed his beer can aside and clamped two hands on Danny's T-shirt, nearly lifting him right off the ground. "You're dead, Ford! Do you hear me? Dead!"

The group closed in on Danny, and he prepared to feel pain like he never felt before.

Then a voice piped up from behind him.

"Yo, Danny!" the voice called. "There are some people here to see you, dude!"

Tanner froze, leaving Danny to hang. Danny managed to turn around just enough to see Doberman, his vampiric grin flashing more wickedly than ever.

On either side of Doberman stood Johnny and Kevin.

And behind them about twenty skate rats of varying size, haircut, and rage.

"Hi, guys," Danny said lamely, waving.

Tanner dropped him. Danny backed away as Doberman and his crowd filtered out onto the patio, eventually flanking Tanner's group. Then surrounding it.

Johnny and Kevin moved in beside their brother. Danny felt new adrenaline flowing, the adrenaline of relief.

Doberman stepped into Tanner's face. "You were crumpling my friend's shirt. Explain yourself."

Tanner scanned the faces of all the skate rats. Danny saw weakness in his face for the first time. "It's our problem, pal. This has nothing to do with you."

"See, that's where you're wrong," Doberman said, scowling. "'Cause this is my house. Which makes this my patio. Which makes this my party. And as a gentleman host, that means I'm responsible for the guest list. Do you follow?"

Tanner nodded robotically. Danny noticed a drop of beer hanging from the end of his nose.

Doberman continued. "That means one thing. No scumbags allowed. Especially scumbags who give my honored guests a hard time. Guests who have earned the right to call me their friend." He shot Danny a quick, encouraging look. Then he got even farther into Tanner's face. "Do we have a problem with that?"

Tanner wiped the beer from his nose. Took a deep breath and licked his lips. "No. No, I guess we don't."

"Good." Doberman nodded, satisfied. "Now, pick

up your beer cans and get off my land. All of you."

Tanner eyed Danny and his brothers with contempt, then did as he was told. As he and his friends made their way back over the dune, he turned and pointed at the Fords.

"We'll be seeing you again," Tanner vowed. "Once you're on that volleyball court, you're fair game. We're not just going to humiliate you; we're going to hurt you. Mark my words."

"Looking forward to it, Tanner," Johnny called after him.

Tanner St. John only turned his back and disappeared over the dune.

When they were gone, a huge round of cheers and applause erupted from the skate rats. They high-fived Danny and Doberman, clapping their backs and making Danny feel like he was some kind of celebrity.

Raven stepped up and gave Danny a huge smile. "I can't believe you!"

"That I did so well?" he asked.

"No, that you were going to let them beat you up!" she said, giggling. She fell into his arms, and they kissed again. More hootchy-kootchy sounds rained down from all directions. Danny burst out laughing and broke their kiss.

Doberman then pulled Danny close and smiled. "You know what? You need a meaner haircut."

Seventeen

THE PARTY CONTINUED harder than ever. The guests were fired up, having seen the evening's entertainment. Doberman put on the Dustmites, and a mosh pit broke out in the living room. Danny and Raven caught up with Johnny and Kevin in the kitchen. Kevin was elbow deep in a bowl of cheese puffs. Johnny had already emptied a bag of pretzels. But to his credit, he'd managed not to spill many crumbs on the pale green tile floor.

"What are you guys doing here?" Danny asked. "How did you find me?"

Johnny shrugged. "We realized how lame we were being—"

"How lame *you* were being," Kevin corrected, reaching for a cracker from a tray on the kitchen island. "I was being pretty cool."

Johnny continued, ignoring him. "And then we got a phone call inviting us to this wild party at some strange address. It turned out to be Doberman."

"A party sounded pretty good at the time," Kevin added, hacking a hunk of cheese off with a plastic fork. "A good way to meet people."

"And a good way to make amends with our brother," Johnny added, offering Danny an apologetic smile.

Danny returned the grin. "Done deal, bro."

They bumped fists to make it official.

"Now," Johnny continued, standing and offering his hand to Raven. "I don't think we've been properly introduced. I'm Johnny. Danny's my loser brother."

Raven shook his hand, nodding. "I know. He is quite the loser. I'm Raven."

"So I hear you have a higher GPA than me," Johnny joked. "How is that possible?"

"I don't know," Raven said. "Maybe we'll find out this fall when I enroll at Spring Valley."

Johnny's jaw dropped. He gaped at Danny. "Is she serious?"

"Oh yeah, I forgot to mention that," Danny replied, his eyes twinkling.

"Sounds like destiny to me," Kevin commented, eating his cheese.

Danny and Raven shared a playful look. "I don't know," he said. "I think destiny is what you make it."

They walked out from Doberman's house onto one of the many decks overlooking the sea. Danny held Raven close, finally knowing that she wasn't going anywhere for a while. It was a wonderful feeling.

"So Doberman put you up to this?" she asked, gazing out at the waves pounding the shore.

"Yeah," Danny confirmed. "He thinks you're pretty special."

"I guess so," Raven said distantly, as if she wanted to avoid the question. "He can be pretty possessive."

Danny turned her toward him and looked into her eyes. "What is it?"

"It's nothing. . . . I . . ."

"What?" Danny pressed. "Is it Doberman? Did you two have a thing or something? He said he's known you for a long time."

Raven didn't answer.

Danny swallowed hard. "That's it, isn't it? He's your ex-boyfriend. Oh, that's just great."

Raven shook her head. "No, Danny, that's not it. It's like he tries to dictate everything I do just because I live here for the summer with him."

Danny couldn't believe what he was hearing. She lived with him? "What are you talking about, Raven? Why did you wait to tell me this?"

"What do you mean?" Raven asked, obviously confused. "Tell you what?"

"That you're shacked up with your ex-boyfriend, that's what!" Danny exclaimed.

Raven burst out laughing. Danny blinked. Now he was confused. "What's so funny?"

Raven grabbed him by the T-shirt and pulled him close. "Dobie's my *brother*."

Danny paused. Let it sink in. Recognition flooded him as her words finally registered. Then he started laughing himself. Raven kissed him through the laughter until they were quiet again, listening to the surf in the distance.

"So where do we go from here?" Danny asked softly.

"It's a long summer, Danny," she replied. "Let's just enjoy it."

Danny nodded, gripping her hand tight. "That sounds good, Raven. Really good." Then he leaned in close. "But I just have one question."

Raven's eyes were expectant. "What?"

A smile crept up Danny's face. "Your last name. And maybe Doberman's first name? And, um, your phone number."

Raven giggled. "Hey, you already know where I live. Isn't that enough?" She giggled again.

"You know what else?" Danny said, leaning closer. And closer.

"What?" she asked.

"You've already seen my tattoo. When do I get to see yours?"

Closer.

Closer still.

She gently pulled his head to hers, kissed him lightly on the cheek, and whispered a single word into his ear.

"Patience."

Do you ever wonder about falling in love? About members of the opposite sex? Do you need a little friendly advice but have no one to turn to? Well, that's where we come in . . . Jenny and Jake. Send us those questions you're dying to ask, and we'll give you the straight scoop on life and love.

DEAR JAKE

Q: *Do you think it's possible to fall in love with someone you've never met? I'm totally in love with the lead singer of a rock band—a really famous one. Even though I've never met him, I have seen him in concert and his songs make me feel like I know him. I'm trying to figure out a way to meet him, like getting a backstage pass. I don't want to date anyone at school, since I only want to go out with him. My friends tell me I'm being dumb. Am I?*

JQ, The Philippines

A: Crushes are never dumb. But, I think I understand why your friends are concerned. You don't want to date guys at school because you only want to go out with the rock star. But you've never met this guy, and chances are you probably won't! Enjoy his music, ooh and ahh at his face on a poster, go to his concerts and sing along at the top of your lungs. But keep in mind that it's his music and his image you love—not *him*.

Q: *Okay, I want the straight scoop: do guys only like blond girls with good bodies? That seems to be the case at my school! I have curly brown hair, freckles, and I'm not exactly a skinny-minny.*

MS, New York, NY

A: Okay, I'll give you the straight scoop: no! I, for one, being a guy, can tell you I like all kinds. The first girl I ever loved had curly brown hair, and she wasn't a skinny-minny, either. Sometimes it will be a smile that attracts a guy to a girl. Sometimes it will be her laugh. Sometimes it will be that she loves to read. And sometimes it will be her looks. Chemistry doesn't depend on a certain hair color or body type!

DEAR JENNY

Q: *My new boyfriend keeps asking me to wear makeup and "girlier" clothes, like skirts and dresses. I hate makeup, and I feel dorky in skirts. I don't want to lose my boyfriend, but I don't want to have to glop stuff on my face and wear clothes that make me uncomfortable, either. What should I do?*

DW, Baton Rouge, LA

A: You've hit on the keyword: uncomfortable. Doing anything that makes you uncomfortable, especially when you're doing it for someone else, usually just makes you *more* uncomfortable. Try telling your boyfriend straight out that makeup and dresses just aren't your style. If he persists in asking you to change your appearance, then perhaps you should think about changing your boyfriend!

Q: *My parents hate the guy I'm dating just because he looks tough and has a tattoo. I keep telling them that they don't even know him (they've only met him once for, like, a minute). Mike is the sweetest guy*

I've ever met, and I really like him. How can I get my parents to see past his "look" and realize he's a great guy?

AH, Dayton, TX

A: I suggest you ask your folks if you can invite Mike to a family dinner so that they can get to know him. If dinner seems too much, then perhaps you could all go somewhere together, such as a carnival or baseball game. Once your parents have the chance to see that he is a great guy, they'll probably be able to see past the "tough" exterior.

Do you have any questions about love?
Although we can't respond individually to your letters,
you just might find your questions answered in our column.

Write to:
Jenny Burgess or Jake Korman
c/o 17th Street Productions,
an Alloy Online, Inc. company.
33 West 17th Street
New York, NY 10011

Don't miss any of the books in *Love Stories*
—the romantic series from Bantam Books!